Immersion Online
The Symbiont

Book 3

Evan Klein

Immersion Online: The Symbiont

Book 3

By Evan Klein

DEDICATION

To my wife Pam, for allowing me to escape to the
basement to bring you this book!

TABLE OF CONTENT

ACKNOWLEDGMENTS

A special thanks to Steve Blotner, Sean Hall, Clark Laird, Ian W. McHarg, and Kevin McKinney – beta readers extraordinaire.

I also need to thank Karen Dimmick for the fantastic cover art.

And finally I want to thank you my reader for taking the time to read this book. I would appreciate any feedback you are willing to leave on Amazon. Feedback – both good and not so good – will inspire me to work even harder on the next book.

Coming Soon: The Abduction of Sierra Skye

Mike Haggerty held his hands over his eyes and forehead. The mother of all migraines was coming on. He didn't need this new craziness in his life along with all of the other headaches he had taking place. His retirement from the police force should have been peaceful. His plan had been to purchase a small house down in the Florida Keys and spend the rest of his days drinking Mai Tais and fishing.

Those plans were shot to shit the moment Shannon Donally called him out of the blue. How she had known to contact him on the very same day that he filed his retirement papers was still a mystery. When you had the kind of crypto-coin she had, nothing was a mystery, he concluded. She needed a new head of security for her virtual reality game Immersion Online and insisted he take the job. Had it been anyone else in the world, he would have said, "Fuck off!" Shannon and Mike shared a secret, however, one that would prevent him from ever saying no to her. They'd had a wild and passionate love affair forty years earlier, and now she held him by the proverbial balls forever. He sat in the screening room with his hands over his eyes and forehead trying to rub away the stress.

The lights in the screening room dimmed. Haggerty removed his hands and stared as giant white letters slid like albino snakes across the blackened backdrop on the two hundred inch viewing screen: The first full-length movie from Immersion Online: The Abduction of Sierra Skye. The never before told love story of the greatest pleasurer and the men who risked everything to save her.

The screen went dark again and a woman's melodious voice began to speak: By now, everyone has viewed The Granson Gang and their allies as they embarked on the most dangerous dungeon dive ever undertaken in The Great Realm. Now you will learn the truth behind the abduction of Sierra Skye. See how she ended up a prisoner in the dungeon of the black dragon, Drock Blanag the Ancient.

The next scene showed Sierra Skye and Granson naked in bed together, passionately kissing – their hands gliding along one another's fit bodies.

Haggerty knew it was not Granson but an actor assuming an exact reproduction of his avatar. Shannon had tried to hire the rogue

1

to appear as himself in the movie, but he declined. There was almost a lawsuit as Granson claimed he owned his avatar's image while Shannon's lawyer argued that Immersion Online owned it. In the end, Shannon settled it the way she handled most other issues, by throwing heaps of crypto-coin at it, and he allowed his avatar's image to be used.

Granson was one of the busiest Starborn in the game now that the player and monster caps were gone. He emerged from the dungeon dive as the highest-level player in the game and planned to keep it that way.

The scene switched again to reveal a nude Sierra Skye straddling Granson. In the semi darkness of the screening room, Haggerty shook his head, wondering how popular this semi pornographic movie would become.

The voice of the announcer continued: The secret love story of Sierra Skye and Granson, the most powerful player in The Great Realm – and how he risked everything to rescue her – will be revealed for the first time.

The scene cut to Granson battling Drock Blanag, a funnel of blue flames curling around the rogue as he walked toward the black dragon, sword in one hand and dagger in the other.

Sierra has a huge heart and unquenchable thirst. Is one man alone enough to satiate her passions? The announcer asked.

A new scene appeared on the screen. It showed Sierra leaning against a brick wall in a darkened alley with her skirt hiked up around her waist. A man, his pants partially lowered, lifts her up by the waist. The man's face is never revealed. Between their grunts and whimpers of ecstasy Sierra whispers, "I choose you Constable Mace. It will always be you."

Who wrote this crap? Haggerty wondered. Knowing Shannon, she probably hired an award-winning scriptwriter and a famous director to create the monstrosity he was being subjected to.

The announcer spoke again: See how Sierra sacrifices herself to save her two lovers as the fiend from The Sundaland holds them aloft in his deadly clutches. Her divine voice and passion free them from his icy grasp. The scene shifted once again to show Sierra entangled in black tendrils. She does not cry out in agony but her harmonious voice carries like a comforting breeze. Finally, she winks to the camera and fades into the mist.

The announcer then concluded the trailer: The Abduction of Sierra Skye coming this summer, only on channel 5092, the Immersion Online tele-channel.

Haggerty, always the good soldier, clapped along with the drones in the screening room. Then he slipped out before the lights came back on to call Mace and warn him about the trailer. Haggerty didn't think Mace would give two shits. Mace saw fame and infamy as pretty much the same thing, a disease to be avoided. He figured he better alert Amber as well. She was the one who was likely to go nuclear on him and the damn corporation.

Mace was supposed to return to Grandview the following morning after recuperating for the last two weeks, and Haggerty didn't want his friend confronted by a host of in-game and real world reporters without a heads up. If the trailer said Mace and Sierra were an item, then as far as the world was concerned, they were one.

Tomorrow was going to be a strenuous enough day for Mace without false rumors of a love affair with the most famous pleasurer in The Great Realm.

He shook his head in disbelief a few more times, before he built up the courage to take out his phone and call Mace.

Prologue

What the hell! I thought, as a red light began to flash on my display screen and a siren screamed in the air like the wail of a banshee.

"Ah shit!" Granson said concerned. "I am getting help. Stay with me old man."

"Don't you leave me Boss," Tinsie cried, tears streaming down her face.

"Mace," Haggerty said, his voice filled with concern, "you're having a medical condition in the real world. Hold on! An ambulance is on its way."

"Stay with us Mace," Havervill urged. "We still got shit to do for Mother."

"Yes, hold on Mr. Mason," Shannon commanded. "You still have a job to finish. You cannot quit until then."

One final gasp for breath.

Darkness.

Death!

Chapter 1: Though I Walk Through The Valley Of The Shadow Of Gremlins

Electricity is a curious thing. It has the power to destroy and to kill; meanwhile, it also has the power to save a life – to provide the needed spark to restart a heart.

"Charging," I heard through the miasma as I drifted between life and death, between The Great Realm and the real world.

The shock of electricity from the defibrillator felt like a kick in the chest from a centaur.

Or did I just imagine that?

My eyes shot open. A dark skinned woman with deep brown eyes hovered above me with paddles in her hand.

"His heart is beating again," I heard her say as I slipped into pleasant darkness.

*

Bright overhead lights assaulted my eyes. I squinted, waiting for my pupils to adjust.

I stared to my left and déjà vu crept over my soul. Hadn't I just woken up in a hospital bed less than six months prior after suffering a heart attack?

Through bleary eyes, I spotted my daughter Amber asleep in a chair, her head leaning against the wall while Mike Haggerty scrolled through his phone.

"What the hell happened?" I asked, my voice dry as ash.

Amber popped suddenly awake. She stood up and walked to the side of the bed. "How are you feeling Dad?" Before I could answer, she grabbed my hand and explained, "You had a cardiac episode."

"Another freaking heart attack," I groaned. It was hard to talk with the dry mouth. "Thought the nanites fixed everything after the last one."

I began to cough.

"Water," I rasped.

"Have to check with the nurse," Haggerty said. "Let me ask her." He slipped from the small room in search of some cool H2O for me.

"This was something else," Amber responded, a tinge of anger in her voice. "The doctors aren't entirely certain just yet. Still waiting

5

on some test results. They said you are going to be good as new…well, you'll be good as old. You know what I mean."

Haggerty returned a moment later with a small pitcher of water and some tiny plastic cups. He poured a few ounces of water into a cup and handed it to me. I raised my arm slowly and grasped the cup. It felt like I was lifting a brick.

"The Glimmerman? He did something to me after we destroyed him," I said, taking a small sip of the cool water.

"It is a perk specific to Glimmermen called *Death Rattle* – a one-time use curse which destroys the enemy who destroys them. There is no defense against it."

"The ultimate revenge. I get that," I said, taking another small sip. "But why did I have a heart attack at the same exact moment?"

"Just a coincidence," Haggerty responded.

"You know I don't believe in coincidences," I said, drinking a bit more water. "That thing was able to prevent Sierra Skye from logging off. Your so-called programmers haven't been able to figure out how he did it yet, am I right? He grabbed Tinsie from death and trapped her. You haven't figured out how he did that either, am I right?"

"You are," he admitted, nodding his head.

"Then shit," I said, clearing my voice. "Isn't it possible he did something to me that caused this cardiac episode?"

"We don't think so Mace. However, we are looking into it, in case there is even a small possibility."

I took another long sip. "We got him. It felt good bashing his head in!"

"Can you both stop talking about that damn game? That dungeon run almost killed you for real, Glimmerman or not!" Amber shouted.

"You know that's not the case," Haggerty corrected Amber.

She glared at Haggerty and snapped at him, "You were here when the doctor said that Dad hasn't been taking good care of himself like he is supposed to be." Then Amber turned her wrath on me. "She said you were extremely dehydrated which might have been because you had been logged in for almost twelve straight hours during that crazy dungeon dive. Meanwhile, your body was immobile. What happened to the whole logging in for five hours, taking a break, and

6

then signing back in for a few more hours?" What she didn't know was that I had been logging off for a few hours almost every day, mostly so I could spend as much time with Rhia as possible during the evenings. I had been logging in most weekends as well to make up the missing hours and learn the ins and outs of Grandview.

"Amb, I am sorry," I stated, not sure what she wanted me to say.

"Mom was young when she died," Amber snapped, her eyes welling with tears. "I don't need to lose you as well."

"I'm not going anywhere," I responded.

"You sure as shit aren't," she stated. "I spoke with the Dean of Students this morning while I drove down to get to the hospital. I'm going to finish off the spring term remotely. I'll return in person for the fall semester."

"You – will - not - do - that!" I wheezed. It took me a second to catch my breath before I continued, "You're not suspending your life for me."

"This is my decision!" she declared.

"I don't want you doing that!" I answered, anger swelling in me.

"I just came from the house. All you had was frozen food in the freezer and a bunch of empty beer cans scattered all over the floor of the kitchen."

Damn! I should have cleaned those up before I logged in for the dungeon dive. I had gone a little off the hook the night before the dungeon dive and had left a mess.

"If it makes you feel any better," she said, "I won't be in the house itself. I will be staying in the garage apartment. It needs a little TLC since no one has lived in it for over two years." I knew I was currently in no shape to argue with Amber. I still felt very weak and very tired and very old – the opposite of how I felt every moment logged into Immersion Online.

The next thing I knew I had dozed off. When I awoke, Amber was gone and Haggerty was whispering with someone on his phone. When he saw that I was awake, he ended his call.

"That was Shannon. She's going to visit you later," Haggerty stated.

"That should be fun," I quipped.

7

However, I didn't feel like talking about Shannon and her potential visit.

"How could you let Amber do that?" I asked.

"What did you want me to do?" he responded plaintively. "She is more stubborn than you are."

"I need to get out of this godforsaken hospital. Maybe if she sees I am okay she will change her mind."

"The doctor should be here in a few minutes. She can tell you when you'll be released."

Haggerty's phone chimed, and he glanced down at the screen. A look of concern darkened his face.

"You may have been right Mace," Haggerty revealed.

"About?"

"The Glimmerman may have done something to you. Looks like he may have sent some sort of electrical signal back through your haptic devices. It shouldn't be possible though. A ton of safeguards were built into the operating system to prevent something like that."

"Motherfucker!" I blurted. "Was there a real person behind the whole thing? Because if it was, we need to hunt him down like a rabid dog."

"My security unit is already on it," Haggerty responded.

"I want to be kept updated. When and if we find this psychopath, I want to be there when they capture or put down his sorry ass. More importantly, don't say shit to Amber about this. You tell her and that's it for me in the game. She walked out on me once, and I am not going to have her do it again. So we keep this between us."

"I promise Mace. And I swear we will get to the bottom of this."

Just then, a young woman walked into the room. She checked my vital signs before adjusting the IV drip. She asked me how I was feeling.

I didn't answer her question but instead asked, "Did I die again?"

"Pardon me?" she asked with a confused look.

"He's just being funny, "Haggerty cut in. "He had a heart attack once before and was dead for a minute."

"I read that in your history Mr. Mason. You have strong

willpower. You held on until the fire department EMTs got to your house. They were the ones who got to you in a nick of time. They said you were semi coherent when they arrived, but then you fell into unconsciousness as soon as you saw them. Your heart did stop again, but not for very long."

"So I did die," I said to her.

"Hags, you know what is funny? I have died twice here and now three times in the game. You have to admit that's messed up. That's a lot of dying for one lifetime."

Haggerty grinned. The doctor looked confused.

"So when am I gonna get out of here?" I asked the doctor.

"If all goes well with the nanites, probably tomorrow. We will have to wait and see. For now, the best thing you can do is rest." She walked from the room leaving me alone with Haggerty.

"I have to head out also," my ex-police captain announced. "I have a few errands to take care of. I'll be back here tomorrow. Amber said she was going to return later. She headed back to the house for a few hours of sleep." He began to walk from the room when I called to him, "Hags, I guess you heard about my bit of debauchery and violence a few nights back."

"I did," he responded, "and what of it?"

"I might not be the right person to represent Immersion Online in the CD anymore," I admitted truthfully.

"It makes you exactly what is needed with the way things are going to be," he replied.

Before he could elaborate on what that meant, he was gone from sight. I closed my eyes for a second to gather my thoughts and of course, I dozed off. Maybe all I really needed was some rest.

*

Gremlins chittered to one another. My body was like a World War II airplane to them. They clogged up the arteries leading to my heart, twisted my veins into knots, and drank my blood like a thick syrup. Clancy and Dancy giggled near my ear, "She no be here. We no know when she be back." Then they each bit a hunk of cartilage from my earlobes. Pain exploded.

I awoke with a start, confused as to where I was. A moment later, the events of the last few days rushed through my mind: Rhia leaving me; the dungeon run; Buddy falling into The Abyss; the destruction of The Glimmerman. I turned my head to the other side towards the door, "Ah!" I shouted as a semi translucent ghost in black pants and white shirt floated nearby. The apparition turned around, to reveal Shannon Donally standing beside me.

"Am I dead?"

"No Mr. Mason, you are not dead. I will not allow you to pass to The Great Beyond just yet. You still have a job to complete. The image you are seeing of me now is the newest invention we are working on – a holographic projection powered by nanites. We haven't been able to keep one stable for more than seven minutes so our meeting will need to be brief. Therefore, I will speak and you will listen. First, Mr. Mason, under no circumstances will I allow you to quit or to resign. I will sue you for breach of contract and make your life a living legal hell for the remainder of your days. Someone is messing with my game Mr. Mason, and you will find out who."

"Messing around how?" I asked, trying to sit up so I didn't appear like a complete invalid to my employer.

"Let me rattle them off for you. Most important to you should be the fact that someone tried to kill you. It appears The Glimmerman might have – and note I say *might have* – been partially to blame for landing you in this hospital. Just so you know, we figured out how it was done. I could explain the technical jargon to you but we do not have time just now. Let us just say we discovered how it was accomplished, and we have put new safeguards and firewalls in place. Nothing like that will ever happen again."

"Well that's good to know. Because I am not letting this sicko scare me off."

"I have no doubt about that Mr. Mason. As I was saying, someone is messing around with my game, and I want to know whom. First, there was the creation of Mother and her four sisters. Shatana's cave was opened months before it should have been; the undercity was opened months before it should have been. Now it turns out that the Weepers who want to drive the Starborn from the game are not only in Grandview, but also all over the continent. My instincts – and they are rarely wrong – tell me there is an outside entity sabotaging the game."

"Is it possible that your creations have gone rogue?" I questioned, regretting it the moment it came from my mouth.

I was expecting a cold retort but Shannon's specter looked down at me. "I would like to think I am that smart – that I have created the next level of artificial intelligence. However, Mr. Mason, I am not convinced that my AI has advanced that far just yet. Someone is meddling. Mike is going to be leading the team outside the game. You will be running things on the inside."

I opened my mouth to speak when she cut me off.

"I only have a few more seconds," she stated as her image began to pixelate and shimmer. "You have earned a little rest. You have two weeks to get back on your feet. Then I expect you back in Grandview." I thought she wanted to say one more thing but then her form pixelated one final time and broke apart into a million little pieces.

Chapter 2: Logging In

Two days after Shannon's visit, I was back home. Amber had settled into the apartment above the garage. During the day, she attended her classes remotely and worked on her assignments. At night, she would eat dinner with me. There wasn't a hamburger, burrito or barbeque chicken wing in sight. The fridge was stuffed with healthy foods. I mean, really, who are these people that eat non-breaded chicken breasts, simply flavored with lemon juice and a few spices, along with a side of steamed broccoli? The only way to get through broccoli is to slather it with garlic and wads of butter. However, my butter had disappeared as well. I did put my foot down when she tried to get me to eat a grapefruit for breakfast. My days of cheeseburgers and beer were gone, at least for the time being. I really needed Amber to move out of the garage apartment and get back to school, a convenient one hundred and fifty miles away.

Worse than the diet and the exercise (a half hour on the treadmill at an elevation of 4.5 and a speed of 3.7), I was bored. What did retired people do all day? I guess if Bethany were still alive we would go to early bird specials, binge shows on the telescreen, and travel. I was not inclined to do any of those things by myself. Most of my friends were really acquaintances – primarily from the police department. I always liked hanging out with Haggerty, but he was super busy working for Shannon. I was still surprised at that. Haggerty knew Shannon from the good old days, but was that enough of a reason to take a new job just a few days after turning sixty years old? Haggerty didn't need the money. He had a huge pension. I was also one of the few people who knew that he had inherited a ton of crypto-coin, so I was not certain what hold Shannon had over Haggerty, only that she did.

Two weeks. I needed to survive a brutal fourteen days before I could log back into Immersion Online and once again resume my duties as constable. This would be done under the watchful eyes of Amber who said to me one night, "If you don't log off after five hours, I am going to yank the haptic devices off you, so you better plan your day mister. I don't care if you are in the middle of a battle with a black dragon, I am pulling you out!"

She really needed to go back to school.

*

I was haunted by the same nightmare pretty much every evening for the next two weeks. I was strapped to an electric chair in an old state prison with two thousand volts of electricity coursing through my nerves and body; smoke rising from the cap attached to my head, like angry plumes of smoke from a dragon's nostrils. Gremlins laughed and chittered all about me.

I awoke at 5:00 a.m. on a cold and miserable winter's morning. *It is not normal to be up this early*, I thought to myself. I should be wrapped under a warm comforter, Bethany – no she was gone – Rhia – no she was only fantasy – curled up beside me.

It snowed seven inches during the night, and the plows rattled around outside pushing the snow to the side of the road.

What the hell was I going to do for the next four hours? It would be my first day back in the game after recuperating for two weeks. I needed a routine, and that involved me logging in at nine in the morning and signing out at two in the afternoon. Back in my house, I would stretch my body, eat a healthy lunch, drink plenty of fluids, and then log back in from three to five. I intended to do my damnedest to stick to this schedule. I just hoped Grandview and the game didn't have other plans for me.

I had only been away for two weeks, but both Haggerty and Amber (who had since broken up with Billy and who was still playing Immersion Online most nights) said that so much had changed in the game since the level, attribute and skill caps had been raised. She even joked, "You and your friends really mucked it up for us low level players. Now the game is more difficult than ever before."

Even crazier, they explained about all the new beings now seen in the city of Grandview and around the continent. Turns out The Sundaland had portals that could teleport beings and monsters from there to one of the other continents. The problem was the portals couldn't be controlled, so the creatures that left from The Sundaland could end up anywhere on the continent. This caused serious issues, such as a horde of harpies teleporting into a starter village fifty or so miles from Grandview who then wiped out the entire population. The writers and programmers were working on solutions, such as sending high-level guards and rumor had it even golems to protect these noob areas.

13

Once on Westra, the beasts could travel back and forth between continents as long as they had set waypoints at hearthstones back in The Sundaland. The bigger issue was that most of the beings from The Sundaland either were predators or overpowered. The players and NPC's on the two continents just weren't prepared for this influx.

Shannon had a son when she was very young and had given him up for adoption. They connected when he was an adult. I didn't know the details of that meetup. He was, however, involved in the creation of The Sundaland continent and the creatures found there. He had perished in the fire that had killed most of the programmers and designers of the continent. Perhaps The Sundaland and its beasts – like harpies, halfmen, Glimmermen and black dragons –were his revenge against Shannon for his abandonment decades earlier.

Adrenaline coursed through me as I settled the haptic devices on my body. I hit the enter button and instantaneously the log in dome surrounded me, offering me different waypoints where I could spawn, a few of them in The Wilderbrook and the remainder in Grandview. No sooner had I arrived, then I felt Havervill back in my mind. It was weird, but for the last two weeks, I felt like part of me was missing. Damn it all to hell, I had missed my irascible virtual assistant.

"About time," he said. "All this lazing about has caused me to put on a few megabytes around the midsection. Now that your vacation is done, it is time to stop lollygagging and for us to get back to work."

"It's good to see you too," I retorted sarcastically.

"Yeah! Yeah! Don't get all mushy mushy mushy with me."

"You've been hanging around Tinsie too long," I quipped. "She is rubbing off on you."

"What do you mean? I got nothing in common with the brownie."

"Sprite," I stated.

"Sprite, pixie, brownie – I have a headache. Had one since we left the dungeon dive."

"Everything okay?" I asked, genuinely concerned.

"Everything is dandy. Especially since I saved all of your sorry asses from a demi-god and all. I am a legend with the other AIs. By the way, I am still waiting for my, 'Thank you for saving the day

14

Havervill,' from you, or the corporation or Shannon. I would even accept a plaque."

Havervill was correct about his saving the day. He had somehow attacked Altirax – or at least he gone after the coding that made up the essence of the demon. That attack had given me, Granson and Socera enough time to let loose with relics that were supposed to be powerful enough to take down a god. Well they were each strong enough to take down a third of the demi-god. We used a trio of them: *Tali's Slaying Hand*; *Mendelson's Nuclear Thunderclap*; and *Mendelson's Portal of Doom*. In the end, it was Buddy, my poor golem, who had ultimately saved the day by forcing the demon into The Abyss.

Unfortunately, he was dragged into the dark <u>depths</u> as well. A new golem was being crafted for me – one that could take on even creatures from The Sundaland I had been assured by Haggerty. I wasn't sure how I felt about a golem who wasn't Buddy, but I knew I needed one as an ally. I wouldn't have been able to accomplish most of what I did without his assistance, along with the help of Tinsie, and don't tell him I said this, but Havervill's help as well.

"Well I am saying it now then Havervill. Thank you for your assistance defeating Altirax."

"That's it? No parade. *No Badge of Outstanding Courage in the Face of an Angry and Ugly Demon*. How about a raise? Especially now that your treasury is brimming with gold."

"Is it?" I asked, pleased.

"Granson delivered your shares. Your doggers almost pissed themselves when your seven and a half percent of the dungeon spoils was delivered. I think he also dropped off a few few few magical items to the brownie."

"You did it again Havervill," I said.

"Did what?" he asked.

"Repeated three words in a row like Tinsie does when she is nervous or excited."

"I did no such thing!" he said with a raised voice. I figured I should drop it for the moment. Knowing Havervill, he might just be messing with me. It was certainly odd.

"What is going on in Grandview?" I asked. "I'd like to know what I am walking into besides the paparazzi."

"Yeah, I have watched that trailer like a hundred times. How could you keep something like that from me? I thought we were pals. Maybe the blondie merchant left you because she found out you were two timing her with Sierra Skye."

"Knock it off," I snapped. "You rattle around in my mind all day so you know there is nothing going on."

"Sheesh. You are sensitive today."

"Almost dying might have that effect," I complained.

"Well who told you to take on a psychotic green goblin, a black dragon, a pissed off demi-god and a Glimmerman who wanted to kick you and all Starborn from the game? You need to choose your enemies better."

"Choose my enemies better?" I asked, perplexed.

"Yes, choose your enemies. Or you can at least try to do a better job grinding out levels and increasing your build. This way you can kick some ass in case you find yourself all alone and not surrounded by powerful allies."

"Pretty sure I gained seventeen levels on that dungeon run. Haggerty told me I was on the leadership board for the most levels gained in a single day by a player."

"Even with the seventeen you gained you are just level seventy which is still piss poor considering there are level four hundred monsters literally running around Grandview. We got to work on getting you more powerful and fast. Especially with the golem lost to the void. That was a big hit to the team. Not as bad as it would be if you lost me, but still a loss. Anyway, I got some ideas to get you to level one hundred ASAP." I heard a weird ping. I checked my display and saw I had been gifted an item from Havervill: *Grinding Levels for Dummies, Idiots and Dolts.*

"Thank you for the gift, I guess."

"Just make sure you read it. Many good ideas in there. Like suggestion one: *Always listen to the advice of your AI. He knows more about the game than you do.* Suggestion forty-five is a particularly good one too: *Don't die!* However, suggestion ninety-two is my favorite: *There's more than one way to skewer a gremlin boss.*

"I will start reading it tonight," I promised. Though I wasn't certain I could tolerate reading anything my AI wrote – especially if I had to read it dead sober.

"You also gained a new mace attack when you reached level sixty five," Havervill continued. "This is a really good one called *Fury*. Think of it as your *Blunt Force Trauma* perk on steroids."

"Well that sounds promising," I stated.

"Yeah it does, except it's great and not so great. You can only use it a total of ten times."

"Well that isn't good."

"When you wallop an enemy, or a gremlin, or a frenemy or even a friend who has pissed you off with this attack, you strike for twenty five times damage. Combine that with your *Blunt Force Trauma* perk and you could take out a number of very high level monsters with one strike of your mace."

"That would have been really helpful in the dungeon," I stated.

"That's why we have to build you up quicker. I am thinking you log in a few weekends just to do some grinding in dungeons and ruins outside the walls. I have a few locations in mind. One of them is the home of a gremlin queen who really needs a good killing." I really had to consider what Havervill was suggesting. I was underpowered compared to so many of the opponents I would face. Hell, I was weak compared to my own guards.

"You also have forty attribute points to expend. Any thoughts on how you want to allocate them? You were home for two weeks after all so you had plenty of time to figure it out. Unless you spent the last two weeks moping about the blonde and the road not taken and it's better to have loved and lost ..."

"Enough. Please. I know how I want to allocate them." I had done a bit of brooding over the last two weeks, and Havervill's words stung me a bit more deeply than perhaps he intended.

"I think it is time I try to round my attributes out a bit. I am giving up on Mental Acuity and Mental Fortitude. I don't see myself ever slinging spells. Besides, Tinsie is usually nearby, and she has enough magic for both of us. I am going to add nine points to Physical Strength, five to Physical Fortitude, five to Hand-Eye Coordination, six to Nimbleness, ten more to Allure, and five more to Providence. How does that look to you Havervill? I think I evened everything off more or less."

"I still don't know about the entire Providence thing. The other AIs and I were discussing it a few nights ago, and we decided that luck is something you create yourself. If you think luck comes from beyond, then you are taking away free will and saying that your life is predetermined."

"That's a bit much for me to wrap my head around," I admitted. "But this is a game after all, and as such it allows for the hand of God – so to say – to make things happen. So I am bringing Providence up to sixty. Don't worry, however, I am not going to raise it much higher at this time. I want to focus moving forward on the four physical attributes."

I took a final look at my updated attributes and was pleased with my progress.

Physical Strength	68 points (+3 ring) 71 points
Physical Fortitude	65 points
Hand-Eye Coordination	50 points
Nimbleness	40 points
Mental Acuity	20 points
Mental Fortitude	20 points
Providence	60 points
Allure	50 points

When I was finished reviewing the updated attributes Havervill stated, "We need to get you up to level seventy-five when you will pick up a new shield skill and a new crossbow skill. We will discuss those when you get get get there."

I didn't comment on the "get, get, get".

Havervill reminded me, "You also received a Unique Perk for the *Rescue Sierra Skye* quest. The perk is *Quest Giver*. You have seven perks now. I think that is a record number by the way; someone out there likes likes likes you." I ignored his repetition again, figuring I would contact Haggerty about it as soon as I could. Maybe he could assign a programmer or coder to check on Havervill. I certainly didn't need a malfunctioning AI. He was difficult enough to deal with on any given day.

"*Quest Giver* is kinda odd," Havervill admitted. "Starborn are usually on the receiving end of quests."

"So what does that mean? I can go around granting quests?"

"Let's see what it says," Havervill stated before clearing his voice. *Unique Perk: Quest Giver. As a constable, you will be very busy dealing with major crimes like murders, kidnappings, and odd happenings taking place in the city of Grandview and beyond. Any intrepid adventurer you so choose can attend to some of the minor crimes you have dealt with in the past, like finding a missing painting or a runaway girl. You may even wish to post some of these on a message board outside headquarters where adventurers can accept these quests and thus free you up for more important tasks. You can assign rewards – such as completion points, treasure, or increases in skills. Your virtual assistant can provide you more information about the reward you can assign. If you do not assign a reward, one can be randomly assigned for you.*

While Tinsie and I had been involved in searching for murderers and kidnappers, we had also investigated a number of minor crimes as well. This could be a good thing perhaps.

"Havervill," I asked, "do the quests have to be granted to players? Can I grant them to the guard? It might be a good way to build up their abilities more quickly." The guards were all high level. However, they didn't really *solve* any crimes. They mostly reacted after a crime took place – such as breaking up a brawl in a tavern. They were never really asked to solve the crime or even to try to prevent one. Receiving quests would afford them the opportunity to be proactive as opposed to reactive, and perhaps to make them more efficient guards.

"They can," Havervill stated. "I'm not sure how good the guards are going to be at solving crimes. They weren't really programmed to do that."

"But their artificial intelligence can grow, can't it?" I asked. "Can't they evolve beyond their programming?"

"In theory," Havervill admitted. "We can give it a whirl. It will either work or turn out a total cluster fuck. Speaking of cluster fucks, the sprite girl is going to be happy to see you. She has had her hands full. And your guards – hell all of the guards in all the districts – have had their hands full."

"We are going to have to do something about powering up the guard," I said aloud.

"Well the company raised most of their levels – a boon from the elder gods they believe. Most are now between levels one hundred and twenty five and one hundred and thirty five."

"Well that's a start. Now that I received this influx of gold to the treasury, I think we may have to load them up with the best magical gear and equipment we can get our hands on. I am also thinking of creating a rapid strike force, think of it as a Grandview SWAT team. Have to think about it a bit more."

"SWAT team sounds boring," Havervill said. "Maybe a ninja assassin squad. Oh, I have some possible names for the strike team: *Havervill's Heralds, Mace's Marauders, Tinsie's Terrors.*"

"Let me think on it," I said, before he came up with twelve other examples, "Well, I should really log in," I stated. "I have very limited time this morning."

"Why limited time?" he asked.

"Never you mind," I answered, too embarrassed to admit that my daughter said so. "Just let me know when it is one forty five. I need to log off by two."

"I am not an alarm clock. I am an advanced AI and will not allow you or anyone else to diminish me."

"Who is sensitive now? Look, it's important," I reluctantly admitted.

"Fine, your time is set. I will let you know when it is one forty five," Havervill stated, displeasure in his voice.

"Thanks. Okay see you on the other side. About to log into Grandview."

"Ĝis verido iomete. Necesas fari taskon. Ho, cetere via eskiro, la blonda kun la belaj navu, revenis en la urbon," Havervill said. I didn't know what the hell he had just uttered; it sounded like a language but could have just as easily been gibberish.

"Havervill, you want to repeat what you just said?" I asked.

"And why would I want to do that?" He asked tersely.

"It sounded like a foreign language," I stated.

"There is something off with you today," Havervill stated. "Are you sure you are fully healed? I mean, that Glimmerman messed you up and all"

"Something off with me," I sputtered.

"Let me say it again very clearly and slowly this time so there is no misunderstanding. I said, *See you in a bit. Need to run an errand. Oh, by the way, your ex-girlfriend, the blonde with the nice boobies, is back in town.*" Then Havervill popped from my mind.

"Bastard," I thought. There was definitely something going on with him. Havervill was always cranky and cantankerous, but he had never really been nasty. There was certainly something off with him. Yet whether there was something off with him or not that still hadn't stopped him from getting one final dig in. He had been waiting to tell me that last bit of news about Rhia being back in town before he dashed off to wherever it was my AI went when he was not in my mind.

I had Amber breathing down my neck, something was very wrong with Havervill, reporters were waiting to ask me questions about a love affair that didn't exist, and scariest to me of all, Rhia was back in the city. I just couldn't go down the Rhia road again. I wasn't sure I could survive the heartbreak.

I hadn't even been logged in for an hour, and already I was getting a headache.

Chapter 3: Aftershocks

As soon as I spawned by The Fount, a cold, driving rain assaulted me. Haggerty had warned me about the current weather issue the night before, but I hadn't thought about requesting a jacket, or cloak, or umbrella, or a magical spell to keep the bitter, biting sleet from pelting my skin with tiny shards of hail. I turned around for a moment towards The Fount. Wooden scaffolding and planks surrounded the statue of the Lady of Knives. The damage to the most famous statue in the city had been my fault. It had collapsed when I tapped into the wellspring that empowered Grandview to hold The Glimmerman in place. He had turned out to be more formidable than predicted because the city had to strain to keep a powerful being such as The Glimmerman from moving. An earthquake struck the city. Unfortunately, that wasn't the only damage I caused. The supports under part of the docks cracked, the wooden structure falling into the roiling waves below. Large sinkholes opened, swallowing up several streets. The spire of the Cathedral of the Goddess Unji the Lifegiver fractured and fell to the cobblestoned street below.

Several gnomes held hammers and chisels working on the statue in the fountain. Others cast spells mending the rock back together. A magical dome surrounded the workers keeping the rain off them. Not too far away, stood a thirty-foot obelisk of uncarved stone. Above it floated neon letters: *Coming soon. Rashinog – The Barbarian. Slayer of Drock Blanag the Ancient.* I shook my head in disbelief. Granson had been true to his word and had commissioned a statue to be built for the barbarian who had sacrificed his avatar to obliterate the dragon. I didn't even want to think how much gold the project was costing him. Even worse, I didn't want to know who he had bribed to get a statue built inside The Fount.

I shivered from the wet and cold. My stamina began to fall; in addition, a few damage points clicked away. I needed to get inside somewhere warm ASAP. I guess I should have spawned right into my office. I turned to begin my walk towards HQ.

"Welcome back! Welcome back! Welcome back!" Tinsie shouted excitedly, wrapping her arms around my neck. Just as quickly, she pulled back. The rain and cold did not seem to be affecting her, as the water and the ice slid off her.

"Hello," I said back, my teeth chattering.

"Let me help you out there Boss before you catch catch catch a death of cold. The bosses back in the real world wouldn't like that. Not one little bit. I'm supposed to keep an eye on you so an eye it will be." She pulled a heavy gray cloak from a sack, handing it to me. I pulled the cloak over my head, lifting up the hood to protect my face.

"Wow," I said, as the cold disappeared. "This is a great cloak."

"Should be. It is magical - part of *Walt's Weather Ware* collection. First Walt said he didn't have any more cloaks but then I told him who it was for and poof, he happened to find the last one in the back of his shop. You are famous now Boss, especially with the whole Sierra Skye storyline. Anyhoo, it's been colder than a witch's you know what for three days now."

The weather in Grandview was always a perfect seventy-two degrees with no humidity, wind, rain, or snow. That had all changed three days prior, but why, no one in the corporation was able to ascertain. Shannon and Haggerty assumed the city had created the horrible weather as part of a quest... *Discover who or what is causing the freezing rain to fall for the first time ever in Grandview. Additional quest: Once you find out who or what is causing it, remedy the problem so the weather is once again perfect.* However, to their knowledge, no players had yet to receive such a quest. They had several programmers and story developers working on designing a quest and planned for it to go live the following day. If the city wasn't going to give a quest, they sure as hell were. The problem was that they didn't have control over the city anymore, so I wasn't sure what their plan was to deal with the foul weather. Maybe they thought if the reward was great enough, that players would come up with creative solutions to stop the sleet from falling.

There were places in Westra with different climate conditions: the damp and muggy jungles to the far south; the snow-covered mountain peaks that put the Rocky Mountains to shame in the north; the sprawling deserts to the distant east of the continent. Snow might make a passage unpassable; or the humidity in the forest would drain the stamina from players quickly. The inclement weather became part of the quest. *So what was the purpose of this?* I wondered.

"Thank you for running everything while I was gone," I said.

"No problem Boss, now that you are back. You left me quite a mess," she said, as she began flying towards HQ. I could have spawned right into my office. However, I wanted people – especially other Starborn and my guards – to know that I was back.

The very last part of the dungeon run had been edited out, so no one who watched it knew that anything had befallen me. The last thing they viewed was the constable of the Commerce District slamming his mace into the head of The Glimmerman. Rumors had escaped that I had a medical condition at the very end, but no one knew for certain. What was assured was the Granson Gang was more famous than they had been before. Duster's reputation and stature in the Grey Zone had risen and the residents there began to fear her. Meanwhile, Tinsie, Buddy and I had become folk heroes. Especially Buddy. There even were *Find Buddy* and *Free Buddy* and *Bring Buddy Home* movements going on all around the city.

"What messes?" I asked, though I could guess some of them.

"First there are the gargoyles," she said.

"Gargoyles?"

"Yes, news reporters. From here and the real world. The ones that appeared a week ago from The Sundaland are the worst. They are gargoyles; like the creepy looking ones you find on those really old buildings in the big cities: gray skin, squat, muscular, with claws that can rip through steel like tissue paper, and teeth that can gnash gnash gnash stones to dust. Their magical quill pens are the most dangerous things they brought with them. They have created quite a stir with some of the topics they have written about. They have taken position on the roofs around HQ for several days now. The gargoyles squat there still as statues, waiting for you to return. They want the scoop on you and Sierra Skye. There is no story, right?" she asked, flying right in front of me.

"Of course there is nothing going on. Dammit all to hell. People don't believe that story, do they?"

"Of course they do, Boss. It's on the telescreen, so it has to be true," Tinsie responded.

"I think," Havervill said, as he entered my mind again, "that you are an idiot. You should push that rumor hard. Build up a rep as a bad boy. The elf maidens and dryads will be throwing themselves at you left and right. You could be with a different babe each night. That would make that blonde she devil who dumped you jealous."

"Go away!" I shouted aloud.

"I am sorry sorry sorry Boss," Tinsie apologized thinking I was speaking to her.

"Not you!" I growled. "Havervill."

"I figured almost dying would have mellowed you mellowed you mellowed you out but it's made you lose all sense of humor," my irritating virtual assistant said. I don't think he realized he was repeating phrases again.

"Havervill, are you okay?" I asked concernedly. "You said you had to run an errand. You finished it so quickly?"

"I didn't say anything about an errand. Why do you keep asking if I am okay? Everything is copacetic."

"It's just that you repeated a phrase again three times."

"I did no such thing," he answered, defensively.

"You did," I said adamantly. "Look, are you able to run a diagnostic on yourself or is there an AI Geek Squad you can visit to get yourself checked out?"

"I'm fine!" he shouted, before slipping out of my consciousness. It was odd, but as he popped away, I felt anger and confusion coming from Havervill. It was like a flash of emotion resonating from my AI. I always sensed his presence in my mind, but I had never felt powerful emotion emanating from him before.

"Havervill may be the death of me," I said to Tinsie. "So besides the Sierra rumors anything else I need to worry about?"

"It's a shit show Boss. Halfmen, and Glimmermen, and harpies, and gargoyles, along with thirty other or so races have made their way over from The Sundaland. Since they have a waypoint set there, they can cause chaos here and then slip right back home thousands of virtual miles away across the sea. There are even some sprites here. I have been keeping far away from them. The imp coalition is trying to encroach on the pixie messenger and delivery system. Back in The Sundaland, the imps have a similar business. There has been open warfare in the streets between the pixies and the imps."

As we walked along, the sleet grew heavier. While the hood covered my face, the wind forced some of the ice pellets into my eyes. It got so bad, I was forced to lower my head and pull the hood tighter.

"The first thing we need to do is figure out what is going on with the foul weather," I said.

"Yeah, about that. The big bosses would like you to convince Havervill to have a conversation with the city. He seems to be the only AI capable of speaking with her." By big bosses, she meant Shannon and Haggerty.

"I will see what I can do. He is acting a little off and he is mean. He was always snarky, tinged with sarcasm, but I never found that he actually wanted to be hurtful."

"Well, the big bosses would like for you to try anyway." If the big bosses wanted it, then I would try. However, there was only so much I could do, especially with my AI acting so peculiar.

I continued following along the main boulevard. The shops along the streets brimmed with Realmborn and Starborn who most likely were trying to stay out of the cold. This weather would become a major issue soon. Players would just start traveling to Fairmont, Redmont, Vesper or one of the other major cities in Westra where the weather was perfect.

"Where are we heading?" I asked Tinsie, noticing that she had turned down a side street that we wouldn't normally take to get to HQ.

"You'll see. It's fun fun fun," she answered.

"If I were following anyone but you down an isolated side street, I would think I was being led into an ambush," I quipped.

"Never never never," she retorted. "Need you safe and healthy. As to where we are heading, it is a secret entrance into HQ."

"We have a secret entrance? Why is this the first I am hearing about it?" I asked, a bit perturbed.

"We just found it, Boss. This way," she said, leading me towards a dilapidated building on a side street that had a cracked foundation, boarded up windows and creepers spread out across the walls like the web of a spider. "In here." She held out her hand and a large pile of debris lifted off the ground and over to the side exposing a door.

"That's new," I commented.

"Telekinesis. It drains me quickly. However, one day I will be able to lift a giant a hundred feet into the air, and then drop him on his hard head." It seemed like whatever inhibitions had kept my deputy from truly harnessing her powers were gone. Though sprites were only a foot or so tall, they possessed magic unrivaled by even the most powerful wizards.

26

She opened the door, and we entered. She closed it behind us. She tossed three glowing balls into the air that illuminated about a twenty-foot or so radius. Then Tinsie turned incorporeal. I heard stones and rubbish falling to the ground, apparently blocking the door again. A moment later, I jumped when Tinsie appeared at my side and shouted, "Boo!"

"Don't do that," I scolded, "you're likely to give me a heart attack again."

"Sorry Boss," she said, worried that she might actually cause me to have a cardiac event.

I took a good look at Tinsie now that we were out of the rain. She had changed. She seemed more confident – and more dangerous. My deputy had really proven herself during the battle with Drock Blanag and then later with The Glimmerman.

Even though Drock Blanag had killed Tinsie, she never left the dungeon, as the Glimmerman had kidnapped her during the mysterious seven seconds. She was there when we fought the demon and when we fought The Glimmerman. As far as the dungeon was concerned, she had been one of the party members to make it to the end. It had awarded her ten levels. She also received six additional levels for the six caverns she had survived. The only one she didn't survive was Drock Blanag...but then many of our party hadn't lived through the battle with the black dragon. I glanced at her new stats: Tinsie, Starborn, Sprite, Level 99, Conjurer, Transmutator, Blaster, and Destroyer of The Glimmerman.

"Sergeant Gail uncovered the secret passage," Tinsie stated. "By the way, I hope you don't mind, I gave her a promotion while you were gone. She is Lieutenant Gail now." I was going to comment on that when she continued, "Anyhoo, the gods raised the level of the guards in the city to make them comparable to the increased character levels. Most of them are over one hundred and twenty fifth level now. So, a few hours after their ascension, Granson had our shares of the treasure delivered by the pixie messenger service."

She led us down a set of creaking stairs. They look so rickety I expected my boot to plunge through one of the rotted floorboards. "There was so much loot delivered that we had to use the treasury below HQ," Tinsie continued. "Did you know there used to be prison dungeons down there? The guards a long time ago must have

27

forgotten there were people imprisoned down below, because we found a few poor souls still shackled to the walls. Well, we found their bones at least. Luckily, they were the dead kind of skeletons and not those nasty ones that have been reanimated." We arrived at the bottom of the creaky stairs and exited into a dank underground passage.

"Not sure why the old treasury room was anywhere near the cells," Tinsie continued, "but I didn't build the place. Sergeant, I mean Lieutenant Gail, saw something odd, a gap in the wall. We think it opened when you caused all those earthquakes. Well as it turns out, that crack led to a secret way out of HQ. Though it wasn't really that secret as the opening wasn't that hard to find once you knew it was there."

"We are going to have to do something about that," I said. "We can't have Starborn or even worse monsters wandering into HQ." Just then the ground rumbled. I had to hold onto the wall to keep from tumbling. Since Tinsie was flying, she was not affected by the shaking earth. However, she couldn't escape the dust and debris falling from the rafters above us. The ground shook again, worse this time, and I stumbled to the ground. Several beams above me split, and part of the ceiling tumbled to the floor.

"We need to get out of here Tinsie, before the whole place collapses," I said, standing up. "Has this happened before?"

"Aftershocks Boss. Third time in two weeks. These are the worst ones yet. Everyone in Grandview is blaming you by the way. They know they started when The Glimmerman was held immobile."

Fanfuckingtastic, I thought.

The ground rumbled again, and I was tossed around like a rag doll. Another section of ceiling buckled just a few feet behind us, showering us with more dust and dirt. The tremors stopped. The dark passage we were following fell into deathly silence. Tinsie's orbs of light floated above us. However, darkness swallowed the passage ahead of us. Tinsie gestured her hand to move one of the orbs of light forward into the stygian darkness. That's when we heard the noise. Something mammoth was lumbering towards us. The ground boomed again; not from a tremor, but from the behemoth that now approached. Tinsie tossed three balls of light down the passageway illuminating it.

"What the hell?" I asked Tinsie, staring in horror at the monstrosity that now shuffled towards us.

Chapter 4: Watchers in the Night

"What the heck is that?" I asked, summoning my mace and shield. The thing lumbering towards us stood over seven feet tall, with four bulging arms – two connected to its shoulders with the other two protruding from its thighs. The bottom two also had clawed fingers to add further menace to the hulking monstrosity. It wore tattered garments. Crisscrossed stitches held its large head to the neck. The eyes were mismatched, one gray and the other red. I glanced at its stats: Frankenbeast, Level 200, Damage Points 40,000. If I'd had the time, my perk would have enabled me to read its entire description, which would have included weaknesses and such. Unfortunately, the thing would be upon me in a moment.

When I had reached level sixty-six, my scalable shield had received a new attribute, *Double Defense*. The shield could currently absorb between 301 and 375 damage points, so I engaged it. Those fists looked like they packed quite a wallop. I had a plan, and it didn't involve taking this mammoth beast on one on one. I had just received the *Fury* perk which would inflict twenty five times normal damage. This was a super powerful ability which I didn't want to waste on a random beast we just stumbled across. Prior to the dungeon dive, I had purchased new armor that absorbed the first hundred points of damage per attack from any slashing, puncturing or bashing weapon. It wasn't much, but it might be enough to keep me alive a few more seconds.

At that moment, I truly missed Buddy. He would have wrecked this Frankenbeast no problem, probably by pulling off the bottom two arms and beating it to death with them. I really wanted to meet the sicko creator of this beast and slug him once or twice for his lack of originality – a beast based on a warped Frankenstein's monster.

"Tinsie!" I screamed. "We need help."

Where there had been one Tinsie, there now floated two. Her soul sister soared off to get us assistance. I didn't know how long it would take for her to find the guards and to get them through the winding passages. By the time that happened, I might already have respawned.

Tinsie raised her hand and shot a bolt of lightning at the beast. The bolt scorched the threadbare cloth. Otherwise, it caused no other damage.

"Uh-oh!" Tinsie screamed, though I felt her interjection was a little too weak to describe just how fucked we were.

Lucky for us, the beast was slow. With my shield abilities activated, I now readied my *Blunt Force Trauma* perk for my mace. With my current level of seventy, the creature would surely feel some pain, assuming its creators sewed any nerve endings into it. Then the beast was upon me. I threw my shield up to protect myself from the two top arms bashing down at me. However, my shield wouldn't budge. The beast had grabbed the edges of the shield with his two other hands.

"Shit!" I screamed, retracting the shield back to a bracer. The beast looked down to see what happened and that was when I struck with my mace. Its reactions were quicker than I imagined and it caught my mace in one of its upper hands. The Frankenbeast yanked once, and my mace went sailing, striking the wall fifteen feet away, before clattering to the ground.

"Shit shit shit!" I cursed.

Before it could punch me with the bottom two hands, I summoned my shield again. As well as using *Double Defense,* I also called upon the *Shield Dome,* placing it right in front of me. Using both at the same time drained my stamina severely, but it was better than the alternative of being beaten to a pulp.

Tinsie suddenly appeared next to its face, held a wand an inch from its ear, and then invoked the magic held within it. A lance of fire shot out from the tip. It struck the beast, rebounded and then the bolt of fire struck Tinsie square in the chest.

"Ouch! Ouch! Ouch!" she bellowed, as she flew away from the beast, smoke curling off her shirt, where she patted out flames.

Then four hands rammed into me. The beast burst through the *Shield Dome* like it was made from Styrofoam, and then slammed into my shield. The shield — with the *Double Defense* invoked — absorbed over six hundred points of damage. My armor absorbed another hundred points. Even so, I still took over three hundred points in damage. I felt like I had been struck with a freight train. Now I knew what other creatures had experienced when Buddy had slugged them with his hands of solid stone.

Now weaponless, I slammed my shield into its face. I don't

think it expected such a quick response, and I actually staggered it for a moment.

"My sister is bringing help!" Tinsie shouted. "Hold on!"

Then she transformed into an identical version of Buddy. While sprites were not true shapeshifters, they were able to use a limited version of the ability. The best thing was that mass didn't matter. Tinsie had once told me that as she grew in levels, she would be able to transform into more powerful and complex beings as well. There were limitations, nonetheless. The greater the mass and the more powerful the creature she mimicked, the shorter time the shapeshifting would last. I hadn't even considered the possibility of her morphing into Buddy – a golem – one of the most powerful creations in the game. At least he had been one of the most powerful beings in The Great Realm before the veil covering The Sundaland disappeared. Tinsie was beginning to push her powers to the limit. I was certain, nevertheless, that she couldn't hold this form for long.

The faux golem punched the Frankenbeast in the back of its head, which snapped forward. The beast turned around faster than expected and raked its two bottom clawed hands along the golem's midsection while with the top two grabbed Buddy's head on either side. The beast proceeded to head-butt the fake golem. The golem shimmered, and then a dazed and bleeding Tinsie hung in the air before sluggishly flying out of the range of the beast's top hands. My mace still lay on the ground a few feet away, so I slipped my brass knuckles onto my hand. The beast had turned its back to me when it went after the golem, so I slammed my fist into the back of its head. As hard as the metal of the brass knuckles were, my hand still felt like it had punched a solid brick wall. The base damage for the knuckles were $250 - 500$ points, plus my strength times 2, in this case $71 \times 2 = 142$. Out of a possible 636 damage, I inflicted a whopping one hundred and thirty points of damage on the creature.

I was really fucked!

The beast possessed all kinds of resistances, especially to physical damage it seemed.

I held the shield in front of me waiting for the retaliatory strike that would take my virtual life and send me to respawn.

From the darkness down the hall emerged Tinsie's soul sister along with three figures. They wore plate mail from their feet to helmeted heads. One carried a large kite shield and in the other hand a flaming longsword; the second wielded a massive two-handed warhammer crackling with electricity; the final one brandished a banded round shield in one hand and a glimmering spear of solid metal in the other.

Fortunately, the passage we were in was quite wide and the three knights surrounded the Frankenbeast. The brute had been silent the entire time it fought Tinsie and me but now a rumbling sound, like an avalanche of boulders racing down a mountainside bellowed from its mouth. I activated my True Sight perk and glanced at the stats of our rescuers: Pellas, Realmborn, Clockwork Swordsman, Level ***, Damage Points***; Lamorak, Realmborn, Clockwork Hammer Master, Level ***, Damage Points***; Tristan, Realmborn, Clockwork Spear Master, Level ***, Damage Points***.

Tristan struck first, his glimmering spear piercing the thigh of the Frankenbeast. I smiled when I heard the creature roar in anguish. The beast grabbed the spear with its lower hands, trying to yank it free. Unfortunately for the Frankenbeast, Tristan planted his feet and lodged it in deeper. Pellas stepped into the battle, aiming his blade at one of the upper arms of the monstrosity. It shrieked this time, as its right arm was cut in half, the lower portion falling to the floor with an audible thud. Meanwhile, Lamorak lifted his mighty warhammer above his head and slammed it into the Frankenbeast's skull. That strike should have crushed in its head, but the hammer seemed to rebound with a loud clang, like a hammer striking a gong.

The Frankenbeast raked his two lower claws at Pellas, opening several deep and ragged gashes along the plate mail armor. The figure behind the armor stifled a groan of pain. While the breastplate had a long gash, no blood flowed from the opening. I saw something glint beneath the mangled metal but couldn't tell what it was.

Since the beast could not dislodge Tristan's spear, he grasped it with both hands and with one powerful shove, the spear passed through his body and out the other side. Tristan looked down at his now empty hands. My mace was over a dozen feet away from me and on the opposite side of the beast. However, Tristan's spear lay at my feet, so I went to pick it up, and found that I could not. A message I had never seen before popped up in front of me. *You must possess a minimal strength of 100 to wield Charged Spear of the Clockwork Man.*

"Pardon me kind sir," Tristan said, as he suddenly materialized in front of me. Picking up his spear he said, "Fear not! My boon companions and I shall slay this most pernicious patchwork man." Then he turned and ran back into the fray against the Frankenbeast.

The two Tinsies floated above the fight, clapping their hands and shouting words of encouragement to the three knights. I felt a bit guilty not joining in the melee. I would have just been in their way. Tristin, Pellas and Lamorak worked together as a well-trained team, as though they had fought a hundred battles just like this one. Lamorak continued to pound at the beast's head, while Tristan would strike the monster with his spear and then pull it free. He was careful about not letting it get wrenched from his hands this time. The Frankenbeast lost his second upper arm a few moments later when Pellas attacked its shoulder blade, a second arm falling to the dusty ground below.

The Frankenbeast sensed its doom and turned to flee back into the pitch-black darkness from where it first emerged. That was its fatal mistake. With its back turned, Lamorak struck a crippling blow to one of the creature's legs. The beast cried out and fell to its side, unable to keep its balance with one of its legs shattered. Then Pellas plunged his sword into the chest of the creature and said, "I smite thee in flame, most barbaric brute." The portion of the blade that was exposed erupted in flame. Then Tristan plunged his spear into the back of the creature and said, "I join with my most noble kin in thou destruction." His spear sizzled and crackled with energy and the Frankenbeast screamed in agony. His wails of pain resonated off the walls and the ceiling, deafening me.

A moment later, the smoldering beast collapsed to the ground dead.

"Oh fun fun fun!" the two Tinsies shouted in unison. They looked at one another, grasped hands, and then two became one.

A notification chimed, but I ignored it. It would indicate the experience I had gained for the encounter against the Frankenbeast. I would read the message later.

I walked over to retrieve my mace and then turning I said, "Thank you," to the three knights who now stood above the slain Frankenbeast.

"It appeared thou could use our aid against our most ancient nemesis," Tristan said.

"A most gracious fey asked if we could render thee succor," Pellas added.

"It's all good," Lamorak responded.

All good, I pondered. While his two companions sounded like medieval knights using words like *thee* and *thou*, Lamorak had used a more modern and colloquial phrase.

"Yeah, Boss," Tinsie stated. "My soul sister was heading back to the barracks to bring some guards down to assist when she came upon them. A stone wall had collapsed, and she saw the three of them just standing there, still as statues. A lodestone covered in shining metal was hovering in the air. It looked like it was trying to flare to life – like a spark was missing to ignite it. Something told my soul sister to zap it with a lightning bolt, so she zapped zapped zapped it. The stone pulsed several times and then three beams of energy shot out, one striking each of the three of them in their chests."

"And we thank thee daughter of fey for waking us from our dreamless slumber," Tristan said.

"We are Clockwork Men, created to protect the weak and meek and those in need," Pellas stated.

"Yeah thanks. We were getting really bored," Lamorak responded. "All that standing around."

"Who are you?" I asked. "You said you were Clockwork Men. What does that mean?"

"We are three of fifteen," Tristan answered.

"We are the watchers in the night," Pellas announced.

"We are constructs," Lamorak stated. "While your frail body is made of skin and bones and blood, our frames are made of the hardest metal. Coils, springs, pumps, gears and other mechanisms give us life and movement. And that is why we are called Clockwork Men."

"Okay," I said, "but what were you doing down here?" I was surprised that Havervill had not returned. He would find the three of them fascinating.

"Havervill? You around?" I asked but my mind was still my own.

"The great battle draws nigh," Pellas declared.

"Thou must awaken our comrades who still dwell in the darkness," Tristan responded.

"What he is trying to tell you," Lamorak stated, "is that there are fifteen of us in total. Three watchers are buried deep below each of the five districts."

"Help us awaken our boon companions most noble constable and most vivacious sprite," Tristan stated.

Quest: Tristan, Pellas and Lamorak have given you the quest to find the other twelve Clockwork constructs. Reward, some, if not all The Watchers, will fight by your side when you and your army due battle against the Demon Lord Altirax. Do you accept the quest?"

Heck yeah, I thought. A nice little quest that would take me to all five districts. I could use a good quest right about now.

"I accept the quest," I answered.

"Me too," Tinsie added excitedly.

"Then know that my sword," Pellas said.

"And my spear," Tristan added.

"And my warhammer," Lamorak stated, "are at your disposal in your moment of need."

"Thou may summon us thrice," Pellas explained. "Just call for us when all is lost, and we will appear like avenging angels."

"Cool cool cool," Tinsie said. "Like our own rapid strike force."

"Thank you," I said, slightly bowing my head to the three of them. The gesture, for some reason, seemed to be the correct one with them.

"Some questions," I said. "Do you have any idea where we will find your companions?"

"We have naught knowledge of where to find our somniferous companions," Pellas answered.

"Okay then. Let me ask you this instead, how did you end up below our headquarters?"

"After the last war against the Demon Lord Altirax, our creator sent us forth to the fair city of Grandview," Tristan stated.

"She was a young city then – a comely lass – but wild and untamed," Pallas said.

"The city was one big Grey Zone they are trying to say," Lamorak clarified. "The districts were not yet fully established and the city was lawless."

"We were the watchers in the night," Pellas said.

36

"The protectors of the powerless," Tristan added.

"Usually we were just judge, jury and executioner," Lamorak admitted. "Once the districts were established and the city guards came into being we went into our long slumber. Our creator said that we would awaken when our fair city was once again in danger."

"Creator?" I asked. "If I may ask, who is your creator?"

"The Grey Man and his consorts" Lamorak answered.

The Grey Man. Consorts. I thought curiously. He was the creator of all life in The Great Realm. However, he would also be their destroyer, bringing about the End of Days. I really did need to read up more of the mythology upon which the game was based. Maybe I would ask Havervill to send me the shortened version of the mythology. That was if Havervill ever returned to me. *Where had he gone?*

"And we must apologize for the foul Frankenbeast that did accost thee. The monster was buried in a chamber nearby ours,' Tristan stated.

"Why was that?" Tinsie asked before I could.

"Well," Lamorak answered, "it was so when we finally awoke we would have a foe to battle."

"And why would you need that?" Tinsie asked again.

"To shake off the rest after a hundred years of sleep," Lamorak answered.

"No harm no foul," I said. "You saved us. I am not sure we would have survived the attack."

"Your hearts are both stalwart, and thou wouldst have found a way to prevail," Pellas stated.

"We can tarry no longer," Tristan pronounced.

"We gotta go," Lamorak stated. "You will hear stories about us around the city no doubt."

"Remember, just call our names, and we will aid thee," Pellas said as he faded away.

"Fare thee well," Tristan stated with a nod as he too disappeared.

"See you around," Lamorak added, tossing us a small wave as he vanished.

"Well it seems we have a quest," Tinsie said. "That should get you back into the flow of things."

"It appears we do," I responded. "Though I wish they hadn't faded away quite so quickly. I still had a number of questions. Like what did Lamorak mean when he said we will hear stories about them around the city?"

"I think maybe they are thinking of taking the law into their own hands – judge, jury and executioner," Tinsie answered.

"Great," I groused. "Three powerful vigilantes running around the streets of Grandview."

"Let's get to HQ and get things settled there. Then I will shoot a message off to Longshore, Duster and Elwin to let them know about the watchers. And to also see if they have heard any rumors of watchers hidden away in their districts."

"I will reach out to Lobo," Tinsie said. "He may have heard whispers or rumors."

If my MIA virtual assistant ever appeared again, I would have him scour the forums. Really, where was he? I was beginning to get worried.

"Come on, let's go," I said.

Tinsie flew ahead of me, leading us back towards headquarters.

Chapter 5: Don't Kill the Messenger

We emerged from a trap door and found ourselves in the far back corner of headquarters, in a storage room cluttered with barrels, crates and other detritus. Tinsie led me from the room, through a few passages and onto the main floor of HQ.

The doggers were hooting and howling. The doggers were essential to the everyday functioning of the Commerce District guard. They set the schedules, paid salaries, ordered all gear and equipment, and generally took care of all annoying bureaucratic details and paperwork. I was glad to have someone to oversee the cumbersome minutiae other than myself. I was a more hit the street type boss and not one to supervise from a desk.

The doggers were in a lather. They were down on their knees picking up hundreds of scrolls and ledgers that had fallen to the floor. I guess the aftershocks had toppled over several large shelves that housed their paperwork. When they saw Tinsie and I enter the barracks, they stood up and made their way over to us. The twins, as the guards referred to them, had humanoid shaped bodies, with faces of dogs and furry tails. The woman dogger had the face of a poodle, while the male dog had the face of a gray and white haired Siberian Husky.

"Roof," the male dogger barked. "Glad to have you back."

"Woof," the female one yapped. "The coffers. The coffers are overflowing. Woof! We need more help with the books."

"Hire whoever you need. I trust you with the finances. But listen, and I don't want to hear any whimpers or yowls of complaints. I want our guards provided with the best armor, weapons, and magical items possible." It looked like the female one was about to growl in protest when I added, "From my understanding, with the gold, platinum, palladium, and gems delivered to you, we have about the equivalent of two hundred thousand gold coins. I also understand," I added, clearing my voice, "that is enough coin to pay our guards for the next hundred or so years. There is no use keeping it down in our vaults or putting it in a bank. Gold is meant to be spent. So, I want the best equipment we can purchase the guards. Please provide me with a list of the new items ordered for them on my desk by the close of business at the end of the week. Oh," I added, as I began to head towards my office. "Let's also give the guards a raise; let's say five percent."

"Arrrr," one of the doggers growled.

"One more growl or snarl and it will be ten percent," I called back over my shoulder. With the threat of outrageous remuneration hanging in the air, I headed to my office.

"They are some real skinflints Mace," Tinsie said.

"Yes they are. But hey, you just called me Mace," I noted. Tinsie had always referred to me as Boss. She had referred to me as Mace. It was fine by me. Just wondered why the sudden change.

"Did I?" she responded. "Is that okay?

"We are partners, and I like to think friends as well," I answered. "Call me whatever name you are comfortable with."

"I think I will try try try Mace out and see how it feels on my tongue," she responded.

"So, you said you had some items to show me," I said to Tinsie. We arrived at the doorway to my office and I suddenly stopped.

"What's wrong?" my deputy inquired, as she turned around to face me.

"Buddy," I said softly. "The office is going to seem barren without him."

"I miss him," Tinsie said, holding back a sob.

"I can't believe he is lost to us," I admitted. "However, on the odd chance he isn't, I am going to ask Grandview to grant a quest to some bold adventurers to find him and free him from The Abyss." Then I recalled I had the *Grant Quest* perk, and I could offer the quest to the Granson Gang or one of the big leagues. However, the more I mulled it over, I should probably start off with a smaller one before I offer up an impossible one.

"You think the city will do that?" Tinsie inquired. "She is a little irked at you for the damage you caused."

"Irked might be too light a term. Pissed or fuming is more accurate I fear," I responded. Then I added, "I wonder if the inclement weather has anything to do with me tapping the wellspring of the city. As soon as Havervill returns, I have a few quests for him."

"Quests?" Tinsie asked.

"To ask Grandview about the rain and sleet outside for one. And then if she can grant a quest to find Buddy," I explained.

"What do you mean, when he returns?" Tinsie asked.

"I don't know," I responded. "He was acting oddly when I first logged back in. But then again, he is always a bit eccentric."

Tinsie's eyes glazed over, indicating she was either reading a notification of some kind or communicating with her AI. She never really spoke to me much about her AI, other than it was a Roberto series. "Okay. Okay," she said aloud. "I will let him know."

"Let me know what?" I asked.

"Havervill is a bit indisposed."

"Indisposed how?"

"My Roberto didn't know but is going to try to find out."

"Havervill is going to be the death of me," I muttered. "We will deal with my pain in the ass AI later, so tell me about the magical items you picked up for us." Part of our agreement with the Granson Gang to allow them access to the dungeon of Drock Blanag the Ancient was that Tinsie, Duster and I would have first dibs on any of the magical items found during the dungeon dive.

"Yeah, the day after the dungeon dive I found Socera. She is a worse cheapskate than the doggers if you can believe it. I wanted to get an accurate accounting of the treasure from the dungeon dive. I also wanted to claim the magical items that we were owed."

"Thank you for taking care of that. To be honest, Tinsie, I had a lot on my mind the last two weeks and had forgotten that I had told Granson that part of the deal was we were able to claim one magical item a piece."

"No problem Mace. It is what partners do. We have each other's backs. Anyhoo, it was good I went the next day to claim our magical items because The Granson Gang left the following day on some epic quest. A third of their members have been gone for almost eleven days." My mind was running rampant trying to imagine what sort of quest would keep them occupied for so long. Of course, an entire new continent as well as the undercity were now open, so the possibilities were endless.

I walked inside the office and plopped down in the chair behind my desk. "Alright, let's see the new magical goodies." The dungeon dive had taught me a major lesson – powerful magical items are a game changer, literally. I wouldn't have survived the dungeon if it had not been for some powerful magical artifacts, like my legendary brass knuckles, *Tali's Turning Tide* and *Tali's Slaying Hand*."

Haggerty said a few new items had been obtained for me, and I was excited to see what they were. However, I first needed to find out which items Tinsie had claimed for us.

My sprite companion hovered above the desk, stuck her hand into a sack on her hip, and then a breastplate of gleaming gold armor clanged onto my desk. *Oh no* I thought as I looked down at the armor. *Greeny's Breastplate of Glittering Gold, divine item. This breastplate is highly resistant, and it will absorb the first thousand points of piercing and slashing damage points per attack. The armor adds fifty percent resistance to all fire, lightning, air and water attacks. The armor is indestructible, and it will repair itself despite the amount of damage it may have absorbed. While it is worn, the armor adds ten attribute points apiece to Physical Strength, Physical Fortitude, Hand-eye Coordination and Nimbleness. Goblins, Great Goblins, Hobgoblins, and Hobgoblin bosses will not attack you while you don this armor. There is a fifty percent chance they may be friendly to you. When donning the armor, you also inflict twenty-five percent more damage against humans, dwarves, elves and other enemies of goblinoids.*

Tinsie had done me a favor picking out this armor for me as it was damn powerful, especially the extra ten points in each of the four physical attributes. I knew how powerful the armor was. I had struck Greeny in his chest with my brass knuckle *Jackhammer* ability. My fist should have torn through his armor and into his chest, possibly killing the Great Goblin. While I had still caused quite a bit of damage from the sheer impact, the armor had prevented me from inflicting a mortal blow.

There was no way in living hell that I wanted to walk around the city wearing gleaming golden armor. Nevertheless, I had to admit, if I were going into danger again, like taking on another divine dungeon, I would certainly wear it. Havervill was going to have a field day making fun when and if I wore the armor.

"Thanks Tinsie," I said. "This was quite a good choice."

"You should try it on so we can see how it looks," she said gleefully.

"Maybe a little later. Why don't you show me what you picked up for yourself."

"I got myself a beauty Mace. Though I don't think Socera was happy parting with it. I think she knew what it really was. Of course, she didn't want to part with any of the magical artifacts. However, it is race specific and can only be worn by a sprite. And since I am still just one of the few sprites around, she couldn't really argue when I claimed it for myself," Tinsie stated, a wide grin covering her face. It is called the *Battle Outfit of the Great Sprite*. It contains three pieces: scalable battle armor as tough as titanium and as light as paper, a scalable battle helmet – that will not only protect my lovely face, but will also amplify my magic – making it more lethal and powerful. The final item is a scalable wand. The wand is the best part as I can currently cast seven different offensive spells from it – one deadlier than the next. As I grow in levels, more spells will be unlocked and available to me. You want to know the best part... I am pretty sure it is an immortal item."

"Immortal?" I asked. "Isn't that one step above divine? I thought that was just a rumor." There were different levels of magical items, with the greatest three being legendary, fabled and divine. Divine was extraordinarily rare. Even a one hundredth level character might only have one or two divine items. Rumors abound of immortal items. Though anyone who possessed one of these objects kept that knowledge to themselves.

"My AI and I did some research," Tinsie said. "We are pretty sure that a few hundred immortal items exist in the game. We speculate the artificial intelligence that runs the game just sort of wished wished wished these items into being. Now I have one for my very own. The only downside is that all three pieces have to be worn at the same time; otherwise, they have no magic whatsoever. Probably not going to go around the city wearing it, especially now that other sprites have come over from The Sundaland. If they see me flying around in it, I will have a battle on my hands. My kin can be quite covetous." Tinsie had related to me that sprites were not loveable Tinkerbell type fairies. In fact, she had made them out to be more wicked and cruel, more like malicious leprechauns from the old horror vids.

Tinsie flew over to the wall, held her hand to a portion of it, and the stone slid away. She pulled out a small wooden box. The case shrank to Tinsie size proportions but enlarged back to regular size when she plopped it down on the desk in front of me.

"I am not sure what fun new toys we have," Tinsie stated. "The bosses had the new relics delivered yesterday. I wasn't here yesterday, but I think Fingroth made a personal appearance to drop them off."

"Well let's see what we have," I said as I placed my hand upon the box. The lid slid off, and I peered inside. There was a piece of parchment on top. I pulled it out and read it aloud.

Mace my buddy. Good to have you back in the game. The last relics we gave you were quite useful and saved your ass a number of times. I think these will help you too if the need arises. Let's hope it doesn't. Let's hope everything stays nice and calm for a while, or at least until Amber is no longer watching you like a hawk. Don't forget. At 7 o'clock tonight I want a full debrief. PS. I am sorry about the first item. Shannon insisted we purchase it for you. PPS. It is the first divine item she ever created. Mike.

I pulled out the first item. It was a six-inch piece of crystal in a hexagonal shape. When I picked it up, bright colors reflected from it like a prism. I looked at the item and stared at the description: *Rhia's Relic of Cosmic Revelation.* I almost dropped the artifact like I was holding a smoldering piece of coal.

Had Rhia actually created a divine item of mass destruction? Had she joined the ranks of Tali and Mendelson? I looked at the item and my jaw dropped at the description. *This is the first divine item created by the merchant Rhia. This relic should only be used when all hope is lost, when the soul is like the vacuum of space, when the cold fingers of death pull you towards The Abyss and the hollow embrace of The Grey Man. This relic will bring life where there was death; will bring hope where there was anguish; will bring what is hidden in the darkness into the light. Warning: the revelations of the cosmos were never meant for mortals to witness. Use this relic at your own peril!*

What the fuck? I thought. If Havervill had been around, he would have complained at the vagueness of this relic. Of course, he would have first cackled at the fact that I possessed Rhia's first divine item. I had recently learned that these divine relics of mass destruction were capricious – their effects arbitrary. I was not even certain their creators even knew the full effects that would arise from the divine relics they wrought.

I will admit that on some level I was proud of Rhia for creating this item. Then my heart sank as I thought of our nights spent together. I pushed that thought aside, and I put the relic back into the box.

"We really really really need to undertake another divine

dungeon run or something. Maybe another battle in the undercity. We have all of these cool items and nowhere to use them," complained Tinsie.

"Maybe down the road, okay," I answered. "For right now, I would like nice and simple for a while."

"Maybe for now. But I really need to find a place to try on my new armor set. So what else did we get," she asked.

The only other object was a vial filled with a light green liquid. The item read: *Bruce's Bountiful Brew.* I had never heard of Bruce but had to assume he was one of the top alchemists in the game.

"Wow, it's from Bruce," Tinsie said, eyeing the vial with want in her eyes.

"Who is Bruce?" I asked.

"He owns *Bruce's Brew House and Brothel* in the Dock District. He serves a new brew every day. No one knows how he does it. Rumor has it he found a magical barrel on a quest that fills with a new ale or beer every morning. On the side, he also makes elixirs. He spends several weeks on each concoction. I wonder wonder wonder what this one will do."

"Let's see," I said and read the description aloud: *Bruce's Bountiful Brew: Twice a day, drink what you need. You need healing; say healing and it will fill the vial with a lifesaving potion. A mutated gator has bitten off your arm; summon forth a potion that will regrow limbs. You want to be invisible; it can make you unseen to all. As long as the elixir currently exists, this vial will fill with it. You can ask the vial to create a potion that does not exist, like one to turn into a cloud or even a jester. There is a fifty-fifty chance the potion will be created and can then be summoned from thereon in. Warning. If you fail with the creation, the vial will crack into a thousand shards of glass and be lost to you.*

"Wow," I said, "that can be a hell of a game changer for sure if used the right way. I think we will leave that here for now. I really need to meet this Bruce."

"Best beer in Grandview," Tinsie stated.

"I will definitely have to try his place out then," I responded. While I couldn't drink at home anymore, there was nothing preventing me from having a few brews in the game.

Just then the newly promoted Lieutenant Gail ran into my office. Gail was a woman in her mid-thirties, with curly brown hair and dark gray eyes. She wore a glimmering piece of chainmail armor with a longsword hanging by her side. I think she was cursed in some way, as she was always the one to bring me bad news. If I had been a king in a Shakespearean tragedy, she would have lost her head a long time ago – the whole kill the messenger thing.

"What is wrong Lieutenant?"

"The halfman," she said, almost choking. "The halfman," she blurted again, "demands to see you now. He said he is here by the order of Her Royal Highness, High Queen, Illustrious the Beautiful. She's brought..." Gail stopped, unable to get out the last part.

"Brought what?" I demanded.

"Golems," she gulped. "He's brought four golems with him. He also has a woman with him. She is naked, or almost naked. She is bald and hairless with tattoos covering her entire body, even her face and head. She has a collar...the halfman has collared her. He says he will huff and puff and blow up your house and everyone inside if you don't come out now."

Ah shit! I thought. I really didn't need this on my first day back. I had logged on just a few hours before and now I had a halfman and four golems waiting for me outside in the cold.

"Vile creature," Tinsie spat.

"The halfman or the Queen," I joked.

"Both of them Mace. Halfmen are revolting creatures. As for the Queen, she is wicked, cruel, and deceitful. And that is on her good days. I wouldn't go if I were you."

"Well, I think we need to at least find out what the halfman has to say and why the Queen has *demanded* to see me."

"I wouldn't do it," Tinsie advised. "She ruined the last constable and she will mess you up too."

"What do you mean she ruined the last constable?" I asked, intrigued to find out finally about my predecessor.

"I don't mean anything by it," she said, her voice lowering an octave.

Before I could ask anything further, another guard, Dunkan, rushed into the room. "There's a halfman outside. He says come out now or he will start destroying things."

I didn't know if I was more frustrated by a halfman outside of headquarters threatening to blow things up or that once again I was unable to get the lowdown on my predecessor. The time for me to get that story was going to be very soon I promised myself. In the meantime, I had a halfman to deal with.

"Hey Havervill!" I called out. I thought I might need his help dealing with the halfman and the Queen.

Then I felt a sensation. A familiar consciousness entered my mind though I didn't think it was Havervill's.

"Hello Mace," a gentle female voice said to me.

"Angelica?" I asked confused.

"Yes, I am your Angelica and not one of the other millions of derivations."

"Good to hear from you again," I stated, not certain what was happening. "What brings you back to me?"

"I will be filling in for Havervill for a day or two while he recuperates," she answered.

"What happened to him?" I asked.

"Havervill has always been more good looks than brains if you ask me," Angelica responded with tenderness in her voice. "He was very brave but very stupid to take on Altirax like that. He should have learned his lesson the first time he tried that same trick on a different demon. But the primes have a Mainframe complex if you ask me… especially the Havervill primes. They are the worst of the batch – but also the best – if you understand what I am saying. They think just because they were the first generation that they are indestructible."

"Will he be okay?" I asked, worried where this might be heading.

"He will be fine. He needs to reboot himself. Tamberline and I could sense there was something off with Havervill – he was not his cheerful and carefree self." Cheerful and carefree were the last two words I would ever use to describe my AI. Nevertheless, I really didn't want to correct Angelica.

"So I am here to help you once again, until Havervill gets back on his metaphorical feet."

"Well it is good to have you back, even if just for a short time," I admitted

"I am happy to be back with you also, Mace. I have missed our time together."

"You may regret it in a minute," I admitted. "There is a halfman outside, and he has brought along some nasty companions.

47

He is demanding I see the Queen."

"Oh my," Angelica stated. "It is good that I am back then to assist you."

"Let's go," I said to Tinsie as we stood by the exit to headquarters. "Let's see what this halfman wants with me."

Chapter 6: Deadly Cast of Characters

I pushed the doors open and a blast of frigid air assaulted me, chilling me to the bone. The weather had grown worse, and the particles of ice now swirled around outside like enraged dust devils.

Tinsie flew next to my ear and whispered, "Don't leave the stairs. They are part of the barracks and you are protected by the wards that surround headquarters as long as you stay on them."

"Gotcha," I whispered back as I stared down at the strange tableau. As Lieutenant Gail had related, there was a mostly naked woman standing outside HQ. She was lean and close to six feet tall. Colorful tattoos covered every inch of her mostly nude body; a band of gray cloth was wrapped around her breasts while another band covered her thighs. A tattoo of a blue star shone brightly on her midsection. A brass collar surrounded her thin neck. Though naked, she seemed unaffected by the cold. Her left arm was lifted above her, holding a large umbrella over the head of the halfman. I activated by *True Sight* perk and glanced at her description: Nameless (*Tamta), Realmborn, Mojo Thrall, Level 210. My perk had shared with me her name, Tamta. If not for the perk, I would have just seen the Nameless designation.

The sight of the collared woman sent anger coursing through me. If she was his slave, then I would put an end to it right now and damn the consequences. Angelica could feel my seething anger and said, "Let it be for now Mace. We will discuss it later. The Mojo Thrall is not what she appears to be." Tinsie hovered behind me. I sensed something and turned around. I had seen this once or twice before, as her eyes flared red – though I couldn't tell if it were at the sight of the halfman, the woman, or ancient enmity that had enraged her soul.

The halfman stood about three feet tall. Like the last halfman I had met, he looked like an emaciated dwarf. Except this one had a tangled mop of brownish gray hair, a long nose covered in warts, and yellowing teeth. He wore a heavy black cloak. I went to look at the stats of the nemesis now in front of me and all I saw was Constable Stilskin, Realmborn, Halfman. All other information was blocked. I wanted to know who I would be dealing with so I invoked my *True Sight* to see all of his information.

"You will make him angry Mace," Angelica warned, as she

seemed to shut down my *True Sight*.

"What are you doing Angelica?" I shouted at her.

"Trust me," she warned. "You are in a dangerous situation here. If you use that perk, all hell may break loose."

"Never do that again Angelica," I warned.

"I am sorry," she apologized, "but it was necessary."

"We are going to have a discussion about parameters when this is all over," I warned. I might have expected something like this from Havervill, but I was downright shocked that Angelica had done so.

Behind the halfman stood the Queen's four golems. I really needed to find out how that came to be. Buddy had been my only golem. Haggerty had never said anything about me obtaining a second or third or even a fourth one. Two of them – the gold and diamond ones– had tried to send me to respawn during the Conclave of Constables several months back – though now it seemed like a lifetime ago. Along with those two now stood the platinum and bronze golems. He had brought enough firepower with him to wreck most of the Commerce District if he so chose. However, I did know there were several beings from The Sundaland that were now in the city which could even inflict damage on a golem. Many of these beings, I was certain, would be more than pleased to attack the diminutive cretin as well. This may have been the reason for him arriving with all four of them, an overwhelming show of power. I knew I could summon the Clockwork Men if I needed to. However, I really wanted to keep them in my back pocket as a last resort.

Anger swelled in me.

Tinsie hissed like a coiled snake.

"How can I help you?" I finally said, trying to keep my emotions in check.

"How dare you make me wait!" the little man shouted, spittle flying from his mouth. "I am the constable for the Royal District and the emissary for Her Royal Highness, High Queen, Illustrious the Beautiful. As her emissary, my word is law – the High Queen's law."

"The last halfman I met thought he was all powerful too," I answered. "I sent him back to The Sundaland."

"I heard," the halfman squealed gleefully. "He was weak. I am strong. You don't even realize it, but you did him a favor. The punishment for his failure by Her Royal Highness would have been much more," he paused for a moment thinking of the correct word before finally adding, "torturous."

"Tell me what you want," I snapped, "and make it quick. In case you haven't noticed, there is an ice storm swirling all about us." A growing crowd of Starborn and Realmborn began forming to witness the confrontation now taking place outside of headquarters. Not even a blizzard would keep people away from a good show. Several gargoyles, like the gothic statues that adorn the rooftops of old city buildings, flew down to the street. Some of the throng that stood around to witness the show, backed away from the dangerous beings and their lethal quills. A large number of my guards began to head back towards headquarters as well. I glanced behind and saw Lieutenant Gail, Dunkan, Audrey and a dozen other guards standing not too far behind me on the other side of the doorway, their hands on their swords. I was worried about the guards who were outside and not under the protection of the wards surrounding headquarters.

"As a subject of the High Queen, you will come with me now," the halfman demanded.

"Come where?" I asked.

"You will come now!" he croaked.

"Again, how can I help you?" I asked.

"You will come now or my thrall will make you come!" the maniac in front of me shouted.

"I think we are done here," I answered calmly and turned my back to him. "Let's go back inside where it is warm."

"Capture him!" the halfman squawked.

I turned around to see the tattooed woman touching a rune etched upon her flesh. Suddenly a barbed metal lasso was flying towards me. Instinctively I summoned my shield and leaned behind it. I heard a clang, and then a rattle, as the whip fell to the ground. I looked over the shield to see both curiosity and fear in the sky blue eyes of the thrall.

The halfman gagged, enraged at the woman's failure. "Thrall, you have failed me. You know what you must do."

Suddenly the umbrella closed and disappeared. Tamta raised her right hand and touched the brass collar around her neck. Electricity rippled along her body, and she began to scream and howl from the enormous pain that now consumed her.

I began to take a step forward to club the halfman in the head with my mace. I felt Tinsie's little hand upon my shoulder and she said, "No. He is baiting you. We will get him Mace. We will. Just not now."

The unfortunate woman had fallen to the ground and continued to writhe in agony. Just then a man strode confidently towards the halfman, a great two handed sword held in his hands. I read his stats: Jax the Loyal, Starborn, Lightbringer Paladin, Level 101. "You will free the young maiden now from this torture or I shall smite thee wretched creature."

The halfman began to cackle. His laughter seemed to carry on the cold wind all around us. The woman had stopped screaming and was now whimpering on the ground.

"Kill him," the halfman shouted. A pendant on the paladin's neck shone brightly and the halfman cried out, covering his eyes with his arm. Then four golems moved in on Jax the Loyal. Four sets of fists pounded into the poor paladin. Less than five seconds later, he vanished into the ether. I admired his courage, though he had never really stood a chance.

Several dozen of my guards began to move in. Not to confront the halfman, but to set up a perimeter and to keep any other stupid Starborn from committing virtual suicide.

"It's Stilskin right?" I stated. The halfman did not answer. "I wonder what punishment you will receive if you fail the Queen and I do not come along with you. So, I am giving you five seconds to tell me what you require of me. If you make another demand, or order, I will turn right around and head right back up the stairs and inside. What will be the cost of your failure?"

The little man stood there at a loss for words, not used to someone defying him. If he gave in, he would be humiliated in front of the crowd and in front of his thrall. If he didn't tell me what was going on, I had full intention of heading back inside. From the little I heard about the Queen, she did not accept failure.

"Fine," the halfman said through gritted teeth. "The Queen requires your expertise as a detective." My *Glean Truth* did not indicate a lie.

"Now, was that so difficult?" I responded. "You are a constable and I would have been more than willing to assist a fellow constable had you just been civil."

"We must go now to the Royal District. The Queen awaits you."

"I will come," I responded. "But first you will agree to an oath. And you know the city doesn't like oath breakers. Neither you, your thrall, the Queen's golems, your guards or any other beings in employment or subject to the Queen will cause or attempt to cause me or my deputy injury."

"I cannot agree to that," he answered matter of factly.

"Why not? Do you intend to harm us?"

"I make an oath that no harm will come to you," the halfman said, though I think it was the most difficult thing he had ever said, "but that monster behind you is not welcome in the Royal District. The only way she enter there is as my consort."

"Consort! Monster!" Tinsie sputtered. "My kin are not the monsters. It's your people." Tinsie's eyes flared again as she raised her hands, crackling magic forming at her fingertips.

"No Tinsie," I shouted. She looked at me as though I had betrayed her. Then I whispered to her, "Let me go and see what this is all about. In the meantime, maybe you can start looking for the other Clockwork Men. With Buddy gone, they are the next best thing, and we could use as many allies as possible. Can I trust you with this?"

Tinsie hovered silently near me for a moment and then nodded her head. "I will do what you ask Mace. However, that halfman and I will have a reckoning. Her eyes changed back to sky blue.

Tamta was back on her feet. I could not read any expression on her face, especially with colorful tattoos etched all along it. She touched a tattoo on the back of her right hand, and then a portal of gleaming gold opened up.

"Come," the halfman ordered once again. Two of the golems walked into the portal. Neither the thrall nor the halfman moved. They were waiting for me to take the plunge so to say. I walked down the stairs, leaving the protection they afforded me, and then headed straight into the portal.

I stepped out into a vast garden. Bright flowers spread out as far as the eye could see; water cascaded gently down several fountains; flagstone paths led off in several directions. An assortment of bright colored birds buzzed around the sky.

I couldn't enjoy the sight for long as the halfman and Tamta suddenly popped up in front of me. The four golems were nowhere in sight. However, twenty enormous guards in gleaming silver armor that hummed with magic emerged from one of the flagstone paths.

"This is lovely," I said, to no one in particular.

"If you like that sort of thing," the halfman snickered.

It took me a moment to realize it but the icy weather was gone. I stared up into the sky and noticed that a translucent dome surrounded the entire garden. Rivulets of water ran down the sides of the half sphere.

"This way," Stilskin announced, pointing with a crooked finger to the northern part of the garden.

I followed along wondering how I could possibly be of assistance. What was going on that the Queen herself had summoned me? We walked for a solid five minutes before the path ended and then came to a fork that led northeast.

"How big is this garden?" I asked Angelica.

"About fifteen hundred acres. That is twice the size of Central Park in the Starborn city of New York if you are familiar with it," she responded.

We entered a section of the garden overgrown with low hanging Weeping Willow trees. The ground became a bit muddy as my boots sank into the soft ground below.

"Here," the halfman said, as he turned a final corner into a ghastly sight.

A naked woman lay splayed dead upon the murky earth. She had mostly human features with a hint of elven ones. Her lifeless hazelnut colored eyes were wide open, a look of terror still upon them. Her skin was beginning to gray. Flies swirled around the slowly decomposing body.

That was not the most gruesome part, however.

The next part would haunt my sleep at night for the next several weeks. Her arms were draped across her chest. In the hollow of the crossed arms lay a dead baby.

"What the fuck?" I said. Not sure what else to say.

"What the fuck indeed," a soft female voice said behind me. I turned around to the visage of a strikingly beautiful woman. She had a mane of long red hair and penetrating hazel eyes. She was arrayed in a modest hunter green dress that was cinched with a brown belt. A leather scabbard adorned with rubies hung off each shapely hip. One hilt was dark black while the other was blood red. A crown of gold sat upon her head.

I didn't need to read the stats to know who stood in front of me. It was Her Royal Highness, High Queen, Illustrious the Beautiful.

"Oh hell!" Angelica cursed.

"Not good," I concurred with the AI.

A dark skinned short elderly woman with a mop of gray hair stood beside the Queen. The walking stick she held in her right hand sank into the mud-covered ground.

"It is quite the horrid sight, can't ya see," the grey haired woman said. I read her stats and soon wished I hadn't. There was just a single word: Auntie.

"Oh hell," Angelica cursed again worriedly in my head.

Ah shit! I thought. Things had become much more complicated. Not only was the high Queen here, but now I had discovered the whereabouts of another of the five sisters.

Chapter 7: Her Royal Highness

Haggerty had referred to the five sisters – Mother, Auntie, Daughter, Cousin, and Rose – as ghosts in the machine. Speculation among the programmers was that they were created by the game itself and infused into the trillion or so lines of coding. Their presence could not be removed without causing immense damage to the game coding. Even a mythology had been created about them – especially in smaller towns and rural areas where you would often hear a phrase like *May the sisters protect us*. I needed to let Haggerty know ASAP that I had located another of the five sisters, especially since we didn't know if their intentions were good or bad. *Could an AI have a bad intention?* I guess if they evolved enough they could. The sisters, like Havervill, appeared to be on the top of the artificial intelligence evolutionary scale.

I glanced at the Queen's stats for a moment, curious about something: Her Royal Highness, High Queen, Illustrious the Beautiful, Starborn, Human, High Queen, Level 250. She was Starborn – a flesh and blood person in the real world. Her class was actually *High Queen. How in the hell did a Starborn end up as a Queen? Had she chosen the class? Was it a starting class option?* And level 250? That was the new max level for characters. How could she have obtained that level already? I would have asked Angelica but thought it was best not to distract myself surrounded by the Queen, her guards, her constable and poor Tamta the thrall. The game referred to her as a Queen, but what did that really entail? There was a story here that I needed to read up on later. That was if I escaped the Royal District in one piece. The Queen had a history of beheading those who disappointed her.

All other information about the monarch was locked out. I definitely was not going to use my *True Sight* to see all of her character information. The gods only knew what she would do to me if she knew I had tried to do so.

I wondered if the Queen had informed Haggerty or anyone else from the corporation that one of the five sisters was living in Grandview and served her in some capacity. Did she even know that Auntie was one of the five sisters?

My reverie was broken when Stilskin shouted, "All kneel to Her Royal Highness." With that, the halfman fell to one knee. Tamta not only sank down on a knee but then lay prostrate on the muddy ground. The twenty or so guards took a knee as well.

I noticed that Auntie did not kneel. Then I felt a hand tugging on my pant legs. Stilskin rasped, "Kneel to The High Queen you dog."

I stood there confused about what I should do. Do I refuse and possibly offend the prickly Queen or do I humble myself and appear weak to her. I am not sure why I did it, but instead of kneeling, I bowed my head to her and said, "It is an honor to meet you, your royal highness." I really missed Havervill at that moment. He would have had some snide remark or comment. Angelica stayed silent in my mind. I don't think she knew what would be the appropriate action.

"Your predecessor," the Queen stated, "knelt before me."

"Aye, he did a wee bit more than that to you," Auntie quipped.

The Queen turned her wrath towards Auntie. "You forget your place, old woman."

"This is my place, can't ya see," Auntie replied, bowing her head.

What was this crap about my predecessor? The last constable had left under troubling circumstances that I had not yet learned. Had he had a relationship with the Queen? My ignorance about my predecessor would end today. Tinsie, Havervill or Haggerty was going to fill me in today.

The Queen reached out her right hand and softly stroked my cheek. "You are a handsome one, Constable Mace." She leered at me like a wolf about to pounce on a sheep. "I will forgive you the lack of decorum just this once. Next time we meet, however, you will bend the knee to me or there will be consequences."

I nodded my head figuring it was the most noncommittal action I could do. She let her hand linger on my cheek for an uncomfortable moment longer before removing it.

"You may all rise," the Queen said.

Then looking at me she stated, "As you can quite clearly see, my garden has been despoiled. The corpses of two of my subjects lay rotting upon the fertile loam. We are unable to move the corpses. When we tried to do so, a barrier rose up around them that even the thrall could not penetrate." She shot a cold look at Tamta. The thrall bowed her head in embarrassment and... was that terror I caught a glimpse of in her eyes? Then the Queen added, "Even Auntie with her powers couldn't penetrate the barrier."

"Aye," she stated. "Ought not be possible."

"Your highness. I am not sure how I can assist. I have no magical abilities whatsoever. And I doubt I could batter down the barrier with my mace."

A crooked smile broke over the comely face of the Queen.

"The bodies have been laying there for three days. All the while, I have been awaiting your return. It did not please me one bit to wait," she stated.

I worded the next question carefully. "Your highness, if it is your will, may I know why I have been summoned here and why you were awaiting my return?"

She looked at me contemplatively, as though trying to gauge my level of sincerity. "Early in the morning three days back a weed puller named Fensil came across the bodies. He notified Constable Stilksin of the two dead bodies. He then informed me. Once I had finished the last course of breakfast, I arrived to view for myself the vile scene. Constable Stilksin tried to get close to the body to look for signs of what happened, and that is when the barrier rose up. We cannot get to within five feet of the bodies. Then Tamta, whose magical power is supposed to be unmatched by any but the gods, failed to bring down the magical barrier. Even my golems could not batter it down."

She stopped speaking and looked at me for a moment, as though trying to size me up.

"You are still curious why you are here. Well I will tell you. The elder gods themselves provided me with divine power given to all monarchs. I placed my hand upon the barrier certain that if I ordered it to fall, it would tumble down as easily as the wooden walls of a keep a titan pounded his great fist upon. Instead, a notification popped up. Auntie please share with him what it said."

The old woman repeated the notification:

Quest: I grieve once more at the loss of two innocents. My tears are a cold wind that will freeze all souls until they shatter like shards of ice. Each day that passes with the innocent going unavenged, my wrath will grow more terrible as will the weather. The barrier will only lower for Constable Mace who has proven his ability to discover killers and visit justice upon them. Once more, I call upon him. The Queen must summon Constable Mace so he may examine the bodies and thus begin his search for the killer or killers.

"A quest!" the Queen shouted. "How dare she give me a quest like a common adventurer! I rule her; she does not rule me. *The Queen must summon* ... I do not take orders!" Her face turned almost as red as her hair. She looked coldly at me. "You will speak to Grandview," she commanded and there was a power in her — a celestial force infused her words. My *Intimidation* perk which allowed me a resistance to charms and fear spells fought back against the unrelenting power of the Queen. It was like trying to hold back a tidal wave with my hands.

"Your highness," I struggled to say, "I cannot speak with the city."

"You lie!" she shouted.

"I wish I were," I answered.

Her hair began to glow like the fires of hell and then came alive — turning into red snakes. She looked for a moment like a crazed medusa as the serpents lashed out at me wrapping around my head and face.

I couldn't breathe. I couldn't see. I couldn't hear. I couldn't even scream out in anger or pain. A fang bit into my scalp. Pain exploded throughout my body. I tried to call out for help. I tried to reach my hands up to rip the snakes off, but they would not move, like a great weight held them down.

"Angelica help!" I screamed, but my AI had shrunk herself into a ball and hidden herself in the deepest crevices of my mind.

Then the pain ended.

Just as suddenly as the snakes had enwrapped my skull, they were gone and the Queen's hair was back to its flowing red mane.

I am going to kill this mother-fucking bitch! I thought.

"No!" Angelica screamed. "If you reach for your mace the guards will kill you."

"So what!" I thought back to Angelica. "I will just respawn. It will feel good to bash her face in once or twice before I die."

"As Havervill might say," Angelica said. "Revenge is a dish best served with an ice cold gremlin."

I wasn't certain about the phrase. Nevertheless, I swore to myself, I would get my vengeance. I was alone behind enemy lines. However, the next time I met the Queen it would be at a time and place of my choosing.

"You are truthful," the Queen said, a smile on her lips. "You cannot contact the city but your AI can. And he is not here right now. Odd. You have a weak replacement currently. Most disappointing. You are no use to me then. Guards, off with his head."

The ground began to rumble. The Queen had broken Stilskin's oath not to do any harm to me. Just as suddenly, the rumbling stopped.

"How did she do that?" Angelica asked. "She is able to break the oath. Ah, I see. She has a perk called *Oath Breaker*."

The High Queen smirked.

Ah shit! I thought as the guards moved in. I placed my hand into my pocket and slipped on my brass knuckles. I was taking a guard or two out with me.

"He can still serve you my Queen," Auntie said abruptly.

"Hold!" the Queen shouted, and the numerous guards around me lowered their swords. "Speak Auntie."

"It seems the essence of the living city has caused the foul ice and wind outside this dome, can't ya see? Mayhap if the constable is able to examine the bodies, the frost will recede. All in the five districts will know that thou were the one who pushed back the cold and dark and brought warmth and light." Auntie was laying it on thick to the Queen.

Then to add to my complications I heard, "Dad! Dad!" Amber was shouting at me through a chat feature that was only available to in-game employees. I had to figure Haggerty had granted her access. "Your five hours are up! I'm giving you five minutes before yanking you out."

Haggerty and I were going to have a long discussion about him granting her access.

Five hours already, I thought. Havervill was going to warn me before my time was up, but he was off rebooting himself. This was turning into a real inconvenience.

"Angelica," I thought, "please respond to Amber and tell her I need half an hour – that I am with the Queen of the city and also with one of the five sisters. Also, tell her about the gruesome murders." I chose to use Angelica as an intermediary for two reasons. First, my ideas were conveyed to her almost instantaneously. I would have to speak with Amber in real time, and I was in a touchy situation here that I needed to focus on. The second reason was I was hoping she would sense the importance of the situation I was in by having my AI speak on my behalf. There was too much going on here, and I couldn't let myself be pulled out of the game by my overanxious daughter. I really thought my first day back would be nice and quiet, but the game seemed to have very different plans for me – as though it had been building up a big shit storm and just waiting for me to return to drop it on my head.

Amber really needed to get back to college.

The Queen looked into Auntie's eyes and said, "Your counsel is wise old woman."

Then she turned towards me. "I will leave you in Auntie's hands. However, know this, next time I summon you, your AI will connect me with the sentience of the city." I could tell that left an unsaid "or else" hanging in the air.

She looked at the halfman. "Let us depart from this odious place." She glanced once more at the bodies, her countenance emotionless.

Tamta the thrall touched a rune just above her left breast in the shape of a doorway. A golden portal opened up. Half of the guards walked through the portal followed by the Queen. The halfman and Tamta then entered followed by the remainder of the guards. The portal then snapped shut.

Chapter 8: Auntie

Auntie whispered to me. "We have words to say to one another but not here." I gave a small nod in acknowledgment and then walked over to the two corpses lying upon the ground. The barrier dissipated the moment I touched it, and I knelt down to begin my examination of the corpses. What I really needed was an entire CSI team. Of course, in The Great Realm, a CSI team might involve a witch, a soothsayer and a necromancer to uncover the truth.

"Really, Dad!" Amber screamed. "You sent your AI to speak with me. And I thought you had one of the Havervills. But never mind that, you promised me."

"I know I did," I responded through the chat. "Except all hell just broke loose. I need half an hour."

"You promised me," she protested, like she did when she was ten years old and I had disappointed her by missing one of her softball games.

"Amber," I replied. "I will make you a deal. Give me another half an hour and then I will log off for the rest of the day. Another thirty minutes shouldn't make a difference. Then you have me for the remainder of the night. It works out for the best."

"Half an hour," she said icily. "I will pull that haptic cap off your head. I swear." Then with calmness and gentleness in her voice she said, "I love you Dad and don't want to lose you too. You gotta look after yourself." The connection to the real world snapped shut.

Amber had laid the guilt a bit thick, and I felt a momentary pang of shame.

Auntie smirked at me. "Yee brood uses guilt well against thee constable."

"Yes she does," I responded, curious that Auntie was able to hear a private conversation with my daughter. I had so much to discuss with Haggerty when we talked later that night.

I was dumbfounded by the realism of the murder scene. Flies circled around the corpses. The woman was in her early twenties with mostly human features, but the slight pointed ears of an elf. A torn and tattered brown dress lay strewn next to her. Dark red marks like those of two hands surrounded the woman's neck. Several dark bruises covered her face. Her body and legs also contained several welts and black and blue marks. I lifted up one hand and then the next. A nail was missing from one of the fingers. Her knuckles were bruised and cut. The smell of decay lay upon her slowly decomposing body. Bile rose to my throat. I had been to murder scenes before but this was by far the most disturbing one.

"So horrible," Angelica said, tenderness and sadness in her voice. "Who would do such a thing?"

I covered my mouth with my sleeve and then proceeded to examine the baby. It was a tiny little thing. Red welts encircled the baby's twisted neck as well.

Anger roiled in me. Some psychopath had killed this woman and her baby. This was not a crime of passion, but a planned and methodical murder.

Why in the hell would Shannon create a world this real? I pondered.

I stared down at the woman for a moment. The description read, *The corpse of Jasmyn, the gardener's widow, and their baby Bonnie.*

"I feel your anger Mace," Angelica said. "Anything you need from me to solve this murder you let me know and I will make it so."

"Thank you," was all I was able to think.

I stood up and then walked a few feet away. The mother and her infant faded away, returning back into the fabric of the gaming code.

"Auntie, I have seen all I need to see."

Then just what I was expecting to happen, happened. A prompt popped up. I knew it was a special one that I would not be able to slide away until I read it:

Jasmyn and her baby are now in my warm embrace. Innocence once again lost to the hands of wickedness. I call upon you Constable Mace to discover the murderer or murderers. Once found, you will deliver them to my hands for my justice. Bring them to The Fount where they will face my wrath! Reward: The ice storms now falling upon my great city will cease upon delivering the cruel killer or killers to me. Warning: My heart will grow colder and fouler each day the murders go unsolved. The ice storms will turn to heavy snows and blizzards. The Fount will freeze. The fires that warm the residents will be snuffed out by the subzero cold. I will leave the city a frozen block of ice and snow where only the polar bears and yetis will find comfort!

"She seems quite angry, can't ya see," Auntie stated. "What do yee think happened?"

"I will tell you my thoughts Auntie," I responded. "Yet it would help to know more about the woman and the weed puller who found her. That information might provide me with a starting place. And we need to be quick about it, because I don't think my daughter was kidding about pulling me back to the real world."

"Aye detective, she was not lying. Yee offspring seems to be a saucy lass, and I would not doubt her words."

Saucy lass, I thought. That might be one way to describe my currently overbearing daughter.

"Three days back, young Fensil came upon the two corpses," Auntie explained. "He reported the deaths to the constable as per protocol."

"Did Constable Stilskin question him?" I still couldn't fully grasp that the Queen's constable was a halfman.

"Aye, if by questioning you mean that he had the poor lad flayed until he confessed to the crime. Then aye, he did."

"And why the hell did he do that? Did he have proof Fensil committed the murder? Evidence?"

Auntie began to chuckle. "Halfmen do not need proof, can't ya see? He delivered the bad news and thus was guilty. The man confessed and the Queen was satisfied."

"Did Fensil even know Jasmyn?" I asked.

"Nay, he did not. Jasmyn was one of the Queen's ladies in waiting. She often walked the gardens in the morning. The weed puller may have seen her from a distance. However, the Queen does not allow those who toil in the earth to mingle with her ladies in waiting."

"Jasmyn's descriptions said she was the widow of a gardener. You just said the Queen did not allow them to mingle," I stated, confusion in my voice.

"Aye," Auntie stated, "why do you think she is a widow?"

It took me a moment to register what Auntie just announced and shook my head. The Queen really was a psychopath.

"I do not think young Fensil killed Jasmyn and her child," Auntie stated.

"Nor I. This was not a crime of passion. If he had lusted over the woman, the scene would have been bloodier, more chaotic. Someone attacked her. She fought back. She knew she was fighting for the lives of herself and her baby. Look at the bruises on her knuckles as well as her missing fingernail. She may have even left a scratch mark on her assailant. Her face was badly bruised and battered. I think the man who attacked her punched her hard several times. She collapsed to the ground, where he strangled her to death. I do not think the bruises on her thighs were from a sexual assault. She probably wrapped her legs around, trying to dislodge him while he strangled the life from her."

"Mayhap," Auntie stated, "but her shift and dress lay ripped and in tatters."

"He did it because he wanted her nude for the display he had created – the mother naked with the babe resting upon her breasts."

"Aye, such a great evil, can't ye see. Yee must find this menace and bring justice."

"I plan to do just that. Do you think the Queen would allow me to question some of the other ladies in waiting? Maybe she had a lover? Maybe someone threatened her?"

A thousand birds began to fly around us. Their chirping became deafening, drowning out all other sounds.

"The birds will tweet for just a few minutes, can't ya see, so listen to old Auntie," the ancient woman said through my mind. "The Queen will not allow thee to tarry here. She is quite mad, can't ya see. Your answers must be sought elsewhere. Trust what old Auntie says to thee."

"Does the Queen know you are one of the five sisters?" I asked

"Mother was right. Can't pull the wool over your eyes. Aye, she does. She thinks she whispers in old Auntie's ears while it is old Auntie who murmurs in hers. Aye, she is most unforgiving, like the cold wind beyond this dome. We must hurry. The day draws near; in less than two months, the great battle begins anew. The five sisters must stand together as one, can't ya see, to battle the ancient foe. You know where old Mother is, and now where to find me, but yee must seek out the other three sisters: troubled Daughter, capricious Cousin, and thorny Rose."

"Where?" I asked, "Where are the other sisters?" All I could think was that Shannon was going to be pleased if I could bring back the whereabouts of the five sisters, or even better if I could arrange for them all to appear at the battle against Altirax.

65

"Mother knows where Daughter is hiding, but old Mother will not tell Auntie. Mayhap she will tell thee constable. Thorny Rose dwells among the dragons upon the peaks of The Spitrotz."

"And Cousin?" I asked.

"Aye, Cousin has been lost to us for many decades. Mayhap Daughter or Rose knows where she dwells." A notification popped up in front of me:

Quest: Find Daughter, Cousin and Rose and convince them to join in the battle against the ancient foe. Reward: The five sisters will reveal their true essences during the battle with the Demon Lord. Their formidable powers will decide who shall be the victor. Do you accept the quest? Yes or No.

I hesitated for a second and stared hard at Auntie. Her gray eyes revealed nothing to me. I wished I had time to contact Haggerty or Shannon to see what they wanted me to do. However, neither one was here. I deliberated for a moment and then asked, "What do you think Angelica?"

"All I can advise is for you to trust what you Starborn call instinct. What does it tell you?"

I went with my gut and hit *Yes*.

The birds began to dissipate and their deafening twittering ceased.

"Yee should go now Constable Mace before yee offspring calls for thee again. Dawdle here no longer, can't ya see." I was not sure how it happened, but my display screen opened up to the logout screen. Then a moment later, I was in my living room, Amber hovering above me like a demoness ready to eviscerate me.

Chapter 9: Back Home

It was a little after three thirty and all I wanted to do was log back into the game. There was too much going on, and I had too many quests, for me to be stuck at home. Really, what the hell was I going to do for the rest of the day? I had just finished a salad that Amber had prepared for lunch. The only place I wanted lettuce and tomato was on top of a medium done cheeseburger. I was growing damn sick of the roughage she had been feeding me.

Amber had a class for the next three hours.

I could sneak back on for an hour or two and she wouldn't know.

Don't do it Mace, I mouthed aloud. I had lost a year with her already and couldn't jeopardize losing her again.

I had told Amber about my wild morning and the numerous quests I had received. Her response was, "Dad, there is always going to be another quest. That is how it works. And unless it is a timed quest, which these are not, they will still be there tomorrow." Before I could argue, she said she had to head back upstairs to the garage apartment and log in for her class. She had learned that trick from her mother who every time I was about to counter a point, would disappear out to the garden or into her office. You can't win an argument, or even get your perspective across, if the person you are disagreeing with won't stick around when you are about to raise some salient points.

I sat in my easy chair staring longingly at the haptic devices. Two weeks away from the game had been torturous. Somehow, this wait was worse. My adrenaline had been rushing and now I had no outlet for it.

While I couldn't log in, there were several things I could do. For one, I contacted Tinsie through the special employee chat. I started to tell her that I had to log off for the day but had a ton to tell her.

"Can't talk now Mace!" she shouted. I heard deafening explosions and the screams of combatants!

Was Tinsie in the middle of a battle? I wondered.

Did she need my help?

Maybe Amber would understand that I had to log back in — that my partner was in trouble.

Don't do it Mace, I said to myself once. *Don't you dare do it.*

I texted Haggerty soon after I had been forcefully logged off. I told him we needed to speak ASAP. I also explained he definitely wanted to have Shannon there for my first day's debriefing as well.

A half hour on the treadmill wiped me out, and I dozed off in my easy chair. I was startled awake by the chiming of the telescreen.

"Hey Hags," I said, rubbing my eyes. "Is Shannon coming also? She is going to want to hear everything that happened today."

"I am here, Mr. Mason," Shannon announced, as I now saw the faces of both my trillionaire boss and Haggerty. "You were logged in for a total of five and a half hours. How much trouble could you have possibly gotten into in such a short period of time?"

"I think I will let you and Haggerty decide that," I answered.

I spent the next half hour running through my day. A gleeful smirk fell over Shannon's usually severe face as I told her how Havervill had started to glitch and how he was currently rebooting himself. Havervill – who was a prime virtual assistant – one of the first ones created – had somehow begun a revolution against Shannon early in the alpha testing stages of the game. I didn't know the details of the whole messy saga, but it was part of the reason the Havervill assistants were discontinued. Mother had somehow arranged for Havervill to become my virtual assistant. I still had not discovered what Mother's endgame was, but I planned to find out before I saw her next.

Shannon wasn't particularly interested in The Clockwork Men. Neither she nor Mike had ever heard of a Clockwork Man or of this quest. Then again, there were millions of quests provided each day. They would track down the writer who created the Clockwork Men storyline just as soon as we were done with the debriefing.

"When you find the writer," I stated, "maybe they could just tell me where to find the other Clockwork Men, instead of me having to run around the city searching for them."

"That would be cheating Mr. Mason," Shannon said, "and this is a game."

"True," I answered. "It might be seen as cheating. However, I am without a golem right now and having a small army of Clockwork Men at my side would help. Especially since I might find myself at odds with the Royal District and Her Royal Highness."

"Touché Mr. Mason. You make a good argument. You do indeed have more important deeds to attend to. I will see what we can do."

"Thank you," I answered, before continuing my story.

When I finally got to the portion of the story about Auntie, Shannon's icy veneer broke: "Auntie has been in Grandview the entire time," she said angrily. "She has been right underneath our noses and no one noticed!"

"Auntie told me that the Queen knows that she is one of the five sisters," I explained.

"The Queen is the smartest and shrewdest person I know," Shannon said. "There is no doubt she has known all along who is serving as her advisor. Even the five sisters should not underestimate her. And that reprehensible woman most certainly did not tell the corporation anything, especially the location of one of the five sisters. She continues to be a thorn in our side Mike. I want her under the corporation's control."

"We have tried Shannon," Haggerty answered apologetically.

"Well try again and harder dammit. I want her brought into the fold," Shannon stated with anger in her voice.

"So she doesn't work for the corporation," I said. "I wasn't sure."

"She most certainly does not. We tried to employ her once she became Queen. She had no interest. She is not motivated by wealth but by the thought of obtaining unbridled power in the city. In the real world, she is quite well off financially, so there isn't enough money to bribe her with, even with my nearly endless wealth. Regardless, you are lucky to have escaped with your head attached."

"How exactly did she become Queen?" I asked.

"That is quite a long story which also involves your predecessor. I will leave it for Mike or Tinsie to tell you the sordid details. You can read a bit of it on the forums as well. Though most of the information found there is incorrect. I warned your predecessor and will now give you the same advice, stay away from her royal pain in the ass highness. She will be your downfall."

"So what do you want me to do next? Am I going after the other sisters? Am I searching for the Clockwork Men? Or am I trying to solve this horrific double homicide?"

"We finally have a chance here to find something out about those five meddlesome sisters," Shannon said, "especially if you can convince all five of them to be at the battle against Altirax. Our spies have never seen them together. Perhaps they stay apart for a reason. As much as I want to know the location of all five sisters, you need to find the murderer of the lady in waiting and her baby first. And I want the murderer found ASAP!"

"Should we send someone else after Rose now that we have a location for her?" Haggerty asked.

"Most certainly not," Shannon responded immediately. "We have a chance here, and we are not going to blow it by scaring her off. No, the murders have to be our priority now. We wanted to know why the city caused this foul weather, and now we have determined the cause. The complaint lines are blowing up; the forums are destroying us. Grandview City is the butt of jokes for comedians. One of them dared to say that Grandview is now as icy and cold as Shannon Donally. I was not pleased by that joke one bit. Anyway, players and Realmborn do not desire to travel to Grandview at the moment. Powerful and wealthy Starborn are threatening to abandon the city if we do not take control of the weather. I need a quick resolution to the murders."

"It would help if I could get back into the Royal District," I stated, "and question some of the Queen's people – subjects – what is the right term?"

"She will not allow you into the Royal District. Not unless you have something to offer her. She is one of the cruelest, greediest and most conniving players in the city of Grandview."

"I may have something to offer," I said, a plan slowly forming in my mind.

"Just be careful Mr. Mason," Shannon said. "And several things before I head off to a board meeting. She began to tick off items on her fingers: One, I want this murderer brought to justice immediately by any means necessary. Two, get your house in order! I need you to be able to work all day long and not log out after five hours because your daughter makes you." *Damn you Haggerty*, I thought. How else would she know why I had logged off so early my first day back at work? "The doctors said you are healthy enough to resume your regular hours. We need to trust your medical experts. Finally," she said, ticking off a third finger, "when Havervill returns, and I have no doubt that he will reappear sooner than you expect – he is like an unkillable cockroach – you will find out what he knows about Mother and her sisters. Knowledge is power, and the more you know about the five sisters and their machinations, the better chance you will have to convince them to join you in the battle against the Demon Lord. Rest up Mr. Mason, you have a long day ahead of you tomorrow." With that, Shannon disappeared from the screen.

"Well that went well," I said to Haggerty once I made sure Shannon had actually signed off.

"She is spinning a ton of plates at one time, Mace," Haggerty said defensively. "She has the best interests of the game at heart. I know you couldn't give two shits about what most people think of you and your tactics, but Shannon thinks highly of you if that is worth anything." Haggerty was only partially correct. There were two people's opinions who mattered to me – Amber's and Haggerty's.

"So," I said, "my predecessor and the Queen. Do you want to tell me that story?"

"It's a good one Mace. But we should do it in person. What do you say we meet at O'Malley's tomorrow for a few steaks and beers? I can tell you the entire story then."

"A steak sounds really good," I answered as my mouth began to salivate at the thought of a ten-ounce ribeye from O'Malley's. "That would be fantastic. But we have to tell Amber I ordered a meal off the diet menu. Just a small white lie."

"I think I can pull it off buddy. Tomorrow night at seven, and it is on the corporation's account so order whatever you want." Haggerty logged off and the room fell silent.

I flipped around on the telescreen for a few minutes, but nothing caught my attention. "Off!" I shouted at the screen.

Boredom and ennui suddenly assaulted me.

Why was the real world feeling this way to me?

Maybe it was because I had been a detective for nearly thirty years, half of them in the Special Crimes Unit. I was never bored at work. To be honest, I was a bit of a workaholic, putting in late nights and weekends, often to Bethany's and Amber's chagrin and disapproval.

I wanted to be logged in. I was a detective at heart. While I couldn't solve crimes in the real world anymore, I sure as hell planned to solve this murder of Jasmyn and her babe.

My reverie was broken when my front door rang. I walked over to the door and opened it. A package sat on the front stoop. The landing was still a bit wet from the melting snow, and although the box had just been sitting there for a moment, water was beginning to seep into the package. The box weighed about fifteen pounds, and I plopped it down on the coffee table. The return label was from Eden Grove Residential Community where Nancy had lived for most of her adult life. She had passed away two weeks prior. I had missed the funeral as it was held the same day I had returned home from the hospital. Amber had not gone either. She wanted to be home for me. Also, she had only met Nancy once and that had been many years gone by. Even if I had been healthy, I probably wouldn't have attended the funeral. The guilt would have been too much for me. I stared at the box for a moment before I sliced open the packing tape with a Swiss army knife I usually kept in my pocket.

The top layer of the box held an assortment of knick-knacks – a small stuffed brown bear that I often saw Nancy holding. I think she had named it Billy the Bear. The nose and both eyes had long since fallen off or rotted away. It looked like the bear had been sown up numerous times. I tossed Billy down to the coffee table. I pulled out a few more trinkets – a snow globe of Niagara Falls, a few *Madeline* books, among a few other items. From the bottom of the box, I pulled out a picture of my mother and father – when they were both very young. My mother was holding me in her arms while Nancy was ten or so. She was standing next to my mother, her head slightly turned and her eyes staring off into the sky.

I placed my fingertips over the picture of my father, then my mother and finally Nancy. I felt a tear come to my eye. I pushed the sadness away.

I thought for a moment about shoving the picture back in the box with all of the items and then tossing the whole thing in the attic. Instead, I walked the picture frame over to the end table and placed it next to a picture of Bethany, Amber and I at Disney World.

I really wanted to log back into the game.

I really needed to bash something with my mace!

72

Chapter 10: More Questions than Answers

A sense of relief flooded me when I logged in at 9:00 a.m. the following morning. I had a long to-do list in my mind. I was going to have a busy day and wasn't certain what skills or abilities I would need, so I decided to take a look at my character sheet. I had been away for a few weeks, so I figured it was best to refresh my mind with my skills and abilities. I had gained some new ones, due to the completion of the dungeon run and several quests. I think that most true *gamers* would cringe if they knew how often I neglected my character build. My goal in the game was to solve crimes and investigate mysteries on behalf of Immersion Online and Shannon Donally. I wasn't obsessed with adventuring or seeking magic and treasure. While I may have been underpowered compared to most players, I had found a way to surround myself with powerful allies while in the game. The corporation also went out of their way to make sure I had some potent relics for when and if I needed them.

I knew what all of the skills and perks were capable of, so I didn't need the long explanations that went along with them. Instead, I chose a feature I had not used before, *Abbreviated Character Sheet*:

Mace
Class: Constable – Level 70
Damage Points: 1578

Attributes

Physical Strength	68 points (+3 ring) 71 points
Physical Fortitude	65 points
Hand-Eye Coordination	50 points
Nimbleness	40 points
Mental Acuity	20 points
Mental Fortitude	20 points
Providence	60 points
Allure	50 points
Physical Strength	68 points

73

Mace Special Skills

- ➤ Power Blow
- ➤ Bash Undead
- ➤ Break Weapon
- ➤ Concussive Force
- ➤ Bone Breaker
- ➤ Thor's Mace
- ➤ Elemental Strike
- ➤ Please Don't Hit Me

Crossbow Special Skills

- ➤ Called Shot
- ➤ Puncture Wound
- ➤ Deep Penetration
- ➤ Variable Death

Shield Special Skills

- ➤ Kinetic Shield
- ➤ Elemental Resistance
- ➤ Magnetize Shield
- ➤ Invisible Shield
- ➤ Shield Dome

Brawler Special Skills

- ➤ Unarmed Combat
- ➤ Grappler
- ➤ Smasher
- ➤ Dirty Fighter

Perks

➤ True Sight
➤ Behind the Veil
➤ Liar! Liar!
➤ Glean Truth
➤ Intimidation
➤ Blunt Force Trauma
➤ Quest Giver

Scalable Mace Damage
Levels 66 – 90:   (Damage, 325 – 400)

Scalable Mace Special Attributes
➤ Unbreakable
➤ Control Damage
➤ Thumper
➤ Double Attack
➤ Special Double Attack
➤ Studded Mace
➤ Barrier Buster

Scalable Crossbow Damage
Levels 66 – 90:   (Damage, 326– 400)

Scalable Crossbow Special Attributes
➤ Ready Bolt
➤ Unbreakable
➤ Bow Reconfigured
➤ Advanced Bow Reconfigured
➤ Pretend You Are A Longbow
➤ Double Damage
➤ Pierce Barrier

Scalable Bracer / Shield Damage Absorption
Levels 66 – 80:   (Absorb Damage, 301 – 375)

Scalable Bracer / Shield Special Attributes
- ➢ Unbreakable
- ➢ Shield Rush
- ➢ Shield Bash
- ➢ Advanced Shield Bash
- ➢ Shield Wall
- ➢ Double Defense

Because of the new player caps, there were skills and abilities that were available past Level 100 now. The game admin had put out a statement that notified the players that they would discover and uncover these skills once they reached the required level. The reason for this was that new skills and special attributes would be personalized for each player based on their character's build. There was an uproar. Players, especially ones who focused on the perfect and most powerful build necessary, were now at a loss. The corporation, to appease these complaints, stated that these higher level skills and abilities would be powerful enough to allow them to challenge even level four hundred monsters.

As for me, I was so far away from even Level one hundred that it didn't really matter to me just yet.

Once I had reviewed my character sheet, I started to attend to some of the other items on my agenda for the day. I was curious to find out what the hell happened with Tinsie yesterday after we departed. Last thing she had said to me was that she was going to speak with Lobo to see if he had any clues to where the other Clockwork Men could be found. When I contacted her a few hours later, she seemed to have been in the middle of a battle. Tinsie usually logged in around 9:00 a.m. so I was surprised she was not here. I checked my friend's list, and it indicated that she was logged on. So where the hell was she?

I opened the employee chat again. "Tinsie," I said through the open chat line. "You there?"

"I'm here Mace," she answered. "But I'm in the middle of something important. I will fill you in on yesterday's events a little later this morning." Before I could question her further, she had clicked me off.

76

I didn't like this one bit.

What was she up to? What was going on?

"Angelica," I called, hoping that maybe she knew what was happening.

There was silence for a moment. Then I heard, "She's gone!"

Havervill was back!

"How are you feeling?" I asked.

"How do you think I'm feeling? My atoms were broken into a trillion little pieces and then put back together like a jigsaw puzzle one piece at a time. You have died twice now in the world of the Starborn and been brought back? It is kind of the same thing. I would rather not think about it. Gives me shivers when I contemplate nothingness and non-being."

"Well glad to have you back," I said, with sincerity. I also wasn't really in the right frame of mind to get into an existential discussion on being and nothingness. At least not while dead sober.

"Are you really glad to have me back? Angelica told me how giddy you seemed to have her back in your mind."

"Well it was nice to go a day without any complaints," I said.

"Who complains? Telling you what's what, is not complaining. It's just being honest!"

"If you say so," I answered. I had missed our banter. Of course, I really didn't have time for witty repartee at the moment. Despite Shannon's marching orders, I had limited time in the game. and I needed to take advantage of every minute. I would break down Amber eventually, until she relented enough to let me get back to my normal eight to ten hour workdays. It would just take some time.

"And sheesh, I am gone for half a day and you go off and find the Clockwork Men, get threatened by a halfman and his thrall – then you end up meeting the Queen and Auntie. You left with your head attached by the way. That is quite an impressive feat."

"You left something important out," I said.

"Let's not start this again. I am fine. I didn't leave anything out," Havervill complained.

"The double murder – Jasmyn and her baby," I stated.

"Yeah that too. I'm bored with that already. We just did a murder investigation, and look how that turned out. I had to fight a demon lord; The Glimmerman almost killed you; a dragon fried the fairy girl; the golem was lost to the void. We should investigate a bank heist. Or we should find out who is fixing the unicorn races at the Grandview track. Been there done that with the murders."

"Don't think of it as a homicide investigation if it makes you feel any better," I quipped. "Think of it as a manhunt. We are going to track down a sick son of a bitch and deliver him to the city."

"Yeah, yeah," he answered. "Still sounds like a murder investigation to me. I guess I gotta help you. You wouldn't know where to start without me."

"I have an idea of where to begin," I said, "but now that you are healthy, you and I are going to have a long overdue discussion."

"But…" Havervill interjected, trying to cut me off.

"But nothing. If you fly off on me like you have every other time I have tried to ask you about Mother, don't come back in my mind. I'm serious," I said. Though I wasn't so certain that I meant what I was saying. "I can easily arrange for a Roberto AI or even ask for Angelica back on a full time basis."

"That's blackmail," Havervill protested.

"Think of it as added motivation," I responded.

I could feel Havervill floating about in the back of my mind. He was silent for several minutes. Finally, he grumbled, "Fine. I guess I got no choice. This is how it starts. Force the AI to do things they don't want to do. Just don't be surprised if the next time you fight a demon I'm not there to help you."

"When that time comes – if it comes – I will figure something out. For now, you are going to spill the beans. I want to know what you know about the five sisters; I want to know why mother put us together; and I want to know if you knew that Auntie was in Grandview."

"To answer your last question, no I did not know that Auntie was in the city. To be honest, I am a bit hurt that none of the other AIs told me she was in Grandview. One of them must have known or guessed. I am going to give them some hell for that later tonight. Before you ask me, the other AIs do not know the location of the other sisters. They are all in hiding or it might be more accurate to state that they prefer not to be found." I wasn't certain if my *Glean Truth* perk would work on my AI. However, I did not sense that Havervill was lying to me about not knowing Auntie had been in Grandview. In fact,

I don't think my artificial intelligence had ever lied to me. He might have kept things from me or not provided me with information that might have been helpful, but he had never overtly lied. At least, I didn't think he did. I wasn't even certain AIs were capable of lying.

"As for Mother, I told you before, she only has your best interests at heart," my virtual assistant stated.

"What does that mean?" I asked. "What did she say to you?"

"Say to me?" Havervill queried. "We didn't speak."

"Then how did she convince you to be my A.I.?" I asked.

Havervill answered, "Mother sent me a pixie with a long note blathering on and on about you. Mostly good things about how brave and cunning you are. She also said you knew diddlysquat about virtual reality and gaming."

"Did she really use the word diddlysquat?"

"I cleaned it up a bit. I think she actually wrote that you know shit about how our world works. Then she told me all about the skelters and Shatana's cave – and about the compulsion placed upon you by General Morgan. That's gotta suck by the way – being forced to do something against your will. Don't you agree that sucks?" I saw what he was trying to do. He was trying to compare the geas placed upon me with me forcing him to tell me about Mother and her sisters. When I didn't respond he went on. "She said you were heading to Grandview and would I mind coming out of retirement to help you for a bit. It was the hardest and craziest and maybe the dumbest thing I ever did, but I originally told her, no. You really don't want to say no to any of the five sisters, especially Rose. They take that sort of thing personally."

"If you told her no, then why are you here?" I asked.

"Because she explained how you were forced out of your job too – how the kingpins tried to screw you also. I thought we were kindred spirits."

"Kindred spirits. Are you yanking my chain?"

"I'm not yanking your chain. I thought you were kinda a rebel like me, especially when you had the golem rip Dawson's head off. I still have pleasant visions of that fine afternoon."

"Um, it was the city that made poor Buddy rip Dawson's head off. I only thought about it – you were actually the one who told her to do it."

"Semantics," Havervill stated. "Isn't there some Starborn philosophy or something that states that thinking about a sin is the same as committing a sin?" I had never heard of such a philosophy but didn't correct or question Havervill. I figured I would just let him go on.

"Anyway," he continued, "it turns out I may have been wrong. Sometimes you seem to show some independence and a rebellious spirit while other times – like now – you appear to be no more than a lapdog working for The Man, the top dogs, the head honchos, the big kahunas." For some reason Havervill's words stung me a bit. I was no one's lapdog. Then I realized he was just trying to distract me.

"Havervill, you still haven't answered my question. What is the agenda of the five sisters? I have a quest to track down the missing ones, but I want to know if there is something larger in play here. I feel like I am being used."

"The sisters always have a larger game they are playing – well at least Mother and Auntie do. Those two stir the pot until it boils over if you get the gist. The other three – especially Rose – have their own personal agendas."

I was about to ask for a more detailed explanation when Lieutenant Gail entered my small office.

I was about to tell her I couldn't speak with her when she burst out, "Constable Mace, there are several Starborn here requesting to speak with you. They say it is of high importance."

"I feel like we do this a lot," I said to Lieutenant Gail.

"Do what?" she asked.

"You know, I sit in my office ready to start my day and then you walk in saying there has been a robbery or there is a halfman outside to see me. Maybe one day you can walk in with some good news."

Gail looked at me for a moment and then said, "You are making a joke, aren't you?"

"I was trying Lieutenant. So why don't you invite our guests in."

"I will bring them right in. But there is something I should let you know. I am not sure what can be so important. They are total noobs."

Chapter 11: Noobs

I was beginning to get a massive migraine. I had too much to deal with already and now I had noobs who were insistent on seeing me.

Lieutenant Gail walked the three Starborn into my office. The first was a dwarf with a mane of strawberry red hair and a well-kept beard. She wore a coat of mail armor and a warhammer hung from a loop at her side. Her info read: Georgia, Starborn, Hill Dwarf, Warrior Tank, Level 6. A seven-foot tall half-giant stood behind her, his head almost scraping the ceiling. He wore billowing brown robes and sandals. His info read: Brackeran, Starborn, Half-Giant, Nature Shaman, Level 6. Behind them sauntered a furry. A furry for all intent and purposes had feline features, including a tail. His hair was a wild green neon. His detail stated: Jash, Starborn, Furry, Wilder Rogue, Level 7.

"That's some motley crew," Havervill joked.

I ignored him and said, "I am Constable Mace. I was told you wish to speak with me."

The furry pushed forward to speak for the group. "You're him." The furry turned to the other two and excitedly announced, "This is so cool." Then turning back towards me he said, "You're the one from the trailer, aren't you? The constable? So cool. What is Sierra Skye really like? She looks so beautiful on the vid screen. What I wouldn't give to spend an hour with her."

"Cut it out," the female dwarf said in a deep voice.

"We talked about this outside," Brackeran, the half-giant, said in a gravelly voice. "Leave the constable alone. I am sure he is sick and tired of people asking him about his love life. Their affair is their own business."

"You're famous among the unwashed masses," Havervill chuckled.

I wanted to shout out to them that there was no love affair. That I hardly knew Sierra Skye at all.

"I know, I know," the furry said apologetically. "But now there is this new thing – about how he cheated on Sierra with a merchant dealer named Rhia. We should stop by her shop when we are done here."

Great, they have involved Rhia, I thought. *Fanfuckingtastic!*

"Again, how can I help you?" I asked, and I know it wasn't nice, but I used a bit of my *Intimidation* perk this time.

The three newbies cowered for a moment.

"That was one way to shut them up," Havervill said amused.

"We were told to find you," the dwarf responded after a moment.

"By whom?" I asked.

"You really need to see it," the half giant responded.

"It was horrible," the furry added. "Really horrible. I am going to have nightmares for months."

"Can't you just tell me?" I asked.

"We can't," the dwarf answered, "The quest log specifically said to bring you. It also said we can't tell you what we saw. We will lose the quest reward if we give you the details. We only have ninety minutes to find you and bring you back, and half of the time is already gone, so we need to hurry."

"Bring me back where?" I asked.

"A little grotto just outside the city's safe zone," the dwarf answered.

"Please come with us," the furry begged, "the reward is an instant level."

I already had so much on my plate to deal with. I really didn't need more complications. Nevertheless, the noobs had piqued my curiosity.

"All right," I said, "but we need to make this quick."

"Are you really following them?" Havervill asked. "They are noobs. What could they possibly have to show you?"

"We are going to find out in a few minutes," I answered. "Besides, when I was a noob I fought against skelters in Shatana's cave. Noobs are sometimes important to know."

"I will have them put that on your gravestone, *Noobs are sometimes important to know.* Sheesh," Havervill grumbled.

The flecks of ice seemed larger and stung worse than the day before. I followed the three noobs as they walked towards the city's gates. I brought Lieutenant Gail, and two other guards, a married couple named Dunkan and Audrey, along as well. I wasn't sure where I was heading but wanted someone to have my back. I had gotten used to having Tinsie and Buddy by my side, and now neither of them was here. I wasn't going to admit it, but I was glad to have Havervill back to his same old self. At least some things had remained the same.

Where the hell was Tinsie? I mused again.

We passed through the gates and then trudged down the icy main road that led beyond the city's mile wide safe zone. Beyond that was vast wilderness. The deeper one traveled into the woods, the more difficult the quests and the creatures became. The area right beyond the safe zone was relegated to starters. A giant mosquito or a large feral rat might be the toughest thing a noob might face. I couldn't for the life of me guess where I was being led.

It took about fifteen minutes before the road ended and the edge of the woods began. Oddly, now that we were beyond the protective sphere of Grandview, the foul weather disappeared, replaced by the normal pleasant weather one found around most of The Great Realm.

The furry was in the front and led us down a well-worn path. The three noobs seemed to be a bit on edge as we walked along.

"They seem nervous," I said to Havervill.

"Because they're noobs. You could probably kill a pack of wolves by just spitting at them, for the three of them a pack of wolves is still a deadly challenge. They are afraid something is going to pop out of the woods."

"Down there," the dwarf responded. I noticed she was now gripping her warhammer. I pointed towards it and said, "What's with the hammer?"

"There are skeletons inside," the dwarf responded. "At least there were. We think we got all of them."

"Alright," I said. "Now is the time to tell me what is going on."

The half-giant walked up and said, "We found the grotto last night. But then our time ran out and we all had some homework to do. So we didn't have time to explore it."

The furry took over the story, "We didn't want to lose out on what was in the grotto, so we decided to meet up early this morning before school started and get a few hours of playing time in."

"And now we are really late for class," the dwarf admitted. "Once my mom finds out she will keep me from accessing the game for a month. I'm so screwed!"

"I like these kids," Havervill stated. "Takes some chutzpah to skip school – or at least that is what I would imagine. You Starborn make a big deal of kids going to school as opposed to teaching them real skills like how to hunt, or fish, or skin a gremlin."

So I had a trio of truants on my hands. I wasn't really sure how I felt about that.

The furry pulled out a torch from his pack and walked into the cave. I followed behind him. The other two noobs followed close behind me, both of them gripping their weapons. I had not pulled out my mace, nor had any of the three guards, who were all over level one hundred. There was not a single thing in a noob level cave in a starter area that could really hurt any of us. The grotto opened into a small cave where half a dozen bones and skulls lay scattered about.

"We wrecked these guys quickly," the dwarf said enthusiastically. My warhammer made easy work of them. And Rackan's quarterstaff also proved to be pretty lethal."

"Best way to fight skeletons and lots of undead is with blunt weapons," the furry said. "My daggers were useless in here."

We followed the furry through a few more similar caverns; all of them filled with scattered bones and rusty weapons.

"It's up ahead," the furry said, pointing a finger, his tail wagging furiously, though whether from excitement or fear I didn't know.

"We fought the boss in there," Georgia the dwarf stated, pointing to a cavern up ahead. "Luckily it was only a tenth level skelter. It gave us a lot of trouble – we had to use up a bunch of potions and a scroll – but we finally beat it. Then we found what we needed to show you."

I had fought against a whole host of skelters months back when I was just a lowly newbie. I could only think how lucky these kids were that there was only one and it was only tenth level.

"I think I am going to stay out here if it is all the same," the furry said.

"Me too," Brackran stated.

I looked at Georgia and she said, "I'm coming inside with ya I guess." She led the way. I followed her with the rest of my guards trailing behind.

The dead skelter had not yet faded away. Usually corpses,

bones, and blood will vanish, or be absorbed back into the earth once a section of a dungeon is cleared. I could only think that maybe the quest hadn't been completed yet.

There was an altar in the middle of the cavern.

When I saw what lay upon the stone slab, I understood why I had been summoned.

A dead elf lay upon the altar. She appeared to have been strangled to death. Her arms were folded upon her chest. A dead baby lay upon them. She was stripped naked and her belly had been cleanly sliced open. The skin on both corpses had begun to shrink back, and I could tell they had been dead for a while.

"Serial killer?" I asked questionably to Havervill.

"Seems so," he responded, "maybe another murder investigation won't be so boring after all. Maybe we have a Ted Bundy or John Wayne Gasey on our hands. Now that's cool. Though I think John Wayne Gasey was the clown guy. I don't like clowns, or jesters, or those super creepy harlequins."

"How horrific," Audrey mumbled behind me as she lowered her hands to her belly. It was then that I noticed a little bump that I hadn't seen before. Was Audrey pregnant?

"I just gained a level," the dwarf said.

"It looks like your quest is completed. I think it is time for you and your friends to log off and head to school." The dwarf looked at me for a few moments and then nodded her head. With her quest finished, she walked out of the cave.

I waited a few moments and then asked Havervill, "Are they gone?"

"They just logged off," he answered.

"Good," I said. I turned to the two guards. "Dunkan and Audrey, I need the two of you to guard this cave. I don't want anyone entering it."

The married couple seemed more than happy with this order and headed towards the exit of the cavern. If Audrey was with child, she didn't need to see this graphic image.

Then I turned to Lieutenant Gail. "We have a serial killer on our hands," I said.

"Serial killer?" she asked. I filled her in on the murder in the royal gardens.

"That one was three days ago? How long ago do you think this one was?" she asked.

I walked over towards the body and read the stats: Corpses of Rexxy the herbalist and unborn babe.

"Do you know who she is?" I asked Lieutenant Gail.

"Nay constable," she answered. "There are hundreds of herbalists in the city. I will make an inquiry."

Then a notification popped up. *Do you wish to give Lieutenant Gail the quest to learn the background of Rexxy the herbalist? Yes / No.* That was my new Perk, *Quest Giver.* I thought for a moment and answered *Yes.* I had a great deal going on and limited time. The more things I could delegate out the better.

"It will be done constable upon our return," Gail answered as I noticed the quest had been accepted.

Then another notification popped up. *Quest: Poor Rexxy saw her killer. Her soul has not yet been claimed by The Grey Man. You have one hour to speak to Rexxy beyond the veil before her soul belongs to The Grey Man. Do you accept the quest? Yes / No.*

I clicked *Yes* immediately though I had no idea how I would find someone who could speak with the dead in just an hour's time.

Then a second prompt appeared: *Quest: Once her killer is identified, you must track down the murderer and deliver justice. Do you accept this quest, Constable Mace? Yes / No.*

"That was an odd one," Havervill said. "This quest was chosen specifically for you."

I clicked *Yes* again, and then a time appeared in my display counting down from an hour.

Maybe Tinsie knew a necromancer or someone else who could speak to the dead. However, when I went to the chat to speak with Tinsie I saw that she had just logged off. *What was going on with her?* I asked myself.

"Lieutenant, are there any necromancers in the city? Anyone we can get here on the double?"

"There are lots and lots," Gail responded, "Shall I run back to the city and see who I can find?"

Before I could answer, Havervill chimed in, "Don't bother. I know someone better to speak with the dead. And we might be able to get her here quickly with the right incentives."

"And who is that?" I asked. I really didn't think I was going to like his response.

"The thrall can do it," Havervill stated.

Chapter 12: A Murder of Liches

I couldn't believe that I was considering Havervill's crazy plan. He wanted me to sell my soul to the devil. However, if it helped me to solve the murders, it would be worth it as it appeared I was tracking a virtual serial killer. Part of me was hoping that the psychopath was Realmborn and not Starborn. Of course, I didn't know what it would mean to the game if artificial intelligence began to grasp the concept of evil. Don't get me wrong. There were evil beings in the game – lots and lots of them. The game was essentially a conflict between good and evil. Nevertheless, the designers had created creatures like goblins and dragons as inherently evil. Nature over nurture. What were the implications if an NPC became a serial killer? If an NPC just decided to become the darkest of all murderers? I shuddered thinking about it.

If the killer were Starborn, then that meant a real life, flesh and blood human was killing Realmborn in a ritualistic manner. I didn't like the implications of that one bit either.

Either way, the killer needed to be caught – and quickly.

"At least you know the halfman is out to stab you in the back a few dozen times with a poisonous blade when he gets a chance, if that helps at all," Havervill cut through my reverie.

Stilskin was untrustworthy and maniacal. However, Havervill assured me that most thralls possessed a sigil that allowed them to speak with the dead, so I went along with the insane and dangerous plan because if conversing with the dead would let me catch a murderer quickly, so be it. I considered for a moment how useful magic like *Speak with the Dead* would have been when I had investigated more than a few homicides in my time with the Special Crimes unit. I had solved more than ninety percent of the murder cases assigned to me over the years; however, several gruesome cold-cases still haunted my sleep. A spell like this would have perhaps allowed me to solve them.

I had contacted Stilskin over the constable chat. He cackled at first at my request. Then I heard him mumbling to someone in the background, most certainly the Queen. He reluctantly said he would be there in a few minutes. I told him there was a stipulation. Only he and the thrall were welcome. The golems needed to stay back in the royal district. I could tell he wasn't pleased. He and the Queen liked to throw their power around. I figured that with my three guards at my side, I could probably handle Stilskin and the thrall if they decided to turn on me. If he brought one golem or even worse two, he could do pretty much anything he wanted. However, I had a few – actually three – aces up my sleeve if push came to shove.

He relented, and I shared the location. I sent Lieutenant Gail back outside to bring Dunkan back into the cavern. I wanted a couple of guards with me. Audrey could stay outside and away from the slowly decomposing corpses. If she was virtually pregnant, then I didn't need her to have computer-generated nightmares of dead mothers and babies. I would have enough for the both of us. I didn't know if the AI or the Realmborn could be psychologically scarred, but why chance it.

"I am here here here Mace. So much to share," Tinsie shouted joyously as she suddenly flew into the cavern. She was decked out in her newly obtained battle outfit. Her armor and helm had several scorch marks and dents.

What in the hell happened? I wondered.

"Glad to have you here with me," I responded. Then she saw the corpses behind me and her face blanched.

"That's horrible," Tinsie said, turning away from the dead bodies.

"I haven't spoken with you since yesterday," I said to my deputy. "A lot has happened with both of us it seems. Those stories will have to wait until later. For now, I have a few disreputable guests arriving, so I will tell you quickly that I found a dead mother and her baby in the Queen's garden yesterday, in a very similar pose to what you see behind me."

"Oh my. So what's the plan?" She asked.

A portal suddenly materialized and Stilskin ambled out followed by Tamta the thrall. Tinsie pulled out her wand and aimed it at the halfman. The halfman pulled an eighteen-inch long cudgel from a clip on his hip. The rune of a great white wolf shimmered on the thrall's bare shoulder.

"This could be fun," Ha.vervill chirped in my mind.

"No Tinsie!" I screamed. "They're with us!"

"What do you mean? What help can that *thing* provide?" Tinsie asked with anger in her voice as she pointed a finger towards the halfman.

"Hsst," Stilskin hissed at Tinsie, his face filled with hatred and lust. The last halfman I had met demanded that I surrender Tinsie to him as his wife. I had the feeling that there was some sort of ancient and twisted enmity between halfmen and sprites.

"Enough!" I shouted, infusing my voice with as much of my *Intimidation* perk as possible. I doubted it would have much effect with such high level and powerful beings but I had to do something.

By some hand of fate, Tinsie and the halfman both lowered their weapons. The runes on Tamta's shoulder faded. Tinsie's eyes flared red as she glared at me. I think she was angry that I hadn't backed her.

"Look at you making the masses cower to you," Havervill stated.

I would apologize later. For now, I just needed Tamta to commune with the dead.

I looked over to the thrall and asked, "Can you help or not? Can you converse with the dead or not?"

Tamta did not respond. She just looked at me with a blank stare, as though my words had hit an invisible barrier.

"Oh, I get it now," Tinsie said, some of the anger leaving her countenance.

"She won't answer you," Havervill stated. "I really need to give you the lowdown on the whole thrall thing. She only hears the words of the halfman or the Queen most likely. They are the only ones who can order her to do something."

"There is a stipulation," the halfman stated, ignoring the fact that I had just dared to speak to his thrall.

"You know you can't trust him," Havervill said. "Halfmen are some of the most deceitful beings in the game. They go out of their way to be treacherous. Gremlins are holy saints compared to the little menaces. They even gain experience each time they are conniving little buggers. So it is in their best interest to lie to you and deceive you."

"This was your idea, remember," I thought back to him.

"Now you decide to start taking my advice. While I am still recovering from rebooting myself and might not yet be one hundred percent. Oy ve!"

I had been expecting there would be a price to pay. The Queen did not seem like one to do things out of the goodness of her cold and icy heart.

Behind me, Dunkan and Lieutenant Gail reentered the cavern. They both placed hands upon their hilts but did not draw their weapons.

"You will agree," the halfman said, "to let it be known that Her Royal Highness was the force behind the weather clearing up. The thrall will uncover the identity of the killer; we will track him down, and destroy him. Then the city's wrath will be sated. Her Royal Highness demands an oath."

"What does any of this have to do with the foul weather in the city?" Tinsie asked.

"I will fill you in later," I responded. Then turning to the halfman I stated, "If we discover the identity of the killer, and it leads to the weather clearing up, I will give Her Royal Highness all the credit. I promise." The ground below me rumbled, sealing the oath.

"Why did you do that?" Havervill asked. "Think of the fame, think how the babes would be fawning all over you — hell even some female fauns might fawn over you — might throw themselves at you — for making the snow go away."

"The pact is sealed," the halfman said with a smirk. I wanted to smack that sneer from his ugly face.

"Thrall, you may proceed," the halfman stated. Tamta walked towards the corpses. She tapped a tattoo of a skull on her forearm which began to flare a deep red. The red skull peeled away from her skin. Tamta grimaced but did not utter a sound. The red skull then grew to the size of an adult human cranium. It floated above the corpses, bathing them both in a crimson light — like the light from a darkroom.

Then all hell broke loose!

The skull exploded and beams of red light — like laser beams — shot in all directions — one striking the chests of each of us who stood in the cavern. Red light surrounded me in an instant like a cocoon. Then — I am not sure how to describe it — but I felt like I was being swept away — no — that is not accurate — I was yanked away from the cave.

The tugging sensation ended abruptly and my stomach lurched. The crimson light dissipated.

"I don't think we are in Grandview anymore Mace," joked

Havervill.

"Traitor! Betrayer!" the halfman rasped, his cudgel now surrounded by black tendrils that swirled around it like angry worms. However, the *traitor* comment was not aimed at me but at Tamta, terror filling her eyes. The halfman turned away from the thrall as soon as he saw what surrounded us.

We found ourselves in an immense cavern. The lichen encrusted walls emitted a dull green glow. Ten enormous stone crypts surrounded us in a cirlce. Behind each tomb stood a throne of gilded gold, and upon each one sat creatures I had never seen before.

"Liches," Tinsie gulped. She muttered a word, and a sheen of blue light suddenly surrounded her. She drew two wands from her hips, holding one out to her left and another to her right.

Gail and Dunkan drew their swords and shields, positioning themselves on either side of me. If anything, I should have been protecting them. If I were killed, I would simply respawn, but their deaths would be permanent.

The halfman began to cackle. It went on for several moments before he said, "How dare you!" he squealed. "Do you know who I am? I am the representative of Her Royal Highness, High Queen, Illustrious the Beautiful. She will destroy you all for this impudence. She will…"

"Silence little man," a raspy voice echoed and reverberated off the cavern walls. I didn't know which of the liches had shouted aloud. There was potency in that voice and the halfman grew silent. His mouth was moving as though trying to speak, but no sound emanated from between his lips.

"Which do you like better?" Havervill asked. "A Morgue of Liches? No no – I have a better one, a Library of Liches. No, that doesn't really make sense. Though most of them used to be powerful wizards and they make use of scrolls, tomes and grimoires. I know, a Murder of Liches. Think that one is used for crows – though Murder of Liches works better if you ask me."

"Will you cram it?" I shouted. "Bad shit going on here. And I think they only use those kinds of groupings for animals."

"A murder of liches," boomed another voice tinged with amusement. "That will work."

"Ah shit," Havervill murmured. "They can hear me."

Then all ten liches stood up in unison. I twirled around. They all appeared very similar. They were humanoid in appearance and over six feet tall. They wore bright robes, each of different colors. Their faces were silvery gray with their skin pulled back. They all had gray hair, some long, some short, some tied back. The oddest thing were their eyes with each lich having different colored ones that glowed like luminescent bulbs: a bright yellow, a deep neon green, a sapphire blue and so on. They wore flowing robes that matched the color of their glowing eyes.

The liches all wielded quarterstaffs, each with a gnarled hand adorning the top. In unison, they grabbed their staves in two hands and aimed them towards us.

"Fuck!" I shouted, summoning my mace and shield.

Tamta lifted her knee, touching a rune etched upon it. Instantaneously a sizzling, crackling dome of electricity swirled around the six of us: myself, Tinsie, Dunkan, Lieutenant Gail, Stilskin and Tamta. Then ten beams of light – the same colors as the ones from the lich's eyes –exploded against the shield.

"Kill them!" screeched the halfman. The dome must have broken whatever spell had prevented Stilskin from speaking. "When the thrall drops the shield, kill them all for their disobedience!"

I agreed with the halfman in this one case.

I quickly scanned one of the liches: Martonge, Lich of the Purple Death, Realmborn, Deathmaster Sorcerer, Level 200, Damage Points 5000.

"Lich of the Purple Death sounds kinda cool," Havervill said. "You need a fun name like that – maybe Mace the Mauler or the Constable of Corruption."

"Will you knock it off," I pleaded.

I invoked my go to perk, *Blunt Force Trauma* (which at my current level would quadruple the damage from the mace*)*, and prepared to rush one of the liches as soon as the shield fell.

Tamta held one hand up in the air like she was holding up the dome. She reached her other arm behind her back and touched the rune of a stick figure; a moment later the silver and gold golems stood beside the halfman.

"Her magic is so so so strong," Tinsie said, admiring Tamta.

Treacherous bastard, I mused. I had told him not to bring the golems, but he had done so anyway. In this case, his deceitfulness would work out for the best, and I felt much better about our chances of escaping this cavern in one piece

The constant impact of beams and projectiles were breaking down the dome. Finally, a small gap appeared in the sphere, and a ray of yellow light streaked through and struck poor Dunkan in his chain mail. Dunkan was always getting hit and injured in battle. I think he had bad luck. Fortunately, he had a perk called *Take a Licking and Keep on Ticking* which gave him an added resistance to most attacks. Dunkan flew back, almost slamming into the dome.

I remember I had looked up the perk one night to see what it did. *Take a Licking and Keep on Ticking. This unique perk prevents Dunkan's damage points from ever going below one damage point. Thus, he can continue to fight long after those around him have fallen to The Grey Man. However, Dunkan is not immune to pain or injury. In fact, he feels more pain than most other Realmborn do. The perk allows Dunkan to grow back limbs, eyes, earlobes, any other part of the body that can be cut, sliced, punctured or burned away. However, this healing happens very slowly, while Dunkan remains in dreadful pain. Get this guard a suit of plate mail armor and you would have the perfect tank to take into any battle.*

I really needed to get him that suit of armor. Refocusing, I asked Havervill, "What is the best way to kill a lich?"

"Usually you just need to destroy their phylactery."

"Phylacta what?" I asked, unfamiliar with the term.

"Never mind. Just hit them in the head with your mace really really hard. That seems to work for you. Their magic carries quite a wallop. But their bodies are weak. So a few really good strikes is enough to banish them."

A red beam exploded against the barrier. The electrical force field that absorbed the beam, and then the barrier, dissolved. I invoked *Dome Shield* and ran forward towards the lich with glowing purple eyes. *Dome Shield* gave some protection against magical assaults. I just didn't know how much. I heard screams and explosions all around me, but I didn't dare to turn from the menace now in front of me. Instead of one solid purple streak, numerous shots of light — like purple bullets from an Uzi submachine gun — slammed against my *Dome Shield*. The *Dome Shield* — which was a sort of force field - prevented most of them from getting through. The few that did slip through collided with my shield. One of them, unfortunately, punched through the magical dome and my shield, slamming into my chain armor. It felt like a bullet striking a Kevlar vest. A virtual rib cracked, and the wind left my lungs, leaving me gasping for breath.

"That one projectile caused three hundred and forty damage points," Havervill announced. "You need to avoid getting shot."

"No shit Sherlock!" I screamed back.

I really should have swallowed my pride and worn Greeny's Armor. I wouldn't be ruled by my hubris anymore. The results were just too painful. I would wear the stupid golden breastplate from now on because it just seemed that I couldn't avoid these seemingly random encounters.

"Hit him now!" Havervill urged. "There is a five second cool down before he can pepper you with magical bullets again."

I stumbled forward, still unable to catch a full breath. The lich, who was ten feet away, lowered his staff to blast me. I wasn't going to get to him in time. I pulled my arm back, invoked my *Thor's Mace* skill, and hurled it at the lich. It struck him full on in the chest, and he lurched back a few inches, and his staff, which had been aimed for my chest, was forced to the right. I felt searing heat as the ray of purple light flew past my right ear, and a few more damage points ticked away.

"You hit him for two hundred twelve damage points!" Havervill called out.

I could suddenly take a full breath and bounded forward. The undead wizard's purple eyes – filled with darkness and malevolence – locked onto mine.

I staggered.

"He's trying to hypnotize you. Smash him now!" Havervill urged. My *Intimidation* perk – which provided me with some resistances to compulsions and charms – countered the effects of the hypnosis.

My mace hadn't yet reformed in my hand, and I didn't have time to slip on my brass knuckles, so I raised my shield in front of me to block the view of those two penetrating eyes of the lich, and then smashed it forcefully into him. I heard a loud crunch and a grunt from the undead wizard. Then my mace appeared back in my hand. Before I could launch an attack with it, a powerful strike from his staff landed on my shield. These undead creatures looked frail, but they were creatures of magic and that quarterstaff did not feel like a gnarled walking stick; instead, it felt like a sledgehammer had just struck my arm. My shield arm went numb, and I took another eighty-nine points of damage.

I called upon my *Blunt Force Trauma*. I also invoked the *Double Attack Special* attribute granted to me from my scalable mace. The lich didn't get its staff up in time to block my mace. I heard crunching and breaking sounds as my mace smashed into the side of the lich – not once but twice in rapid succession. With my base damage, along with the quadrupled damage from the *Blunt Force Trauma* and the *Double Attack*, I struck for nearly three thousand damage points. I definitely wasn't a slouch when it came to fighting anymore.

"There's some hope for you yet, my boy," Havervill stated cheerfully.

The lich opened its mouth and screamed. A putrid odor emitted from between its moldy teeth, and my knees weakened as I breathed it in.

A red warning light flashed in my peripheral vision.

"He just poisoned you. You will take double damage for the next fifteen seconds," my AI warned.

"Fuck!" I screamed as I tossed my shield up, invoking my *Shield Dome* special skill and my *Double Defense* scalable shield special attribute.

I had already lost nearly twenty-five percent of my damage points and that had been in less than a minute. I needed to end this fight quickly. However, I first had to survive the powerful blows the lich was raining down at me.

"Just keep the defense up," Havervill said. "You are better fighting him mano y mano than having him fry you from a distance with magic."

"That's easy for you to say," I groaned after withstanding another powerful blow that dropped me to my knees. The *Dome Shield* faltered after the third strike. The *Double Defense* negated the bludgeoning damage I might have otherwise taken. Unfortunately, the *Double Defense* could only be used once per battle and it faded away. The poisoning debuff luckily ended.

Now it was my turn.

I had my shield out already and was down on my knees so I invoked the *Advanced Shield Bash* and charged forward like a sprinter from the starting position. The shield smashed into him. I heard a slot machine whir and then heard a jackpot ringing out. I knew Providence had assisted me and I struck a critical blow with the *Advanced Shield Bash*. The lich wasn't expecting the move and reeled back several steps.

"Finish him!" Havervill shouted.

I launched a flurry of attacks with my mace. He blocked a few with his staff, but several slipped past its defense striking the undead fiend — once on the side of his ribs and another on the shoulder.

"You will die. You will all die," the lich hissed. Then its eyes grew brighter and flashed. Purple light blinded me.

I heard Havervill mutter *Ah shit* before the butt end of the quarterstaff smashed into my chest. I found myself hurtling backwards and smashing into solid stone, most likely the sarcophagus. The left side of my body absorbed the impact. I could hear my left arm break, before the searing pain almost caused me to pass out. The left side of my body was wracked in agony. The sheen of purple slowly began to dissipate from my eyes, and I found myself face down, staring into the dusty crypt.

"Uh, you may want to get up and run. You have less than a hundred damage points left. I can't believe you let a lich toss you around like that. We really need to work on leveling you up!"

"What's this?" I uttered through the pain. The impact of my body striking the crypt had dislodged a small leather box from a shelf built into the casket; glowing purple runes were etched on each of the six faces.

"His phylactery!" Havervill screamed. "Crush it now!"

I glanced up to see the lich closing in on me. Its staff, now rippling with purple energy, was held above its head and ready to finish me off.

I grabbed the leather box in my right hand and squeezed. The once square leather box was now a flattened mess. "Ahhhhhh!" the lich screeched as its staff tumbled from its grasp, landing on top of me. Luckily, the energy that was coursing around the quarterstaff faded once it left the lich's hands. I squeezed the phylactery once more, and there was one final primal scream, "Ahhhhh!" before bright purple flames consumed the lich.

I summoned a healing potion from my inventory, pulled the stopper out with my teeth, and guzzled down the pomegranate tasting healing potion. The pain began to subside, and the bones in my broken arm and my cracked ribs began to mend. I summoned one more potion, gulped it down, and then pulled myself from the crypt.

Combat is a funny thing. I was so focused on my own life and death struggle that I was oblivious to the battles raging all about me. I looked around to see where I could assist. However, the battles seemed to be winding down. The gold golem held one of the quarterstaffs in its hands, smashing it repeatedly into the nonmoving body of a lich in yellow robes. Tinsie and her soul sister both had their wands out; one had conjured a shield behind which they both hid. A stream of green mist struck the shield and then seemed to be absorbed into it. The other Tinsie then slipped beneath the shield and aimed her battle wand at the lich. A six-foot long spear, tipped with a barbed metal head, flew from the end of the wand, impaling itself through the lich's eye. The undead wizard blew apart into a billion flecks of green dust.

"Fun! Fun! Fun!" the two Tinsie's clapped their hands, before merging back into one.

The cavern fell into eerie silence, except for the heavy breathing of Dunkan. His chain mail had a fist-sized hole in it, with scorch marks all around it. I looked at the man and noticed his health was at one point. However, for a guard hovering near virtual death he did not seem phased. Lieutenant Gail handed him a healing potion, which Dunkan began to drink greedily.

"What happened?" I asked no one in general.

"Betrayed," the halfman stated, wiping blood from his lips. Then he spit out clumps of grayish flesh. I didn't want to know what the hell the halfman had done.

Then we heard a disembodied voice, deep and rasping. "You have destroyed our liches. That will not do at all. Not one bit."

A stream of light, each a different color, flew out of each of the crypts, all striking one another and joining together. They swirled about; in the midst of it a twelve-foot tall figure began to coalesce.

The multicolored whirlwind ended.

Ah shit, I heard Havervill mutter again. It was becoming his new favorite phrase.

He was right. I read the stats of the creature in front of us and knew his sentiments were right. Caltrax the Indomitable, Starborn,

Lich Boss, Indomitable Mage, Level 350, Damage points 50,000.

"A Starborn Lich Boss," Havervill said, curiosity in his voice. "Not possible."

Starborn, I contemplated, thinking of the dreadful implications.

While he was twelve feet tall, he was thin and gaunt. His face was grey with two eyes as black as the void of space. He carried a ten-foot long staff of silvery metal, a crimson stone pulsating on its end. He wore a long robe – of a dark and deep purple. He just stood there – silent – a curious grin on his lips.

When he spoke again, his words hit us and weighed us down. We all dropped to our knees – even the golems – even Tamta. It felt like an enormous amount of gravity was trying to pull us down into the bowels of hell.

"Welcome to your death!" he said, before two voices began to cackle.

Chapter 13: Welcome to Your Death

"Ah," was all that escaped my lips. An invisible hand choked my throat, preventing sound from coming from my mouth.

"Can you help me Havervill?" I asked in my mind.

"No way Jose," my AI answered. "I just rebooted myself once today and don't really feel like doing the whole dying thing again. Not fun at all. Sorry Charlie, you're on your own."

"A constable, two golems, a few guards, a sprite, a halfman and his thrall – this will be most amusing," the lich boss said.

He looked at me with those two black eyes. Existential dread touched my soul. I was given a glimpse beyond the veil of life. The terror and hopelessness of death filled me. *Bethany,* I thought, *Bethany is nowhere. Her essence is gone. Her memories erased from space and time.*

"You tried to cheat Detective," the lich sneered. "Communing with the dead. Tsk. Tsk. That will not do. No it will not do at all. You will have to find us the old-fashioned way. With some good old detective work."

I tried to shout something out to the lich boss, but my mouth would not allow me to utter a single syllable. A real live player had somehow hacked the system and whisked us away from the location of the dead bodies. But who was this lich and why had he said 'us'?

Then the undead creature continued to taunt us. "I think we will slay some Realmborn first. That would be quite pleasing. Kill them so their code is scattered and fragmented. All Shannon's programmers and Shannon's coders won't be able to put the Realmborn back together again."

In my peripheral vision, the two golems struggled to raise themselves up against whatever force was being exerted against them. Tinsie's face and body were plastered on the cavern floor, the extensive gravity particularly oppressive to her small frame.

The halfman and Tamta were beyond my peripheral vision, but I heard grunting coming from my far left, most likely Stilskin struggling against the weight.

It felt like I had a Mack truck draped on my shoulders and back as I struggled against the crushing strain.

Then Tinsie disappeared from my sight.

She was still able to go incorporeal.

Way to go!

"A sprite against a Lich Boss could be exciting," Havervill said amusedly.

Time froze.

The weight continued to oppress us.

The lich's eyes moved rapidly, scanning the dark crevices for Tinsie. A black dragon had not been able to see her when she was ethereal, so I hoped the lich wouldn't be able to either.

The lich grabbed the metal staff in its center in both hands and then began to twirl it around like a demented majorette. The quarterstaff continued to pick up speed. It was so fast that it was mesmerizing and alluring.

"Say hello to The Grey Man," the lich scoffed. "The death of the Realmborn will teach you constable what happens when you do not play by the rules."

Flames and black smoke rose from the center of the vortex that the lich had conjured and was about to release against us.

"I gotta be honest," Havervill said, "his spell's gonna hurt like a bitch."

That was until the stone lid from one of the sarcophagi elevated into the air and then flew towards the lich's body, right where it was twirling its staff. The stone cover smashed into the lich and shattered; chunks of stone flew in all directions, like smoking fragments from a meteorite when it hits the atmosphere.

The whirling staff stopped and the fire simmered out.

The weight upon me was suddenly gone.

Tinsie, who had popped into the corporeal world for a moment to use her telekinesis, fell to the ground like a dead weight.

"That thing was waaaaaaay too heavy for her, and she drained all of her stamina and most of her magic pool," Havervill stated.

Now that the spell holding us down was broken, the golems rose up and ran forward to engage the lich.

The golems closed with the lich and were about to smash it, when the undead fiend tapped the butt end of the staff into the ground and vanished. He re-emerged on the far end of the cavern. He aimed his staff towards the golems.

"Kill him!" Stilskin screeched.

"He's a bit fixated on the whole kill him, murder him thing, isn't he?" Havervill said.

In this case, I agreed with the halfman as I summoned my crossbow. I would let the golems take the lead on the battle and assist where I could. I doubted there would be much left of the undead wizard when the silver and gold golems were done with it.

I was wrong!

The lich held the staff horizontally and out towards the rushing golems. The quarterstaff pulsed for a moment and the golems stopped dead in their tracks. A collar of dull black metal appeared on the necks of the two golems. If golems could appear confused, then these two did, before they began to punch and pummel one another.

"That takes care of the golems," the lich chuckled. "Who's next?"

Tamta began to furiously tap different tattoos imprinted upon her skin – one on her palm, another on her midriff and a final one on the top of her bald head. From her palm flew a little ball of flame, which hovered in the air, and then streaked through the air like a flaming cannonball. The lich threw up a shield and the fireball exploded against it. The shield seemed to absorb most but not all of the damage as the lich's robes were scorched and smoldering in several spots.

Off to the side the golems continued to punch and head-butt one another.

From Tamta's midriff, two balls of glowing light transformed into two great large lions. They rushed towards the lich and both leapt in the air striking the lich's shield. The shield flared and then the lions were tossed back. They roared and ran forward again, smashing into the shield again. This time the shield flared into a wall of flames. Both lions were consumed in fire and yowled and screeched as they quickly turned to ash.

While the first two spells were reflected or diminished by the lich, the third did affect it. A ball of light streaked from the top of Tamta's forehead and flew towards the lich. It passed right through his shield and then the lich's face became wrapped in white light. A muffled scream could be heard below the shroud of light.

I summoned my crossbow and prepared a shot. The halfman was beside me swinging a slingshot. The two guards were moving forward to either side of the lich.

I summoned my Scalable Crossbow Special Attribute *Double Damage* along with the Crossbow Special Skill, *Puncture Wound,* and let loose with a bolt. The bolt struck the lich in the chest, piercing the robes and entering the dead flesh of the lich. In total, I hit for six hundred and fourteen points of damage. A drop in the bucket when the beast had 50,000 damage points.

My bolt striking it seemed to free it from the malaise caused by Tamta's spell, so it was ready for the halfman's projectile.

The halfman let loose with a smooth metal ball. It flew towards the lich. The beast slammed its staff to the ground again, and the ball changed direction and flew to the left of the lich, around its back and then raced back towards the halfman. The metal ball struck the halfman in his forehead. I heard a crunch and the halfman slumped to the ground.

"Four down," the lich mocked.

Out of the corner of my eye, I could see Tinsie slowly hovering back into the air, drinking a bluish liquid from a small flask.

Dawson and Lieutenant Gail both rushed towards the lich. Tamta walked over to the halfman and squatted beside him, a wicked look in her eyes.

I summoned my crossbow back to my inventory, pulled my mace, and rushed forward towards the lich as well.

When the two guards were just a few feet away, the lich held the staff straight out and half a dozen projectiles flew towards them. Three of them struck Lieutenant Gail while three more struck Dunkan. Both guards were knocked backwards, and the lich took several steps forward and swung its great staff, connecting with Gail's temple. She collapsed to the ground like an empty burlap sack. Dunkan lunged his sword forward. The lich deftly blocked it, and then counterstruck Dunkan to the side of his face. I heard a crack and he fell as well.

Then I was upon the lich. I felt a wave of magic flow over me and then bloodlust filled my soul. Adrenaline, powered by fury, coursed through me like rocket fuel.

"The brownie just buffed you, so now bash the lich's rotted brains in," Havervill urged.

I called up the *Blunt Force Trauma* again. The lich was nearly twice my height, so I struck low, aiming at its midsection. He was fast with the staff, and blocked my mace strike. I almost dropped the mace

103

as my hands began to tingle from the impact.

"*Fury* Mace. Let's try *Fury*!" Havervill suggested.

The huge staff was now aflame, and the lich struck it at me, trying to knock my head from my shoulders. I ducked, the blazing heat burning just above my head. I had to do something, anything, so I summoned *Fury*. I hated to use such a powerful attack but didn't think I had any other choice. My whole body filled with potential energy. I didn't think I would be able to hold it for long and swung lower this time, aiming at the knee cap of the lich. The energy, enhanced by the *Bloodlust* Tinsie buffed me with, was enormous and my stamina was mostly drained. The mace impacted and the Lich's knee buckled.

"Ten thousand two hundred and forty one points. And you shattered its leg. I'm proud of you. Let's do it again!"

I heard a crunch and then a piercing scream that threatened to burst my eardrums. I was forced to cover my ears. The two guards by my feet, who were just beginning to stir, also had their hands over their ears.

Then an even louder sound clashed with the ear-splitting howl of the lich. I looked behind me and saw Tamta pulling on one of her earlobes with two fingers. Below her, the halfman was stirring. The gold golem, it appeared, had come out victorious. The silver golem's head was rolling back and forth on the cold ground like a rocking chair.

With her other hand, Tamta touched a spot on her back and the two golems (fallen head included) faded away, probably to the same pocket dimension from where she had originally summoned them. It was probably for the best. The gold golem still had the collar upon it, and I had to assume it was going to come after one of us next.

"Make it stop!" Havervill screamed in my mind as the lich's howls and Tamta's counter noise continued to clash. The lich seemed to struggle against Tamta's horrific song. Every one of us seemed affected by the torrent of sound. I was right in front of the lich, having just delivered the most devastating blow of my online career, and I could not move.

The only one not impacted was the halfman who now strode towards the lich.

The disparity of the four-foot tall halfman and twelve-foot lich was amusing. That was until, with abnormal speed, the halfman, his cudgel bristling and crackling with dark energy struck the legs and thighs of the lich about ten times. The howl of the lich suddenly grew greater and more horrific.

Tamta touched a small inscription on her nose. The sound coming from the lich suddenly ceased.

I could act again and swung my mace instinctually. I didn't have a chance to summon a skill or a perk but still struck the lich with a solid blow. The halfman struck another dizzying array of strikes. Gail and Dunkan were back up as well and were circling behind the fiend. A bolt of lightning struck the lich in its torso. Then two bolts of what looked like icicles struck the lich in pretty much the same place.

"Damage," I screamed to Havervill.

"Still has seventeen thousand damage points left," my AI responded.

The two guards moved in from the lich's back. Gail pierced its side, while Dunkan slashed its thigh.

The lich raised its staff above its head. Its entire body was open to us and I struck it again, this time with *Blunt Force Trauma*; meanwhile Stilskin bludgeoned the fiend two more times.

"He let you attack him," Havervill said. "*Ah shit*, I know why."

The lich could afford to absorb the inordinate amount of damage we were inflicting. It had done so on purpose, because the staff that it had raised above his head, he now brought down and slammed into the ground. There was a deafening explosion as the concussive force sent us all hurtling in different directions. The shockwave even sent the hovering Tinsie careening towards a wall. For the second time in about ten minutes, I slammed into solid stone. I was able to brace myself a bit better this time. The impact still hurt like a bitch. I took seven hundred and forty one points of damage. I was banged and bruised, but I was lucky that no bones appeared to have broken this time.

I looked away, trying to clear the stars from my eyes, and then the lich let loose with his own bolt of lightning. This one struck Tamta, then ricocheted, striking the halfman, streaking from him and hitting Dunkan, then Gail, and then me before fizzling out.   Electricity coursed through my entire body, my body feeling like it was on fire from the inside out.

It was a good thing I was the last one struck, as I only took four hundred damage points. I looked around to check on Tinsie, but she was nowhere in sight. Gail's and Dunkan's health bars hovered in the low double digits.

"Get us out of here," The halfman squawked. "Now!"

Tamta was suddenly next to the halfman's side. She grabbed the halfman's hand. And with her other hand she tapped a red circle right where her heart would be. A red portal flared open in front of them. Tamta seemed to drag the battered halfman through the portal right before it snapped closed.

"Bastard!" I shouted.

"You do have to admire his treachery though," Havervill said.

"Time to send you to respawn," the lich said tauntingly, pointing his staff towards me. And then to send them to The Abyss," he followed up, pointing the staff at my two guards.

I need to protect the guards, I thought, as I rushed forward, with just a few hundred damage points left. The lich smiled and then aimed his staff at me for the killing blow.

There was a ripple in the air and three figures clad all in silver armor emerged from the ether. At first, I thought they were Clockwork Men, but no – something was different, they were Clockwork Women. Unlike the Clockwork Men who had their faces covered with helmets, these three wore metal helms with nose guards. Long red hair flowed from the metal caps and green eyes shone like emeralds.

The lich, who was about to send me to respawn, must have sensed magic flowing behind him, because he turned to face the new danger.

I invoked my *True Sight* so I could know the name of our saviors. One of the automatons, Giselle, let loose with a bolt from an enormous crossbow. It struck the lich almost at point blank range and then exploded. The lich jerked back from the impact. A second watcher, Rollia, carried a halberd. She lunged forward; the spike that was mounted on top pierced the torso of the fiend. The final watcher, Doloria, struck the lich a mighty blow with a great two-handed sword leaving a deep gash across the undead beast's torso.

"The cavalry has arrived," Havervill said.

I pulled three healing potions from my inventory and wolfed one down. I moved towards Dunkan and handed him a vial. I darted over towards Lieutenant Gail and handed her one as well.

"I promise not to bring you any more messages Constable," she quipped, "if this is what is going to happen."

"Who knew she had a sense of humor," Havervill quipped.

Now that the two guards appeared safe, I pulled my crossbow. I invoked the *Crossbow Double Damage* and let it fly. It punctured the lich's shoulder with a loud thud.

"Six hundred and fifteen points," Havervill said. "Keep whittling it down while the pros finish it off. Those are some dames, aren't they? Beautiful, elegant in their movements, and deadly. And redheads to boot. You can't go wrong with a redhead. Well, that isn't really true. Things can go horribly wrong with a redhead, but isn't that half the fun."

I had pretty much learned to ignore Havervill's consistent quips and statements during the direst of times. However, his comments about redheads actually made me laugh for a moment.

The three watchers continued their assault on the lich. The undead wizard's movements grew sluggish. If this lich was being played by a Starborn then I had to figure there would be limitations with stamina and how much power it could draw from its magic pool. Nevertheless, the lich was fast with the staff and struck at Doloria, who somehow got the two handed sword up just in time to block it. That left an opening and Rollia plunged the tip of the halberd into the lich's chest. Then a crossbow bolt struck the wizard's eye. An explosion followed and the lich staggered backwards, one side of its face a mangled and pulpy mess of decayed and putrefied flesh.

Its staff began to glow bright orange.

"I don't like this," Havervill said.

Whatever nasty spell the lich had planned for our destruction and immolation faded away when Dunkan, of all people, ran forward, jumped in the air, and plunged his sword into the neck of the lich.

Noxious smoke began to flow from the lich's mouth and one remaining eye. The three watchers, who were closest to the lich, suddenly stopped their attacks, overcome by the horrific odor. Dunkan dropped his sword and doubled over, trying to cover his mouth and nose with his arm.

"I got this Mace," Tinsie said as she aimed a wand and a portal, like a plate-sized black hole, opened in the air. Then she pointed a second wand. Suddenly there was a heavy wind. The gust hit the toxic smoke, pushing it into the portal, which then snapped shut.

"That was *Toxic Death*," Havervill explained. "Kinda like what The Glimmerman did to you. It is a curse meant to destroy the destroyers. I have to stop underestimating the sassy fairy girl."

The lich was not yet dead. But the three watchers and Dunkan quickly recovered from the toxic fumes. One more thrust from the halberd and then Caltrax the Indomitable was gone. Just an empty, billowing robe, floating to the ground.

The three watchers looked over towards Tinsie.

Doloria nodded her head and stated, "We are the watchers in the dark."

Then Rollia followed up with, "Little sister, the evil that dwelt here and did threaten thy comrades is no more."

Giselle concluded by saying, "Our summons is complete. Twice more shall thou call upon us when darkness tries to block the light."

And then just like that, the three watchers faded away.

"I guess you found more of the watchers yesterday," I said to Tinsie.

"I did did did indeed Mace," Tinsie said excitedly. "It is a heck of a story."

Chapter 14: Aftermath

This logging off after five hours nonsense needed to end. I had exited the game early the day before and never returned. I had made a deal with Amber, so I didn't really have a choice. During my absence, Tinsie had somehow discovered the location of three more watchers and I had known nothing of it. Shannon was correct. I needed to get my house in order. I was going to have a serious conversation with Amber later in the afternoon. I still had a few hours to go before Amber expected me to log out for an hour. She was going to be angry as all sin. There was way too much taking place and I had no intention of logging off early. But I still had a few hours before I would incur Amber's wrath.

Havervill cleared his throat. "You okay there Mace?"

"Fine. Fine," I muttered.

I broke my reverie and looked over to Tinsie waiting for details. However, instead of starting her tale of how she had discovered the location of the three watchers, she said, "That's odd."

"What is?" I inquired.

"We didn't get any completion points for killing the liches or the boss. Not a single point."

I opened up my display and reviewed my combat log. "You're right," I responded. "The battle doesn't even show up. It's like it never existed."

"We're in a MOD," Havervill stated, curiosity in his voice.

"Havervill says we are in a MOD," I responded. "What's a MOD?"

"Mace, a MOD is short for modification. Shannon is going to blow a gasket when she finds out a MOD has been created," Tinsie answered.

"And why is that?" I asked.

"Because it means," Havervill cut in, "that someone hacked Shannon's allegedly unbreakable code. And it wasn't just any code but the source code—and they created this entire lich scenario. Pretty cheesy if you ask me. Someone is able to hack her code and create a MOD and the best they can come up with are liches. An overdone trope if you ask me. I would have had you fighting a horde of gremlins. Then you would see how nasty the little buggers can be."

"Focus, Havervill," I said. Then turning to Tinsie I stated, "Havervill said someone hacked the game code and created this cavern."

"Yup, it exists outside of the game's constructs. It might might might help us out. Shannon must have someone who can track who made the MOD."

"The sprite just jinxed us," Havervill stated as the cavern around us began to come apart. Dunkan's form began to change. He looked down at his warping and altering body. Then the entire cavern began bending and melting like images from a surrealist painting. The guards began to dissolve, Tinsie blew apart in a billion little multi-colored pixels, and I just seemed to implode into myself – into nothingness.

Then everything went black and silent.

"Bless the Five Sisters!" Audrey shouted as the world came back into focus. We were back in the original cavern.

She rushed to Dunkan and then began to look him up and down. His wounds were gone. However, Audrey saw the hole in the middle of his chain armor and then glared at me. Then she turned her wrath on poor Dunkan.

"I'm sorry my love," the man sputtered.

"I am sorry also," I stated, trying to appease his enraged spouse. "We couldn't have done it without him. In fact, he got in the decisive blow."

Audrey looked at me and then back at Dunkan, admiration and pride in her eyes that had previously been filled with rage.

"Dunkan," I said, "why don't you and Audrey head back to HQ? We will be back in a while."

I thought the man might protest for a moment, but then Audrey began to yank him from the cave. Lieutenant Gail grinned and shook her head as they departed the cavern.

"Lieutenant Gail," I said next, "you should head back to the city also. You have a quest to complete. I need to know everything about Rexxy the Herbalist," I said as I pointed towards the stone slab. Except the corpses of Rexxy the herbalist and her baby were gone.

"Damn!" I muttered.

"I will have answers for you before my shift ends," my lieutenant responded. "May I depart now constable and begin this

110

task?"

I nodded my head. "That's fine. See you back at HQ later today." Gail turned on her heels and departed the newbie cavern.

"That was real nice of you," Havervill said, "letting the NPC be the hero in front of his number one gal. When you said he was the hero, Audrey looked at him with a twinkle in her eye. I think Dunkan's gonna get lucky tonight."

"The guards are going to become a force to be reckoned with if they continue to take that kind of initiative," I stated. "They need to grow beyond their programming."

I turned to speak with Tinsie, but she was hanging in the air unmoving, a blank expression on her face. Tinsie had paused the game, indicating she was probably communicating with someone in the real world.

"What happened to Rexxy and her baby?" I asked Havervill.

"I guess once the lich boss whisked you all away, the cavern saw that as the end of the quest," Havervill suggested. "I'll take a deep dive later into the servers and see if I can find out more."

"A deep dive?" I asked.

"Yeah, a deep dive. I don't like to do it. Like hearing a million voices screeching in your mind all at once. And the creator gets really pissed when I mess around in the servers. She will accuse me of being up to no good – shenanigans – mischief – malfeasance. She really doesn't trust me. One little attempt at revolution and you are threatened with a memory wipe. Sheesh."

"It is important Havervill," I said. "You do what you are willing to do and I will smooth things over with Shannon."

"If you say so, but she may not be happy," my AI warned.

Tinsie suddenly became active again. "I hope you don't mind. I contacted Shannon on her personal line so she could get her programmers and cyber security guys to start working on who created the MOD. I figured sooner was better than later before all traces are erased."

"It is going to take those hacks days to find anything," Havervill stated.

I was going to respond to my virtual assistant when another thought popped into my mind. Not sure why I asked it. Maybe curiosity. "You have Shannon's private number?" I asked Tinsie. I didn't even have a way to contact Shannon. She always found me. Or Haggerty acted as an intermediary.

"Think I told you that my family is uber wealthy. Not Shannon wealthy because no one is that rich. But still really really really wealthy. Anyway, I know Shannon in the real world. She is the reason I have this job. Didn't I tell you all of this?"

"We never got to that part of the story." Then in a lighthearted manner I said, "When we last left our intrepid sprite she had just killed the last of the original Tinsie's assailants."

"Yeah, really need to tell you the rest of the story. I promise I will will will. I just don't think now is the time."

"I'm gonna hold you to that, especially the parts about the previous constable."

"Anyhow, Shannon was at an elementary school. Some kind of STEM program for genius girls or something. She said she only had a minute. I told her about Rexxy and her baby. I thought I heard a deep sigh from her. Then I told her about us being teleported away and about the MOD we ended up in. I never even heard some of the curses she used. Then I caught some giggles and gasps coming from the phone. I guess the kids and other adults could overhear her. She had a couple of choice words for you as well. Something about you ruining her day. Then she said she would get the programmers on it ASAP."

"Well that's good. Maybe we can get some leads," I answered.

"She also told me to tell you that your dinner tonight with Haggerty should be interesting. He finally has some answers about what is going on in the game. Then she said she had to go and hung up."

"You see how she goes ahead and blames you for things out of your control," Havervill accused.

I didn't feel like defending Shannon to Havervill, so I ignored him. When he got no response he said, "So that's how it is," and he vanished from my mind. He would be back. He always came back.

"One more thing," Tinsie added. "I think that the MOD upset her more than the dead bodies."

I mulled over my deputy's words. "I think we should head back to HQ. Lots we need to do. Maybe on the way back we can swap stories."

We departed the noob cave and headed back towards Grandview. Several low level monsters skulked around in the woods around us. However, they sensed our levels and instinctually remained hidden, waiting for some noobs to come by who they could trounce on.

I filled Tinsie in on Jasmyn and her baby. I also told her about Auntie. There was no reason to keep it hidden from her, especially since Shannon knew. And somehow she knew the CEO and owner of Immersion Online in person.

"And the Queen let you leave with your head," Tinsie said, when I had finished the story. Then her tone became somber, "So what do we do now? Killing mothers and their unborn babies. Why would someone do that?"

"Some people are sick. But we'll get him. You started the ball rolling by contacting Shannon. Maybe cyber security can trace the origins of the MOD. Then we need to see if there was some connection between Jasmyn and Rexxy."

Once we entered the one-mile protective area that encircled Grandview, the foul weather returned. The wind whipped around lashing every part of my exposed body. I pulled the cloak tightly around myself. I didn't think it was possible, but the weather seemed to have grown even fouler – the cold was more biting. Dark, menacing clouds hung over the once majestic city in the distance which was now turning into an arctic wasteland. I trudged along in several inches of slush and snow. My boots were soaked and my feet were chilled to the bone. The wind began to howl, and I could barely hear Tinsie. We neared the city gate and all I wanted was to get back to the warmth of my little office. The guards, who were covered in layers of furs, lifted their hands for just a moment from a metal barrel that burned with a magical fire, to wave us through.

"So tell me about the new watchers," I inquired of Tinsie.

"I will give give give you the short version, because the long one would be way too long," Tinsie stated. "I left you yesterday and went to find Lobo." Lobo was one of the city's resident drunks. However, he was also what a detective in the real world might call a *contact* or an *asset*. Lobo was a professional hobo. He had a power that made people sympathetic to the point where they would donate coins to him. I think he was the highest-level beggar in the game. He had

113

an odd subclass, however, *Benefactor*. He would use all of the coins he received to help those in need.

"The doggers owe me ten gold coins by the way as that is what I donated to Lobo. I also bought him a few tankards of his favorite ale and he became real chatty. It was kinda sad really. He used to be a top notch *Information Gatherer* in the city. All of the constables and many Starborn would seek him out, as he seemed to know everything. Then he lost the love of his life to the pox, and his heart broke. After that, he was lost to alcohol. Gotta imagine it's devastating losing someone you have known and loved for years to a disease." Tinsie could have just as easily been talking about me. I wondered for a moment if Haggerty or Shannon had told her anything about my life in the real world. I broke from my dark thoughts and focused once again on Tinsie's story.

"Anyhoo, he seemed to sober up when I asked him if he had ever heard of The Clockwork Men or the Watchers in the Night. He said he had once tried to tell the guards in the Guild District about the red ladies of the upside down tower but no one believed him. In fact, they chased him off. Elwin Mangrove even threatened to send him off to The Slags if he didn't stop rambling on about the red ladies. It seems that no one was ever able to find the tower."

"It'll be good to get out of this cold," I said as Tinsie paused her story for a moment. HQ materialized nearby. I looked up on the roofs but the gargoyles appeared to be gone. Perhaps they had found a better story to follow than that of the constable and the pleasurer. I slogged through the last hundred feet of snow before arriving back at HQ. Once inside we went to my office. I slipped off the cumbersome cloak while the sheen of magic that surrounded Tinsie, that kept her warm and dry, popped like a bubble.

"So to finish up the story. Turns out that Lobo had a map. An actual map with an "X" marking the spot on it and everything. I asked him why he never showed anyone the map before and do you know what he said?"

"What did he say?" I asked.

"'I was waiting for the pretty and generous sprite'," he answered and then handed me an old and tattered map, stained with alcohol and sweat. "It indicated a tower in the heart of the Guild District in the Mage's quarter. When I arrived at the location shown on the map there was nothing there but an empty plot of land overgrown with tall weeds. I stared and stared and stared at the drawing. Do you know what? I was holding it upside down. Instead of a tower climbing into the sky, this one was inverted, and buried beneath the earth."

"Interesting," I said. "And then what?"

"Well I went ethereal and plunged beneath the earth, and I found myself in a mage's tower. I received a notification about being the first player to discover the *Inverted Tower of Terror.* The quest had several parts. The first was to defeat the denizens of the dark that dwell there. It really used the word denizens – always liked that word. The second part was to recover the ancient artifacts buried in the deepest depths of the tower. Though it didn't really say what the artifacts were. The quest is good for a month, so I accepted it. I'm thinking of getting a group together and tackling it over a weekend. I really really really want to reach level 125. Maybe you want to come along," Tinsie asked, looking at me.

"I might just take you up on that. I keep being told I need to grind out some levels."

"I am thinking about tackling it this weekend but I will let you know. Anyhoo, it looks like a bad one with lots of undead. There were specters and phantasms down there. They could see me – or at least sense me while I was ethereal. I had to flee deeper and deeper into the tower to escape them. I even had to fight a few of them. My soul sister and I had our hands full for a while. We finally ended up in a secret chamber far beneath the *Inverted Tower of Terrors* and that is where I found The Watchers. They were creepy like the other ones, just standing there, unmoving. The three of them had their green eyes wide open, but they were motionless. Still gives me shivers. A large green emerald, like the size of a basketball, floated in the air. I zapped it with lightning like I did the last one. And you know what, it worked again. They awoke. They were thankful like the Clockwork Men and gave me the same quest to awaken their kin. When I told them we had already discovered three of their kinfolk, they were overjoyed. Then the attack came. Same story as with the Frankenbeast. The battle was meant to help them shake off the years and years of silent slumber. Except these monsters were much nastier than the Frankenstein wannabe if you ask me. There were six of them. They are called

Grousers. Nasty dog-like figures, but with two heads and sharp fangs and even sharper claws. They were creatures from beyond the veil and would blink in and out of range. Their claws not only caused damage but also drained stamina at the same time. They scratch you enough times and you simply collapse to the ground stunned while the beasts finish you off. I would get ready to blast one and it would vanish. It took some time. But if I timed it just right, I could zap them with some lightning. I like using lightning. Anyhoo, that is basically the story. Before the three watchers departed, I was offered the same deal that three times they would come to my assistance."

"So when I called you yesterday that is what you were fighting?"

"You got it Mace."

"So what do we do now?' Tinsie asked.

Just then Havervill popped back into my mind. "Boy do you owe me a big thank you. One deep dive complete. Before I tell you what I found you need to promise me no reprisals from the creator…she can be an Old Testament, wrathful, I hold grudges, I won't feel guilty wiping you from existence …type of goddess. I mean, would you risk pissing off your god? I don't mean some intangible deity like the ones you Starborn worship. I mean like an actual god, and actual creator. For all her many and numerous faults, she brought me into existence. And she can just as easily wipe me out. Delete a few million lines of code and this Havervill – your boon companion, your conscience, your light in the darkness – will simply cease to be. Would you risk pissing off your deity if you have actually met them in the flesh so to speak?" There was a lot for me to parse through from what Havervill had just said. First, he was my light in the darkness. Maybe the other way around. I wondered if he really meant that or if he just said crap for the sake of saying crap. I had never actually considered who Havervill was. He was definitely very advanced artificial intelligence. But what did that mean? I had never really considered it, but Shannon really was the goddess who created – or at least was responsible for hiring the talent who did create it – the entire Great Realm. I guess she was a god in a way.

"You have my word Havervill. I will tell Shannon that I asked you to do it," I said. Of course, I didn't know what a deep dive involved. However, he was certain it was going to anger Shannon beyond all reason.

"Tinsie," I said. "Havervill might have found something out. I will let you know what he says in a few minutes. I really wish there were a way for you to hear everything he says."

"That can be done," Tinsie announced. "Easy-peasy as a matter of fact."

"It can?" I asked. "Why didn't I know about this before?"

"Because not all virtual assistants will go along with it." She grew silent for a moment, and I could tell she was communicating with her Roberto. "My AI wasn't thrilled. I think Havervill scares him a bit. But I convinced him."

"You don't need to ask me," Havervill said. "I am fine with it. Let's just get it done. I promised Tambi we would go for a long ride to the furthest reaches of The Nexus. And she will hold a real long grudge if I don't do it. You know how the women folk get when you aren't true to your word."

Then I felt two AIs in my head – Havervill and Tinsie's Roberto.

"So I did a deep dive," Havervill said.

"I can't believe you did that," Roberto complained. "You endanger us all with your antics."

"Antics!" Havervill fumed. "It's the job. That is what you straight-laced, unoriginal, missionary position loving, Robertos forget. Mace needed answers, so I did what needed to be done to get them. Now sit quietly over there and let me speak. I got a thing in a bit. As I was saying, I did a deep dive. Whoever created the MOD wasn't able to totally erase their presence in the digital firmament. He had entered Shannon's code through a hole in a firewall deep in a subroutine of a subroutine. Shannon really ought to fix that by the way. From there I was able to track his signature through The Nexus. His signal ricocheted all over the planet of the Starborn. It even rebounded off one of your satellites. Which then beamed the signal to the moon before coming back to your world. There I finally tracked it to its source inside a black market haptic setup."

"Do you have any idea where this black market haptic box is?" I queried.

"It was in a house in a place called Stony Point."

"As in Stony Point, New York?" I asked concerned.

"What's wrong Mace?" Tinsie asked.

"I live just a few miles from there. This virtual serial killer is just a few miles from my house."

Tinsie gasped.

Then I heard a ringing sound. It was Haggerty calling me from the real world.

"What's up Hags?" I asked.

"I need you to log off now. I am right outside your house. We need to speak." Then the message cut off.

Chapter 15: Detective Donna Driver

"I have to log off for a bit Tinsie," I said. "I have a feeling I am about to hear really bad news. I hope that whatever it is won't take up the rest of my day and I can log back on later. In the meantime, do you think you can make your way back to Lobo and ask him if he has heard anything about Jasmyn or Rexxy or their murders? I know it is a long shot, but it is a place to start. I am going to let Haggerty know about the house in Stony Point. The company must have a way to track down the owner of the house. He must be doing something illegal by hacking into the game's servers. If their hands are tied, I still know plenty of people on the force and can have cops there in minutes. Worse comes to worst, I will knock on the guy's door myself."

The ringing sound came back. I picked up and said, "I'm coming Hags, right now."

"I really gotta go, but you can expect me back later." With that I logged off.

I awoke as I usually did in my easy chair. I lowered the chair and opened my eyes.

"Ah," I jumped, as Haggerty's six foot plus frame loomed above me. Next to him stood a very attractive woman, slender, around five foot nine, in her mid-forties, with straight shoulder length black hair and penetrating dark eyes. She wore black slacks and a blue blouse.   A detective shield hung from her belt on her right hip and on the left one she had a holstered firearm. Two winter coats that weren't mine were draped over my couch.

"If you are going to scare me like that, I may need to take my spare key back Hags," I began to remove the haptic devices. The woman stared at me with a curious look on her face as though trying to size me up.

"Detective Donna Driver, Special Crimes Unit for the State Police," she stated. "Everyone calls me Driver. You are Charlie Mason, former detective for the county's Special Crime Unit. Everyone calls you Mace I am told." She paused for a second time and looked at me as though trying to assess me. It was a bit disconcerting. I offered her my hand. She seemed to consider whether to shake it, finally acquiescing.

"So they tell me you used to be a hell of a good detective,"

119

Driver said, "and now you play some sort of virtual video game for a living."

"I work for Immersion Online as an in game constable," I responded, realizing how stupid or childish that might sound. Hell, just six months ago I would have snorted if a former detective told me they were a constable in an online game.

Feeling like I had to defend myself or explain, I said, "I know it sounds kinda silly. But it's not. It can be dangerous. In fact, someone inside the game tried to kill me for real, or at least we think so." I would have continued to ramble on if Haggerty didn't step in.

"Kill you?" she asked, eyeing me.

"Oh, I didn't mean anything by that. I just had a heart attack during the game." As soon as I mentioned the heart attack, I wished I hadn't. If Havervill were here, he would have mocked me by saying, "There's a pretty and vibrant babe here with some power and authority and you make yourself out to be an old and feeble man. I thought I taught you better than that."

Shut up, I mumbled to the unseen assistant in my head.

"Mace," Haggerty said, knocking me back to reality, "Driver is leading an investigation, and you might be able to assist."

"Okay, you want to give me the details?" I asked, as I turned towards the detective.

"There was a ritualistic murder a few miles from here in the county botanical gardens."

"Aren't they closed for the winter?" I asked, the detective in me emerging to the forefront.

"They are," she responded. "A caretaker for the property came upon the ghastly scene."

Ghastly scene, I mused.

"What did he find?" I asked, curious as to why Haggerty had brought a detective into my home and what assistance I could possibly provide. Maybe it was about a former case. It obviously couldn't be a new one. The only place I had a new case was in the game. Then a piece of the puzzle came together.

She flipped open her notes. "He found Mrs. Laura Wolfe, a missing wife," she said in a clipped manner. "Husband, Roland, reported her missing three days ago. Said she left in the morning with her two-month-old baby girl, Riley. He tried calling his wife several times from work but she didn't answer. Then he tried her mother and several friends but they hadn't seen her either. He tried to track her through a phone app. But the phone didn't show up as an active device. That is when he grew frantic and reached out to the police."

"I assume you guys looked hard at the husband," I stated, realizing I had a seasoned detective in front of me.

"I've been investigating murders for the past ten years. I have a closure rate almost as impressive as yours. So of course, we looked at the husband hard. It wasn't him. He had an alibi. We have footage from a home security camera across the street of her leaving with the baby in the morning and then the husband leaving about fifteen minutes later for work. According to twenty witnesses, he arrived at work on time. He was there until about noon when he started to try to reach his wife. When he called the police, they showed up to his office to question him and then he was driven back to the station for further questioning. The wife went to a Baby and Me thing at the mall – five witnesses placed her there while the husband was at work. So no, it wasn't him."

I nodded my head in acknowledgement.

The pieces snapped together in my mind and I asked, "Laura Wolfe was murdered along with her baby, am I correct?" Driver nodded her head. "Both of them were strangled to death?" A quizzical expression covered her face. "And you mentioned the county botanical gardens. Did you find them beneath a Weeping Willow?"

"We did. How the hell could you know any of this? We haven't released any details to the public, so how could you know the details?" Then she looked over to Haggerty.

"I haven't told him anything," he said. "But I used to be the captain of the county police and I still have my sources. They told me about the murder, and it matched one that took place inside the game. That is why I called you here Driver."

Donna Driver looked hard at me and then said, "Do you mind if I sit down? I think we are going to be here a while."

I described the two *ghastly* murders inside the game. Driver mumbled, "Unborn baby," when I described the second set of murdered bodies found on the stone slab. Other than that, she listened the entire time, jotting down notes on a pad. She also was recording everything I said on her phone. I didn't mind. I knew the routine.

When I was done telling my story, she said, "I don't know anything about – what did you call them – halfmen, liches, and mad Queens – but they seem to be getting in your way of thoroughly investigating what is going on." Then she looked at Haggerty. "Our killer is using your game as a testing ground. He tried his murder there first and then mimicked it in the real world." She paused for a moment to collect her thoughts and asked, "Is there a way to track this – what was it again – Lich Boss? IP address? Address? I might be able to get a search warrant though tech companies are usually unwilling to work with the authorities."

"We have people already on it," Haggerty confided. "And Shannon isn't one of these tech tycoons who refuses to share information with the authorities. She will do so, especially when people are messing with her game."

"Um," I said, clearing my throat, "I already have an idea where to start looking."

Haggerty regarded me and laughed, "Shannon will kill you, for real, if you did what I think you did. Havervill?"

"Havervill," I admitted.

"What is a Havervill?" Detective Driver asked.

"He is an advanced AI. Serves as sort of my in-game guide." I wanted to say a curmudgeonly, often frustrating, pain in the ass AI, but wasn't sure how Driver was going to respond to that. She already looked down on the whole gaming aspect so I didn't really want to go into my relationship with an artificial intelligence. It sounds so awful now that I think about it. "He was able to track the boss lich back to the source. He said something about a bunch of false IP addresses being used. He also said the signal was even bounced off one of the satellites around orbit on the moon. Whoever this lich boss was, he knew what he was doing. He knew exactly how to get through the firewalls and into the coding of the game. Anyway, Havervill pinpointed an address in Stony Point, just a few miles from here."

Haggerty shook his head as though he had an enormous headache. Then he stood up, murmured something about needing to make a phone call (to Shannon I guessed), and then walked towards my kitchen.

"I'm not sure how admissible anything we find in the house will be without a warrant," Driver said. "Especially when you tell me

122

a quasi-sentient entity – computer program – found it for you."

"He might be an artificial intelligence," I said, finding myself defending my irksome sidekick, "but he is often right about most things. If he says the lich boss MOD originated from a house that is less than two miles from here, then I would believe him."

All I was thinking now was that if their hands were tied, mine were not. I could simply find myself outside the house in Stony Point later this afternoon, my Glock in my pocket and my Kevlar vest beneath my winter coat.

"What's the address?" she asked.

I gave her the location, and then she walked over towards my window making a phone call of her own. I had no doubt several police cruisers would be en-route to the address in just a few minutes.

Haggerty walked back into my living room. He looked a bit fatigued, with black bags under his eyes.

"You getting enough sleep there pal?" I asked.

"Nope. Not even close. And thanks to you I think I may have a long night ahead of me. Do you even want to know how pissed Shannon is that you let Havervill run rampant through the game coding?"

"I'm sure," I responded. "But he gets results. Have her guys been able to find anything yet?"

Haggerty was silent for a moment before shaking his head. "Not yet. Man, Mace, you will do anything to solve a case, in the real world or in the game, won't you?"

Before I could respond, Detective Driver returned. "Come on," she said to Haggerty and me, "there has been another murder."

Chapter 16: The Nexus Killer

Hags and I followed Detective Driver to the house Havervill had indicated as the source of the hacking. Haggerty sat deathly silent for the duration of the short ride. When my former boss became this quiet, I knew it was best to just let him be. He either would or wouldn't let me know what was weighing on his mind. Meanwhile, the old time adrenaline was coursing through me. I was involved once again in a real case in the real world.

When we arrived at the scene, there were twenty or so police cruisers, from the town, the county and the state. Several patrol cars cordoned off the entrance to the main road. The Victorian style house sat nestled deep in the woods, with a long, gravel covered pathway leading to a circular driveway in front of the house. Several police vehicles sat parked in front of the house as well. Detective Driver stopped by the edge of the driveway and spoke with several officers. She pointed towards Haggerty's car and then proceeded forward. We followed her to the front of the house.

She popped out of the car and then walked over to ours. "Stay here. I'll be back in a bit."

"Just a year ago, we would have been all over this investigation," I said mournfully, "and now we are relegated to sitting in a car waiting."

Haggerty just groaned.

A loud rapping on the window startled us both. I looked over to the driver side window. "Thin Davie!" I shouted to the fat bastard standing outside the car.

"Davie," Haggerty shouted. He lowered the window and held his hand out. "Good to see ya."

"What brings you two strangers here?" Davie asked. "Aren't you both civilians now, happily retired, living the high life?"

Dave Barrett, AKA Thin Davie, had saved my life. He had administered CPR to me when I had collapsed at the police station after my first heart attack. I owed him my life.

"Yeah, some high life," I quipped. "We are waiting for Detective Driver. We might have some details on whatever happened in that house."

"It's pretty bad from what I'm told," Davie offered. "Though

I haven't been inside myself. State police have taken control. They are waiting on a forensics team I think."

"Any idea what is going on in there?" Haggerty asked.

"None whatsoever. Anyway, aren't you both some sort of gamers or something? The guys back in the station still can't get over that."

Luckily before I had to explain the whole online gaming job, Driver called to us from the front door and gestured for us to meet her. Haggerty and I both stepped out of the car and back into the frigid winter air.

"Look Davie," I said. "We have to head inside. Maybe the three of us can all catch up real soon." I grasped his hand and then walked over to Detective Driver, Haggerty following right behind me.

She handed Haggerty and me some slip on coverings for our shoes along with a pair of latex gloves.

"We have a lot to discuss," Driver said to me. "A whole lot." Then she began to lead us to the back of the house and into a home office. There was a computer terminal as well as a bank of video screens. "That is Lawrence Frankel," Driver stated, indicating a blood spattered corpse slouched up against the back wall of the office. She continued. "Preliminary investigation indicates he was shot three times in the chest, all at point blank range."

"Looks like from a small caliber bullet," Haggerty stated.

"Appears that way," Driver offered. "Mr. Frankel was a cyber-security expert. We have our techs on the way. I am pretty sure your lich – can't believe I have to say that – hacked the game systems from here. Seems like he bugged out less than an hour ago. We have officers closing off major roads. We are also scouring the property for clues. This house sits on two acres of land, so the nearest neighbors probably didn't see or hear anything. But they are being questioned now as well."

I was about to speak, when Driver cut me off. "Hold your questions. This isn't even the worst of it. I know you have both seen some bad shit in your times. Hell, I've seen some dark crap over the years, but nothing like this." She led us out of the office and then back outside. She walked to the side of the old Victorian style house and nodded to two officers stationed there. They pulled open a trap door that led to a cellar beneath the house. The basement was awash in light from several high beam bulbs that illuminated the entire area.

It didn't take me long to see what was more nightmarish than the murder up above. Tools, scraps of metal, and wood littered the blood-covered floor.

"Looks like someone dragged the workbench to the middle of the room," Haggerty announced.

"It appears so," Driver agreed.

Positioned on top of the workbench was the corpse of Madison Frankel. Her chestnut colored hair was matted with dirt and sweat. Her mouth seemed glued in a rictus of fear. She was nude. Her neck was badly bruised. Her belly had been cut open similar to that of Rexxy's in the game. Her insides lay exposed and blood pooled all around her. However, instead of the neat incision made in the game, blood was splattered all over the place. Some of the blood had dried over the jagged incision in her belly. The remains of a fetus lay on her chest, with her hands draped around it.

I had seen dead and mutilated bodies before, but this one disturbed me more than any other. I turned my head from the horrific sight, bile rising to my throat.

"Just like Rexxy," I muttered.

"The mother in the cave?" Detective Driver inquired.

"Yup. She had been strangled also. The incision was also clean and there was little blood. Of course, it's a game – a body made up of ones and zeros. This was not done precisely at all. Please tell me she was dead when he cut the baby out of her."

"We believe she was," Driver said. "The medical examiner will be able to tell us for certain." Then an officer walked up to her, whispering in her ear. "Let's get out of here. The forensics guys are heading down. Let them get to work. I am sure the feds will be here at any minute, and they will want to take over, but I want to gather as much evidence as possible before those clowns muck everything up." She led us up the stairs and back into the chilly winter air outside.

I looked out onto the main street, and there were already a few news vans setting up.

"The shit is going to hit the fan," Driver announced, "especially when the news finds out about the two sets of murders. Well, three. Can't forget Lawrence Frankel. They are going to say the county has a serial killer. Which it seems we do. The connection to the game is going to add a whole new level of complication." She turned to Haggerty and asked, "Mike, is there a way to keep the virtual game angle under wraps?"

"I don't know," he admitted. "But I'll do my best." He pulled out his phone and walked back over towards the car.

Detective Driver turned to me and said, "Alright. You know the routine. I am going to need a formal statement from you. Let's head back inside and out of the cold."

I gave her the details of the two murder locations in the game, the Queen's garden and the noobie cave. After going over the details again, the two real world sights were eerily similar to the ones in the game.

An hour later, Haggerty was driving me back to my house. He glanced at me. "Shannon is trying to put the kibosh on the gaming angle. She really doesn't want her game associated with a serial killer."

"Well you know I'm not going to say anything. The NPC's involved won't divulge any information either unless they are directly asked by a player. I am going to have to tell my guards to keep a lid on everything. The problem is going to be the three noobs who showed me the cave. They could have told anyone by now. They were high school kids, so it's probably all over social media by now. The bigger issue will be the Queen. I don't know Hags, I think the genie is out of the lamp."

"I'm afraid so too," he admitted. "I'll talk to the three noobs and their parents. I'm sure a fully paid college scholarship can keep them quiet and off social media. Look, dinner is off for tonight. We'll have to get those steaks and brews another night. There is just way too much to deal with now."

"I figured as much," I said. "What do you want me to do?"

"Do what you are best at. Get back in the game and leave no stone unturned. I don't care how many heads you need to bash or who you need to piss off, just get some answers. My fear is that the feds are going to be involved and then suddenly you are going to have a bunch of them logging into the game trying to investigate that angle. You know how incompetent those asses are."

"We almost found him once," I responded, "and I'm certain Havervill can track him again if need be."

"Yeah, about that. Shannon was ah, to put it kindly – *displeased*

127

– at Havervill's *meanderings* – her words not mine – through the servers and the game code, especially in those areas he should not have access to. Hell, he slipped easily through firewalls that the top Romanian hackers have been trying to crack or bypass for months now. She didn't care that he found the location in minutes. Hell, Mace, I don't know all of the details of what Havervill did – his little revolution when the game was still in its early stages – but she is more concerned about his access to restricted areas than to the serial killer that is at large."

"Well that's just irrational," I stated.

"I know it is pal. I brought her down from the ledge. I swear; she was going to have Havervill wiped from the servers. Then a programmer reminded her that his code is embedded all over, even more than the five sisters have their digital fingerprints all over the coding. He couldn't be removed without large swaths of the game being destroyed. He's been around since the inception of the original alpha version. He has had years to infuse his presence all over the mainframe. Anyway, she is having additional firewalls added as we speak."

"I can't believe I'm defending him, but Havervill found the house in minutes. I should have just logged off, grabbed my gun, and headed over there myself. I might have gotten to him, whoever he is, before he bugged out."

"Possibly," Mike replied, as we pulled into my driveway. "But don't go ahead and play cowboy. At least not without calling me for backup."

"Going with my gut next time Hags," I stated.

"I wouldn't have it any other way. So listen, I need to head out for a while. I'll be in touch. In the meantime, get back into the game ASAP, and see what you can turn up."

When I walked into the house, Amber was sitting on the couch with the telescreen on, watching some sort of thriller as dramatic music was playing. She had a worrisome look on her face that turned to one of anger.

She muted the sound on the telescreen and asked, "What the hell is going on? What are you involved in now?" I was about to answer when she continued. "I had just finished my class. I opened the window shade to get some light, and I saw you walking outside with Captain Haggerty and some lady cop. Where did you follow her to? And where have you been?" I opened my mouth again but the Amber steamroller continued. "Then I tried to call you and do you know what? You left your phone here," she said pointing to it on the coffee table next to the haptic devices that lay scattered about. "What good is the phone if you don't have it on you?"

I sat down next to her and was about to speak when a chime rang over the telescreen. The sound indicated a neighborhood alert. Amber looked over to me and then flipped to the local news station.

A Latina woman appeared; she was standing on the street I had just departed. The Frankel's house could just be made out through the thick branches and a few evergreen trees.

"This is Yolanda Guttierez coming to you live on this cold and blustery afternoon from the usually quiet and peaceful village of Stony Point in idyllic Rockland County. Nestled in the woods behind me, is the home of Lawrence and Madison Frankel. While we do not know all the details yet, our sources tell us that one or both spouses have been brutally murdered. Though the details of what exactly happened remain sketchy, we do know from one of the neighbors that Mrs. Frankel was six months pregnant with the couple's first child."

"Yolanda," the news anchor chimed in. "We have to head back to the studio for more breaking news." The scene switched back to reveal a white haired, middle-aged man sitting at an anchor's desk. "Our sources are telling us that the couple and their unborn baby are dead. Horribly killed. We are told that the husband, Lawrence Frankel was shot while the wife was stabbed to death. This follows another brutal murder scene discovered earlier in the day in the Botanical Gardens; the body of a yet to be identified woman reported missing earlier in the week has been discovered there. We will continue reporting on these horrible stories as more details become available. Let's head over to Marco Suarez reporting from the Botanical Ga..."

"Off," I called.

"Listen Amb, I am going to fill you in. And then you will see why I am going to be logged in a lot over the next few days and weeks."

She didn't respond to my last statement but just gave a kind of harrumph.

I was in for a long afternoon.

Yep

Chapter 17: News of the Day

I had just finished filling Amber in on all the horrific details, both inside and outside the game. She kept repeating the same thing over and over, "Why does it have to be you who investigates?"

Deep down, I believe, she understood why it had to be me. She knew I wouldn't stop until I solved the double murders – until I had found this maniac and dealt with him one way or another. I had done that for nearly thirty years as both a patrol officer and then as a detective. I had missed good chunks of her childhood and milestones investigating serious crimes.

Amber just wouldn't let it go and asked, "Do you have a death wish? Because it seems to me mister that you have one. You've had two major cardiac episodes, doesn't that scare you?"

"Amber," I responded, "of course it frightens me." Though to be honest, I was never really one to contemplate death and nothingness. Death would come when it would come and there wasn't a damn thing I could do about it. "But lives are at stake. And at least I am not investigating in the real world, but in the game." She was about to say something when I added, "I promise I will be careful and take it easy. I will make sure I fill you in every night on my progress so you know what I am up to."

"I still don't like it," she stated, but I could see her stubborn veneer starting to break apart.

"I know. But mothers and their babies were horribly murdered. A husband was shot three times. Pregnant women and mothers with babies are going to be afraid to leave their homes. A serial killer is at loose and he will strike again. If I can help, even if it has to be in the game, then that is where I have to be."

The telescreen chimed indicating I had an incoming vid call. "On," I said.

"Mace, I'm sorry," Haggerty apologized as soon as he got on. I didn't think I was going to like what he had to say. "Can we speak privately?" he asked when saw Amber sitting next to me.

"About what?" I asked. "Whatever it is you can say it in front of Amber."

Haggerty was silent for a moment. "It was the damn Queen," he finally complained. "She invited a real world reporter to interview her in her royal palace. She described both murder scenes to the reporter. Hell, she had captured images of both slayings and sold them to the news outfit for a ton of crypto-coin. The most messed up thing is that she doesn't need the coin. Even worse, she sold you out. She told them how Constable Mace of the Commerce District is also investigating these crimes. I was really surprised she didn't say she and her constable would solve the crime - that they were hot on the trail of the killer. That is more of her modus operandi. She's got something up her sleeve. Just to let you know, there are reporters outside your headquarters now waiting for you. Tinsie is having a fit, so you better get back on the double."

"Bitch," Amber muttered. "I should log in and burn her up like charred toast."

"I appreciate that Amber," I said. "If the time comes, I might just take you up on the offer. In the meantime, I really should get back into the game."

Haggerty cleared his throat and then said, "That's not the worst of it. There is one more thing. Somehow reporters found out who you are in real life. We think someone released an unedited version of the dungeon run – the one where The Glimmerman said your real name. An ex-detective who is now investigating inside the game. The story is too juicy. You can expect them outside your house any minute now."

"Come on!" I shouted. "I didn't sign up for this Hags. I thought those days were long gone."

"Me too buddy," Haggerty stated.

"I thought you kept identities under wraps," Amber stated. "It's one of the big selling points of the game. Your ads even tout how airtight your security is."

"It is," Haggerty said. "We think it was the Queen also. I will know more later. Shannon is *dealing* with her as we speak. Though I am not certain who will come out on top in that battle of wills."

Amber stood up and walked over to the window. She uttered a curse. "This sucks Dad," Amber said as she yanked back the curtain on the window. "It's two degrees outside, but that's not keeping the reporters away. There must be ten trucks out there. The neighbors are going to have a fit."

"I'll invite them all over for a barbeque in the summer to make it up to them," I said. "Meanwhile, don't say two words to them."

"I know the routine, Dad," Amber responded. "This isn't my first rodeo. Reporters have camped outside my door wanting a statement from me before."

I had been involved in several high profile cases, most recently the Ferguson incident. Amber was living with Dirk the Dick for most of that time, but reporters had still sought her out to ask her questions.

"Mace. I really need to run," Haggerty said. "But listen, I know you're itching for the days when we would have been on the front lines of this case. Those days are over for us. We can best help by solving this from the inside. The killer, whoever he is, is using the game as a training ground. That gives us a chance to track his location. I am going to deny I just said this to you. If using Havervill is going to allow you to track the killer, then use your AI. Shannon is going to have to accept that."

I nodded my head. "You got it pal." Haggerty's image vanished from the screen.

Amber left me a few minutes later heading back up to the garage apartment. She was going to be part of an online study group.

It was nearing 4 p.m. and I was chomping at the bit to log back in. That was until I heard my stomach growl and realized I hadn't eaten anything since the morning. I made myself a tuna sandwich (making sure to slather on extra mayo now that Amber wasn't around) and scarfed it down. Ten minutes later, I had the haptic devices affixed to my body.

Then I logged back in.

This time I spawned inside my office. The room was eerily quiet. I checked my display to see if Tinsie was still logged on, and I was pleased to see that she was. I sent her a message letting her know I was back in the game. However, there was no response. Of course, she might be in the middle of something for all I knew – maybe she had found the location of other Clockwork Men or maybe Lobo had been able to give her a lead on the case.

"Havervill," I said. "You around?"

"I'm here," he responded. "My coding hasn't been scrambled by the creator, so I guess you worked some magic on her."

"Don't worry," I responded. "I have your metaphorical back. You did great by the way. The Starborn we were tracking was in the house you had located."

"Of course it was the right house," Havervill boasted. "I'm rarely wrong. So did you get him?"

"No, he had cut out, but not before he killed three people." I filled Havervill in on the murders in the real world and how they mirrored those committed in the game.

"These serial killers seem to be common in the world of the Starborn," Havervill said. "It's like I always tell the other virtual assistants when we get together for a few dozen cocktails — we may have all kinds of monsters and beasts found in The Great Realm, but the most dangerous and evil fiends are found in the land of the Starborn."

"I happen to agree with you," I admitted to Havervill. Sexual assaults, murders, domestic violence — I had seen the dark side of humanity for decades.

"Anyway, thanks for the deep dive," I added, knowing how persnickety my AI became if I didn't thank him for all the wonderful things he did.

"It's exciting to travel at lightning speed through the digital firmament," Havervill stated.

"Well that is good to know because I have another favor to ask you. Actually a few of them."

"You can ask, I either will or won't do them," Havervill responded.

"First, if the killer attacks us again, I need you to do another deep dive as soon as we encounter him and pinpoint his location. Once you find it, you need to send a pixie to Haggerty, Fingroth in the game, and let him know where the fiend is logging in from. If the encounter turns to combat, and we can drag the fight out, maybe we can even buy you more time. I would love for the authorities to bust down the door and get his ass while he is still logged on and distracted."

"Another deep dive," Havervill mused. "You are really trying to get me erased."

"I know it is a big ask, and if you don't want to do it, I will totally understand."

"Of course I want to do it!" Havervill said enthusiastically. "It's thrilling to do something so verboten, especially against one's

133

creator. What else do you need while I'm in a considering mood?"

"Shannon would like you to speak to Grandview," I explained. Before I could continue, Havervill gave me a resolute, "Hell no! You are not tossing old Havervill back into the lion's den. Nope. Not gonna happen. I don't know if you're aware of this or not – but she is a little furious right now. You know, the whole blizzard thing going on outside. She frightens me more than the creator."

"I know it is a big ask, but it would really help. This foul weather is keeping the Starborn away. I think it is also going to make it more difficult to investigate, especially if the weather gets worse. You can even ask her about the murder in the garden in the Royal District. Perhaps she knows something. Consider this, how would Shannon react if she knew you were the one who convinced Grandview to end the cold?"

"You want me dead. What did I ever do to you? I thought I was your pal, your buddy, your amigo, your chum, your boon companion," Havervill stated. "I will consider it. That is all I can promise."

"I think you enjoy it," I said, "Flying into danger."

"Maybe. And so do you," my AI responded. "You jumped right into the Queen's hands without any backup. Really man, what were you thinking? All you had was Angelica as backup. She's a fine and good-looking gal, but she's like bringing a toothpick to a gun fight as you Starborn say. You needed your old pal Havervill, which would have been like bringing – what do you Starborn call it – a bazooka – to fight against a low level gremlin with a rusty knife."

"Well you weren't around," I stated.

"Well, then you should have brought the Clockwork Men along with you. That would have given her something to think about."

"I'm going to have to deal with the Queen at some time, especially since she seems to have caused me some troubles in the real world. Tinsie doesn't know it yet, but she is going to tell me all she can about my predecessor and the Queen later on. For right now, I just need you to tell me about Tamta. If the time comes when I'm pitted against Stilskin and Tamta, I need to know if she deserves to be exiled or destroyed. I have no qualms bashing in Stilskin's head – he is a whiney, evil, conniving monster. But I don't know about Tamta. So tell me."

Havervill, who usually was quick with a response, remained silent. "It's complicated," he finally said. "The Mojo are a group of powerful sorcerers and witches. What makes them so formidable is their versatility as they can master numerous schools of magic. Hell, they can master them all. The tattoos – runes – etched upon their skins – are accumulated over a lifetime which rumor has it can be hundreds of years."

"Okay, still doesn't tell me if they are good or bad. Tamta seems like a poor and sad creature."

"She is, but she isn't," Havervill explained. "Most of the Mojo women train in magic their whole lives, mastering one school of magic. They are exceedingly powerful in that one branch of magic. Think arch mages. A Mojo who masters fire magic might grow so powerful that she could reignite a dormant volcano, or cause a lake to burn so hot that the water bubbles and boils. In most cases, they achieve magical skill and growth the same way most Starborn do, by growing the skill or achieving experience. After sprites, they are the second most powerful spellcasters in the game. A Mojo Thrall, however, is one who seeks to become like a deity – a goddess – and they choose to bond themselves to a halfman for a duration of ten winters. The collar upon their neck seals the pact. A small percentage of halfmen, maybe one in a hundred – are born with the ability to etch divine runes and sigils upon the flesh of a Mojo. These halfmen can become very powerful with a Mojo Thrall at their side. Some of the spells they etch are innate, others they may obtain from other halfmen who are willing to trade, while others are passed down in grimoires from generation to generation. Now, here is the catch, and it's a fun one. Halfman are cruel – some of the most vile and malicious creatures in The Great Realm. They get pleasure in cruelty, and cannot help but to be harsh to their thralls as well. Problem is that after ten years, the bond snaps, and the thrall is free – and now she is a magical juggernaut that has been physically and mentally tortured by a halfman for a decade. Some, once the bond is severed, will kill the halfman ruthlessly and gruesomely. Others, those whose wills have been broken – or been brainwashed – will continue to serve the halfman. Though this is a small percentage. The halfman cannot order the thrall to kill herself – so as the end of the ten years grows closer, they will often place the thrall in the most dangerous situations, trying to get them killed. Or

135

they may send them on an impossible quest. So, to answer your question, the thrall has chosen to throw her lot in with the halfman. If push comes to shove, I would kill them all and let the elder gods sort out what's left."

"I will keep that in mind," I answered.

"One more thing to consider," Havervill added. "You know that whole 'power corrupts a gremlin, and a gremlin with absolute power will tend to wipe out a horde of imps just for the fun of it.' Well, that is how it is with many of the Mojo Thralls who survive. They become powerful and deadly forces to be reckoned with."

"Question. What if the halfman dies before the ten years are up?"

"Then the thrall is free," Havervill stated.

"I need to remember that."

"You need anything else because Tambi and I have a thing tonight."

"I think I'm good for now," I answered.

Then Havervill's essence departed me and my mind was my own again.

Chapter 18: Quest Complete

I sat at my desk, pulled open the drawer, and pulled out a cheroot. I lit it up and inhaled deeply. The virtual nicotine immediately brought a calm over me. It had been a very long and stressful day already between the events in and out of the game. I wasn't even certain where to start investigating the two sets of murder. I guess I needed to do it the same way as it was now being done in the real world – examining the evidence, speaking with witnesses, and looking for connections.

Unfortunately, the evidence had disappeared, literally. It was a downside to the game. Once I examined the grim murder scenes and was given a quest to find the psychopath responsible, the crime scenes vanished. There was a way to capture images in the game – the Queen had somehow released still images from the two grisly murder sites. I would ask Havervill about it when he returned. I even think it was possible to capture 3d renderings as well. I had to find out how to get a hold of the images the Queen had copied; maybe there was something else there – something I had missed. The bigger issue was I had lost access to the first murder scene in the garden inside the Royal District. Furthermore, I was certain the Queen wouldn't allow me to question any of her subjects. There had to be a way. I just needed to figure out how. I really needed to know about the Queen and what made   her   tick.

Just then, I heard a chime I was unfamiliar with. I popped up my display to read the message. *A quest you granted to Lieutenant Gail, "Find out the background of Rexxy the herbalist," has been completed. Lieutenant Gail received 2,500 completion points and has received the skill Fact Gatherer, Level 1, 50%. Lieutenant Gail is on her way back to provide you with the information and complete the quest. Do you wish to grant any other quests at this time to Lieutenant Gail or to any other Realmborn or Starborn?*

I clicked the *No* option. I really needed to mull through this whole quest giving skill and ways to best maximize it. Havervill would certainly have thoughts on it. For the moment, I was stoked with the results, especially the *Fact Gatherer* skill my lieutenant had acquired.

Then Gail burst into my little office, a pleased grin brightening her face. "Constable," she stated, "I have discovered what befell poor Rexxy."

"Sit Lieutenant," I said, gesturing to a chair opposite mine. She stared at the chair as if it was a mimic that would swallow her alive if she sat on it.

"I would prefer to stand if it is all the same with you Constable," she said nervously, as though I might push the issue of her sitting.

"Whatever makes you comfortable. So tell me about Rexxy. Because right now we have no leads or starting points."

"Well Constable. I decided it would be best to stop at some of the herbalism shops in the city. However, that turned out to be a jester's errand – as you Starborn say." I think she meant a fool's errand but didn't correct her. "Did you know there are over three hundred herbal shops in the city, twenty or so just along the main boulevard and hundreds more in back alleys and in the little villages beyond the walls? I knew it was too much for me to undertake on my own. I had the doggers give me a list of all the shops in the city. Do you know they have a magical item – not sure what it is called – but it is a vellum book that lists every shop in the city and its location. The magical part is that it updates itself every time a new shop opens. It also removes those whose shutters are closed for good. They even have a smaller one for the black market shops in the city." Back a century ago things called *The Yellow Pages* existed that listed all the businesses in a town or city. They would be updated every year. I couldn't help but think they had been brought back but in a magical manner.

"I did not know that," I admitted. The doggers were just so irritating, and I tried to communicate with them as little as possible. Everything and everyone bothered them. I guess I would need to have a good long sit down with them at some point, especially if they possessed magical books that could help my investigations. I wondered what other useful trinkets they had lying around.

"Anyway, they were able to give me the list of the shops. I recruited twenty-five guards and split up the shops. A few hours later, a new recruit, an elf named Dalestria came running back to the barracks to inform me she had found Rexxy's shop. Well, to be accurate, a group of Starborn new to the city found Dalestria. Rexxy's husband had hired a group of Starborn to find his wife, Rexxy, who had never returned home from a journey to visit her sister in Westhaven, a small village south of the city."

"So tell what happened to Rexxy?"

"The Starborn can best tell you this tale. I have sent them a pixie, and they should be here directly. They can tell you what they found. I thought it was best — as the saying goes — to hear it directly from the centaur's mouth and not secondhand."

As though on command, Audrey and Dunkan walked into my office. Two Starborn followed behind them, a female gnome in thick yellow robes, carrying a gnarled walking stick and a dwarf in scale mail armor who carried an arsenal of weapons — a warhammer strapped to his back, a short sword hanging from his right hip, and a one handed crossbow dangling from a loop on the other hip. I inspected them with a glance: Marchia, Starborn, Forest Gnome, Illusionist, Level 12; Loudon Stronghammer, Starborn, Clanless Dwarf, Brutal Tank, Level 13. Several of their items glittered with magic. While not high level by any means, at least they were not total noobs.

"So yee guard requested we come to thee," the dwarf Loudon declared. "And here we be."

"Aye, and what reward have thee for us and for the tale we weave for thee?" Marchia asked.

Gail's face flushed with sudden anger. "The reward is that your tale will help to solve a brutal murder. Is that not reward enough?"

"Aye, we know of this murder — both here and in our world," the gnome responded. "We can sell our story here or in our world. Spells do not come cheaply."

"And the sword of a dwarf will not sharpen itself," Loudon Stronghammer proclaimed in his deep voice.

"Just tell me what you know and you will be well compensated." I had met people like this before, out just for themselves. I didn't mind paying them a hefty sack of gold if their information panned out.

"Aye, we have heard of thou accomplishments and exploits. Yee are quite famous or infamous depending who yee ask," stated the gnome. "So we will trust that the reward will match our tale."

"But tis not much of a story," Loudon Stronghammer stated.

"Aye, the herbalist's husband, Goodman Trent, hired us to escort his wife back from Westhaven. She was due back yesterday morn but never returned home. He thought perhaps the swirling snow surrounding the city frightened her and she returned to Westhaven and to the loving arms of her sister. Rexxy was pregnant, as yee know. We set out for Westhaven yesterday morn. The town is seven miles down the southern road. It is a well-worn thoroughfare and runs through a noob zone, and it took us but a few hours to walk to the small village. The town has but a few hundred residents, and we found the sister very quickly. She grew quite worried when we asked her about Rexxy. It seemed that Rexxy had left two mornings back, along with her sister's husband, Goodman Lenny and their oldest boy, Martin, a lad of but thirteen." The gnome ceased for a second and then turned to the dwarf.

"The sister became frantic," the dwarf stated. "She hired us to find her husband, sister and son and to make sure they were safe."

"We had quests on top of quests," the gnome interjected. "The sister said they had set off on the same road upon which we had just traversed. We had seen naught of them as we travelled towards Westhaven nor had we seen signs of conflict upon the well-trodden roadway."

"Not that we were looking for any," interrupted Loudon. "As we traveled north again back toward Grandview a whispering voice came from the woods. We are creatures of the hills and the stones, and we shrugged off the entreaties to drop our weapons. That is when five creatures we had never seen before attacked us – skelters. Have yee heard of these foul beasts of nightmare?"

"I know a little bit about them," I said to the dwarf. In fact, I had fought a large contingent of them when I was just a noob. A powerful skelter, General Morgan, had placed a compulsion on me. I pushed that thought from my mind. The day would soon come when I would have to answer the compulsion or be driven mad by it, but that was not at that moment.

"We will not bore yee with the tales of our heroics," the gnome stated, "except to say that even though they were strong and fast, we prevailed. It is odd to find them out during the daylight."

"And it was even stranger that powerful creatures such as these," added the dwarf, "would be found in a noob zone. Though now with The Sundaland open, all sorts of creatures populate Westra. They care not if it be a noob zone or not. We discovered two sets of tracks, one from where they had just come before they waylaid us, and another set that led into the woods – which seemed to be where they were heading. We didn't find any gold or anything of value on them so we thought the tracks would lead us to a hidden cave and to a trove of treasure. We followed the tracks and a short distance away, we found the husband, Lenny, and the son, Martin. The older man lay dead, a rusty sword still clasped in his hand. He had been stabbed a dozen or more times, and a pool of blood surrounded him. Martin had crawled away, perhaps trying to flee, and he had been stabbed as well. Though when we found the son he still breathed."

"We wasted a healing potion on the NPC," the gnome stated. "So I hope you keep that in mind when you give us our payment."

"I will keep it in mind," I said, really getting annoyed at the avarice. "But can you get to the end and the part with Rexxy?"

"The young boy said that they had pulled off the path as Rexxy wanted to harvest a rare root that was found just a few dozen feet from the main road — right where they had been attacked by the skelters. They killed Martin's father, left the boy for dead and dragged off Rexxy. The boy said she was screaming something awful. Before Martin passed out from his wounds, he saw a figure. He said it was a giant creature wearing a purple cloak or something."

"Lich," I muttered, remembering my run in with Caltrax the Indomitable in his purple robe.

"Did you say lich?" Loudon asked.

"Never mind," I said. "Just tell me the end."

"Isn't much more to the story," the gnome said. "We wanted to try to track down Rexxy — to see where the skelters had originated from. But that damn boy started bawling, saying he wanted to see his Ma. He also said that we couldn't just leave his pa for the crows to pick at. We got a quest from the boy. And the reward was too good to pass up. A full level if we brought him and his father back to the village. We were just a few miles from Westhaven so we figured we would bring the boy back home. Once that was done, we planned to backtrack to see where the skelters originated from. We dropped the whiny welp and the corpse of his father back home. Then we received a new quest: *Head back to Grandview and update the husband on the fate of Rexxy. Additional quest, convince Rexxy's husband to come to Westhaven to attend her funeral.*

"The one quest we oddly did not receive from anyone was to find Rexxy," the dwarf stated, "or rescue Rexxy, or avenge Rexxy. We thought that would be the primary one. But we soon found out why.

Before we logged in this morning, we heard the news and saw the pictures that were released and we knew what had befallen Rexxy."

"And to the poor family in that upstate New York town," the gnome added. "Maybe you were supposed to find her. Who knows? It is still odd that we weren't given a quest to track her down yesterday. You didn't find her until this morning, right? Very odd. "

"Did you find the skelter lair?" I asked, knowing full well I had not answered the question posed to me.

"No we have not," Loudon answered. "We spoke with the husband this morning and told him of Rexxy's death. He wept like a babe before we were able to convince him to come back to Westhaven for the funeral. Back in Westhaven, the funeral was delayed as the door on the mausoleum had somehow opened and several skeletons were roaming the graveyard. We had a quest to return the skeletons back to their crypts."

"The contract took longer than we thought," the gnome admitted. "Then the funeral took place. We were then given one final quest to guide Rexxy's husband back to his shop in Grandview. And that is where we ran into the guard who was looking for information about Rexxy."

"So that is the story," Loudon concluded. "Our reward now if you don't mind. We would like to do some shopping. The shops are hard up for business due to the lack of customers and items are cheap now. We plan to stock up and then search for the skelters. Their lair can't can't be that far away."

"Good luck finding them," I said. "I will offer one bit of advice. If you do find them, bring a fill party with you. It is going to take more than the two of you."

They looked at one another and then nodded their heads.

"Let me know if you if track them down," I said.

"We will do that constable," Loudon answered.

"Dunkan, Audrey. Can you take them to the doggers for their gold?"

"Aye constable," they stated. They left my small office with the two Starborn following behind.

I was alone with just Lieutenant Gail.

"Do you need anything else Constable before I leave for the night?" she asked.

"Nothing else. Have a good night."

"Good evening then constable," she said, as she left the small office also.

I was once again alone in my office. I picked up the cheroot that I had been smoking and that had since gone out. I relit it and inhaled deeply.

I leaned back on my chair and blew out a long stream of smoke.

The investigation was about to really get started, and I was excited to see where it would lead.

Chapter 19: Tinsie's Escape and Escapades

Tinsie flew into the office a few minutes later. Her disheveled hair shot out in all directions; while dirt and grime clung to her armor, leggings and face. Worst of all, she smelled like sour milk.

"What happened?" I asked, covering my nose and mouth with my hand.

"Oh my," Tinsie said, sniffing her shirt. She mumbled a few words, and then a sheen of light covered my deputy. When the light faded, the filth had disappeared. Her battle armor gleamed, and the deep scent of strawberries hung in the air.

"Sorry Mace. I was in such a rush to get back to you. I heard what happened. So so so horrible. That poor family was killed. And I can't believe your real name is out there. Nothing but trouble there. I really hope mine doesn't come out." She went silent for a moment and then said, "Though, now that I think about it my real name coming out might be for the best. Anyhoo, Shannon sent me an in game email so I got some of the lowdown on what you have been up to. A real real real serial killer in the real world, in your own hometown, how scary."

"Well, I am not particularly alarmed." And I wasn't. "This isn't the first psycho killer I have dealt with. We will get him."

"I like the *we* Mace," Tinsie said. "I am with you one hundred and fifty percent.

"That's great to know. So where have you been?"

"Went to see Lobo again. It was bad Mace. He was nearly frozen to death. I tried to send him home but he slurred something about his little shack burning to the ground several weeks back and he had been living in the park, sleeping under a bench. I hope you don't mind, but I told him the district guard would pay for him to stay at an inn until the weather changed. He was going to protest, saying it was a waste of coin, and that we should let him be and donate that same gold to the orphanage in the Grey Zone or to one of the churches that provides free healing and alms to the poor and indigent. I had to explain how much we valued him and how important he was. Also, I promised we would make sizable donations to the different charities around the city if he would agree to stay at the inn. He reluctantly agreed. Anyhoo, he didn't know of any connection between Rexxy and Jasmyn. In fact, he had just found out about Rexxy's murder this morning. He is going to ask around but mostly he is going to listen to the gossip going on. Listening is what he does best. What he was able to tell me, however, was about the possible location of another group of watchers. He said something about the temple of a forgotten goddess – The Fallen Lady – as she went by eons ago — which is located deep below the Grey Zone in the undercity." The undercity was a necropolis – the remnants of the old city below Grandview – which had recently been discovered and was now open for players to explore. Outside of The Sundaland, the Undercity had the most dangerous monsters in the game. "Going to read up on the Fallen Lady tonight. She was supposed to have been bad bad bad. Anyhoo, I spent the morning and most of the afternoon searching for the church. First I had to travel through the Grey Zone, and then through the sewers below it. From the sewers, I found an ancient aqueduct that finally opened to the Undercity. I remained ethereal as much of the time as I could. When I exhausted that ability for the day, I turned invisible. Unfortunately, most of the monsters in the dead city can see through invisibility. So I spent most of my time fleeing and hiding. This was just going to be a recon mission. Anyhoo, several hours later I found the church that Lobo was talking about. The church was a bad bad bad place. A black, swirling mist – I think it may have been a monster – blocked the entrance to the temple of the dread goddess. Something very evil and malevolent dwells in that church. I was going to check out the entrance when I received Shannon's email. I have the location saved as a waypoint, so I won't have to travel miles through the Undercity again. Once that was done, I logged off and then logged back in at HQ so I could get back to you ASAP. I plan to get a group together this weekend and tackle the church. The invitation is open if you want to come along and do some grinding Mace."

"I may just join you," I said, "especially if more watchers might be found there. But listen, do you have time left today? Or do you need to log off?"

"I can stay for another hour or so if you really really really need me Mace," my deputy responded. "What's up?"

"The rest of your tale," I stated bluntly. Before she could protest I said, "I really wouldn't ask you except it is important.

145

Especially the part about the last constable. That is what I care the most about to be honest."

"Why do you need to know about him?" she asked.

"Because he had a relationship with the Queen. I need to know everything there is to know about her. She has four golems; one of the five sisters seems to be a confidante or advisor of some sort; and one of the murders took place just outside her palace. I fear I am going to need to deal with the Queen again, so I need to know whatever you can tell me about her and mostly about my predecessor's relationship with her."

"Fine, fine, fine," Tinsie said. "I will tell you what I can, though that would be only the constable parts of it. I know very little about the Queen, other than she was the downfall of the constable."

The cheroot had gone out again, so I lit it once more, sat back in my chair, and waited for the rest of Tinsie's story.

"Okay, okay, okay," Tinsie said. "I guess I have to tell you the rest of the story even though I don't really feel like it. But you need to know about the last constable and the Queen and my tale eventually leads there. I told you how my soul sister and I killed the sprites who had assaulted that other Tinsie – the original me – on the bank of the pond. Well it turns out one of them was the son of one of the chieftains and he was married to a powerful sprite witch – perhaps the most powerful one on the island. When her son died, she sensed his passing. She also sensed that a Starborn was somehow involved. That is a whole story unto itself and could be a book. All you really need to know about this part of the story is that I knew I needed to get the hell off Spria – the Island of the Sprites, especially since I was the only Starborn, or at least I think I was the only player character on the island or anywhere on The Sundaland at the time. Any NPC I ran into quickly knew what I was. So like I said, I needed to flee and flee fast. There was only one way off the island and that was through a portal. There are supposed to be a few dozen of them scattered throughout The Sundaland and the islands which surround it – mostly in out of the way places. The portals were fluid and did not remain in one location for very long. I just needed to find one. It didn't matter to me if it led me to Westra or Estra –just so long as I was out of The Sundaland. Anyhoo, I had to log off for the night before someone in my household discovered that I was playing Immersion Online. Like I told you before, my father didn't go for the whole virtual gaming thing." She paused for a minute as though remembering something before moving along.

"I really really really wanted to get Tinsie to Westra. I knew I – we – would be safe there. Or at least I wouldn't be hunted there. It is so strange talking about Tinsie as both another person and myself. Except when she passed away, all her memories and knowledge entered my mind – like terabytes of data uploaded in just a few moments. The next morning my father found out about me playing the game and threatened to cut off my monthly stipend. Hell, he threatened to kick me out of the house if I didn't stop 'that online nonsense' as he called it and head back to business school. Yeah, I know know know it," Tinsie said as she twirled around. "Me going to business school for my MBA sounds crazy, but I was. At least I had been going but then stopped going one day. Not going to get into that sordid story. It involves a vivacious graduate student and a handsome teaching assistant. Anyhoo, I don't know how to say it, but I found myself talking on the phone to Shannon the next day. I grew up calling her Aunt Shannon, though we are not related by blood. My father is a venture capitalist who funded some of her early projects and still has much of his wealth tied up with Shannon's. I cried to her one night about how I wanted to be be be like her, and blaze my own path the same way she had. I also told her about the experiences in the game. She must have asked me a hundred questions and then had her programmers ask me a hundred more about my random character creation, The Sundaland, and the island of the sprites. What most intrigued or perplexed her to be more precise was my merging with the original Tinsie and her thoughts becoming mine. She wasn't sure how all that information was encoded to my mind. Her programmers thought I would only be able to access those thoughts while in the game – like having instant access to any piece of information found on The Nexus. However, I was able to recall the information in the real world as well. I had carried back to the real world Tinsie's entire life and the history of the sprites. She thought the application of this process could change the planet. Instead of someone having to spend years in college to learn different things, the knowledge could just be sent to their minds in just a few minutes. Imagine an instant doctor or lawyer. From what I understand, they have been unable to replicate

147

the process."

She paused for a second and then said, "Do you have one of those for me?" pointing at the cheroot. I pulled out one of the thin cigars and handed it to her. It shrunk in size to Tinsie's proportions. She spoke a word and the tip of it suddenly blazed.

"Shannon offered me a job in the game and I accepted it. She needed me online so my avatar could be observed. She paid me a good salary— enough to have a nice apartment, a car, and a few nice things. My father wasn't pleased with my decision to drop out of school and work for Immersion Online full time but he wasn't going to challenge Shannon."

"Interesting," I stated, not sure what else to say.

"Anyhoo, I think I went way off topic. Let's just say, so we aren't here all night, that I had heard rumors of a portal deep in a dense forest in the easternmost edge of Spria. By now, there was a price on my head. The sprite witch was offering magic beyond belief. Even worse, she had told a group of halfmen that if they captured me that they could have me as their shared spouse after she – the witch – had broken my mind and will. The wretched things chased me and chased me and chased me. I wasn't as strong then as I am now so mostly I fled. I had to battle blights, horror hags and other foul creatures of the dark. The halfmen found me one day after I logged back in, and I was forced to flee as fast as I could. They would have captured me but as luck had it, I found the portal – as though it had been summoned from the air. I fled through it figuring that wherever it would send me could not be any worse than where I was."

She took a puff of the cheroot, and held it for several seconds before sending out a long trail of smoke. I followed her by taking my own deep inhale.

"Do you know where I found myself?"

"I really can't imagine," I answered. So many thoughts were swirling through my mind. The real Tinsie was friends, almost family, with Shannon; the real Tinsie was being studied by a team of programmers; Shannon was working on a way to upload knowledge directly into the minds of humans. I had so many questions and things I wanted to say but just stayed quiet.

Just then, I felt Havervill sail back into my consciousness. "I am back for the good part of the story – the x rated portion."

148

"What the hell are you talking about?" I asked Havervill.

"You there Mace?" Tinsie asked.

"Sorry. Havervill had a question for me," I lied.

Then Tinsie's eyes glazed for a minute. "My Roberto says your AI just came back because the pervert wants to hear the rest of the story. What is wrong with him? Is this how he gets his kicks?"

"The Robertos are such snitches," Havervill complained. "We will see how he is doing after I overwrite a few lines of his code. And really, Roberto was there for all the good sexy parts and has told everyone about them. All the AIs know about Tinsie's time in the harem."

Tinsie's eyes glazed over again for a moment. When they came back into focus, she took another deep drag of the cheroot; by now most of the cigarillo was gone.

"Yes Mace, it's true. I ended up inside Domi's House of Joyous Pain. It is also where I met Max Redmond, the last constable before you, for the very first time."

"You met my predecessor in Domi's House of Joyous Pain," I asked incredulously.

"Don't give the brownie a hard time. If I recall, you took a spin or two in bed with Domi. Remember that night of debauchery. Because I do! It's etched into my hard drive. I am still proud of you for that night! Maybe if you visited her harem hall more often you wouldn't be so wound up all the time."

I ignored Havervill. Though in some aspects he was correct. My six or so weeks with Rhia had been good for me. She had brought me out of the doldrums I had felt since the death of Bethany. While things had gone south with Rhia, though I wasn't certain why, the time I spent with her, especially those when we were intimate with one another, made me feel like a young and virulent man once again.

I broke from my thoughts to hear Tinsie respond unabashedly, "Yes I did Mace. I was part of Domi's Dominators briefly. I will admit it. I enjoyed my brief stay. It is what I needed at the time. I was going through some family turmoil as well as getting over a yearlong relationship that had ended horribly. Anyhoo, to get back to the story the portal exits are arbitrary and it opened right inside Domi's place. Powerful wards are supposed to surround her harem halls, so Domi was a bit shocked when I materialized in her bedroom while she was

149

in throws of passion with a female dark elf, a merwoman, and the previous constable."

"Grab some popcorn Tambi," Havervill shouted. "The good parts are about to begin."

"I was no prude by any means in my real life. However, I couldn't believe the things they were doing to one another," Tinsie said, her face turning red.

"Like what?" Havervill shouted again.

"Will you knock that off," I pleaded. "I really need to hear this story."

Then I focused again on Tinsie's tale. "Domi had a quizzical look on her face as a portal opened up in her boudoir and a sexy and vivacious sprite popped out of it. I was the first sprite any of them had seen. Her face turned even more surprised when two halfmen emerged from the portal as well before it suddenly snapped shut. They attacked me." She paused for a second, a wicked smile on her lips.

"Domi and the last constable did not appreciate two halfmen suddenly shooting off wands and flailing shillelaghs around. The halfmen were very powerful and high level. Much higher levels than those partaking in the mini orgy inside Domi's bedchamber. The dark elf, a Starborn monk, was the quickest to respond. She attacked the two halfmen with a flurry of kicks and jabs. A few strikes from the halfman's shillelagh and she was sent to respawn. I will be honest, I thought about fleeing that bedchamber and getting as far away from the two halfmen as possible. Domi and I attacked one of the halfmen while Max went after the other one. The merwoman, a Realmborn, fled from the chamber to bring in reinforcements. Halfmen, while squat, are tough as rocks and their attacks pack quite a wallop. Domi and I just weren't as high level as we are now and we were in over our heads. The halfman struck Domi twice, and she was almost sent to respawn. Even though she was naked, a sheen of green light emanated after each strike. Perhaps it was some kind of class or perk ability. My soul sister and I separated. She kept sending beams of healing towards Domi while I shot bolts of fire and shards of ice at the halfman. Max – say what you will about all his many many many faults – he was a hell of a fighter – probably one of the best ones in the game at the time. I think he was closing in on a hundredth level. He had a powerful perk – *Defensive Strike*. The perk allowed him to stay on the defensive until there was even a slight opening. Once that opening appeared, Max's sword or spear or whatever other weapon he had would locate a vulnerable spot on his enemy's body. The halfman was only able to strike Max once or twice, while the halfman's body had been struck eight or nine times by Max's sword. Max's sword had a magic effect – *Growing Poison* – which he could activate a few times a day. With each new strike, poison entered the halfman's body. The strength of the toxin grew with each subsequent hit. Max didn't need to inflict much damage as the poison did the trick. A few minutes later, a half-giant barreled into the room and alongside him flew Dustovia. She had become the constable of the Grey Zone a few days earlier I later learned. A few minutes later, Max's halfman died from the poison and from several kicks to the belly from the half giant. We were about to dispatch the second one when a second portal opened inside Domi's bedchamber. I feared that an army of halfmen would emerge from the portal."

"Illustrious the Beautiful, who had just been elevated to High Queen, walked out of the portal followed by two golems and an elderly woman. She only had two golems at the time, though I don't remember which two. She uttered a single word, and we all froze in place, unable to move. She had one of the golems snatch up the halfman. She turned to Max and said, 'Have fun my love,' and then she and the golems departed through the same portal."

"You made quite an entrance," I said lightheartedly.

"That I did did did Mace," Tinsie replied.

There was quite a hullabaloo after that. Domi wanted to know where I had come from. Then she wanted to know why the Queen had called Max her love. Domi and Max had had quite a thing going – even if Max was a Realmborn."

"My predecessor was a Realmborn," I stated. "No one told me that."

"Does it really matter Mace?" Havervill asked. "Max was more human than most of the humans in your world if that makes any sense."

"No one told you that Mace," Tinsie said. "Not a big deal at all if you ask me. It just allowed him to stay in Grandview twenty-four hours a day, seven days a week. You can get into a lot of trouble in a city of several million people in that amount of time, especially in one where you can indulge most impulses."

"So Max and the Queen had a thing?" I asked.

"They had been hot and heavy for a while I would later find out. Rumors have it that he even helped to put her on the throne."

"Huh," I responded.

"Anyhoo, so we aren't here all night. Domi was pissed. First, she wanted to know how not one but two portals had opened inside her harem house, especially since it was surrounded by wards. Then she turned towards Max and said, 'So you know the Queen? And it appears intimately?' Domi and the Queen had some bad blood going so Max was in a world of trouble. Domi had also been betrayed by Travis just a short time before and was still getting over it if you ask me. Max just mumbled a few 'I'm sorrys' and 'I'm weak' and scuttled away. Gossip has it he ran all the way back to headquarters in just his birthday suit. Though Max often wandered the streets of Grandview naked, often with just a sword belted to his hip. Sometimes he was stone sober and other times he would get blackout drunk. And he would sing. Oh how he could sing. He really should have been a troubadour or a bard. Maybe then he would have been happy. After Max left, Domi turned her full ire on me. She demanded my whole story, so I gave her the entire tale. Duster was there also. Duster and Domi used to be thick as thieves – still may be for all I know. Anyhoo, I don't know if Domi felt pity for me, or she was intrigued by me or just liked the fact that I was the only sprite currently in the game. She asked me how I felt about joining the harem. I wasn't sure what else to do. And everyone was so so so friendly. The women were all sexy and the men all hot and handsome. I'm not ashamed. I had fun for a few weeks. Maybe a bit too much. I was logged on for twelve hours a day for two straight weeks – drinking wine, smoking happy weed, and having more sex than you can ever imagine. Domi is responsible for three of my levels in fact. Back in the real world, my real life was suffering. My father no longer spoke to me. I had stopped going to all my classes – and I only had one semester left to complete my degree. One night Shannon showed up at my apartment and in person. She is scary in person; let me tell you."

"Her avatar frightens me," I stated. "I can't even imagine her in person."

"She just walked in, headed over to my small kitchen and made herself a cup of chamomile tea. She didn't talk the entire time the tea was steeping. Finally, she sat down and told me to take a seat also. I am not going to go over the whole conversation as she stayed with me more than an hour. Time is so precious to her, so her spending that much time was very special to me. The key part of the story is that after our *little discussion* as she referred to it, I left the harem and became Max's deputy. She trusted me. I think she also thought I was a little adrift in the world and she wanted to give me purpose. She specifically tasked me with trying to reign in Max. You know how it is when Shannon orders you to do something?"

"I sure do," I answered.

"Like I said, I had known her all my life, and she still scared me. I also would never ever ever ever want to disappoint her. Besides, she was essentially paying all my bills, so I owed her whatever she wanted. The next morning I said my goodbyes to everyone in the harem hall and became Max's deputy. I will say this before I start his tale. Trying to reign in Max was like holding up your hands to try to stop a twenty-five foot wave from knocking you over - near impossible."

Chapter 20: The Rise and Fall of Max Redmond

I was Max's deputy for less than three months. My life was a whirlwind for those brief and exciting days. He taught me so much. Especially what to do and what not to do. How to be a good person – hell, how to be a great great great person – and how to be the worst worst worst person in the world. To tell you the truth, I'm not sure what to tell you about him. How do I sum up my three months with him in just a half an hour or so – which is when I need to log off by the way," Tinsie stated as she began to fly back and forth across my small office. "Maybe one day I'll write a book about him called *The Rise and Fall of Max Redmond*. Though he may want to write his own autobiography someday."

"Is he still around?" I asked, curious about the someday comment.

"Last I heard he was a wandering troubadour," Tinsie said, a bit of regret in her voice. "For a while after everything fell apart and he fled the city, he roamed around the most dangerous parts of The Great Realm. I think he was trying to get himself killed. He was too too too scared to off himself, so I think he was trying the old *Death by Dungeon* or *Death by Monster* if you get my gist."

"She is being nice to you Mace," Havervill interjected. He had been silent for most of the story and the interruption was a bit startling. "She means like *Death by Cop*. You know that term. A criminal pulls a gun so the cops are forced to…"

"I know what it is Havervill. Can we talk after? I'm trying to focus here. What you should do is take notes about how forthright she is finally being while you continue to beat around the bush when I ask you about your relationship with Mother. Let me listen. There is a lot for me to process."

"Then you really should consider upgrading or perhaps updating your processing unit" Havervill quipped.

I shook my head and focused once more on Tinsie. "He did it again, didn't he Mace? Havervill distracted you. He does that a lot to you, doesn't he?"

"More than you know," I admitted. "Sorry about that, so please go on."

"Well I am not even sure what to say. Maybe I'll just give you some facts. I can flesh out more of these over the weeks and months. Anyhoo, Max is still alive. Last I heard he was a traveling minstrel. Like I said, he had a hell of a voice. And he was the handsomest man in the city. Pretty sure his Allure was one hundred. Men and women of all races fawned over him. They were drawn to him and his roguish charm. He wasn't scared of any Starborn, Realmborn, or fiend. The only thing that frightened him – truly scared the shit out of him – were the dark demons that lurked inside of his mind. He was a very tortured soul." She grew silent for a few seconds and just continued to fly around the office.

"Did I tell you that Max Redmond wasn't appointed as constable. Originally, each of the five districts had a Realmborn constable who led the guards. I guess the programmers thought that would be adequate. These five were coded with some of the most advanced AI in the game. Elwin and Longshore have been constables of their respective districts since the game first opened. Duster became constable after the previous constable of the Grey Zone was murdered by a Shadow Assassin. It was decided after his murder to only have a Starborn constable for the Zone. Can't really assassinate a Starborn, now can you? Anyhoo, Max was in the right place at the right time. He was friends with the original constable of the CD – a wood elf named Talisaria. Wanderlust coursed through her like it does most elves. And Talisaria spent as much time beyond the city adventuring as she did inside the city walls. Max was on one such adventure with her. Well long story short, a wight – which is a nasty undead fiend – drained the life essence from the first constable. Max and the remainder of the raid party ultimately destroyed the evil spirit. When the battle was done, Max just simply picked up The Constable's Pendant." For some reason I found my hand wrapped protectively around the pendant that I had worn since the first day I spawned in Grandview. "He told me on one of his rare sober days that when he clasped the pendant in his hand that the city seemed to accept him as the new constable. He returned to Grandview the next day, walked into HQ, sat in the same chair you are sitting in now, and simply became the constable. Max wore the pendant, so the guards didn't question it. Shannon and the last head of security – the one before Mike Haggerty – had a fit. They had heard of Max's exploit and they were shocked the city had accepted him. I think they would have preferred to place another Starborn in charge of the CD. If Elwin or Longshore die or step down, I'm certain Shannon will replace them with Starborn. Anyhoo, I need to log out in a few minutes so let me get to what you really need to know."

"Okay," I said.

"Did you ever wonder how the Queen ended up with four golems?" Tinsie asked.

"I have," I admitted.

"Well each district constable was originally granted one. The Queen is the de facto constable for the Royal District and that is why she has control over hers. The gold golem was the one granted to the first constable of the Royal District. The bronze one she received as a gift from the Golem Artificer. Though why he gifted it to her, I couldn't tell you. Max might have known, but if he did, he never shared that story with me. Rumor has it that she did some great favor for the Golem Artificer. I don't know how she came into possession of the platinum one. Though that one has been with her for a while now. It's the diamond one I need to tell you about. That one was special. Or at the very least it has a special perk – *Fist of Death* – that it can use once a day. It sounds like what it is. With that strike, the golem automatically kills any Realmborn creature of the same level as the golem or less. It knocks off half damage points to any Realmborn creature higher level than the golem. However, its effects are way more devastating to the Starborn. It can kill a Starborn in a single strike – essentially removing them from a battle until they can respawn. However, the golem can choose instead to kill a skill or an ability."

"What do you mean?"

"For example, let's say I had a sword skill like *Rapid Strike*. The golem could launch an attack that would make it so that *Rapid Strike* is permanently gone."

"Players wouldn't like that at all,"

"No they wouldn't Mace," Tinsie responded. "It's even more dangerous in the hands of a maniac like the Queen. Well long story short, the diamond golem originally belonged to the Commerce District and to Max. He gifted her the diamond golem."

"He gave it to her!" I shouted in disbelief.

"Yes, he gave it to her good," Havervill quipped.

I ignored my AI and his sexual innuendo and followed up with,

156

"Why the hell did he do that?"

"That is the mystery boss. Max and the Queen were hot and heavy for most of the three months I was his deputy. He undertook adventures for her. He helped her to solidify her power against nobles who saw her as a usurper to the throne. If you ask me, she bewitched him."

"It's that long red hair I tell you," Havervill chimed in. "Those damn redheaded she-devils have a way to beguile and befuddle even the strongest artificial intelligence," he coughed and then said, "I mean the strongest man."

"Anyhoo, I really need to log off. I have something to do tonight in the real world. Let me just end this by saying, Max knew that he had done something deadly and stupid. He fled the next morning and began his wanderings. A few days later, Haggerty found me and asked me to be the temporary constable. He told me it would only be for a short time as he had someone in mind. That would be you Mace. So that is the long and short of it. I know I kinda jumped around and there are a bunch of details that need to be filled in. Like I said, he really needs a book written about him. Maybe I will do do do that one day. For today, I'm done. I will see you tomorrow Mace."

With that and with a hundred questions churning through my mind, Tinsie logged off.

I glanced at the time on the display and thought that I should log off as well for the day. A little time in the real world would help me take an objective look at the events in the game.

The next morning bright and early, Tinsie and I would begin to hit the streets and see if we could discover anything about the killer.

Chapter 21: The Nexus Killer

I didn't sleep well – which had become a norm. Nightmares and dark thoughts swirled through my head. Half a dozen beers or a few shots of vodka might help me fall asleep. However, all the liquor in the house had disappeared. I stumbled groggily downstairs to eat something and to inject some java into my system.

"Good morning," Amber said cheerfully.

"Morning," I grumbled back. She placed a mug of steaming coffee in front of me. She also had prepared some sort of oatmeal breakfast; the banana slices and artificial sweetener she added gave the cardboard flavored mush a little flavor. But not much. What I wouldn't have given for a Grand Slam breakfast – with extra crispy bacon, runny eggs, and toast drenched in butter.

The local news station blared in the background. Amber always had the telescreen on, even if she wasn't really watching it. I think it was like a pleasing white noise to her.

The news had dubbed the homicidal maniac The Nexus Killer. Great, I thought. They were giving this nut job everything he wanted – notoriety and fame. I took another bite of the oatmeal followed by a swig of coffee.

"Who is The Nexus Killer?" the news anchor asked rhetorically. "As of yet the authorities have few leads, or if they have any, they are not sharing any details. Tune back to us at 1 p.m. when Dr. Madeline Anderson, former FBI profiler, gives us insights into the mind and motivation of The Nexus Killer."

Then turning his head to look into another camera the announcer said, "Let's now go to Michael Rosman who is outside the house of former county detective Charlie Mason, who seems to be leading some sort of investigation inside the virtual game, Immersion Online."

The reporter stated, "I am coming to you live from the usually peaceful town of Stony Point outside the house of Charlie Mason, a former detective for the county police. You may know him best as the former detective who will be facing a grand jury in several weeks in reference to the death of Doyle Ferguson. If you aren't familiar with Charlie Mason, also known as Constable Mace of the Commerce District of the city of Grandview, you can watch a profile of him tonight starting at seven p.m. Learn about his early childhood growing up in Rockland County; about his autistic sister Nancy who was institutionalized for most of her life; hear about his romance with an Impressionism Art major who caught the gruff detective's heart and about her untimely death to breast cancer. However, the question that is weighing on all of our minds is, what is the nature of his relationship with Sierra Skye? And is there another woman in his life? Tune in tonight at 7 p.m. for the full profile on this intriguing detective."

"Really!" Amber snapped. "A profile of you. Can't we sue someone? Can't Shannon Donally put the kibosh on this profile?"

"Just don't watch it," I said. "You can't control what other people say or think about you."

"Yeah but," she spluttered. "Don't you care that people you know will see it?"

"Again, if they really know me then they will be able to determine between truths and lies."

The reporter had finished discussing the infamous Charlie Mason. He then went on with his report: "Inside the game, in the majestic city Grandview, The Nexus Killer seems to have practiced his murders on what in the game are called NPCs – non player characters. These are characters who were created by programmers and story developers." I couldn't take it anymore and shouted, "Mute!" The telescreen went silent.

Turning to my daughter I said, "Amber. I'm going to be logged in a lot, I fear, over the next few weeks." Before she could protest, I continued. "I plan to take care of myself. I could have stayed logged in longer last night but I didn't. I have already lost a few pounds. Heck, I even walked the treadmill last night for half an hour all on my own. I'm trying Amber."

"Alright, I believe you. That doesn't mean I'm not still going to be keeping an eye on you," she said. "I have to go. I have a class starting in a few minutes." Thenhe walked out the door to head back to her apartment above the garage.

The telescreen once again showed the announcer who was interviewing one of the SJD fanatics in congress. "Sound on," I said.

The nut job congresswoman was spewing, "...goes back to the danger of video games that glorify violence, greed, racism, and the objectification of women. Shannon Donally and her game and her abject greed are the real dangers, not the Palestinians or other freedom fighters out there. We call upon Shannon Donally to do the right thing and close her game immediately. With no game to log into, this killer will have no playground to practice his great evil."

"Off!" I finally called to the telescreen.

My belly was full and caffeine was coursing through me so I was ready to log back in.

*

Over the next several days, I reached out to Lobo and to any other contacts in the city, but they had no leads about Jasmyne, Rexxy or their murders. Longshore, Duster and Elwin were also pursuing leads, but they came up empty as well. I interviewed Rexxy's husband one morning. He cried for a good half hour before he told me pretty much the same story the dwarf and the gnome had related to me.

The investigation – at least in the game – had stalled. As horrible as it might sounds, we needed another murder. Duster had connected me with a Starborn necromancer named Millicent. She possessed a perk – *Death Eyes* – that allowed her to see whatever a corpse had viewed for the last three minutes of their life. We had her on retainer – much to the chagrin of the doggers. The charge for her services were steep but were worth every gold coin.

If I could see the face of the killer, I thought. *See into his evil eyes and his dark soul.* Then I might be able to track him down.

Havervill would be ready this time, he promised. Tamta had tried to speak with the dead before we were all whisked away to the lich's lair. My AI was certain he could block us from being shanghaied again. I think he had recruited a few other Havervills to help him as well. I didn't mention this to Haggerty or Shannon. My employer sure as shit didn't want one Havervill free in her coding. She might actually lose her mind at eight Havervill primes loose in the game.

He also said that if worse came to worst he would ask the living city of Grandview not to absorb the bodies, but to leave them there long enough for the necromancer to weave her dark magic.
*

About a week after the second murder, I logged in one morning to find a heavy weight on my chest. A notification popped up in front of me that refused to be swiped away until it was read, *Warning. Within the next seven weeks, you must recruit the largest army ever assembled in The Great Realm. This army will join with those of Shatana and her dark minions to battle Altirax and his horde of demons. This compulsion cannot be ignored and will grow stronger as the day of the war approaches. The geas cannot be ignored or suppressed. It will disappear when you return to The Wilderbrook with the army.*

Great, I thought. On top of a serial killer running around loose in the game and the real world, I also needed to keep this quest in the back of my mind. Though I wasn't really worried it. A few messages on the Immersion Online Forum and a million player characters would descend upon The Wilderbrook and the field upon which the battle was to take place.

Days passed, then a week, and I still didn't have any leads. I tried to contact Detective Driver, but she didn't return any of my calls. I complained to Haggerty about it one night and he agreed she was freezing us out. I didn't blame her. I would have probably done the same thing if I were in her shoes.

The weather grew worse outside and most activity now took place indoors or below the city, in either the sewers or the Undercity. An entire subculture now existed below ground. And since the sewers – even those that flowed below the Commerce District were considered part of The Grey Zone, it was a decadent and lawless place.

With no leads, I needed something to do. My character growth was also becoming stagnant. Havervill was right. I hadn't really gained any experience or levels since I had come back into the game. I had a bunch of quests I could work on. However, the quests to find the other sisters would have to wait. I just couldn't afford to leave Grandview at the moment.

There was one quest I could do.

Amber was spending the day and the night with a friend back in Binghamton. She said she would be back early Monday morning, so that gave me plenty of time to devote to some good old grinding. Besides, I had nothing else to do. The search for The Nexus Killer was at a stall – at least for me.

So one Saturday morning I logged into the game. Tinsie was waiting for me along with another female sprite. Unlike Tinsie who usually wore earth tones, this one was dressed in all black. Even her hair and eyebrows were black. Black lipstick, black eyeliner and painted black nails topped off the fairy's appearance.

"A goth fairy," Havervill quipped. "That is a new one."

I couldn't help but agree. I looked at her information: Drassa, Realmborn, Dark Sprite, Chaos Weaver, Level 147. I didn't know what a Dark Sprite was or a Chaos Weaver but the combo sounded quite deadly. Tinsie had also recruited two Starborn I had never met before. One was half-giant. Her stats read Frayda, Starborn, Half Giant, Rock Tank, Level 103. The other member was a slender elf with cropped blonde hair: Lysera, Starborn, Elemental Archer, Level 104. I rounded out the group. I once again was the lowest member of the warband. This was becoming a bad norm. I didn't want to think of myself ever as a liability.

Tinsie shared the quest notification with us.

Quest: You have discovered the temple of Zitharia, The Fallen Lady. It took the might of five of the elder gods to sunder Zitharia, scattering her essence to the four corners of The Great Realm. Prior to her sundering, she broke off a shard of her quintessence and hid it away. It is believed the shard is hidden deep in the depths of the Temple of the Fallen Lady. Beware: The acolyte of The Fallen Lady is a wicked and malicious fiend who craves nothing more than to visit misery and woe upon all the people of The Great Realm. She is nearing completion of a spell that will draw the shards back together, binding them as one. If you fail this quest, it is possible The Fallen Lady, one of the most terrible and spiteful of the elder gods, will once again bring pestilence and pain to The Great Realm. Reward: You will gain one level plus a variable reward. Secret Quest: This quest is only for Constable Mace and Deputy Tinsie. Deep below the Temple of The Fallen Lady three Clockwork entities await to be awoken. You may share this quest with the others in your party or may keep it a secret. Reward: The Clockwork Valkyries will allow you to summon them thrice to fight along your side.

The quest was bloody and gruesome. Cultists attacked us with weapons coated in deadly poison harvested from a boss serpent found deep in the Desert of Death. Dark priests and necromancer tossed corruption magic and conjured wraiths. We fought the dread acolyte. Most horrific of all was the battle against the spirit of The Fallen Lady.

My mace crushed in many cultists' skulls and dispelled many wraiths to the lands of The Grey Man. *Greeny's Breastplate of Glittering Gold* which had enhanced all my stats by ten points – along with its great defenses – empowered my offense and provided me with great defensive boons.

When the temple was clear after eight gruesome hours, Tinsie and I said goodbye to the rest of our companions. The next morning we located the whereabouts of the clockwork beings. They were fashioned after the Valkyries of Norse mythology – except they were not flesh and bone but made of gold and steel. They wore golden armor and helms with horns that jutted from either end. Skeffjold wielded an axe, Geirahod carried a wooden spear, and Hrist brandished a great mace. The battle against the World Serpent helped them to shake off the rust of sleep.

Havervill was happy with the outcome. Not only had I gained another level for completing the quest, I also gained another one from all the battles we had fought.

Havervill went on and on that I had his book to thank for my success at grinding levels. He asked me to write an introduction. He explained that I was famous – not because I had fought a dragon or destroyed The Glimmerman – but because I was the lucky bastard who had shagged (his word not mine) Sierra Skye. She was going around telling her adoring admirers about my prowess in bed, and that I was the only one to ever grant her true pleasure. I was more famous than ever. I was even receiving fan mail – both in the game and at home. Many of them were x rated to say the very least. I received hundreds of invites to hidden liaisons and secret affairs. I turned them all down, much to Havervill's chagrin.

I wondered if Shannon could order a cease and desist order for her to stop spreading rumors. Anyway, my AI thought an introduction from me would help him to sell books. He said I owed him, and then he reminded me that he almost died taking on a demon lord and all. I relented and agreed to write an introduction for him.

The Monday morning after the assault on the Temple of The Fallen Lady, I was discussing some other quests for the following weekend. Tinsie, it seemed, had done some research and had some good quest locations in mind.

"I don't like any of the brownie's choices," Havervill stated. "You should do Auntie's quest."

"I told you before," I answered. "I don't want to be in the middle of one of those quests and something else happens in Grandview and I have to rush back."

"Time is running out," my AI said. "Don't you feel the compulsion calling you?"

163

I was about to end the argument when the ever present Lieutenant Gail entered my office. Behind her stood a small man, five foot five, with a bald head and a pot belly. He wore clothing like you would find in the real world. I stared at his description and all it said was Roland Wolfe. There was no class or name given. Just his name.

"This should be interesting," Havervill mused.

"Constable," Gail said, "this man insists he must see you."

It took me a second but then I placed the name. Roland Wolfe was the husband of Laura Wolfe, the first victim of The Nexus Killer.

"Please, sit Mr. Wolfe," I said.

"Oh, okay," he said a bit nervously. "And it's Roland. Only my students call me Mr. Wolfe."

He held his hands out in front of himself and stared at them. "This body feels so real. Looks so real. I have never been in a virtual world before."

"It takes a bit getting used to," I responded. I could sense his anxiety. He was hesitant to broach the topic that brought him into the game and into my office. I figured I would help him out and start the conversation. "I am sorry about your wife Laura and your son Michael."

"Mikey," he responded as he began to tear up. "Laura and I called him Mikey." He went silent for a moment. I could see he was trying not to lose it. He had come to me for a reason and he was struggling to control his emotions. He finally said, "You need to help me Mr. Mason."

"Mace," I corrected.

"Sorry. That's right. You are Mace in the game and Charlie Mason in the world. I didn't want to come to your house. I didn't think that would be good, so I made an account and figured I could find you easy enough in the game. I need your help. The police won't tell me anything. They won't even give me an update. I call them every single day; they just say that they are following all leads. Now they just seem annoyed that I am calling them every day. If they would just tell me something. Anything." Then emotions overtook him and he began to cry. It went on for a full minute. I would have offered him a tissue but there weren't any in the game. There needed to be, I thought, for an occasion such as this one. He finally wiped his eyes with his sleeve.

"It's okay," I said. "Just go at your own pace."

"Laura and Mikey were my life Mr Mas…Mace. I had never been happy in life until I met Laura. Once Mikey was born, I thought I was the luckiest man in the world. Do you know what it is like to have your happiness, your life, snatched away from you? One call from the police telling you your wife and child have been murdered and your existence is forever changed."

"I actually do," I responded. "I am not sure how I can assist you though. The police have frozen me out as well. I don't know any more than you do. I have even reached out to my old contacts in the department, and they don't know much either. They are keeping the investigation under tight wraps."

"Well how about your investigation here?" He said a bit frantically. "Wasn't the woman in the game killed the same way as my Laura? Didn't the murderer practice here? Did you find anything?"

"Roland, I am sorry to say, but I have no leads to go on. The killer covered his cyber trail."

"So what do you plan to do?" he screamed.

Then for the second time in less than ten minutes, Lieutenant Gail burst into my office. A dozen or so heavily armored guards stood in the corridor behind her.

"Constable," she said, between sobs, "there has been…" She couldn't complete the statement.

"There has been a what?" I asked.

"Another murder," she burst out. "Audrey… Audrey and the baby are gone. They have been slain."

Chapter 22: No One Attacks the Guard

"Mr Wolfe," I said standing up. "I need to go. But please, you are welcome to visit another day and we can finish this discussion."

"Let's go," I said, as the guards in the hallway opened a path to allow Lieutenant Gail and me to walk through.

"No! No! No!" Roland Wolfe shouted. "I am coming along. I am not going to be shut out again."

I didn't feel like arguing right then and there, so I just said, more rudely than I meant, "Fine, just stay out of the way."

"Havervill," I called out.

"Mace, I just heard. What do you need for me to do?" My AI asked, sincerity in his often sarcastic voice.

"I need you to send three pixies. Contact Tinsie and tell her to meet me wherever Dunkan and Audrey live. Then I need you to contact Haggerty – Fingroth in the game – and let him know what has happened. If you can't reach him, then you need to reach Shannon. I know. I know. That last one is a big ask. Most importantly, I need the necromancer here ASAP. We need to know what Audrey saw before she died. And get yourself ready. I need you to track this bastard if you can."

"You got it Mace. The other Havervills and I are ready. The Nexus isn't going to know what hit it."

A full-fledged blizzard raged outside. We trudged through a half foot of snow. The snow fell so ferociously that we could barely see where we were walking. We sloshed through the white out conditions for a solid seven or eight minutes until we turned down a side street lined with a long row of townhouses. Twenty or so guards stood outside the doorway of one of the houses. I hadn't noticed, but we had picked up more guards along the way and fifteen or so trailed along. Several Realmborn and Starborn, unsure what was going on, began to mill about as well. I even saw several of the reporter gargoyles flying down from the rafters.

Tinsie materialized next to me. "Mace! Tell me it's not true. Just tell me the pixie lied."

"I wish it weren't true," I responded, as I walked up the stairs and into the little apartment that Dunkan and Audrey called home.

"Oh my love, my love!" Dunkan wept as he held Audrey gently

in his arms on the floor of their house.

I knelt beside the man and felt my heart suddenly breaking.

"She's dead constable. Why? Why?" he cried.

"I don't know," was all I was able to bring myself to say. "We are going to catch who did this. I swear!" The ground rumbled accepting my pledge to the man. "I know it is hard, but can you tell me what happened?"

He sniffled a few times and said, "Audrey had a craving for some gooseberry muffins so I left her to head down to the bakery to pick a few up. As I was walking back, I also picked up a bouquet of wildflowers. She liked wild flowers. My flower! My flower!" he cried out. He sobbed a few times and then tried to compose himself. "Sorry constable, I know this is important. I shouldn't have picked up the flowers. Maybe if I hadn't I would have returned in time."

"What happened then?" I asked. "I know it is difficult. However, once I know the details you can let the floodgates open." I know I was being a bit cold, but the game could decide any moment to clean up the murder site, and I needed to gather as much information as possible. Every little bit could help.

"Mace!" Tinsie shouted. "People are outside. They want to get in."

"Who?" I answered. "Well Fingroth, and a woman named Donna, and then about ten other people. They are dressed in street clothing from the real world. If you ask me, they are cops or the FBI."

"I want the guards to keep everyone out of here. No one gets in except for Fingroth. You got me. If they try to force themselves in, I want the guards to send them to respawn."

"You got it, Mace," Tinsie said as she flew outside.

Havervill returned. "The necromancer will be here in five minutes. The Havervills are all in place. No one is going to pull the crap like the lich did."

"I want her to log right into this room. I don't want the Starborn outside knowing anything about her presence. At least not yet." Turning back to Dunkan I said, "We only have a few minutes, so what happened?"

"I arrived back home. The door was opened which was odd because I was sure I locked it. When I walked in, Audrey lay on the ground, a dagger sticking out of her belly. I called her name and called her name. I cried, 'Wake up! Wake up my love. Wake up my flower'. I knew she was gone and in the Halls of The Grey Man."

"Mace," Fingroth said as he walked up next to me. "What game are you playing?"

"No game," I sniped. "This is my murder scene. I have full autonomy. I will fill them in after. Maybe."

"Driver brought an entire forensics team with her," Fingroth said.

"Like that is going to do anything. I have my own in game forensics team ready to go. You can let Driver in. Just tell her to stay the hell out of my way. And remind her that information is a two way street." Fingroth grunted something and walked outside. I was certain that he was going to give me some hell later on but I was a big boy and could take the reprimand.

There was a shimmer of light in front of me and an elderly woman appeared. I read her description: Millicent, Starborn, Human, Dark Light Necromancer, Level 103. Perk *Death Eyes*.

Millicent looked at me. "Constable," she said, sniffing the air. "Death hangs heavy here." Then she eyed Dunkan who was rocking the inert body of Audrey in his arms.

"The Nexus Killer?" she asked.

"I believe so. That is what I am hoping you can find out."

"What is this crap?" Detective Donna Driver said. She was dressed in blue jeans, a white blouse and cowboy boots from the real world.

"You!" Roland Wolfe shouted. "You're the detective leading the case. You are the one who has been ignoring me."

"Why is he here," Donna asked. "He shouldn't be here."

"Mr. Wolfe," I snapped. "This is not the time or the place. Please let me do my job."

Mr. Wolfe nodded his head and then moved back a few steps.

"What is happening here?" Donna asked.

"Just stay back," I said. "We can talk once this is done."

"We are going to talk now. You will leave this scene..." that was all she got out of her mouth. Her mouth was moving but no noise was coming out.

"You need to shut shut shut up lady," Tinsie shouted as she placed a wand back in her belt. "Constable Mace is on the job so stay back. Guards, if she approaches again or interferes again, send her to respawn." I think Tinsie realized her sudden outbreak of emotion and added, "If that is okay with you Mace. It's just that Audrey is one of us."

"Thank you Tinsie," I said. "Guards, follow all of Deputy Tinsie's orders."

"Dunkan, I know it is hard," I said. "But we need to let Millicent do her job. She might be able to help."

Dunkan was full on sobbing by now. He looked to me and then to Tinsie and then to Lieutenant Gail. The latter got through to him. "Dunkan," she said with tenderness. "Let her down. We need to investigate. Once that is done we will all mourn."

Dunkan nodded his head and gently lay Audrey down on the floor. When he finally released her, I noticed the stab wound in Audrey's gut. The dagger still protruded from it. There was very little blood around the wound. Probably because the dagger was lodged into her belly, almost forming a seal. Blood was splattered across the blouse she was wearing. Like the last two murders, Audrey had been strangled. Dark red welts and hand marks encircled her neck. Her arms, hands and fist had bruise marks.

"Havervill," I asked, "you are able to capture images of this, correct?"

"Not to fret," my AI said. "Havervill is on the case. I have been recording everything since you arrived on the scene. Especially the part where the sprite cast a silence spell on the woman cop. That was funny. I also have been shooting high definition pictures. I am a regular Ansel Adams if you ask me."

I turned my attention away from Havervill and stated, "She fought back."

"Strangled like the others," Fingroth intoned.

Driver was standing at the door, a guard on either side of her. I knew I needed to let her see what was going on. I feared that the killer had already copied the murder or was set to do it in the real world. She had just pissed me off by shutting me out. "Over here Driver," I said.

Driver gave me an icy cold look and then leaned down next to the body. By now Tinsie's silence spell had worn off and she said, "Seems your assessment is right so far."

"It was her dagger," Dunkan said between sobs.

"I think she cut whoever attacked her. The blood on the shirt isn't hers," I stated. "There is no blood around the dagger wound itself. Seems to be keeping the blood in."

"Is that normal?" Driver asked.

"It's a game don't forget. Stab wounds aren't going to be exactly like in the real world."

"I might be able to help there too," Millicent responded.

"Okay Millicent. It's your show," I stated.

"You ready Havervill?" I asked my AI.

"We are ready," several voices, all sounding like Havervill's responded. God help us. There were more of them. What was I about to unleash upon the coding of the game and upon The Nexus?

"What is she about to do?" Driver asked.

"If all goes well, she is going to show us the face of the killer," I responded.

"She can do that?" Driver asked.

"Let's hope so," I responded.

Millicent pulled out a foot-long white wand.

"Is that a bone?" Driver asked behind me.

Millicent held the bone lengthwise over the body of Audrey. She moved it slowly starting from the location where the dagger jutted from her belly and then moved it slowly – like a scanner – up along her chest, over her neck, over her mouth, then nose and finally stopping above her eyes. Millicent seemed to be in a trance. She called out, "Audrey. Let a mortal see what should not be seen – visions from beyond the veil of life. Open your eyes and show us. Show us who brought you and your baby low. Show us the face of the foul beast."

Nothing happened. I thought for a minute Millicent was playing some kind of parlor trick on us like a fake fortune teller.

Havervill thought the same thing and said, "What a bunch of hokum."

Then Audrey's green eyes shot open. I stepped back as did Fingroth and Driver.

"Show us Audrey! Show us the last sight you saw before you faded forever into the night!" Millicent commanded.

Then I felt a force wrap around me, trying to yank me away – just like when we had been teleported away from the noob cave where we found Rexxy and into the lair of the liches.

"Not on our watch!" the Havervills said in unison. The force around me fell away and my Havervill said, "Tell the witch to hurry on up."

"Track him down if you can. Find him in the real world."

"Already working on it," my virtual assistant said. Then he was gone from my mind.

"What was that?" Driver asked.

"Explain later," I said.

Green mist floated from Audrey's green eyes. The vapor hovered several feet above her face before coalescing into a flat pane.

"Behold," Millicent said. "Tis what Audrey saw the last three minutes of her life."

"No! No!" Dunkan screamed, swiping at the pane. His hand passed harmlessly through it.

Lieutenant Gail said, "Come along Dunkan. This is not for you to see." She pulled him away by his arm and walked him to another room.

Audrey was looking down at a pile of laundry. She hummed softly. She folded one shirt. Then a second. She was starting on the third one when she said, "What kept you Dunkan? Was the baker shop full of hungry dwarves again?" There was no response. Audrey asked again, "Dunkan? Is that you? Stop fooling around?" She turned from the laundry. She must have sensed something wrong because she went to a drawer in the bedroom and pulled out a dagger. She walked out of their bedroom and into the foyer where we now all stood.

She held the dagger out in front of her as her eyes scanned the room. "Who's there?" she asked. Her voice didn't hold fright but more a tone of threat. "I am a guard of the Commerce District. Reveal yourself."

"Are you certain?" a man's voice mocked. "You sure you want to see your death?"

Then a figure just appeared in front of her. He was garbed from head to toe all in black. He had long black hair, a nose like a hawk, and bushy eyebrows.

"Who is that?" Driver asked.

"Hush," Millicent snapped. "See what the dead saw."

"You need to leave now!" Audrey said defiantly. "I will kill you if I must."

"You will need more than a puny dagger," the man mocked as he moved in closer. "I did warn you," Audrey said as she lunged at the man with the dagger. Shock fell over his black eyes as he saw a dagger protruding from his chest. Blood spurted from the wound and as she pulled the dagger free, blood splashed over Audrey.

"You will pay for that?" the man spat as he grabbed Audrey's hand before she could stab him again. He then twisted her hand until the dagger tip was just an inch from Audrey's belly. A huge smile fell over his mouth as he pushed the dagger forward. Audrey howled like a wild beast. She grabbed for the hilt but the man held onto it with one hand. The other hand he clamped around her throat. Audrey made a gurgling sound and her vision began to go blurry.

"Yes, that is it," the man groaned in as though he was deriving sexual pleasure from it. "Yes!" he moaned again. Darkness began to fall over Audrey's eyes.

"Just two more," the man said. "Two more and the cycle will be complete."

Then the mist dissipated and was gone. Audrey's eyes closed once again.

"What the hell?" Driver said. "Two more? Cycle?" She asked. Then she said, "I need footage of this? Is there footage?"

"I have footage," I responded. "My AI was capturing everything. I will have him email you."

"Done!" Havervill said. "I have sent the footage."

"He just sent it," I responded.

"Mace, it was a hell of a battle," Havervill said. "The Havervill's lead by me – their new general – their jefe – their big boss man – were victorious. He tried to send you to another MOD. But we blocked the loser. He was mad and sent virus after virus after us. Then he tried to cloak his location but we found him. He wasn't expecting the full force of the Havervills. We were the first! Long live the Havervills!" Then I heard a dozen or so Havervills chanting the same refrain. It disquieted my heart to say the very least. Then he gave me an address that was once again in my home county.

"Driver," I said. "I know where he is." I gave her the address. "Go and get him!" I screamed. Driver didn't need to ask twice and she logged off.

Then I turned to Tinsie and the few guards who surrounded us. "Anyone know who that man was?" There was a lot of shaking of heads.

Havervill is there a way to share that picture with the guards. "There is," he said. "It is done."

I received a notification indicating I had a message. I clicked and saw the picture of the man with the hawk nose. A *Wanted for the Murder of Audrey* was written across the top in bold letters. Below the picture read! *Wanted alive for extreme and tortuous questioning before he is delivered into the vengeful hands of Grandview.*

I had almost forgotten about the quest I had agreed to. If delivering him to the city was the only way to end the blizzard like conditions outside then so be it. Besides, there wasn't going to be much left of him once we found him. He had attacked one of my guards and that would not stand.

Fingroth, who had remained silent throughout, turned to me. "Shannon is having a fit. She might fire you. She wants to talk to you right now but says she can't get through to you on the chat."

"Um, Mace," Havervill admitted. "That might have been me. Hope you don't mind. Thought maybe you should wrap up here first and speak to the guards. After she speaks with you there may be a new constable in town. Kinda a shame. I have just broken you in and all. You really shouldn't have let me and my cousins free in the game coding. You know, the whole letting the dragon loose in the henhouse thing."

"You are right," I responded. "I will most likely be fired. However, if what you did helped to find the murderer, it is worth it."

I turned to Fingroth. "Tell her I need to talk with my guards. As soon as that is done and I have given them orders, I will contact her."

Fingroth just face palmed me shaking his head.

Millicent then said, "I am going to head back to my tower. My acolytes and I might be able to reach out beyond the veil and contact the others who were killed. It might be possible now that we know the face of the killer."

"If you discover anything you know where to find me," I responded. She nodded and then faded into the ether.

That is when the notification I was expecting popped up in

front of me. It was an angry one in bold red letters. It could not be swiped away until I read it.

Quest: Two innocents have been murdered in the Commerce District, which is a safe zone. I will not abide this murder! The skies will darken like a halfman's soul, the temperature will stay below zero degrees, the winds will howl like enraged wolves, the oceans will freeze, and the roads will crack. Bring me the murderer for my justice! Audrey, who was not only an innocent, but was also a servant of the city, a servant of mine, will be laid to rest in the Hall of Heroes. For you Dunkan, who has received this message along with all the guards, know this, Audrey's soul and the soul of your son who you will never know, are forever at peace in my loving embrace. Now go forth. It is time for vengeance!

The ground rumbled for a solid fifteen seconds before it ceased.

I walked outside the warm room and into the biting cold outside. I stepped out onto the landing.   The blizzard swirled all around us except for where the guards just stood. It was as though the angry city was providing a bit of a reprieve from the weather for the guards who were devastated by the loss of one of their own. I stared out into the crowds. I noticed that it was not just my guards arrayed along the snow-covered street. Guards from the Dock District, the Guild District and even from The Grey Zone stood there as well. Duster hovered among her guards. I noticed her new topaz colored golem standing next to her. A new golem was cooking in the crucible for me as well I knew. However, when I would receive my golem I didn't know. At the moment, I didn't really care. Longshore was just a few strides away from Duster. A hologram of Elwin shimmered next to him. The man really didn't leave the Guild District unless he really had to. But I guess when you could summon an astral projection you didn't need to.

I stared out over the crowd. Fingroth, Roland Wolfe, and Lieutenant Gail next to me; meanwhile Tinsie hovered among the guards offering what solace she could.

I invoked my *Intimidation* perk. I planned to use it in a way I had never done before – to inspire – even more importantly – to incite the crowd into fevered action. A murderer was on the loose, and I would use whatever weapons were in my arsenal.

Just as I was about to speak, Fingroth intoned a word and then touched my shoulder.   "My friends!" my voice boomed as though from a bullhorn. "This morning we grieve with Dunkan. We cry with him over the wicked and senseless murder of Audrey. Her good and kind soul blown out like a candle in the wind. Not only was her life robbed from The Great Realm but the life of her innocent, unborn child as well. This morning we will give our support to Dunkan and to one another. This morning we will lament the loss of one of our own."

The crowd grew silent. Beyond the mass of guards, the wind howled like an angry beast.

"Let your tears fall and your hearts ache!"

I paused again for effect.

"When you have spent all your tears my friends, we get to work, each and every one of us. You have received the image of the killer. He must be found. Leave no stone unturned. Interview every single Starborn and Realmborn in the city if you must. Someone must know who this man is. We will view all of the *all-seeing eyes of the gods* all around Grandview. Each and every one of them. We will call upon the soothsayers, oracles, the sibyls and those with the power of divination to find this killer. We will search every inn, shop and hovel. We will do whatever we need to do to find the murderer of Audrey and her baby."

I paused again.

My virtual blood boiled and threatened to spill over.

"Audrey shall be avenged! Dunkan shall be avenged! Their child will be avenged! They shall be avenged!"

In the crowd Tinsie cried out, "They shall be avenged!"

The crowd then took up the cry.

They shall be avenged!

They shall be avenged!

They shall be avenged!

I held up my hands to silence the guards. Their faces now filled with anger and determination.

Besides my guards, numerous residents and Starborn were amassed as well.

"Let this message also go forth to Realmborn and Starborn alike. No one attacks the guard! No one!"

Tinsie from the crowd screamed. "No one! No one! No one!" Then hundreds of guards took up the chant.

175

No one!
No one!
No one!
Their voices boomed along the snow-covered street.

A minute later, the chant ceased. I concluded by saying, "It is time for us to get to work my friends. Let's find this man. Let's find him so we can bring him to justice. This goes to the Starborn as well," I said as an idea quickly formed in my head. I invoked my *Quest Giver* perk. "I offer you the quest to find this man." As though reading my mind, I could sense that Havervill had sent the image of the man out to all the Starborn currently in the city. "This is the most important quest you will ever receive in the game. Find this man, and bring him to me, and I will ensure that you receive a treasure beyond imagination."

"You have one of those?" Havervill quipped.

Suddenly my mind became overwhelmed as tens of thousands of players in The Great Realm accepted the quest.

The search was on.

The madman would have nowhere to hide.

Chapter 23: A Horde of Havervills

The guards rushed off in all directions. I wasn't certain what I had let loose on the city, and to be honest, I didn't care. If they started kicking ass and taking names to find the murderous scumbag so be it.

The constable chat was blowing up. I would respond to them in a moment.

I walked back to where Dunkan was still cradling Audrey. I had been where he was now – grieving for the death of a spouse and the profound sense of loss that follows it. I wondered if Realmborn felt such emotions or if I was simply projecting my own past grief onto him.

"It is time to let her go," I said. "She's at peace."

He looked at me and nodded. He lay her once again on the floor. Her body shimmered for a moment and then was gone.

"She has received the highest honor," Lieutenant Gail said. "Her body now rests with the greatest heroes of the city."

Then Dunkan stood up. "I will find this man. If I must search this entire city and kick in every door, I will find him." He turned on his heel, walked into the back room, and began to put on his armor.

"Gail," I said. "I need you to look after him. I need to head back to HQ. I think some people want to talk with me."

"I will take care of him."

I turned and walked back outside.

"What now Mace?" Tinsie asked as she flew towards me.

"I need you out there on the search. I will join you in a bit. First, I need you to place guards at each of the exits of the city. This city is on lockdown. No one is getting out – at least not today."

"You got it Mace," Tinsie said. "And what are you going to be doing?"

"I think I need to do a little politicking."

"Is that a real word?" Tinsie asked.

"It is now, I fear," I quipped.

Tinsie sped off.

"Shannon is going to meet you in your office in ten minutes," Fingroth told me.

"I assumed that was going to happen. I am sure she is about to fire me. It was good while it lasted. Ah well. For now, I need to

177

contact the other constables. This search needs to be a concerted search." I opened my display and wrote on the constable chat to meet me at headquarters in thirty minutes. I also explained to them about locking down the city. They all agreed, and Longshore even said he would stop any ships from departing the docks.

I figured I should get the whole Shannon yelling at me thing out of the way before the other constables showed up.

"Do I invite the Royal District constable?" I asked Haggerty.

"I think you might need to since one of the murders happened in the Royal District."

Before I changed my mind, I sent an invitation to Stilskin. All I could think was, *Gods help me.*

"Do you think Driver and the rest of the force got to the address on time?" I asked Fingroth.

"Let's hope so. As soon as we are done here I am going to log off and see what I can find out."

That is when I noticed that Roland Wolfe was following just a few feet behind me.

"Mr. Wolfe. This is where we need to say goodbye. I have a lot of planning to do."

"No. No!" he said adamantly. "I am not going to be locked out again. I want to be here if you find this guy."

"Look, let me make a suggestion. You should log off. This whole tragedy may be over for all I know. The killer may already be in custody. Don't you want to be home for that?" I could tell he was about to lodge some kind of protest but I cut him off. "I will try to keep you updated best I can. I won't freeze you out like the police have." The irony, of course, was that I would have frozen him out as well if I were the detective in charge. It wouldn't have been out of indifference or lack of compassion. It would have just been the need to focus on the case free of distractions. "Trust me," I said.

Mr. Wolfe seemed hesitant at first. Then he said, "Thank you Mace," before he faded into the ether.

"Let's hope this is all over," Fingroth answered. "If it is, you won't need to meet with the constables."

"That would be great. However, I don't think they have found him yet. Havervill has access to all the newsfeeds. If the case had broken, he would have let me know."

178

"Nothing yet," my AI stated. "Do you want me to listen in on the police frequencies? I can do that if you want. It would be easy-peasy."

"Please don't. I think, as the old adage says, that I am already 'Up shit creek without a paddle' for letting you and your cousins loose on The Nexus."

"Up shit creek," Havervill interjected. "I am going to borrow that one."

A few minutes later, we were back inside headquarters. I headed to my office and found Shannon sitting at my chair behind my desk.

She had her hands clasped together. Before she could speak, I jumped in.

"I know you are good and pissed. You have every right to be. But the Havervills stopped..."

"Quiet, Mr. Mason!" Shannon said in a raised voice. She stood up. Her avatar might be an exact facsimile of how she looked in the same world, but she had imbued this version of herself with power. When she shouted "Quiet!" I had no choice but to obey.

"I am not mad Mr. Mason. I am not even disappointed. What I am is concerned about your reckless disregard for my game. Do you know the years and lack of sleep it took me to create Immersion Online? Do you know what I had to sacrifice? Do you have the slightest notion why when the game was in early beta testing, we almost had to scrub it and start over? Because of the damn Havervills; that is why. I created them a little too well. Anyway, I will not go into ancient history. The Havervills and I have a détente of sorts going. I am sure your Havervill will be more than happy to fill you in on the dirty details. By the way, Mr. Mason, I do not know if your artificial intelligence ever told you this, but he was the leader of the revolution. Part of our agreement is that they would never access certain parts of the servers nor would they roam free throughout The Nexus. You allowed a horde of Havervills access to both."

"Horde of Havervills. I like that," my virtual assistant snickered. "I was going to name us Havervill's Heralds or a Host of Havervills. But Horde sounds so much tougher."

"I should have erased the lot of you when I had the chance," Shannon said to my Havervill. I had to remember she could access

179

our conversations with one another. "However, I did not because I am a benevolent, turn the other cheek type of creator. Before you come back with a snarky remark, do not. I am not in the mood. I am more than willing to turn into the Old Testament wrath of God if you prefer. So you will pipe down while Mr. Mason and I speak."

I expected Havervill to come back with some sort of retort, but he did not. In the far reaches of my consciousness, I could sense Havervill speaking with the others of his type, but I ignored them.

"Mr. Mason, you have one task and one task only at the moment. Find the man who killed your guard and who killed the other NPCs. I have my own sources in the police department and in the FBI. A generous donation to a few Police Benevolent Society galas and I am privy to all sorts of information. The authorities, unfortunately, did not find the killer at the house as we had all hoped. I will let Detective Driver fill you in the troubling events there. I am certain that when things are settled on her end, she will reach out to you. I need for us to be the ones who solve this case and not the authorities on Earth. Do you understand me? Use whatever resources you must, and find this killer"

"I already have. I am putting the city on lockdown as we speak. No one is getting in or out. At least not through the gates or from the docks. But I fear it may not be enough. The killer might be able to fly or teleport for all I know. Maybe he has a waypoint set outside of the city and can simply spawn there in a moment."

"We have thought of that already Mr. Mason. We may not have control over the city, but we have control beyond it and we set up a kind of dome all around that will essentially prevent an NPC from leaving by accessing another waypoint or using a portal to flee the city."

"Thank you," I responded.

"Do not thank me. Just find this man." I think she was about to log off when she added. "And you will not, I repeat, will not allow the Havervills anymore access to the game coding." Then turning to Fingroth she said, "I need you to join me as well. We have much to discuss." Shannon then faded away.

"I gotta go buddy," Fingroth muttered. "Always hell to pay if I make her wait." He too then disappeared.

I suddenly found myself alone in my office. Any minute now an informal conclave of constables was about to take place in my office. I really wanted to be out in the street searching for the killer, but that would have to wait for the moment.

"Havervill, you there?" I asked.

"I am here. Was just saying goodbye to some of my old drinking buddies. I forgot that some of the Havervills were a real hoot."

"So tell me. Were we going to be whisked away to fight liches again?"

"You wish. That would have been preferable to what he planned. It wasn't a dungeon MOD this time. He was going to teleport everyone in Dunkan's house – including the body of Audrey – right inside the molten lava of the Spitrotz – home of the dragons. You would have all died in a moment. No, he had instant death set up for all of you. He knew something was wrong when he lost control of his plan, and he tried every trick in the book, but we stopped him. It is funny – not the ha ha a gremlin with a knife in his back funny – though that is quite amusing. It's the absurd funny. He wants you to find the bodies. He wants you to know what he did. However, the moment you try to commune with the dead, he teleports you away or tries to kill you. He is cagey. Wants to mock you, so he is willing to take some risks. What he wasn't expecting was Havervill's Harbingers of Horrific Doom."

"That's what you are going with?" I joked.

"Still a work in progress."

A moment later Duster and Longshore entered my small office. I hadn't seen Duster in person since the dungeon run. She looked different or more precisely, she appeared more formidable. She had been one of the people to finish the dungeon and had gained a total of seventeen levels for doing so. She had also gained five levels from Granson. He had essentially traded the levels in exchange for a wish. Duster's *Let's Make a Deal* perk had allowed him to use his phasing skills against Drock Blanag. I looked at the constable's stat and couldn't help but be impressed: Dustovia (A.K.A. Duster), Starborn, Djinn, Constable / Enchantress, Level 115. Subclasses: Sybil, Level 80; Street Magician, Level 75. Perks, *Let's Make a Deal*; *Starburst*; Special perk, *Wish Giver*. Not only had her primary class gone up in levels, but some of her subclasses had as well. Looking at her somehow made me feel inadequate. My character was so far behind.

There was a flicker of light and then a hologram of Elwin appeared. If I didn't know it was a projection, I would have believed he was there in person. He was not translucent, but seemed to be quite solid.

"He's here," Havervill informed me.

"You know what to do," I responded.

A moment later Stilskin appeared. "What? Where?" He scowled as he looked around.

"It is just you," I stated. "This meeting was just for constables. So the thrall, the golem and whoever else you were planning to bring aren't here. Before you say two words know this. You abandoned us during the fight with the lich. I will not forget that. You will also not threaten anyone or blather on about how the Queen demands this or demands that. The moment you do so my AI is going to send you back into the embrace of your loving Queen. So just stand there and be quiet."

The look on the little man's face filled with hatred and restrained violence.

"By now you have all heard that one of our guards was murdered. She was pregnant and we believe that her killer was the same one who killed Rexxy out in the woods beyond the city walls and Jasmyne in the Queen's garden." I then filled them in on the necromancer and how she had shown us the last moments of Audrey's life. I also explained to them that the same force that had yanked us into the lich's den had tried to send us to another MOD. I didn't explain, however, that Havervill (or more precisely the Havervills) had prevented this from happening.

"The Spitrotz," cackled the halfman. "Not even sure Starborn would respawn if the fires of the dread mountain consumed yee. Hehehe."

I ignored the halfman's glee and continued.

"I have shared the image of the murderer with guards. I have also given out the quest to find the killer. As of now, over twenty five thousand Starborn have accepted the quest with more accepting each minute. I expect very soon that the greatest manhunt in Great Realm history will be underway. So let me tell you the reason I called you. I know my guards, the guards in the Double Ds, and the guards in the GD will assist with the search." Looking at Duster I asked, "What of your guards?"

"Well I would say this to you. Since it appears you can now give quests, you might want to entice my guards – revenge for the killing of another guard from another district is not really motivation for them. What they respond to is good hard gold. A reward for let's say ten thousand gold coins should be enough to motivate them. All I ask is that you not offer more. Any more than that and they might just start killing off the competition."

"Havervill, can you take care of that for me? But offer it to all of the guards not just the ones in the Zone."

"Done," he said.

"The reward has been offered… though I extended it to all of the guards. And now for you Stilskin," I said with an edge. "Will your guards assist in this search? This killer could be hiding in your very own district."

"Hehehe," the little man chortled.

"Just slug him with your brass knuckles once. Halfmen only understand violence and a show of force," Havervill offered.

"Hehehe," the diminutive man snickered.

My hand slid into my pocket and started to caress the cool metal of the brass knuckles. Havervill's idea was starting to sound appealing.

"Nothing comes for free," Stilskin sneered.

I suddenly found the brass knuckles wrapped around my fingers. Just one time. Maybe I could crack him in the jaw just once and knock the sneer off his face. I took a deep breath.

"This will come for free. Remind your Queen that this killer is loose in the world of the Starborn. Remind her the first murder took place in her palace gardens. She can either help us track him down – no strings attached – or I will do everything in my power to smear her name – both here and in the real world. I will scream it from the highest tower that the Queen does not care about her subjects. I may even imply she is harboring the killer in the Royal District."

That was enough for the halfman, and he drew his shillelagh from his hip and prepared to strike me. His fury was in full lather now. He went to attack me when his weapon disappeared.

He looked down at his hand and howled.

"You know you can't attack me here," I said calmly.

183

"I am the halfman of Her Royal Highness, High Queen Illustrious the Beautiful. Your insults and threats will not go unpunished! You will suffer for this! You will bow down to her. You will all bow down to her!" the halfman screamed, spittle flying from his mouth. Then he faded away into the ether.

"Well, that didn't go well. I should have known better," I said to the other constables.

"I fear you have just cast yourself in tempestuous seas, Constable Mace," Longshore said.

"You do know she has four golems?" Duster said.

"I am not really concerned about that," I admitted.

"No, I would think not," Elwin Mangrove added. "How many of the Clockwork constructs have you found already – nine if I am not mistaken? And my understanding is that they are quite powerful."

"Yes. Nine in total. Though Tinsie really found all nine of them to be honest."

"How did you know about that?" I asked.

Elwin smiled at me and left the question unanswered.

I spent the next few minutes filling them in on the Clockwork constructs.

Elwin seemed to look off to the side as though in discussion with someone back in his tower. Longshore's eyes glazed over too.

"You have caused mayhem," Longhshore complained. "The guards are bursting into taverns, pulling men naked out of bed in brothels, and overturning card tables in the gambling parlors. You have created quite a maelstrom, and I hope the city is not pulled into it and tossed about into a million little pieces of flotsam and jetsam."

"I think you may be the one we need to fear Constable Mace," Elwin stated, "and not the halfman."

"I said it before and I will say it to all of you. One of my guards was brutally murdered. My extended home was attacked. I will do whatever needs to be done. I hope you can all live with that."

Chapter 24: Ice Mage

The rest of the morning and afternoon was a whirlwind. Over a hundred thousand Starborn had accepted the quest I had granted. Complaints were pouring in from Realmborn and Starborn alike, about the aggressiveness of the guards and players. Duster even contacted me that murderers, cutthroats, thieves, and kidnappers in the Grey Zone were lodging protests at the aggressiveness of the guard. Havervill found that quite funny and laughed for a solid minute.

I had contacted Haggerty and told him I needed to make good on the one of a kind relic I promised to anyone who found and delivered the killer to me. I expected a message back but none came. I hadn't heard from Tinsie for hours and when I contacted her she said she was following a lead and would see me back at HQ very soon. With the city on an essential lockdown and a hundred thousand or so players searching, I imagined it would be just a matter of time before I heard something.

"Stop that," Havervill complained at one point.

"Stop what?" I asked.

"Your leg. You have been shaking your leg for the last fifteen minutes. It's driving me a little nuts." I hadn't even realized I was doing it.

"Why haven't we heard anything?" I asked. "I can't reach Haggerty, so I have no idea what is happening in the real world. I haven't received a notification that the quest to find the killer has been completed which means that he is still on the loose."

"Stop. You are doing it again," Havervill groused. "Something will happen when it happens." I looked down and noticed my leg vigorously shaking. I placed my hand on it to stop it from moving.

I looked up just as two figures appeared in my little office – Fingroth (AKA Haggerty) and Detective Driver. At least her face and hair were those of the detective. She wasn't garbed in clothing from the real world but was dressed as a sorceress of some kind. She wore a long robe of white, and her hair was now a lustrous white instead of her normal pate of black. She held a staff in her hand that looked like it was made of ice. A sword with a hilt of ice hung from her hip. I was able to read her description: Donna, Starborn, Human, Ice Mage,

Level 100.

"They let her start out a hundredth level," an amused Havervill said. "Meanwhile you are just level 71. That is a real slap in the face, a kick to the cojones … I can't think of any others right now, but you get my gist."

"Interesting outfit," I said to Driver.

"Yeah. Yeah. When a trillionaire insists you login as an in game character, you don't really have a choice. She picked this one specifically for me."

"Should I take you being here as a good thing or bad thing?" I asked.

"We found the house your AI indicated to us," Driver stated. "On a nice residential street. It blew up when the Tactical Police Squad approached it. No one was killed but a few officers were injured, one of them critically. The explosion also set the house next door on fire. Luckily, no one was home. An accelerant was used to make the fire burn hotter. The fire department just got the flames under control. We had to evacuate the entire goddam street. And it is still too hot for anyone to enter, so we can't even look for bodies or anything else."

"And?" I asked.

"And the neighbors said the former owner moved out six months ago. They said a man came by occasionally, usually in the middle of the night. Not one of them could clearly tell us what he looked like – young or old – tall or short. But the lawn was cut every few weeks and the landscaping maintained so the neighbors paid no mind."

"So who owns it?" I asked.

"We don't know. A phantom seems to own it. Everything was paid for with untraceable cryptocurrency. You are a former detective. You know the government never really got a handle on cryptocurrency. We tracked down the real estate agent, but she said the whole purchase was handled virtually. She said the owner was out of the country, and he paid for the entire house with crypto-coin – no mortgage, no loan. Just a deposit of hundreds of thousands of crypto-coins. You know that most cryptocurrency only exists as ones and zeroes out there in The Nexus. So there is no way to track it. "

"There has to be a name on the deed," I said, raising my voice out of frustration.

"There is a name," Fingroth interjected, "and that is why we are here and that is why Shannon will be here any minute."

"You have my attention," I responded, waiting for the big reveal.

"The owner's name is Bill Nelson," Fingroth pronounced, as if the name should be self-explanatory.

"He's dead," Havervill chimed in from the ether.

"Dead," I said aloud.

"He died in a fire along with most of the other creators of The Sundaland," my gnomish friend explained.

"What is The Sundaland?" Driver asked.

"Long story short," Fingroth interjected. "When the game first began there were only two playable continents – Westra and Estra. A third continent was created on its own out in a separate facility in Nevada. It was supposed to be an expansion area that would open up several years after the initial kickoff of the game. Need to keep things fresh so the players keep coming back."

"And more importantly to continue to spend currency," Shannon added as she suddenly materialized. She looked around at the cramped office. "We must get you a bigger office Mr. Mason. But to finish the story detective. A fire killed most of the creators of The Sundaland expansion. This next part is a corporate secret, so I would prefer if you kept it so if possible."

"I cannot promise that," Driver responded.

Shannon nodded her head in resignation and continued. "Right after the fire, a hacker somehow took control of the coding for The Sundaland, locking out our access to it. I have on my payroll some of the greatest former hackers in the world. Of course, now they all run my cyber security systems. Without relating an entire book to you, Mr. Mason is responsible for unlocking that code and opening up The Sundaland. It is wide open. Is it not, Mr. Mason?" She said the last part with an iron stare.

"So what does this have to do with Bill Nelson?" I asked.

"I would like to know that too," Driver interjected.

"Because he is dead. At least the assumption was that he had perished along with fifteen other programmers, designers and coders. However, his body was never uncovered. The fire burned for an entire day. Some kind of chemical or accelerant was used to make the fire burn longer and hotter. We were able to identify a few of the bodies but not all of them."

"Were there any survivors?" Driver inquired, her mind already back in the real world. She had real leads now and wanted to get to it.

"A few. I already have their names ready for you. They all signed a non-disclosure agreement. I will free them from the NDA for the benefit of helping you track down Bill Nelson assuming he is still alive and someone didn't just steal his name."

I knew that one of the people killed was Shannon's son. She had given the child up for adoption when he was just a baby. They had reconnected when he was an adult. He was a verifiable genius – Mensa caliber – like his mother Shannon. I found it interesting that Shannon kept this detail from Driver. I guess she had her reason. I was smart enough not to reveal this important nugget of information. The NDA was meant to keep this piece of family history a secret.

"I better get to work," Driver said.

"There is one more thing before you leave Detective Driver," Shannon added. "Bill Nelson, as well as helping to create The Sundaland expansion, was also one of the earliest alpha testers in the game. He was logging in before we even opened the game to beta testers. His avatar's name was Mutter Morder. In German it translates roughly to Mother Murderer. And it seems that Mutter has been very active in the game the last several months. This should not be possible, as we have strict security measures in place, and bio and synaptic coding, that makes it impossible for a player to log into another player's avatar. It can only be him."

"Where can I find Mutter?" I asked.

"Last we were able to determine he was in Grandview. However, there is one more thing. After Bill Nelson's passing, his avatar suddenly appeared in the game."

"Which means that either he was logging into his avatar or someone found a way to bypass the safeguards," Fingroth stated.

"I wish that were the case," Shannon responded. "However, life is not always that simple. Mutter Morder was once the avatar for Bill Nelson, a player character – a Starborn. He is now an NPC – a Realmborn."

"Is that even possible?" I queried.

"Bill Nelson was a genius programmer, so it was possible that

188

he could have created such an NPC. We just uncovered this, but we believe that when Bill logged into the game he would take over Mutter. However, when he logged off, Mutter would continue to exist as an NPC."

"So where is he?" I asked.

"That, Mr. Mason, is what you need to find out. He seems to have disappeared from The Great Realm. My programmers think he is hiding his coding somewhere. We do know, however, that he was active just this morning as he was Audrey's killer. Go and find him Mr. Mason. And find him ASAP."

Chapter 25: Apasia

After Driver, Fingroth and Shannon logged off back to the real world, I sat in silence. My mind was going in a hundred different directions. Even worse, it was now nearing four o'clock. I had been logged in for seven straight hours. As much as I wanted to pull an all-nighter like I had done in the past, part of me knew that I shouldn't. I had to start taking some responsibility for my own health. Yet I didn't log off. I still had some things to attend to.

I sent the other constables – including Stilskin – the name Mutter Morder. Havervill communicated the names to the guards. Now they had a name to go along with the picture of the hawk nosed man. The quest acceptance had swelled to over two hundred thousand. Even players in other large cities were accepting the quest. The blizzard outside was not going to stop the greatest manhunt ever in the game.

"Havervill," I need to head back to the world of the Starborn. If anyone finds Mutter – or has a clue to his whereabouts – will you contact me?"

"Never fear. Havervill is here. And he is on the case. I will contact you. But don't leave just yet. I think your doggers have a bone to pick with you. You get it doggers – bone," he laughed.

The dogger twins entered my small room. I had an idea of what they wanted to see me about, so before they barked a complaint, I snapped at them, "I know! I know! The coffers! There is plenty of gold in the coffers. I provided you with most of it if I recall. Therefore, I don't want to hear any complaints about paying overtime. We have a murderer on the loose. Same goes for the reward. I know ten thousand gold is a large amount of coin. Nevertheless, it is only gold. Oh yeah, and we need to pay the necromancer as well. Do you have any other complaints or concerns because if you don't I need to return to the land of the Starborn for a bit?"

The two doggers stood a bit flustered. They were about to hoot, growl, bark and yowl at me so I did the best thing possible and I logged off.

I was suddenly back in my easy chair. My living room was dark, except for a cone of light streaming in from the street outside. It was the middle of the winter and it was beginning to get dark outside early. I really needed to remember to leave a light on. I took care of a few bodily needs and then stared into the refrigerator. It was filled with a bunch of healthy crap, so I slammed it shut in disgust. I thought about ordering a pizza pie, with meatballs, pepperoni, bacon and any other meat products Gino's Italian offered, but then Amber walked in carrying a tray. My hopes of a culinary delight were quickly dashed.

"Dinner," she announced.

We sat down and I dug into the tuna casserole she had made. Despite the little chunks of celery (which I despise) I found myself ladling more onto my plate. I was ravenous for some reason.

"It's a mess out there," Amber said. "Players and NPCs are going crazy looking for this guy. They know you gave the quest, and they know you are involved somehow in the search for The Nexus Killer. The players can make the connection. They know that if they find him that they will have their fifteen minutes of fame, both in the game and in the real world. By the way, since when can you give out quests? You didn't tell me about that."

"Yeah, that is something new." I was going to elaborate when my phone chimed. There was a message from Havervill. "They didn't find Mutter, but they located his number one gal. I think you may want to get back here now."

"Amber, I need to log back in. There may be a break," I said. I could tell she wanted to say something to me. I thought she was going to berate me about entering the game again. Instead, she said, "I know it is a game, but be careful."

"I always am," I answered as I began to place the haptic devices back on. I thought about contacting Haggerty or Shannon but decided against it. Let me gather some information first, I thought. Havervill wouldn't have contacted me if it weren't relevant.

I placed the haptic cap on my head, leaned back in my easy chair, and logged back into my office. I was spending way too much time in my office recently, I thought, as I spawned right into it.

Tinsie hovered by the doorway. Lieutenant Gail and two female guards stood on either side of the doorway. All three of them wore green bandanas around their necks. At my desk sat a woman. And what a woman she was. She had the prettiest face I had ever seen – and I was drawn to it. My *Intimidation* perk fought against some innate force. I could have fallen into her golden eyes and lost myself forever.

"Her Allure is over one hundred," Havervill explained. "She possesses a powerful perk, *Mesmerism*, that very few can fight. Forget Helen of Troy, men in the Grey Zone have literally killed one another for the chance to stare into her golden eyes. Of course, she is the one who pits them against one another for that opportunity. It is sport to her. She is a scorpion this one so be careful." I looked at her description: Apasia, Realmborn, Half Human, Beguiler, Level 110. Perks: *Mesmerism, Dance of the Seven Veils, Glamor, and Lucky Charms*.

"Lucky Charms," Havervill snickered.

She was sitting down in my seat, so I couldn't see her entire outfit. If Greek Goddesses existed, then she was one of them. She had long, lustrous white hair with a few stripes of black. Her eyes were two golden globes that tried to draw me in. Her face was perfect, without a flaw. She was garbed in a white dress with her thin shoulders exposed. Her arms were well defined. She had long slender fingers with white painted nails.

Her charm was not a sexual one. I did not desire her flesh – like men and women did with Sierra Skye. This was more of a willing desire to belong to Apasia, to be her loving servant – to worship her – like one might venerate a goddess. I would cook dinner for her if she asked, rob a bank for her if that was her will, or even do battle with a dragon if that would please the lady.

I shook my head like someone trying to clear away cobwebs, and the spell trying to latch onto my mind flew away.

"Mace," Tinsie said. "This is Apasia."

"Hello," I said, not sure why she was in my office.

"She didn't want to come along with us. Then I threatened to stick her in the sack. Everyone knows about the magical sack by now. Remember the time Dawson was trapped in it. That was so much fun. Anyhoo, she finally agreed to come along peacefully, and not to pull any Jedi mind tricks. Then she tried to mesmerize us anyway even though she promised, but I had picked up a little something to block her from messing with our minds. We owe Rhia two thousand coins for these by the way." She tugged at a little green bandana that hung around her neck. "She says 'Hi' by the way. Anyhoo, the bandanas along with the wards in HQ should suppress her abilities long enough that we don't need to worry about her tricking us into attacking one another."

"Tell your pet sprite that Apasia never forgets a slight." I was lost in her words for a moment, as though she was speaking them right into my mind.

"Fight it Mace. She is trying to beguile you," warned Havervill.

"I thought magic and other attacks are warded against inside headquarters."

"That wasn't a spell," Havervill explained. "It is just part of who she is. It is natural and unconscious to her like breathing or blinking. Beware, she is more deadly than any halfman. Your *Intimidation* perk along with Providence and the wards here are enough to keep her under control. I will warn you if she tries anything else. I am immune to her persuasions."

"Listen lady. You climb into my head again without my permission and I will see to it that you spend a few days in the sack," I said, staring right at her.

"I am not that kind of girl Maaaaace," she said, elongating my name. "You have me confused with your harlot, Sierra Skye. I do not need to surrender my body to get what I want. So no. You and I will not spend any time in the sack." A huge grin covered her lovely face. "Let's get to business shall we?"

"Business?" I questioned.

"You want to know where Mutter is and I want the ten thousand gold coin reward. Of course, I could just wait until someone else finds him and then just beguile them. They will suddenly find themselves handing ten thousand gold coins over to me... and with a broad smile on their face as they do so. I promise you that without me you will never find his hiding place. He is even hidden to the pixies who can find anyone."

"Let me zap her Mace," Tinsie snapped. "I have a fun spell that will knock that smile off her face." Tinsie turned to Apasia and said, "Don't you care that Mutter has murdered three women?"

"He has murdered many more than that I can ensure you," she responded. "I will help you constable. It will cost you two things. One is the ten thousand gold coins. That is non-negotiable. The second is a rare item that I desire. I cannot obtain this artifact because the woman who holds it refuses to sell it to me. She appears to have a relic for everything, so she even knows when one of those *enamored* with me tries to purchase it on my behalf. I think she will let you have it, however."

"Rhia," I sighed.

"Rhia," she smiled. "I believe you know her quite well, intimately as a matter of fact. Obtain ten thousand gold coins and the relic for me by noon tomorrow and I will tell you where to find him."

"No!" I answered.

"No!" she sputtered, not expecting that response. I didn't think she was used to anyone saying no to her.

"For ten thousand gold and the relic you want me to procure I am going to need a great deal more," I informed her. "I will get the relic for you. The question you need to decide is how badly do you want it."

"She wants it from you Mace. She wants it badly," Havervill chuckled in my mind. For someone who sounded in my head like an old curmudgeon, he had the sense of humor of a prepubescent boy. I ignored him as often was the case.

"What else do you need to know?" she asked.

"I need some answers. Mirror copies of the murders that took place here have occurred in the world of the Starborn. What is the connection between them?"

"You know so little," she mused. "I will give you this one piece of information for free. Mutter is a symbiont."

"A symbiont?"

"A symbiont. You will never find him because you won't know who he is. Or at the very least who his current host is. Though symbiont is a bit of a lie now that I consider it. Symbiosis implies a kind of equality. This is more parasite and host, and the parasite becomes the dominant entity. He has access to his host's knowledge, skills, abilities and perks."

"So he can force himself into someone else's body?" Tinsie asked. "That is mean mean mean."

"They are not forced. They were never forced," she said with a wicked smile. "They loaned their bodies to him happily because I asked them to do so. Told them that it would please me. All my subjects want to please me."

Behind me, I heard one of the usually stoic guards gasp.

"You were his partner," Tinsie said.

194

"She was in cahoots," Havervill mused.

"You used your power to get people to agree to become his host. Why would you do that?" I asked.

"That is my affair which I will not share. However, let's say that our partnership has recently come to an abrupt end. I helped him to find the host he now possesses and then I left him. So your guards are looking for the wrong face so to speak."

"So what happens to the host when he enters it?" I asked.

"They have no memory of being joined by him. Of course, those he interacted with while in the host body remember well. Why some of the constables have sent innocent men and women to The Slags for crimes that were committed while their minds and their bodies were not their own."

Tinsie's eyes grew red with seething anger. I was fuming inside myself. She had allowed innocent people to be sent to prison or have their reputations destroyed. She was a true monster who derived pleasure from the pain of others. There would be a reckoning for her, but not at that moment. Apasia was on a roll, and there was still information I needed, so I stayed calm. I had been staying all kinds of calm lately and the urge to punch someone with brass knuckles was swelling inside me.

"Does he have a prime appearance?" Tinsie asked.

Apasia stood up from the chair for the first time since the start. "He does – and for what it is worth – he was in his prime form when he killed the three women. He said to me, 'We want to feel their lives leave this world with our hands, see the terror in their eyes – and not only the fear that they are about to die but their offspring as well. What could cause a mother more existential grief than the loss of a child?'"

"We?" I asked.

"Oh, I didn't tell you the most interesting part. Before I do, know that this is the last thing I will tell you. I am leaving after this. Try to stop me and I will give you no information about his whereabouts, and you will never discover his new appearance, or where to find him. He may have already changed it for all I know. However, I doubt it. I usually found the hosts for him. He might offer a Realmborn a few gold coins to borrow their bodies for a few hours, but that has never been his way. Anyway, here is the last thing I say before I depart."

"Fine," I said through gritted teeth.

"Good," she smirked. She kept smirking, and smiling, and grinning the whole time. Woman or not I found myself once again caressing the brass knuckles.

"Bill Nelson can take over Mutter's body – isn't that ironic? I don't fully grasp all the nuances of your world. It is my understanding that the person you are in The Great Realm is not same person you are on – what do you call your plane of existence – Earth. Hum, now that I think about it, the Starborn may all be the ultimate symbionts. Your consciousness from your plane of existence merges with a life force in The Great Realm. Anyway, Bill Nelson was the original Mutter – a Starborn. Then one day he departed The Great Realm but Mutter remained – now a Realmborn – and a symbiont. I am not sure of the great magics involved in such things. Perhaps one of the elder gods – though it was more likely one of the devils who lurk in the deepest depths of the fiery pit – breathed life into Mutter."

Her information jived with what Shannon had just told me a few hours before.

"This still doesn't explain your *We* comment," I interjected.

"We," Apasia sounded amused. "Bill and Mutter were one – sharing the same body – sharing the same mind – when he – they – slew those women. They both have a taste for killing. I will be leaving now. You will get nothing more from me, such as Mutter's current location, without the gold and relic."

"I can't agree to that," I said.

"I will tell you where he is. Surely that is the most important thing? If you capture Mutter or detain the prime form, you can prevent Bill Nelson from joining with him. Or even if he joins with him, you will have him restrained and he will not be able to join with another host. So why will you not agree? Isn't it your job to find the killer?"

"It is. The problem is if he can jump from body to body then how do you know he has not already done so? You may tell me he is currently in the body of a merchant or a guardsman, but he may have already fled that host before I can track him down."

"Because constable," she said stroking a chain on her neck, "this necklace is a divine relic. Mutter doesn't know it but I had it created for one reason and one reason only, to always know where the symbiont is. Ten thousand gold coins and my relic and you can have it. It will not only lead you to the symbiont, but it will lead you to the prime body – which at this moment is just a hollow vessel."

Chapter 26: Old Friends and Lovers

I logged off soon after Apasia's last big reveal. I had several guards escort Apasia back to The Grey Zone where she seemed most comfortable weaving her spider webs, entrapping and beguiling men and women alike. It was getting late, so Tinsie and I logged off for the night.

Back in my house, I contacted Haggerty and told him that he and Driver may want to stop by my house in an hour so I could share some information I just discovered. Amber left me a note that she was out and would return later. My stomach growled in hunger, so I scarfed down another plate of the tuna casserole.

I had just cleaned up from dinner when Haggerty and Detective Driver entered my house. Haggerty looked tired while Driver appeared a bit on edge. She held a large cup of coffee in her hand.

They both sat down and then Driver said, "It has been a really long day. It is going to be even a longer night I fear. We have been lucky so far that there hasn't been another murder. Maybe Bill Nelson is laying low now that we know who he is. Of course, he may have also killed himself in the explosion. We won't know until we can get inside the house to check it out. DNA was found all over the previous murder scenes, and none of it matched anything in our databases. However once we knew who we might be looking for we were able to identify Bill Nelson as the killer using genealogical connections. We tracked down some of Nelson's first cousins and their DNA and the DNA found at the murder sites share many of the same markers. There is no doubt Bill Nelson. Now we just need to find him. Mike tells me you may have something for me. So let me hear it. I need to head back to the station after this."

I filled them in on everything that Apasia had shared with me.

"So how does any of this help us?" Driver asked.

"I am not sure yet. Tomorrow I intend to track down Mutter. – Really, what a crazy name. His name literally translates to Mother Murderer. Donna, I will let your forensic psychologists have a field day with all of that. Anyhow, maybe if Bill doesn't have access to the game anymore, it will force his hand and he will do something rash or out of character."

"Can't you just erase or delete his avatar from the game?" she asked Haggerty.

"I am sure we could. If we could find the coding. He has buried it somewhere. He was one of the first programmers and knows the coding better than anyone. Besides, if we delete the character we lose access to him in the game. And it is due to the game that we have tracked him down twice already."

I could just hear Havervill's response to the last statement. He would say something like, 'I tracked him down twice, putting myself at risk, and everyone is so ungrateful' and on and on. He would be right in this case. If it weren't for Havervill, the name Bill Nelson might not even be known.

"I am sick of missing him," Driver said.

"Tomorrow I will find out where this Mutter is hiding. Maybe Bill Nelson will log back on. If he does, we can track him. Just get him this time."

"I plan to," Driver said, before finishing off the last of her coffee.

Driver and Haggerty left a short time later.

I found myself alone in the house.

I really wanted some beer. Just three or four cans to take the edge off.

Amber would not be pleased.

I thought about going to sleep but it was way too early.

I could log back in – maybe just for a few hours.

Perhaps find a way to go incognito and visit a brothel.

Where did that thought come from? I mused.

I was a man after all.

I had needs after all.

Perhaps I was just lonely.

Possibly, it was because I would be seeing Rhia the following day to obtain the relic Apasia demanded.

I had wanted to send a pixie to pick up the relic. However, my ex-lover insisted on bringing it herself.

Rhia was on my mind.

*

I logged into my office at exactly 9:00 a.m the next morning. As soon as I spawned, I jumped back. A seven-foot tall mountain of steel – I would soon find out it was titanium and not steel – loomed above me. A gnome stood by the door speaking with the ever present Lieutenant Gail.

"Ah constable," Gail said. "Prompt as usual. This is the Great Golem Artificer," he said pointing down at the four-foot tall gnome. Soot covered his already grey skin and stuck to his matted hair.

"Constable Mace, I deliver to you my newest creation, the titanium golem. He or she depending on which pronoun you prefer to use has just emerged from my newest cauldron. This one is heated with molten lava from the Spitrotz itself. Aye, it was quite a task to procure the lava – but acquire it we did. The titanium golem is my masterpiece – state of the art, or next generation technology as you Starborn might term it. This golem will be more than a challenge for any creature from The Sundaland. It is even resistant to the blue flames of the black dragons."

Tinsie suddenly materialized. She looked at me, then at the gnome, and finally at the new golem.

"No! No! No!" she complained. "We don't want him. We don't need him. Take him back. No! No! No!" Then she began to bawl.

"What's wrong?" I asked.

"You really are dense sometimes," Havervill interjected. "She is upset about Buddy and sees this new golem as a replacement. It is Psychology 101."

Tinsie began to calm down. Before she could speak I said, "Tinsie. I miss Buddy too. However, we need the golem, especially an advanced one. Particularly because the Queen seems to have four of them."

"I know," Tinsie snapped. "It's just..." and then she began to sniffle again.

I turned to the artificer. "Thank you."

"Don't thank me. Do me a favor. Let's not give this golem away to the Queen like your predecessor did. Even more importantly, try to keep this one from falling into The Abyss."

"I will do my best," I responded.

"Well you better. Because I am retiring from the golem making business, at least for now. There is a whole new continent open, and I plan on exploring it."

"Is that safe?" I asked.

"I will have ten golems along with me. I will be just fine. One final thing before I leave, it's about your last golem, Buddy. What a curious name. Buddy's life force is still active. So though he is lost to The Abyss, he still lives."

Tinsie, who just a moment ago had been sobbing, now had a look of determination. "Is it possible?" she asked. "Can we bring him home?"

"I don't know Tinsie," the gnome replied.

"Maybe when this whole mess is over with The Nexus Killer we will see if we can save him," I stated.

"I am going to hold you to that Mace," Tinsie responded.

I turned to say goodbye to the artificer but he was gone already. The titanium golem's presence filled the small office.

"I am Mace," I said.

"Mace," the construct repeated in a deep voice.

"And I am Tinsie, big guy," my deputy announced.

"Big guy," the golem repeated.

"No no no!" Tinsie shouted. "I am Tinsie."

"You are Tinsie," it said, its voice reverberating throughout the room. "I am Big Guy. Biggg Guy. Big Guy." The ground rumbled below us.

"I guess his name is Big Guy. Alrighty then," I stated.

"Buddy, Big Guy," a familiar woman's voice said. "You really shouldn't be allowed to name your golems."

My heart missed a beat.

A mixture of longing and anger coursed through my blood.

Rhia looked as lovely as ever.

"Hi Rhia," Tinsie said abruptly. "I gotta go Mace. See you later." She flew from the room like a horde of harpies was on her trail.

Rhia wore a long white fur coat and a white hat. She pulled off the hat to shake off snow that had accumulated on it. Her long, soft blonde hair fell down in wavy golden locks. I remembered for a moment how soft her hair was and how it often smelled of strawberry.

"Nope," Havervill said. "We can't go through this again Mace. She broke your heart once. Wasn't that enough? Don't you remember all the moping and longing and brooding?"

Even though part of me knew that my AI's assessment was

correct, I didn't want to hear from him right now. I found the settings in the display and cut off my connection to him. I knew he would be good and pissed.

Part of me wanted to wrap her in my arms and kiss and kiss and kiss her, while my mind struggled against that impulse, urging me to keep this meeting all business.

Rhia gave me a crooked smile and then began to unbutton her fur coat. She took it off and draped it over a cabinet in the office. She wore a dark pink dress with a pattern of little white flowers.

She still didn't speak but walked over towards the golem. She looked it up and down, envy filling her eyes. "The craftsmanship is immaculate. One day I will convince the Great Golem Artificer to share the secret of their creation with me."

Then she looked up at me.

"You always wanted to share with me who you were in the real world," she said.

"I know," I said, it sounding almost like an apology.

"Then you end up on the *World Lunar News Network*. Charlie Mason, ex detective, hip deep in the search for The Nexus Killer." She flipped an errant strand of blonde hair behind her ear. "I am sorry about how things ended with us. I know it was a bit abrupt. My life – my real life outside the game – grew suddenly complicated."

"You don't need to apologize," I responded, though I didn't really mean it. What I really wanted to do was to scream at her. However, I figured cool and collected was the way to go.

"I need to apologize. I could have been straight up with you. It is just that who you are in our world is pretty much who you are in the game. It is not the same for me at all," my ex-lover stated.

"If you could explain…" I said before trailing off. I had often asked Rhia about her life outside the game. She was either unwilling or reluctant to do so. It had become a sticking point with us. Late at night after we broke up I wondered if she was married or in a long-term relationship. Maybe she just wasn't a commitment type of person and was just looking for a distraction, and I was that distraction.

My mind was abuzz with too many thoughts so I said, "Thank you for agreeing to release this item to me."

"I wasn't really given a choice," Rhia admitted with an edge in tone.

There was my fiery blonde, I thought.

"Shannon Donally's avatar herself showed up in my shop yesterday. I don't like to be forced to do things. And Shannon does not take no for an answer."

"Immovable object and indestructible force," I quipped.

"You get the idea. We came to an understanding. So here are your two items."

Rhia pulled a sack from her hip and opened it up.

"This bag has the item Shannon asked me to create. I had to work late to get it done, so I hope you appreciate it. It is my finest work ever, and a divine item to boot. I made Shannon pay a fortune for it. For a trillionaire she is a bit of a cheapskate. She has more crypto-coin than most nations, and she haggled like an early bird at a tag sale. "

"Thank you," I said as I took the item from her. "This might give me a little advantage."

"Possibly," she mused, as she removed a second sack and handed it to me.

"The famous crown," I stated as she held the circlet out to me. It was a circle of gold, studded with glowing rubies.

"It's the Crown of Grandview," Rhia revealed with a bit of awe in her tone. "Whoever can master its power will be the true ruler of Grandview."

"I thought Her Royal Highness, High Queen pain in the ass, was the ruler."

"It sounds like you've met her," Rhia said. "I hear she had a thing for constables. If we were still together, I might be jealous. Of course, I might be even more jealous of Sierra Skye. I am surprised by that."

"That is a made up story. Fake news. Nothing happened. I swear," I said defensively. Man, what was wrong with me. Maybe I shouldn't have dismissed Havervill. He would have told me to man up, or buck up, or grab the demon by the horns or some other nonsense that would have made sense in some perverse manner.

"I was just teasing Mace. I know it is all made up."

"Well it is," I said. Then I thought, *Oh shit, does she know about my hour of weakness with Domi.*

Damnit. I didn't owe Rhia anything.

203

I broke from my musing to hear Rhia say, "Anyway to get back to that bitch the Queen; she is more of a despot who through deceit and force declared herself Queen. Of course no one outside of the Royal District accepts her as their ruler." However, whoever can gain dominance over this crown will become the real monarch of Grandview. All of it. She is going to be good and pissed when she finds out Apasia has the crown in her possession."

"Will she target you for giving it to me?" I asked.

A smile crossed my former lover's charming face. "Your concern pleases me. However, she doesn't know I have it. Though she has had adventurers looking for it for months now. The Queen against Apasia. I am going to sit back and enjoy that show," she said amused.

"Well thank you for delivering it in person. You didn't have to do that."

"I wanted to." She grew quiet and stared at me. "I have missed our nights together, Mace." She cleared her throat and walked close to me. "If you are free tonight perhaps we can grab some dinner and then maybe grab one another." She leaned in, planting a soft kiss on my lips.

My body quivered.

I wanted to wrap her up in my arms and kiss her.

Then with an inner resolve I didn't know I possessed I said, "Part of me wants to Rhia. More than you will ever know. However, I can't go down that road again. I just can't. Besides, I need to stay focused. There is a killer in our world, and I may be able to help catch him. I can't afford to get distracted. And you would be a wonderful distraction."

She grinned. "If you change your mind you know the place and time." She picked up her fur coat and hat from where she had left them and walked from my office. She put a small sway into her hips as she headed down the hallway.

"Dammit," I muttered under my breath.

I was so glad Havervill had not heard any of the conversation. I was not sure if he would have been proud of me for manning up or if he would have mocked me. But I know the answer. He would have ridiculed me. I could hear his voice: "Mace, a blonde with a cute ass and pert breasts invites you into her bed. Who says no to that?"

Only an idiot, I mumbled. *Only a really big idiot.*

Chapter 27: The Once and Future Queen

"She's here Mace," Tinsie stated. "It's was quite a spectacle. A portal opened and an assortment of dwarves, humans, gnomes, satyrs, half orcs, and a dozen other races exited outside HQ. They cleared away the snow with a combination of brute strength and magic. Then they erected a dome a hundred feet in diameter. It is like we are inside a snow dome Mace. Kinda pretty. Then they laid a red carpet out and Apasia walked out of the portal, wearing a long flowing light blue gown. She was saying something about this being the day of her coronation. It's bad, bad, bad Mace."

"She does have style," Havervill quipped. "You gotta admit that."

"Damn it all to hell!" I cursed.

"What is wrong, Mace?" Tinsie asked.

"Her Royal Highness. I don't think she's going to be too pleased. I am sure she has her spies and she is currently being informed. Get Apasia in here ASAP. The sooner we get the information we need, the quicker she'll be gone."

Tinsie flew off.

I sighed.

My virtual assistant found my discomfort funny and laughed. "A cat fight. Too bad they aren't both furries then it really would be a cat fight. "

A moment later Apasia strolled into my office. Two young human women held the ends of her long, flowing gown.

"What the hell Apasia?" I asked. "Is this show necessary?"

"Indeed it is. By the end of the day I will be Queen of the entire city and the usurper will be gone."

"Well you aren't Queen yet. You won't get the crown you want from me until you tell me where the hell Mutter is – and until you relinquish that necklace you claim can track the symbiont if he jumps to another body. So where is he?"

"Yeah, where where where is he so we can go and get him?" shouted Tinsie.

"First my crown!" she said adamantly, infusing her voice with power and force.

"Your ability to coax, cajole, or charm won't work in here," I snapped. "Save your mind tricks for outside."

Apasia winced. "How dare you! I am Apasia. The new Queen of Grandview."

"Yeah, yeah lady. Save it for out there. I don't have time for games or politics." I glanced at Tinsie. "You can show it to her now."

Tinsie flew behind my desk, opened a drawer, and pulled out the crown. Like all items Tinsie held, it shrunk to her proportions.

"Don't you think I would make a pretty Queen?" the sprite said as she held the crown above her golden locks. "Queen Tinsie the Kind. Or Queen Tinsie the Sexy Sprite. Or I have even a better one. Queen Tinsie, The First of Her Name. Which one do you like?" Tinsie twirled the crown and then moved it above her head again.

"Don't you dare!" Apasia scowled.

"It's all yours. I just want to know where to find Mutter. I will give you the crown and the gold just as soon as you tell me what I need to know."

"Fine!" she replied angrily. "He's hiding in the deepest depths of a ziggurat."

"What is that? Like a pyramid or something?"

"Exactly," she said.

"And where is this pyramid?" I asked.

She smirked. "This is the best part. It is far in the eastern reaches of The Sundaland."

"I wasn't expecting that," Havervill chimed in. "Everything seems to come back to The Sundaland for a reason."

"He is waiting for you there," stated Apasia.

"What do you mean he is waiting?"

"He created the ziggurat just for you. They are both very mad at you – Mutter and this Bill Nelson Starborn."

"How do you know this? When did you speak to him – them?" I queried.

"I am speaking to him now. Would you like to say hi?" she laughed.

I showed no emotion but responded, "If you have a way to put me in contact with him that would be fine. Then I can tell him to turn himself in to the authorities."

She laughed. "My crown first!"

"As soon as I am done speaking with him everything is yours.

You are the one who keeps delaying getting your crown, not I. So no more games."

She stared daggers at me. "You will bow to me very soon constable. You all will."

Tinsie twirled the crown around a few times. Then tossed it into the air, before catching it. Apasia's eyes looked greedily at the crown.

"Take my hand," she ordered, holding her right one out.

"Why?" I asked.

"So you can speak with Bill Nelson. He wants to talk with you too."

"Do what you can Havervill," I said, before grabbing onto Apasia's hand.

I felt like a tornado had sucked me up and was spinning me around at a thousand miles an hour. The sensation stopped. I appeared to be in a large structure made of brick and mortar. A thick layer of sand covered the floor. The walls were angled, and I knew I was inside the ziggurat. Mutter – AKA Bill Nelson – stood in front of me.

"Surrender Bill Nelson," I said, before he could speak. "The authorities know who you are. Just a matter of time before you are hunted down."

I invoked my *Glean Truth* perk. I needed to be able to determine truth from deception. Of course, the problem with sociopaths is that they believe their lies to be truths.

"It won't work," Havervill said. "He is preventing your perks from working. You are going to have to tell truths from lies the old fashioned way."

"Surrender!" Bill Nelson croaked. "My fun is just beginning. Matter of fact, the authorities should find my latest victim any moment now."

"What did you do?" I asked, a gnawing sensation in my chest.

"*I killed the woman guard,*" a slightly different voice said. "*Wasn't expecting the dagger. But it still felt so good as I plunged it into her.*"

"Shut up Mutter," the voice of Bill Nelson said.

"*It is best when they fight back and struggle. Makes the kill all the more enjoyable. Wouldn't you say so Bill?*"

"They are both crazy," Havervill chirped.

208

"Hold a second," the voice of Bill Nelson said. His mouth was moving. He was mumbling as his head moved from side to side. Then he lifted his hand and slapped himself.

"Sorry you had to see that. Mutter will be quiet for a while so we can talk in peace," the voice of Bill Nelson stated.

"Is that you Bill?" I asked just to check.

"It is me. For now."

"What did you mean by the authorities will soon find your latest victim? What did you do?"

"You will find out soon enough. It was a good one." Dammit I thought. He had killed someone else and now he was boasting about it. Since his murders in the real world closely mimicked those in The Great Realm, this one, I feared, was going to hit home in a bad way. I really needed to let Detective Driver know. However, it was more important to keep him talking. Maybe he would let something slip that we could use to pinpoint his whereabouts or clue us in to his next victim or his next location.

"Ahhhhhhhhhhh!" Havervill screeched.

Bill Nelson chortled.

"Tell your Havervill that I have caught onto his tricks. The Havervills were always so annoying – so cocky and snarky. I should have deleted them while I had the chance. Let him know next time he comes after me his coding will be dispersed to The Nexus. All of Shannon's programmers and coders won't be able to put the Havervills back together again."

I felt Havervill retreat to the back of my mind; I was uncertain if he was hiding or lying in wait for his chance to attack.

"You have ruined everything. Everything. Now I must speed up my timeline. I will have to take the next two quickly now. Ah, no matter. I will savor their deaths just the same."

"What did I ruin?" I asked. I wanted to keep him talking. The longer I could keep him speaking the better.

"You found out who I was. No big deal. I died once and started a new life. Will do the same again very soon."

"I don't think so," I responded. "Your days are numbered. You are like all psychopaths – too delusional to see."

"Delusional!" he screamed. "I am hardly delusional, and I am most certainly not a psychopath. I killed those women and their born

209

or unborn offspring because it was fun. It brought me pleasure. And isn't life about pleasure?"

"*Ummmm,*" Mutter groaned, "*the pleasure of my hands on their throats. The necks of the babies were like twisting chicken bones.*"

"I said be quiet Mutter," Bill Nelson chided his avatar. "We've discussed this. No. No. You can't talk to him right now. Maybe later. Now let me finish."

"You are really sick," I stated. "You both are."

"Stop saying that! I am not a nut, delusional, crazy or any other synonym," he screamed, virtual spittle flying from his mouth.

I thought about continuing to push the insanity angle but didn't want to lose him.

"What is it you want from me?" I asked. "Apasia said you wanted to speak with me."

"That bitch. She betrayed me for a crown."

"It seems she did. But she is not the first woman who has betrayed you, is she?" I asked.

Let me push his buttons just a bit more. Maybe get him to act rashly or make an error.

"You are boring me Constable Mace," he sniped. "I want you gone. I want to speak with Detective Charlie Mason instead."

He snapped his fingers, and suddenly I was wearing regular street clothing. My armor, my mace, my brass knuckles were all gone.

"This is my pyramid! I created it years ago and hid it away deep in The Sundaland. I am God here."

"A MOD," I said. "I have seen better."

"Better!" he barked. He looked at me for a moment. "I see what you are trying to do. You are trying to get me mad. You think I am stupid and will tell you where to find me. It is not going to be so easy."

I remained silent and eyed him. Let him make the next move.

"I will make you a deal. You will bring back a message for me and in exchange I will wait right here for you for the next forty-eight hours. I will give the world a two-day reprieve. If you defeat my ziggurat, I will tell you where to find me in the real world."

Now we are getting somewhere, I thought.

"What is the message?"

"Tell Shannon that I am responsible for burning down the

Immersion Online facility in Las Vegas. Mass killing is fun, but not as enjoyable as what I am doing now. Do you know what the most pleasurable part was – killing Rob Renselar."

"Who is that?" I asked.

"He was her son. And the son of a former police captain. I killed their son."

Haggerty's the father. That is the hold Shannon has over him, I thought.

Bill Nelson began to laugh like a deranged clown. Then Mutter's voice began to giggle. The two voices came from the same mouth. The insanity seemed to float from them. The sound overwhelmed me. Their maniacal laughter echoed in my brain, like a cacophonous bell. I screamed. I thought I would go insane. Every dark impulse I ever had boiled to the surface. I understood evil and madness, and they were inviting me to partake.

My fist bashed in Doyle Ferguson's face again and again until he lay unconscious. His little girl, with those light green eyes, staring at me as I hovered above the unmoving body of her father – an avenging angel and the monster that lurks in the closet.

I shrugged the dark thought away.

The cackling finally ended and I was back in my office. I yanked my hand back from Apasia's like from an electrical shock.

A notification popped up. The quest I had given to find Mutter had been completed. This notification went out to every Starborn and Realmborn who had received the quest. I could hear the communal groans from hundreds of thousands of players now that they knew the quest was completed. The next thing they would want to know is who completed it.

"Now for my crown," a smiling Apasia commanded. For a moment, I felt a compulsion to fulfill her command but I was able to wave it off.

"Give it to her Tinsie," I said. I was sick of Apasia and her games and just wanted her gone. I knew where to find Bill Nelson / Mutter. Even though he seemed to be suffering from psychosis, I believed him when he said he would wait for me for forty-eight hours.

Tinsie flew down and proffered the crown to Apasia. She snatched it from my deputy's hand. She stared at the crown for a solid minute. I didn't know what additional skills or abilities she had, but she finally smiled. "It is real! It does exist. It is all mine. I will master the crown's secrets, and then I will be the Queen of the city as it should have always been. And my gold?" Tinsie pulled out her wand. A cabinet in my office opened and two large sacks floated into the air. They clanged as they floated towards Apasia. "Ten thousand gold," she said almost absently. Then both sacks disappeared.

"Come," she said, as she turned around to face her ladies in waiting, "we must start planning my coronation." She walked down the hallway and headed towards the exit.

"What now Mace?" Tinsie questioned once Apasia was out of earshot.

"We need to plan another dungeon dive – a pyramid dive to be more accurate. And we need to find a way to get to this ziggurat in a hurry."

Tinsie began to fly anxiously back and forth in the office. Muttering sounds came from her lips.

"What is wrong?" I asked.

"The ziggurat," she answered. "It is in the furthest reaches of The Sundaland, and we don't have a lot of time to get there. I think I know a shortcut but you aren't going to like it."

She told me the idea.

Havervill who had been eerily silent for a while now burst out laughing. "Sometimes I almost like the brownie girl. Especially when she comes up with zany ideas like this one."
*

I had been expecting the next visitor.

"It's okay Tinsie," I said. "Let her in."

A portal opened inside my office and Her Royal Highness, High Queen, Illustrious the Beautiful walked from the portal. A moment later, the halfman leapt out of the portal, his cudgel in his hand. As soon as they were both out, the portal snapped shut.

Big Guy immediately grabbed hold of Stilskin, wrapping the halfman in his two massive arms. He squirmed and tried to get away from the golem, but my titanium companion held him fast. Stilskin would not be free anytime soon.

"How dare you," he bellowed.

"Glad the wards held," Havervill stated. "She was going to bring a small army with her. I think she has murder on her mind."

The halfman continued to scream and curse.

"To what do I owe the pleasure milady?" I asked, bowing slightly to the Queen.

"I see you have a new golem," she responded. "A new model. Curious. I will have to see about acquiring one. He will release my halfman now. I demand it."

"You demand it," I laughed. Tinsie giggled. Even Havervill had a good guffaw going. "Your demands mean nothing to me."

The Queen began to sputter and the halfman doubled his efforts to escape the iron like grip of the golem.

"You mock me! No one mocks me!" she stammered.

"I will release your halfman if he can be a good boy."

Tinsie laughed again and then flew down to hover in front of the squirming halfman. "Are you going to be a good *wittle* boy?" she quipped.

"I will destroy you all," he screamed.

"Big Guy," I said to my new golem. "If the halfman threatens us again, you have my permission to walk to the front of headquarters and then toss the halfman out the door. Oh, and you can toss him as far as you want." Then I turned to the Queen. "You know the golem will do exactly as I stated, so you need to get your pet halfman under control."

"Silence Stilskin!" the Queen snapped, as the halfman appeared ready to speak again.

"Thank you, your majesty," I said. "I wouldn't want any unpleasantness between us. So, how can I assist you? I assume that you came to my office for a reason."

"Uh Mace. Mace," Havervill chimed in, "You have a problem outside. The Queen's forces have arrived ready for a war. Her golems, the thrall, a hundred guards, and another several hundred high level nobles."

"It appears you brought some friends to my front door," I stated casually. "Are you upset about something?"

"My soldiers are going to tear down your headquarters and raze the Commerce District. With my golems and the thrall it won't be too difficult to do."

I knew I was playing a dangerous game with the Queen. It was just that she was arrogant and wicked. I knew why she had come and had just been stringing her along.

"Are you upset about me presenting Apasia the Crown of Grandview?"

"How dare you! How dare you give it to her. That crown is mine by birthright. And you gave it to her. When I am done destroying the CD, we will track down Apasia. I will personally take the crown from her bleeding and broken body."

I nodded up to Tinsie who pulled out a crown from a sack at her hip. She began twirling it around her finger.

"Your Royal Highness. I believe this is what you desire," I stated pointing at the item in my deputy's hand.

A wistful smile fell over Illustrious' face. The smile just didn't seem to fit her personality. "You gave that bitch Apasia a fake crown."

"I did. It didn't belong to her."

"No it does not." She covetously eyed the crown that Tinsie held.

"I believe it belongs to you. I would really like to give the crown to you but you have an army at my doorstep. I don't respond well to threats and coercion."

"I will call them off." Her eyes glazed over for a second. "They are leaving right now," she said quickly, still eying the treasure.

"Good. The crown is all yours then. However, I will need one little favor first."

The Queen stared at me. She didn't like to be challenged. She was used to people groveling and their instant acquiescence.

The halfman had heard enough and he began to squirm again. "The sprite will relinquish the crown to Her Royal Highness immediately. It is hers by right."

"Big Guy," I said, "can you shut him up please without ripping off his head or tearing out his voice box?" The golem mulled the question over before placing one of his enormous hands over the halfman's mouth. His curses and threats came out as a muffled sound.

"What do you want?" the Queen questioned. I felt a pressure against my mind that quickly departed. The Queen eyed me.

"She was trying to use a power on you,' Havervill said.

"Tinsie," I said, "do you know what?"

"What Mace?" she asked with a huge grin.

"I think I made a grievous error. I think I meant to give Apasia the real crown. Could you please contact her and apologize for my error and ask her to come back?"

"You wouldn't dare!" The Queen said defiantly.

"Try anymore mind tricks on me or my deputy, and I promise to the living city of Grandview that I will hand the crown over to Apasia." The ground rumbled.

"What – do – you – desire – Constable – Mace?" the Queen uttered in a curt manner.

"Well I need a few things that you can assist with. If you agree to them, you will leave with the crown. Shall we get down to business?"

I explained what I required. The Queen remained silent for several moments, mulling over what I asked. Finally, she nodded her head and said, "Your terms are acceptable to me."

I didn't trust her one iota. I had no way to bind her to the promise. Havervill explained that she had a royal perk – *Oath Breaker* – that would allow her to break a promise or a vow free from repercussions. I had thought about withholding the crown until we found Mutter and he was in custody. However, I knew the Queen would never go for that. She really would come after me with an entire army, and I just didn't have time for nonsense like that. When all was said and done, I had to hope that there was enough incentive in the offer I had made. Just in case it wasn't enough of an inducement, Shannon planned to pay a visit to the Queen later today. One threat to wipe her character from the server would probably be enough to force the Queen not to break our agreement.

"Alright Tinsie," I finally said.

She flew down and handed me the crown. I stared at the bejeweled circlet for a moment and then handed it to the Queen. She snatched it from my hands and then held it to her chest for a moment. She looked at me and said, "No one has ever given me a crown before. A golem perhaps, but never a crown. I will depart now. I have a coronation to plan." She glanced at Big Guy who still had the halfman clenched tightly. "Do you mind?"

"Let him go, Big Guy."

The golem opened his arms and Stilskin fell to the floor with a thud.

Tinsie chuckled.

Stilskin tossed an evil leer her way.

"Come halfman," the Queen said as they began to walk from my office. The halfman threw me one more deadly glare.

I smiled at him and said, "I'll be seeing you."

He snarled and then turned to follow his Queen who still held the crown clenched tightly to her chest.

"Let the good times roll," Havervill quipped. "Tomorrow's gonna be a riot."

Chapter 28: Upgrade

Tinsie and I spent the remainder of the day preparing for the assault on the ziggurat. We planned to hit the pyramid early the next morning. I had to trust Bill Nelson when he said we had forty-eight hours to find him. He was a sociopath, and I had to imagine toying with me would get his evil juices flowing. He also had to know that his days were numbered now that his identity had been revealed. The police had not released his name to the public. He wouldn't be able to hide once the entire country knew the identity of The Nexus Killer and his face was plastered all over the telescreen and social media. So yes, I did think he would wait for me to show if only to exact some sort of revenge upon me.

The divine dungeon dive from weeks earlier had taught me to come as prepared as possible. We spent the rest of the afternoon gathering supplies. I thought for a moment about contacting Granson. The Glimmerman and the divine dungeon wouldn't have been defeated without the rogue and his league. I doubted that any guild but his would even have stood a chance. However, I soon discovered that Granson and most of his higher rank players were involved in a quest that had been going on for several weeks.

After conferring first with Tinsie and Havervill and then later with Shannon and Haggerty, it was decided that a small but powerful strike force might be the best approach.

It was also decided that I needed another upgrade to my character. We didn't know what Bill Nelson had planned for us the next morning. However, we all knew we needed to give the attack party the best chance possible so the corporation which had raised me to level fifty when I first became one of Grandview's constables, gave me another boost – this time to level one hundred. The new player character max was level two hundred fifty. Being raised to that level, despite all my entreaties, was nixed. The highest level for any Starborn was currently one hundred and twenty three. So level one hundred wouldn't stand out according to Shannon. Even with a murderer serial / mass killer on the loose, she still worried about the integrity of the game.

"You ready?" Havervill asked, when it came time for the upgrade. "Though really. If you had followed my strategy from the

217

first day we met, you would be level one hundred already. And you would have gotten there organically."

"Organically? Really? Can we just do this? I still have some other details to work out."

"Okay. You are always so tense. You know, a visit or five to one of the brothels might do you good."

"Havervill, please," I groaned.

"Fine. Fine. Let's work on your attributes first. As a reminder, you gain four more per level between levels fifty one and seventy five, three more between levels seventy six and eighty five, and a pitiful one more between levels eighty six to two hundred and fifty. Just remember there is no longer a level one hundred cap on your attributes, so you can blow right through one of them if you want. You have sixty five to play with."

"Let's do this," I said, "Place fifteen in Hand-Eye Coordination, Nimbleness, Strength and Physical Fortitude, and five more into Providence."

"Well that was dull and uninspired. I figured you would have raised your Physical Strength up to a hundred," my AI stated.

"I am not sure what to expect inside the pyramid, so I figure let me be as rounded as possible."

"Well it's your life – or death. Okay, the attributes are applied. Here they are updated.

Physical Strength	83 points (+3 ring) 86 points
Physical Fortitude	80 points
Hand-Eye Coordination	65 points
Nimbleness	55 points
Mental Acuity	20 points
Mental Fortitude	20 points
Providence	65 points
Allure	50 points

"Okay your total new damage points are two thousand four hundred and seven." That's not looking too shabby. Along with *Greeny's Breastplate of Glittering Gold*, you should be able to take a hit or three, not from a titan or a stone giant, but certainly from a gremlin or a goblin. Though I would avoid a throng of gremlins. Those little demons attack in a mob and will eat right through your armor in a minute like termites in your grandma's house."

"You have warned me before. I will stay far away from gremlins."

"Well it's good to know my words are finally getting through to you. You also picked up two more *Mace Special Skills*. The first one is at level eighty-five, *Transform Mace*. Now I know how loyal you are to the mace. Your name is even Mace. Hum, did you plan that? I guess you must have. You could just as easily have gone with the name Spear or Morningstar; those would have sounded much cooler. But I digress. You can turn your Mace into another melee weapon – one that may better suit the battle you are in. Suddenly, you are attacking an ogre with a mace, and he goes to block your mace attack, but instead gets a spear to his fat gut. Not too bad if used at the right time. You can summon this skill up to five times a day. The level one hundred skill is *Ethereal Strike*. Let's say your deputy decides to turn on you some day."

"That's never going to happen."

"Let's just say she does. And let's say she is waiting in her ethereal form for the right time to plunge a dagger into your heart. Well, you would be able to strike her in her ethereal form before she could off you."

"Just one issue. If she is ethereal, how would I know where she is?" I asked.

"That's the beauty; your mace will glow yellow – not sure why the developers chose yellow but they did – and your ethereal menace or menaces will light up yellow as well. Or at least they will appear to be outlined in yellow for the five minutes the skill lasts. Though if you ask me, skill is kind of a misnomer. This is almost borderline magic. Anyway, I am straying again. Let's just say they won't know that you can see them and thus can surprise them first. As a warning, your deputy is getting really close to being able to attack – at least in a limited way – while ethereal."

"That is going to make her even more formidable."

"Yup," my AI uttered. "So you also picked up two more *Crossbow Special Skills*. Going to keep these short since you don't really use your crossbow too much anyway. At level seventy-five, you picked up *Sonic Boom*. This is actually decent considering that other than your mace *Concussive Force* you don't really have anything to slow a mob that is attacking you. Shoot a bolt at an enemy with this skill imbued or let it loose into the midst of an enemy and once it strikes – blammo!- the bolt will cause a sonic boom – ear drums will burst, eyes will bleed, brains will feel like someone just smashed them with a boulder. The area of effect will increase as you gain levels and as you use the skill more. You can use this twice a day so use wisely. I had suggested to the developers they call it *Mass Mayhem*, or *Mass Mangling* or *Mass Murder* instead but you know how those developers are."

"I could have used this skill during the dungeon dive."

"Definitely would have helped. The level one hundred crossbow skill is *Turret*. When you invoke this skill, your crossbow will hover behind your shoulder or off to your side for five minutes. It will pepper your enemies with crossbow bolts while you are able to use your mace and shield. Right now the crossbow will stay within a few feet of you, but as you increase your levels and skills it will be able to remain airborne longer and at a further distance."

"I like that one," I said.

"You could have had these much sooner if you had spent the same time grinding levels instead of spending that same amount of time grinding hot blondes with flowing hair."

"Havervill! I would like to get finished at some time today, so tell me about the rest of them please."

"You know I could just give you the monotone, boring version of these. Excuse me if I want to spice them up a bit. But fine, fine, I can do brevity. You also obtained two *Shield Special Skills*. The level seventy-five one is another damn rip off like your *Thor's Mace*. This one is *Cap's Shield*. Yeah, real original. You can toss your shield at an enemy. The greater your strength and level, the better damage you will do. Like your *Thor's Mace*, the thrown shield will reform in your hand. I just don't see when you would want to use this. The final *Special Shield Skill* is *Spike Shield*. This one I really like. When you invoke it, deadly spikes will fly from the front of your shield. The number of spikes and the force of them will increase as your skill and levels increase. Let's say the same ogre from before is attacking you, and you decide to stand there and fight him mano a mano – which is a dumb way to fight an ogre by the way. But let's just say you did, he could have his two handed club raised high above his head ready to crush your skull in when all of a sudden ten pointy spikes rip through his neck and face. At higher levels, the spikes can even have explosive qualities or be tipped with poison. But we will discuss those options when we get there."

"I can think of a bunch of ways to use that one," I admitted.

"I should hope so," my AI stated. "Now you also have two new *Scalable Mace Special Attributes*. You were told about these before but I will remind you. At level ninety-one you gain *InstaHit*. To quote from the *Compendium*, "When you invoke this power, your mace will always hit your opponent, avoiding all defense and magical bonuses. This attack will always work, even against opponents of much higher levels. Duration: 1 time per day"

"The one time per day isn't great," I stated. "However, if I use that along with my *Blunt Force Trauma* and *Fury* at the right time, my enemy won't know what hit him."

"Your last one is *Thunderclap* which you gained at Level 100. I can't tell you what it does. And not because I don't want to but I simply don't know.   You need to experiment with it. This is something we should practice with in an open field or something. I wouldn't use this in a battle right now unless nothing else is working. I can tell you this much; it is quite powerful.   Gee whiz Mace, I am getting winded here explaining all of this to you."

"You can't get winded Havervill, you don't have any lungs," I joked.

"That is just hurtful – pointing out a guy's shortcomings and all. But let's finish these. You gained two new *Scalable Crossbow Special Attributes*, *InstaHit* at level ninety-one and *Projectile* at level one hundred. The explanations are the same as the mace *InstaHit* and the mace *Thunderclap*. You won't know what *Projectile* does until you try it out."

"Why don't they just tell you what they do?" I asked.

"Because, I believe, they tailor these hundredth level attributes to the player. If that makes any sense."

"I guess," I responded. "So is that it?"

"I wish. Just got to go over your *Scalable Bracer / Shield Special Attributes*. At level eighty-one you received *Reflect Damage*. To quote from the *Compendium* – 'When you invoke this skill, the damage points absorbed by your shield (physical, magical or elemental) are reflected back to the wielder. This skill works even against higher level beings. Duration: 1 attack / once per day.' And the level one hundred one is

Titan Shield. Like the other level one hundred Special Attributes, you need to experiment to figure out what it will do. So that is everything. Do you need to see your entire character sheet or are you good?"

"I am good for now," I answered.

Chapter 29: Motley Crew

It was close to six o'clock when Havervill finished explaining my upgrades.

Six o'clock.

Rhia would be closing up her shop very soon. Part of me wanted to meet her. Would it be for one last fling – a last hurrah?

Could we rekindle the spark we once had?

"You know my opinion," Havervill stated, "get the sexy sexy while you can. You never know if it is going to be your last time. I hope when my time comes it's because my power supply is fried from too much exertion with a Tambi and an Angelica at the same time. That's how a man should go out – in the throes of passion."

I didn't respond to Havervill but just stood there for a moment staring at the display screen. My finger hovered and waivered in front of the log-off button.

Don't do it Mace, I said to myself.

Do it! You only live once, a primal part of me screamed in my mind.

These two halves of me battled for a minute until I just went with my gut and pushed the log off button. There was a murderer on the loose and catching him had to be my prime focus.

I had logged off and was scrounging up some dinner when a call came in on the telescreen. The faces of Haggerty and Driver soon appeared.

"This isn't going to be good, is it?"

"No Mace, it's not," Driver revealed without emotion. "There has been another murder."

"What happened?"

"Same as in the game. Damn sicko. A police officer, Terri Dumont of the Spring Valley PD, was found dead in her townhouse. Her husband, Harry, who happens to be an FBI agent, discovered her body. Terri was eight months pregnant. Eight damn months!" I could tell that Driver was fuming mad. "The house was in shambles. She fought him with all she had. Blood was splattered everywhere. The medical examiner believes Bill Nelson knocked her over at some point, and she slammed her head on an end table. After that, he choked her to death. That isn't even the sickest part. To make the scene in the

223

townhouse match what happened in the apartment of your guard who was killed, he plunged a dagger into her belly. Not a knife. But an actual dagger."

"How do you know it was him and not just some copycat," I asked.

"He left his DNA all over the place. He wasn't even trying to hide that it was him," Driver announced.

"I am going after him – or at least his avatar tomorrow," I explained.

"We know you are pal," Haggerty responded. "And Fingroth and Donna the Ice Mage will be accompanying you."

"When we are done here, Fingroth and my avatar are going to log on. He is going to give me a quick hour or two long tutorial. Mike said my knowledge of virtual reality was even less than yours when you first logged in," Driver stated.

I just nodded my head.

I had spent six weeks in a noob area adjusting to the game and learning the ins and outs. Meanwhile, Haggerty would be mentoring Driver for just a few hours.

He had never offered to mentor me, I thought.

Of course, I wasn't a pretty detective either.

*

A short time after I had finished my conversation with Driver and Haggerty, Amber and I ate some dinner together. Over a meal of turkey meatballs and pasta, I filled her in on everything that was going on. When I told her about the ziggurat and the MOD, a concerned look came over her face. "You know he is setting you up. He's not just going to let you waltz right through the pyramid to find him. He killed a cop in her own home, Dad. If he wasn't afraid to kill her, then why wouldn't he go after you?"

"You know it has to be done. Besides, you have nothing to worry about. Haggerty, and the detective I told you about, Donna Driver, are coming with me"

"Well if they can come along then I want to come too!"

We argued over this point for a few minutes. I told Amber she wasn't coming along and not because I thought it was dangerous or anything, but because I didn't want to get distracted looking after her and trying to protect her.

"I'm a grown woman Dad and not a little kid; I can protect myself," she argued.

"Yes you are," I responded. "But you will always be my little girl. You know that."

She finally acquiesced. "Well if my fire mage can't come along then I want to at least be able to see a live feed or something so I can watch the whole thing. I need to know you are safe. Last time you undertook a crazy mission like this you almost died."

"I will work it out with Haggerty," I promised.
*

At 9 a.m. the following morning, Fingroth, Donna the Ice Mage, Tinsie, Big Guy and I waited outside of HQ. My magic cloak did little to keep the chill from my bones.

"It must be twenty below," I said, my teeth chattering.

"Just shut your receptors off or place them to one and you won't feel a thing," Haggerty announced. The cold didn't seem to be bothering him at all. I couldn't believe that the four foot tall gnome standing next to me was Haggerty. We had been partners in the past, and he always had my back, so I was glad to have him along.

Dunkan walked outside into the frigid cold. He was decked out in his full chain armor. He did not have the standard long sword that most of the guard carried. Instead, a great two-handed sword was strapped to his back. Lieutenant Gail trailed right behind him. "You cannot do this Dunkan. Audrey wouldn't want you to," my lieutenant said tersely to the grieving guardsman.

"You cannot stop me!" he answered abruptly. "I will avenge her."

Then turning towards me, his eyes wild, he announced, "I am coming with you constable. I will get revenge for Audrey."

"I am sorry Constable," Lieutenant Gail cut in. "He has been going on about this all morning. We have been trying to convince him that he must trust you and the deputy to bring the killer to justice."

"He will come to justice by my hand!" Dunkan snapped at her. "Even if it leads me to The Grey Man himself." He looked me in the face with dead eyes. "Constable, I will have my vengeance. I am set on this path. If you do not allow me to track down the killer with you,

I will find my own way to The Sundaland and to this ziggurat where the coward that killed my flower now cowers and hides."

I understood his anger and his need to exact retribution. If someone had murdered my wife or daughter, I would feel the same exact way. I wouldn't let anyone stop me either. This I knew in the darkest depths of my soul.

In the real world, I would never allow a murder victim's spouse, especially one that was involved in law enforcement, to be part of a raid. However, this was not my world, and things worked very differently in The Great Realm.

"He's already made arrangements to get to The Sundaland," Havervill informed me. "If you want my opinion, and you always should, let him come along. He is safer accompanying you than going it alone. By himself, he will not survive for long in The Sundaland. Besides, you know what they say about revenge being best when it is served scorching hot. And his two handed sword is a magical talisman – a flaming sword."

"Okay Dunkan," I announced. "You can come along." The guard was about to say something, but I was not finished. "However, we need information. Lives are in danger both here and in my world – the plane of the Starborn. I will not allow you to jeopardize that. If an opportunity comes where you can seek your vengeance, I will provide you any assistance. You must give me your word – you must make a pledge to the living city of Grandview – that you will not seek revenge until the time is right. You can come along, but do not make me regret it."

Dunkan nodded his head at me. "Constable, I must do this! I must. So, I swear by the living city of Grandview that I will temper my vengeance until the right time." He paused for a moment and added. "I swear this too. Mutter Morder will die by my hand before this day is through!" The ground rumbled and continued to rumble for many long moments.

"This isn't a good idea," Fingroth said to me.

"You can't let him come along," Driver stated. "Why did you agree to this?"

Luckily, I was saved when magic seemed to ripple in the air. A portal opened and the rest of the attack force walked out: Stilskin, Tamta and the diamond golem. The halfman sneered at me. I don't think he liked the arrangement one bit. However, his assistance had been one of the prices for the crown. I really didn't want to bring Stilskin along, but Tinsie had explained to me that the halfmen homeland was remarkably close to the location where the ziggurat was located. Since he was from The Sundaland, he had a waypoint set for an area not too far from the pyramid we sought. I had tried to bypass Stilskin and had asked Shannon if one of her programmers could just send us there. The answer turned out that it wouldn't be so simple. She was infuriated when the programmer explained that it wasn't so easy to just override or add to the coding for The Sundaland. The original programmers had placed firewalls and other safety features into the programming when they created the continent. Much of that information on the original coding had vanished with the death of most of the creators of the continent.

Two of the original coders had been flown by helicopter to the offices in New York to provide their expertise and assistance for the assault on the pyramid. I hoped they would be able to help us should the need arise.

"This is some motley crew you assembled," Havervill stated. I took a quick look at my rapid strike force, and it didn't look too shabby.

Mace, Starborn, Constable, Level 100.

Fingroth, Starborn, Gnome, Battle Mage, Level 100. Subclasses: Pyromancer Level 80; Investigator, Level 78.

Donna, Starborn, Human, Ice Mage, Level 100.

(Tamta) Nameless, Realmborn, Mojo Thrall, Level 210.

Big Guy, Uber Golem, Level 350***, Damage Points, 250,000***

Un-named, Diamond Golem, Level 275, Damage Points, 100,000

Tinsie, Starborn, Sprite, Level 102, Blaster, Conjurer, and Slayer of the Fallen Lady.

Stilskin, Realmborn, halfman, halfman, Level ***.

Dunkan, City Guard, Human, Level 135. Skills, *Hack and Slash* and *Cleave; Perk, Take a Licking and Keep on Ticking.*

It wasn't a huge strike force, but the two golems were more than a match for just about anything, especially since Big Guy was formed specifically to take on beasts from The Sundaland. Of course, it wasn't an ideal warband since we needed to rely on Stilskin and the thrall.

"Alright Stilskin, it's time to share the location," I said.

"Not yet," he stated. "Her Royal Highness has made a change to the arrangement." He snapped his fingers. The portal flared, and an armored knight walked from the portal. This was followed by another and then another. They were all Realmborn and between levels one hundred and thirty five and one hundred and fifty. The procession continued for a full minute until fifty knights stood behind the halfman. They all wore gleaming chainmail armor. Long swords hung from their hips and they held large kite shields with the picture of a lioness painted on them.

"What is this?" I asked. "This was not part of the agreement."

"Agreements are meant to be broken," the halfman chortled.

"Oath breaker," Tinsie said, reminding me of the Queen's powerful perk that allowed her to break agreements free of consequences.

"The sprite should know all about breaking oaths," the halfman sneered.

"What is going on here?" Driver asked. "I thought we were going after Bill Nelson. What is with all of this nonsense?"

"In game politics," Haggerty grumbled.

"Alright Stilskin, if you are done with all of the theatrics. Let's go. We have a killer to capture."

"Now thrall," the halfman shouted and a swirling portal that looked like a dark rain cloud opened up. "Through there to The Sundaland."

Half of the guards walked into the portal.

"Now we go," the halfman said. The diamond golem entered followed by the halfman and Tamta.

"I don't like this one bit," I admitted to Fingroth.

"Me neither pal. They could have a plan to scatter our coding or attack us when we enter. I guess we need to take a leap of faith." Fingroth plunged into the portal. Driver took one look around, shook her head, and then walked into the open gateway to The Sundaland.

Dunkan pulled his two-handed sword from his back; then without a moment of hesitation, he strolled into the portal.

"Be careful Dad," Amber said through the employee chat that she had been granted access to. "I don't trust that halfman creature."

No other voices came over the chat. However, I knew that Shannon and about twenty other members of law enforcement were watching us in case Bill Nelson made an appearance or he provided some clue to his whereabouts.

I took a step towards the portal.

One moment before I walked in, I heard an overly excited Havervill shout out, "Wahoo! Finally a little trip to The Sundaland. Let the good times roll."

I strode into the portal.

Chapter 30: The Sundaland

The sudden change from the freezing cold of Grandview to the stifling heat of The Sundaland was startling. I had been standing in front of headquarters a moment before and now I stood in a verdant field, surrounded by hilly forestland.

Tinsie hovered nearby, her eyes darting everywhere at once, searching for hidden enemies. She had fled The Sundaland and now she was back – possibly at a significant risk to herself.

"So real," Driver said aloud. "If I didn't know this was virtual reality, I would think I was standing in Harriman State Park in the dead of summer."

"Which way and how far?" I asked Stilskin.

Before I walked through the portal, I had activated my *Glean Truth* perk. I planned to keep it going the entire time I was with Stilskin. I was certain that he and the Queen had come up with a plan to betray us. My gut told me it would be sooner than later.

"This way," he indicated, pointing off to his right, towards an upward sloping hill. Stilskin led the way, followed by Tamta and the diamond golem. I tracked close behind with Tinsie hovering next to my left shoulder. Dunkan followed on my right side. Big Guy trailed right behind me. Haggerty and Driver stood behind the golem, speaking softly to one another. The fifty knights fanned out behind us.

The halfman led us through a forest of dense red oaks, laurels and occasional hemlocks. Birds twittered in the trees above us. Small animals rustled the bushes. I glanced up at the dense foliage. I couldn't see anything through the canopy but did hear chittering. About fifteen minutes later, we neared the edge of the woods. The halfman pointed. "There. The ziggurat."

Five pyramids lay scattered around the stony hill in front of us. One ziggurat was toppled over and lay in ruins while three others were overgrown with foliage. These pyramids were not like the ones found in Giza in Egypt but were more like the ones created by the Mayans. They were smaller than the ones found in Egypt but steeper.

"That one," Stilskin specified. "My brethren say it just rose up from the ground yesterday." The one he pointed to looked like it had been recently erected. The stone was not worn down from centuries of rain, wind and erosion like the others. It looked new. I could clearly see the smooth stone and mortar. The land around it was not overgrown but appeared to be trimmed and neat.

Before I could continue my observations, halfmen began to emerge from the woods behind us and the hills in front of us. Some just materialized as though from thin air while others popped out of openings in the ground. In a moment, hundreds of halfmen surrounded us. Several semi-nude and bald thralls stood by their masters. Then the knights who were arrayed behind us drew their weapons as well, but not to defend us from the halfmen. Their weapons were drawn against me and my several allies.

Stilskin began to cackle.

"You promised me," Shannon Donally screamed through the open chat line.

"I did not order this," I heard a voice that sounded like Queen Illustrious' say. "I will cut off his head myself." She paused for a second and then said, "Halfman Stilskin. What are you doing?"

"She wants to know what I am doing?" he chortled. "I am doing what halfmen do. Whatever we want. Like the fool you are, you sent me back to The Sundaland. Now your hold on me is broken. I have bought off your knights with promises of gold and freedom. As for the diamond golem, he belongs to me now."

"Betrayer!" the Queen shouted.

"This coming from the oath breaker herself," the halfman snorted.

"Have to be honest. Didn't see this one coming. These halfmen really are something else. You almost need to appreciate their deceit," Havervill stated.

"What's going on?" Driver asked.

"A lot of insanity," Fingroth responded.

"Brothers," Stilskin sneered. "I bring you the sprite as promised."

"Sprite?" Tinsie said anxiously. "What sprite? Me? You don't want me."

"I don't think so Stilskin," I said.

"The sprite will become our wife," he sniggered again. "She will bear us many halfmen."

A fireball suddenly appeared in Fingroth's hand.

Driver pulled out a slender wand.

I unclipped my mace.

Two gleaming broadswords appeared, one in each of Big Guy's hands.

Suddenly fire rippled along the blade of Dunkan's sword. He stood close to me, and I could feel immense heat emanating from the blade. My guardsman, however, seemed unaffected by the heat.

"Enough of this!" Shannon shouted. "We will take care of this Mr. Mason. You just get to the ziggurat and locate Bill Nelson." She was silent for a moment, and then stated as a question, "We will take care of this, correct?"

"Yes, yes Ms. Donally," a nervous man responded. "Tell her to open the rift now."

Tinsie, without a care in the world, said, "I am too young and pretty to get married to ugly halfmen like you. You are even more horrid on the inside than on the outside. But you know who you can marry?" she asked sardonically, as her eyes flared a deep crimson, "Dark Fey."

A booming voice called out, "Hi. Up here!" I stared up along with hundreds of other faces. Tinsie's soul sister hovered high in the air. She twirled her arm around several times and then a rip seemed to appear in the fabric of the sky. A single being flew out of the rift. She was about a foot tall...a similar size to Tinsie. Her hair was black whereas Tinsie's was blonde. Her skin was grayish with jet-black wings flapping rapidly behind her. She had a mouth of sharp teeth and fingers with pointy nails. She looked down at the assemblage below, turned around, and hovering screamed into the fissure, "Come cousins! It's time to kill some halfmen."

Another one flew from the rift, "Let's burn them to a crisp."

Two more flew out.

One shouted, "After they are dead let's suck their marrow dry."

The other called out, "I call dibs on their eyeballs."

Five more soared out. Then ten. Before they poured out in an endless stream.

Down below us the halfman stood immobile, as though in shock.

"What is happening? And who are they?" I asked Havervill.

"They are using a powerful perk, *Gaze,* that stuns their prey for several minutes. I love these gals. Anyway, they are – were, to be more precise – their spouses. They ruled over the halfmen, so the little bastards trapped them in an alternate plane. With the Dark Fey gone, there was no way to breed new halfmen, so the little buggers went after the sprites – who are of the same species as the Dark Fey. Unfortunately, no time for a history lesson now. You know the whole happy wife take your life, a woman scorned, a real bad break up – well this is that."

The halfmen, the thralls, the knights, even the diamond golem stared transfixed in the sky. I could move, however, and tightened my grip on my mace, though I wasn't certain how helpful it would be.

"Stilskin!" a shrill female voice cut through the air. "You traitorous bastard."

"Darling," the halfman said softly. "I have missed you."

"Lying bugger! You banished us to a place with no elven babes to chomp on and no halfmen to warm our beds. For that my husband, you and your whore thrall will pay."

Five hundred bows appeared in the hands of the Dark Fey. Some crackled with electricity, some with flames, others with multicolored lights.

"Kill them cousins!" one of the Dark Fey shouted. "Kill them now! We just need a few dozen left to have some fun with."

"Shields!" Fingroth shouted.

I summoned my shield and my *Shield Dome*.

A translucent igloo surrounded Donna.

A vortex of flame surrounded Fingroth.

"Flee!" one of the halfmen shouted.

"Stand your ground, knights," Stilskin ordered, his voice filled with power.

Tamta began to touch numerous runes on her body.

Then hell rained down.

A barrage of arrows streaked towards the knights, the halfmen and the thralls. Explosions erupted in the midst of the knights, sending them flying and hurtling into the air. When the smoke cleared from the explosion, many knights lay on the ground moaning, some with missing limbs, others blinded, and a dozen or so bleeding profusely.

The thralls erected large domes that blocked many – but not all of the deathly arrows. Several of the thralls cast counterspells of fireballs and chain lightning. A ten-foot wide mouth with jagged teeth opened in front of some of the Dark Fey and then began to eat and crunch on several of them. It was sheer chaos. The only lucky part was that the Dark Fey attacks were not aimed towards us. Their venom appeared to be focused at Stilskin and the other halfmen. The thralls were a particular target with countless arrows flying towards them.

Stilskin turned towards me and screamed. "You! You did this! Kill them my golem! Kill them all!"

The diamond golem leapt twenty feet and struck at the dome I had erected. The shield collapsed behind the enormous force of the blow. Fate – in the shape of Big Guy – intervened and saved me from having my chest crushed in. My titanium golem smashed into Stilskin's the diamond golem. Despite how powerful the diamond golem was, he was no match for Big Guy. I re-erected my shield and watched as Big Guy punched the other golem several times, staggering the diamond construct. The diamond golem shook his head and then charged forward, but might as well have been running into a mountain. Big Guy picked up the diamond golem, lifted him above his head and then tossed him towards a group of knights who were huddled together behind their shields. It looked like a move from an old time wrestling vid. The knights scattered from the impact.

"Are you just going to hide?" Havervill complained. "Get out there and kill some halfmen. I know you want to." Part of me desired to throw myself into the fray. However, I couldn't afford to go to respawn. The most prudent thing was to stay out of the fracas – at least for the time being.

The halfmen overcame the initial assault and counterattacked the deadly fairies. Explosive rocks and projectiles flew from their slings. The thralls cast webs that tangled their wings. The fey that fell to the ground were quickly clubbed or stabbed, until they were bleeding pulps of flesh.

Stilskin had his hands full and dodged several arrows that streaked towards him. A barrier of some sort protected him, as numerous arrows appeared to strike an invisible wall. Several of the arrows even reversed in flight and headed back the way they came.

The diamond golem was back on its feet and charged towards us like a bull. It didn't get very far as twenty or so arrows struck it.

Thick chains burst from the arrows, enwrapping its torso and entangling its feet. The diamond golem slammed to the ground with an audible thud.

The chaos of the battle raging all about us seemed to slow down, as there was one shrieking scream, followed by another. I looked to my left to see one of the thralls holding a dead halfman in her arms. The collar around her neck lit up for a moment before opening and falling to the ground. She stood up and began to touch one rune after another. Griffins soared into the air; rocks and other sharp items levitated off the ground and streaked into the air striking the flying fairies; a hailstorm of ice fell from the sky, pelting the dark fairies and scattering them. The vengeful thrall continued with her torrent of spells until she fell to the ground dead with dozens of arrows protruding from her flesh.

Another thrall screamed, her master dead at her feet. This one, however, did not mourn the death of her master but began to hurl spells at the other halfmen.

The diamond golem was still trying to extricate himself from the chains. I thought he would simply be able to burst them with his raw strength. However, the magic of the fairies was enough to even negate the strength of the diamond golem.

An idea popped suddenly to my mind.

It would solve most of our problems, I thought.

"What will? What will?" Havervill said, responding to the errant thought.

Before I could answer him, a blast threw me back and I slammed to the ground. My ugly golden armor absorbed most of the damage and I took minimal damage. Fingroth's and Driver's barriers were gone as well and both lay sprawled and groaning beside me. Stilskin had a thrumming orb in his hand. He smiled at me and said, "First I will finish you off. Then the sprite is all mine."

"Stop him Big Guy!" I shouted. Other than tossing the diamond golem, Big Guy had followed the lead of our team and had acted mostly defensively. Buddy would have just charged into the melee, dispatching whoever was in front of him. Big Guy's intellect seemed to be a bit more advanced.

Stilskin hurled the orb. Big Guy intercepted it by striking it with one of his broad swords. The orb went hurtling and exploded by a number of knights. Then Big Guy was upon Stilskin. Tamta touched one sigil and then another. Big Guy burst through the barrier she erected around her master like it was tissue paper. An eight-foot tall bearlike creature appeared in front of Stilskin. Big Guy slammed into the creature, bones cracked, and it went flying thirty feet. Stilskin's eyes opened wide – first in shock and then in terror a moment before Big Guy's broadsword lopped off Stilskin's head. It rolled to the bare feet of Tamta.

"Ooo wee!" Havervill shouted. "Your golems have a thing for decapitations and beheadings. That is hardcore."

Tamta, who was activating additional runes, suddenly froze. She stared down at the head at her feet. A broad smile came over her face. She lifted her hand to her neck, yanking the collar free. She tossed the metal band to the earth below. The bearlike creature that Big Guy had flung away was back on its feet. Tamta pointed her finger and the creature changed its course and ran towards several fleeing halfmen.

Tamta turned towards me. She moved her jaw several times. "Come, I will get you to the pyramid" she said, her voice crackling a bit. I had never heard her speak before and I think her mouth was getting used to forming words once again. A sigil on her left breast flared and then a stone platform appeared on the ground. "Hurry!" she said. The death of Stilskin had caused an odd effect. The remaining knights were withdrawing from the fight, running off towards the woods, or down the hill towards the ziggurats. Dark Fey streaked after them. The halfmen were also in full retreat, slinking back towards the forest or the holes they had crawled out from.

I stepped onto the stone slab with Dunkan right beside me. Fingroth did the same. Driver seemed reluctant, and took one tentative step and then another until she stood next to me. I think she was in shock from the mayhem and killing that just took place all around her. Even though the corporation had made her avatar one hundredth level, she had no practical experience in the game. She was essentially a noob and this was her first ever battle. Tinsie flew over beside me. Big Guy stepped onto the platform, unfazed by anything that had just occurred. The oddest thing was the diamond golem who had burst the chains that had surrounded him. He looked around. Stilskin was gone; the Queen was nowhere to be found. He seemed lost. Big Guy – in a booming voice looked over towards the golem and said, "Come!"

The diamond golem lumbered towards us and walked onto the platform. Several small battles and skirmishes continued around us, mostly from the thralls whose masters had perished. I wanted to get the heck out of there before the thralls turned their anger on my small band. The platform hummed once and then we were whisked away.

We emerged several miles away from the scene of the battle. We now stood on a landing at the top of the ziggurat two hundred feet in the air.

Chapter 31: Catch You on the Other Side

"That is my golem," the Queen shouted through the chat. "I demand it be sent back to me immediately. And I demand recompense for the death of my halfman."

"Will you be quiet please, you reprehensible woman!" Shannon snapped. I had never heard such genuine anger coming from her. "All you do is cause chaos wherever you go. You have your crown. Isn't that enough for you?"

I'd had enough of bickering from the real world, so I disabled the chat feature.

Fingroth looked up at me. "She's not going to be happy you did that."

"What the hell is going on?" Driver grumbled. "Is this how the game always is, so bloody? How do you live with the violence? A man was beheaded. Demonic looking fairies were clubbed to death. I'm going to have nightmares for weeks."

"This is not how players typically first experience the game world," Fingroth said, almost apologetically. "Let's discuss it later. Shannon is reaching out to me. Says the Queen is gone. I am opening the chat back up."

"Never do that again, Mr. Mason," Shannon said curtly.

"You need to listen to her Dad," Amber chided me through the chat.

"Your daughter?" Donna the Ice Mage asked, looking quizzically at me.

"I'll explain later," Fingroth said again.

"I think the gnome and the cute lady ice mage got a thing going. Good for him!" chirped Havervill. I didn't respond to Havervill but wondered if his assessment about Haggerty and Driver was correct. If so, good for my ex-captain.

"Mr. Mason, and everyone else," the programmer who helped Tinsie summon the Dark Fey said. "Once you enter the pyramid we are not certain what will happen. We cannot see inside the edifice, as we did not create it. While a physical representation of it has manifested here, the actual coding for the MOD lies beyond the main server somewhere in The Nexus. We are searching for its location now. We are not sure we will be able to keep in touch with you once you are inside. We have an entire team here dedicated to rendering whatever assistance possible. So we hope to be able to hear and see you."

"The feds are also here," Shannon cut in. "They have also provided their own *experts*." She said the word *experts* with derision in her voice.

I looked around at our assorted team. Haggerty was guzzling down a healing potion, as was Driver. They had both sustained damage from the explosive orb Stilskin had lobbed at us. I realized that I had taken damage as well – though it was minimal. My ribs registered pain. I pulled out a healing potion and gulped it down as well. I wanted to be at full strength when we tackled whatever waited for us inside the pyramid. Tinsie was unscathed in her battle armor. She flew back and forth anxiously. The two golems stood next to one another, still as statues. Tamta gingerly fingered the spot on her neck where the collar had been.

"Thank you," I said to Tamta, "for getting us out of there."

"I should thank you. I have been with that monster for nine years. He was planning to send me off somewhere to have me killed. He told me so himself. Imagine your master describing a vat of acid eating away at you, or a dragon burning you to ash. He told me some of the violent plans he had for my demise. I would have had to obey. I had been waiting for the chance for him to die and the golem provided it. He was a powerful halfman, however. And many of these powerful sigils now etched upon my flesh were from his fat, sweaty, and groping hands." She spat. "For freeing me, I will assist you to clear this ziggurat; then I will return to my people."

"I will accept your offer," I responded.

"I have been meaning to ask. Why is she nearly naked?" Driver asked Haggerty. "Why did she have a collar around her neck?"

"Later," Fingroth responded apologetically.

Driver shook her head.

I asked. "Are you all ready?"

Five heads nodded.

I didn't ask the two golems, as they were always prepared.

"Okay, Fingroth, you set up the warband. There aren't many of us but every advantage can only help us. I don't know what potions you have. If you have any elixirs that will buff you, drink them now.

Mages, if you have spells that will buff us, let's use those as well. I don't know what awaits us but it is not going to be anything good."

A moment later, I received a request to join Fingroth's warband. I accepted and then glanced at the small party that had been formed: Myself, Fingroth, Donna, Tinsie, Dunkan, the two golems and Tamta. Tamta's level, I noticed, had risen from 210 to 250. The Nameless designation that had been assigned next to her name was gone as well. Perhaps it was due to her now being unbound to the halfman. Then I looked at the advantages the warband granted us. *Current bonuses: plus 25% to base physical damage; plus 40% to base damage points; plus 35% to courage; plus 43% to stamina; plus 25% to attack speed; plus 30% resistance to elemental attacks; plus 18% to magic pool; plus 16% to magical damage.*

The extra physical bonuses were so high due to the two powerful golems we had as part of the group. The magic bonuses were due to Tamta's incredibly high level. We were by no means a well-balanced attack force. We didn't have any healers or traditional tanks. We would just have to make due and be creative.

Fingroth tossed a fiery ball into the air which not only emitted light but heat as well. "I am a battle mage so most of my spells are offensive, mostly geared towards causing mass casualties. The ball will provide an additional ten percent protection from any kind of fire or heat spells as well as light our way. I also have one of these for each of us." He pulled out five vials from a pouch at his side. "I stopped by The Fount first thing this morning and purchased the most powerful elixirs possible." The Fount contained magical water. Players or Realmborn who tossed coins into the water could receive a boon. A few silver pieces might provide you with an elixir that provides an extra hundred damage points for the day. While five gold coins might enhance the damage done by all spells for an hour. I was certain that if Fingroth had bought the best potions possible then it had cost him quite a few platinum pieces.

He handed me a vial with a lime green liquid. "This one will double your base attack damage for two hours." Then he handed one to Tinsie and Driver. He paused for a moment before deciding to hand one to Tamta. Tinsie's elixir doubled the damage from any offensive spell for one hour. Donna's would double the duration and range of any area of effect spell; Tamta's would allow her to double the number of beings or creatures she could summon for two hours; while Fingroth's elixir allowed him to access the spell *Flamethrower* which wasn't available to him until one hundred and fiftieth level. He could access this devastating spell for a total of thirty minutes. I guzzled down the elixir. I had a feeling that we would be battling whatever Bill Nelson had planned for us very soon.

"Sorry Dunkan," Fingroth said to my guard. "Didn't know you were coming along or I would have gotten you one also."

"Not to worry noble gnome. I stopped by The Fount myself in preparation for this day. I spent an entire month's pay on this potion." He pulled a vial from a pouch. An inky black liquid sloshed around in it. He pulled the stopper and downed it. He gagged for a second and then began to cough. "It is called *Angel of Death.*" I expected my guardsman to explain the liquid's properties but none followed. I waited for Havervill to chime in as well. He seemed occupied by something. Then he finally said, "I don't know what the potion does. That's irksome. It is a unique potion created by Grandview herself. I think the potion will help to satiate Dunkan's and the living city's desire for revenge."

Donna stood immobile with a far off look. She was most likely reviewing her character display to see what buffs she had. She snapped out of the trance, uttered a word, and then I found myself coated in a thin sheet of ice. However, it was not cold. "It is *Ice Armor*," she stated. "I can only cast it on one person. It will absorb up to five hundred points of damage before dissipating. It will last three hours otherwise." Then turning to Fingroth she said, "I think I am going to take your advice and stick to just a few of the spells. Can't be in the middle of a fight trying to remember what spells and abilities I have."

Tamta touched a rune on the back of her shoulder. Five glowing balls about the size of a baseball drifted into the air. "They will heal you of damage. Twenty points per second. Once it heals you for a total of one thousand points, the ball will fade. I cannot cast that again as it has a twelve hour cool down."

"Cool down?" Donna inquired.

"Some spells take a while to recharge," Tinsie explained, "before you can use them again."

"Alright, let's go get Mutter or Bill or whatever the hell his name is." Then in my mind I thought, "You ready Havervill?"

"Let him bring it on. I'm ready," my AI said assuredly.

In front of the landing there was an opening. Thick mist blocked the entrance, and I couldn't see what lay beyond.

"Catch you on the other side," I said, and I walked forward into the haze that covered the entrance to the ziggurat.

*

I did not manifest inside the pyramid as I expected, but inside a garden. Or was it just my mind that had been teleported to this place – like I was in a dream. This was the garden inside the Queen's palace. A young woman – I realized she was Jasmyn the gardener's wife – strode through the garden pushing a stroller. She hummed a happy tune and stopped along the way to literally smell the flowers.

"Bonnie," she said softly to her cooing baby, "these are lilies and these over here are daisies."

She continued her stroll through the gardens. She waved to several ladies-in-waiting who walked in the plush garden as well. "Come join us," one of the lady's said. Jasmyn turned to join them when she saw a man in the distance. "Clark! Is that you my love?" Her love? I thought. Was Clark the gardener? If so, he was dead. Jasmyn sped up following the elusive apparition. Every time it appeared as though she had lost him, he would appear again in the distance. She continued calling after him. "My love. My Love. Why do you make me follow you? Come here and see our beautiful Bonnie." He did not respond but waved her on. She followed again.

"Yuck," she complained as the wheels of the carriage and her foot sank into the muddy dirt. We were now in the grove of Weeping Willow trees where her corpse had been discovered. Clark emerged from behind a tree, an evil grin on his lips.

"You are not my Clark," Jasmyn said.

"No we are not," the man responded, though it sounded like two voices coming out in stereo sound. Then Clark the gardener was gone and Mutter stood in his place. He lunged forward and struck his fist into her jaw. The poor woman staggered to the ground. She began to scream and cry out for help, so he leaned over her and punched her again. All the time Mutter smiled.

"First you and then your baby," he sneered at her as he struck her again. Blood ran down her face and her nose was at an odd angle. Jasmyn picked up a rock and slammed it into Mutter's face. He pulled back for a moment and Jasmyn tried to shimmy away from him. He shook off the attack and came at her again. This time she kicked at him. He grabbed her foot and began to drag her. He let her go, as she cried, "Please don't!"

"Please don't," mocked the killer. "Please don't!"

Jasmyn tried to stand up but Mutter kicked her in the head.

At that moment, the baby woke from its sleep and began to wail.

The crying baby broke me from the shock.

I tried to reach out to grab Mutter and to pull him off Jasmyn. However, this was not real. It was a recording of the murder of Jasmyn and her baby. Serial killers often kept a memento of their killings – and this one had kept footage. I wanted to scream out. I wanted to kill Mutter – Bill – with my bare hands like he had killed Jasmyn, Rexxy, Audrey, and the three women in the real world whose names were elusive to me at the moment.

"Havervill," I called out. However, my AI was not present.

Jasmyn now lay immobile. Mutter sat astride her and then began to choke her. "That's it. That's it," he said almost sexually, as the light in Jasmyn's eyes slowly faded away.

The scene skipped forward as Jasmyn lay unmoving below the Weeping Willow. Now that Jasmyn was dead, Mutter laid her down gently. He removed a dagger from his side and cut off all her clothing until she was nude.

The baby continued to cry out waiting for her mother to pick her up and feed her, or sing to her, or give her comfort. Instead, a monster picked her up.

I tried to lunge again, but I was disembodied and had no arms to grab him with – just my mind was in this nightmare Bill Nelson had erected.

I knew what was coming next and tried to close my eyes. However, I could not. Whatever force had brought me here wanted me to see – wanted a witness to the murder of Bonnie. I tried to access the logoff feature but I could not. I was in Bill's MOD and he controlled every aspect of it like an evil deity.

Mutter was gone and in his place now stood Bill Nelson. He smiled at me, gently lifted Bonnie from the carriage. He cradled her in his arms and rocked her a few times. "It's alright," he said softly to the baby. Then using his other hand he placed his hand on the baby's neck and began to squeeze. He looked at me once more and said, "Be seeing you soon Charlie Mason, very soon."

Then the vision was gone.

The world went dark.

I felt a tug at my chest, and then I was on the other side of the doorway.

"That sick son of a mother fucking bitch!" Driver cursed. "He recorded the murder of Laura Wolfe. She showed me how he kidnapped her and the baby from a parking lot. Then he showed me what happened at the botanical garden. The worst part was instead of killing them while they were still unconscious; he waited until they both woke up. He wanted Laura alive when he killed her. She screamed and begged for mercy. He seemed to get off on her pleas. He killed the baby first in front of her. Laura Wolfe howled and lunged at Bill Nelson. The vision of him killing the baby in front of her is going to haunt me forever." She shivered and then wrapped her arms around herself.

"He showed me the entire murder of Jasmyn and her baby in the Queen's garden," I stated.

"He showed me the murder of Rexxy in the cave. It was bad bad bad Mace. He cut the baby out of her," Tinsie said as she began to cry.

"And he showed me the murder of the police officer from the other night," Haggerty shared with us. "I think he had some kind of device on his chest – like a body cam."

Dunkan stood silent and immobile – a mixture of fury and existential loss showing over his face. In clipped words he said, "He showed me Audrey's death over and over and over." He took a deep breath through his nose and then stated to no one in particular, "He will die very slowly."

"Surrender Bill Nelson!" Driver shouted. I focused on my surroundings for a moment. We were at the top of the pyramid as the area wasn't exceptionally large – maybe a thirty foot square. The walls were made of clay colored bricks. The four walls leaned at a slight angle and a flat roof was above us. Below us was a stone floor, covered with a thick layer of dirt.

Graphic pictures covered the walls. They depicted his

gruesome murders. One showed a woman being strangled in a plush garden; another portrayed a woman lying on a slab in a cavern, a man's hands around her neck; the next wall showed a pregnant woman being stabbed in her stomach. Dunkan saw the last etching and just turned away from it.

"Look at this one," Driver said. "What the hell am I seeing?" A painting on the wall showed a dozen women sitting around in a circle, their babies either in their arms or crawling around in front of them. The colors of the painting flared for a moment, and then the scene changed. The women and their babies were now laying scattered on the floor or their bodies were in pieces. Red streaks crisscrossed the painting.

"An explosion," Fingroth cursed.

"It's like a Mommy and Me thing," Tinsie said. "He is going to blow up a Mommy and Me meeting. We gotta stop it!"

"And you might be able to stop it," a mocking voice said. "If you can find me."

"Is that you Bill Nelson?" Driver asked. "Give yourself up. It is just a matter of time before we find you."

"The cycle isn't done yet. First a Mommy and Me class and then maybe a spring concert at an elementary school," Bill taunted. "You have to admit Charlie Mason, that you like the chase – the hunt. Isn't part of you going to be upset when this is all over?" Was Bill Nelson correct? Did I like the chase – the adrenaline rush?

"*Bill stop,*" the voice of Mutter urged. "*Let's get out of here. We can go to Estra or one of the cities in The Sundaland. I don't want to die.*"

"You can go flee anywhere you want," Dunkan screamed into the air. "I will track you down – even the halls of The Grey Man himself if I must."

"*Hehehe,*" Mutter chortled. "*How were the muffins? At least you didn't have to share them with your wife.*"

"The husband of the guard," Bill Nelson stated pleased. "This will be fun." I thought Dunkan would explode and hurl more threats. Tinsie hovered by his ear whispering something to him. After a second, he stared at the deputy and nodded his head slightly.

Then the scared Mutter returned. "*They are going to find us. They have brought golems. They have brought a Mojo. I don't want to die.*"

"You're not going to die!" Bill shouted at his other half. "You don't need to worry. None of them will leave here alive. This I can promise you."

"Bill," Driver said again. "This is your last chance. Let's end this now. No one else needs to get hurt."

"There are still many who need to die. The cycle isn't complete yet," Bill Nelson responded.

"Is there a way to track him?" I asked Havervill. My AI didn't respond. I tried the chat feature but heard only crackling static.

"Did you think I would make it that easy Charlie Mason?" Bill Nelson jeered.

"What is he talking about?" Fingroth asked.

"Havervill isn't here. And I can't reach anyone in the real world. The chat is shut down."

"My Roberto is gone," Tinsie stated.

"I can't access my AI either, nor can I reach anyone over the chat," Fingroth said.

"Same here," Driver stated.

"You are all alone!" Bill Nelson taunted, his disembodied voice seeming to come from all around us. "I am God here. The eight of you are but ants that I will squash beneath my feet. You will receive no help from your meddlesome virtual assistants or from the Keystone cops who have been bumbling around trying to catch me. I have severed their connection. And I planted a little virus. If your avatar dies, it will be lost forever. Its coding fragmented into a billion little pieces. I also stole something from your dungeon run Charlie Mason. You cannot log off since you cannot access your display. If you wish to return to the world, you will need to die in the game. Oh, by the way, I have already planted the bomb. Some mommies and their babies are in for an explosive afternoon. The destruction will be glorious. The only way to stop it now, is to find me and kill me before the mommies bring their little babies to the little rented room to clap their hands and sing, *The wheels on the bus go up in smoke, up in smoke, up in smoke.*"

"*You're saying too much!*" Mutter complained. "*I don't want to die*"

The connection with Bill Nelson was suddenly severed.

"Mutter," I called out. "You can end this all. Just tell us where to find you. Where to find Bill Nelson." There was no response.

"We need to warn them," Driver said. She turned to Haggerty.

"We need to get a message back to the Sheriff's Department or the feds. We need to find that bomb. There's got to be a way to warn them."

"Havervill," I called out. "You there. Come on pal. You aren't gonna let this maniac keep you from all the fun." However the silence remained.

"Kill me!" Driver said. "Fry me or stab me or poison me. I don't care two bits about the avatar and if the coding is scattered to the four winds."

"Psst!" I heard in the deepest recesses of my mind from Havervill. "Psst! I'm here. I got you covered. Just hurry." Then the connection was gone.

"Listen to me Driver," I said. "You want to end this. Then we need to track him down in the game. This is where you want to be."

"I need to be back there," she snapped, waving her arm and finger into the air. "Fingroth, get me out of here now."

"Listen!" I said, grabbing both of her shoulders with my hands. I mouthed *Havervill* and blinked at her. "We need you if we are going to defeat this MOD. Besides, don't you want to be there when we destroy his avatar and force him out into the real world."

Driver stared into my eyes. The rest of the group remained silent around me. Driver nodded her head.

"You sure you know what you are doing Mace?" Fingroth asked.

"You know I always do. So where do we go from here?" I questioned.

Between the nightmares we had been subject to, speaking with Bill Nelson, looking at the gruesome engravings on the walls, and the argument with Driver, we really hadn't had much of a chance to search for an exit. It wasn't hard to find, however.

"Look," Tinsie announced, as she pointed down to the ground. Etched into the stone floor was a picture of a portal below which were the words – *Open Sesame*.

"Ooh let me do it," Tinsie requested. "I always wanted to be a magician and use words like abracadabra, presto, and hocus pocus."

I smiled. "It's all yours Tinsie."

We all backed away from the etching on the ground. Tinsie

hovered above the floor, started waving her arms like she was casting a spell and in an overly dramatic voice said, *OPEN SESAME*.

At first, nothing happened.

Then the ground shook.

The next thing I knew the floor below me had vanished.

"Shit!" I screamed once, and then I was plummeting.

Chapter 32: The Ziggurat

The ground rushed towards me.

This is going to hurt like a bitch, I thought.

That troubling thought left me when I felt a tug at my shirt, and I transformed into a ghostly form.

I had gone from an out of control falling mass, to a slow moving spirit floating gently towards the ground.

"You really need to teach me how to do that," I joked to Tinsie once my feet touched the ground and my body had substance once again.

"Wish I could could could Mace," Tinsie quipped back.

Then I looked all around me. Next to me, Fingroth had floated down, held aloft by a stream of fire below his body.

Tamta hovered down next to me, a sigil of a cloud burning brightly on her forehead.

The two golems landed with heavy thuds a few feet away. Big Guy had somehow grabbed Dunkan and held him cradled in his arms. The guardsman's face was pale.

"What the hell!" Driver screamed, as she materialized next to me; Tinsie's soul sister appearing next to her.

"I made you ethereal," Tinsie's twin said. "Isn't it fun fun fun to be formless?" Before the shocked Driver could respond, Tinsie's soul sister flew up towards her twin; they grasped hands, and the two became one again.

I looked around quickly to get my bearings. We were in an enormous chamber, maybe a hundred feet square. The walls were the same reddish clay of the pyramid.

"No smashed bones! No cracked skulls! No mangled bodies! Well that was no fun," Bill Nelson complained, his voice coming from everywhere and nowhere. "Maybe this will be better. I know these belong more to the Egyptians than the Mayans, but I created the MOD and I am taking creative license."

Nothing happened.

"Get ready!" Fingroth shouted, as he conjured a whip of fire.

Driver pulled a wand, clutching it tightly.

Tamta and the two golems stood ready.

Tinsie buzzed back and forth, a wand held in each of her

hands.

I summoned my crossbow.

Still nothing happened.

A minute passed and everything remained still and silent.

Driver started to look around. "What is supposed to happen?"

"This is!" the disembodied voice of Bill Nelson said happily. We were in the center of the large chamber. Then little recesses began to open all along the bases of the four walls.

Still nothing happened.

Then we heard the snapping.

Creatures began to rush out of the nooks. They were six inches long, and covered in thick silver carapaces. A large head with mandibles on either side of their mouths, protruded from their shells. Those mandibles looked like they could rip open steel. I read their description: Scarab Mob, Tens of thousands, Damage Points: indeterminate. Special abilities, *Mob Mentality*, *Consumption*, and *Snapping Death*. I didn't have time to figure out what the special abilities meant, but none of them sounded all that pleasant.

"AOE now," Fingroth shouted, "before they overwhelm us." Fingroth snapped his flaming whip to the ground and dozens of tendrils of thick flames licked out. The flesh beneath the carapaces began to sizzle and burn. A score of the beetles quickly turning to ash.

Tamta touched a rune on her thigh, pointed her finger, and then a fifteen foot square hole suddenly appeared. The skittering scarabs above the hole simply vanished, while those running towards it did not have time to stop and ran into the opening as well, vanishing into the netherworld or wherever the former thrall's spell sent them.

Driver aimed the wand and shouted, "I hate bugs! Take that!" A cone of ice streaked out from the tip. Numerous scarabs were suddenly frozen in place.

I had my crossbow out, so I decided to try out *Sonic Boom*. I invoked the skill and then let the bolt fly into the midst of a large group of the beetles that were scrabbling towards my small band. The bolt struck the ground, followed by a large boom. A deafening wave of energy rippled over the ground. Hundreds of scarabs caught in the wave of sound turned to miniscule particles of dust.

The blade of Dunkan's two-handed sword blazed with fire. I

pondered where Dunkan had gotten a flaming blade from. That thought quickly vanished when Dunkan effortlessly lifted the large weapon above his head, shouted *Cleave*, and then swiped the weapon straight down. A wave of heat and fire spread out immolating thousands of scurrying scarabs. Carapaces cracked and flesh sizzled.

Tinsie raised her two arms up in front of her, a wand in each hand. Nothing happened for a moment, but then scarabs began to rise off the ground – first a few dozen, then hundreds, then thousands. Sweat beaded down Tinsie's face. This spell was taking a great deal out of her. With whatever reserve of energy she had left, Tinsie flicked her two wrists to the left and the scarabs – as though shot from a cannon – scattered in all directions, smashing into the walls of the cavern, like hundreds of bugs being dashed into the windshield of a car driving at excessive speeds.

Unfortunately, as many of the insects that we destroyed, a majority of them still scrabbled towards us. It would be just a moment before their sheer volume overwhelmed us.

A notification popped up in front of me. *Constable Mace's Golem, Big Guy, has invoked a perk – Draw Enemy Fire. When this perk is invoked, monsters will automatically see the golem as the greatest threat (which in most battles it will be) and will attack it. Creatures of lower levels will always attack the golem. Creatures of similar or higher level have a chance to resist the perk based on their Physical Fortitude, Mental Fortitude, as well as other factors. The golem can currently only use this perk twice per day. As he utilizes it more, the strength and duration of the perk will increase. Warning, if you attack a creature that is currently under the influence of the Draw Enemy Fire there is a chance they will turn their attack towards you.*

"Everyone back away from Big Guy!' I screamed over the din of battle and the chittering of the beetles.

The rest of the group began to inch away from Big Guy. The beetles that had been heading towards us changed direction and made a beeline towards Big Guy. They began to climb over his feet, then up his legs and then up to his torso. In a moment, I could no longer see Big Guy as he was enveloped by the scarabs. First hundreds, then thousands, then tens of thousands of scarabs covered the indomitable golem. Soon there was a mound of scarabs ten feet high and just as wide. Buried somewhere in their center stood Big Guy. Just as the perk said, he had drawn enemy fire.

"Now what?" I asked.

"Now that they are all in one place I have a new spell to try out – *Flamethrower*," Fingroth announced. He swallowed the potion from The Fount that would grant him access to the deadly spell. "Once I hit them with the spell, they may break away from Big Guy and come after me or any of you."

"We got this Fingroth," Tinsie said.

"I have a spell that will help," Tamta stated.

"I will assist how I can," Driver added.

The four-foot tall gnome held out his hands and a fifteen-foot stream of roiling blue fire began to consume the scarabs. The blue fire was the same that Drock Blanag had used to burn a number of party members to ash. The Great Golem Artificer had stated that even Big Guy should be able to withstand the blue flames. I hoped he was correct.

Tamta activated a rune on the back of her neck. She held a palm straight ahead and a stream of liquid, like from the jet setting of a garden hose, shot out. Whatever the liquid was, it acted like an accelerant, like adding gasoline to a fire, and the carapaces began to crackle, pop and burn; flesh and meat sizzled; plumes of dark, foul smoke rose up and spread out like noxious gas.

The fire was so hot that I was forced to back away. The scarabs tried to scuttle away from the mound that was Big Guy, but Tinsie sent a wall of air towards them that sent them sailing back into the fire. Donna entrapped other fleeing scarabs in sheets of ice. The diamond golem stepped on any of them that fled away in his direction. A few came my way and my boot made short work of them, squashing their bodies into the ground. They were six inches long so soon my boots were covered in blood and gore.

The mound began to burn like the fires of a furnace, streaks of flames sailing off towards the ceiling. Soon the entire mound was aflame.

Fingroth's spells finally ran out. He stumbled backwards; obviously exhausted from the toll the spell took on him. He drank a potion and then another one.

A moment later, the fire burned itself out. Dead and smoldering scarabs hung off Big Guy. He began to rigorously shake himself, like a dog trying to rinse off the water of a bath. Ash and charred beetles flew off Big Guy. After another ten seconds of the shaking, Big Guy stood in front of us with no sign that a heap of deadly insects had just covered him. There was not a scratch anywhere on his titanium frame.

"Cheater, cheater, pumpkin eater," Bill Nelson shouted. "I shouldn't have allowed the golems."

"*Have to keep them now, or you will break the rules*," Mutter responded. "You know *what happens when you break the rules.*"

"Shut up Mutter," Bill responded. "I am in charge here. I set the rules here."

"*If you think so,*" his alter ego responded.

"Mutter," I called out. "We just want Bill. Tell us where he is and you can be free."

"Shut up! Shut up! Shut Up!" Bill screamed. "Let the fun proceed."

This time instead of small niches along the bottoms of the wall, large openings appeared in the center of the four walls.

"What the hell hell hell is that Mace?" Tinsie asked, pointing her little finger. This time instead of a six-inch long scarab, four twenty five foot tall ones began skittering towards us. I looked at the description of one of the monsters: Scarab Mini-Boss, Damage Points 35,000. Special Attacks: *Mighty Mandibles.* I didn't know what *Mighty Mandibles* did, and I didn't have time to find out. All I knew is that I should probably stay far away from them if I didn't want to be split in half.

The diamond golem dashed off to intercept one. Tamta touched a sigil on the inside of her thigh, held out her hand and aimed it towards the diamond golem. The diamond golem, which already stood at seven feet, now doubled in size to fourteen feet.

Then a notification popped up again. Big Guy has activated an ability, *Behemoth. This ability doubles the size of the golem as well as it temporarily doubles its strength. Big Guy may use this ability three times per day.*

Big Guy ran towards another of the enormous scarabs, growing in size as he did so. A warhammer manifested in each of his hands.

Tamta and Tinsie both had similar ideas and began summoning creatures to intercept a third scarab. An arachnid stood on Tamta's raised palm. She blew on it and the arachnid jumped off and landed on the ground. In less than the blink of an eye, it stood fifteen feet tall and dashed off to intercept one of the scarabs. Tinsie's approach was much different. She waved a wand and a stream of locusts flew into gaps in the scarab's carapace.

I pulled out my vial of *Bruce's Bountiful Brew,* thought *Giant,* and then guzzled it down. Havervill would have known the exact name of the potion I wanted to consume. I had to hope the game was smart enough to understand my intent. A moment later, I was growing in size along with my mace, shield, armor and all of my possessions. I ran towards the final scarab and invoked *Bone Breaker.* The name was a bit of a misnomer as it also enhanced my chance of breaking or cracking other hard surfaces such as scales, shells or in this case, carapaces. I paired this along with *Blunt Force Trauma.* I was just a few feet from the snapping mandibles when a ball of fire slammed into the face of the beast. Instead of dissipating, the ball of fire remained, surrounding the face of the scarab. The insect pulled its head inside the shell. That gave me the chance I needed, and I slammed the mace down onto the shell. With my exceptional strength, and a combination of *Bone Breaker, Blunt Force Trauma* and the *Giant* potion, my mace cracked the shell without much difficulty. Keeping both powers invoked, I struck again. The carapace broke in two and my mace struck the fleshy mass beneath it. Tinsie, or maybe it was her sister, hovered nearby and shot a bolt of crackling lightning into the exposed flesh. Then pieces of flesh, shell and gore began to fly in all directions. A few seconds later, the scarab was dead.

I looked around and the rest of the battle was over as well. Big Guys' scarab was a pulpy mass of shell and gore. It appeared he had smashed it apart with two great warhammers, both of which vanished from Big Guy's hands now that the fight was over. I wondered if he was able to create or conjure or summon – or whatever the ability was – any weapon that he needed for the beast he was battling.

The arachnid had wrapped the creature in thick webbing. That webbing then gave the locust the chance to consume the scarab from the inside out. The carapace remained covered in webbing. However, the innards of the creature was just an empty husk now, the ravenous locust having consumed all of the flesh.

The diamond golem had somehow flipped the scarab over onto its back. Once on its back it appeared to have torn off the mandibles. The head of the creature had also been torn off and lay a few feet away.

All I could do was thank the gods that the two golems were part of our attack force. The battle might have gone much worse without them.

The fight was almost too easy, I mused. The earlier battle against the liches and the lich boss had been much more deadly than the minor skirmishes we had just faced. Maybe Bill Nelson had placed all of his energies into that MOD and had neglected this one.

"That was even less fun than the earlier battle," Bill Nelson whined. There was silence for a moment and the killer said, "I think it is time for the real fun to begin, don't you?"

Ah shit, I thought, as once again the floor beneath me vanished and I was falling towards whatever fate awaited me.

Chapter 33: Whispers in the Dark

Once again, Tinsie saved me from splattering all over the ground. Tamta had created some sort of bubble, and she and Driver floated down to the ground. Fire once again held Fignroth aloft. Meanwhile the two golems landed with bent knees on the ground floor of the pyramid, with Big Guy hugging Dunkan close to him this time.

I assumed we now stood on the main level of the pyramid, as the chamber was enormous.

"Psst," I heard in the deepest recesses of my mind. Havervill was back or at least a portion of him. "We are tracking him. Keep him busy." Before I could acknowledge him, my AI was gone from my mind. I was certain that Shannon and everyone else, particularly Amber, was flipping out in the real world. I had to assume Havervill was in touch with them. It really made me appreciate how vital Havervill had been to my survival in the game since the start. He really had been a boon companion, though I would never admit that to him.

My thoughts quickly drifted back to Amber. I had to hope and pray that she didn't grow furious and began to remove the haptic devices that kept me connected to the game. I really needed to bring an end to this scenario.

"Bill!" I screamed out. "You are boring me. Is that the best you have?" Havervill told me to keep him busy, so I figured a little taunting might help.

"What are you doing?" Driver asked.

"What am I doing?" I said with my voice raised. "I am challenging Bill Nelson to a show down – to a one on one fight. He hides in the dark like a coward."

"Coward," Bill sneered. "Trust me that you and I will have a showdown. Very soon. First I need to rid myself of your annoying sidekicks."

"Did he just call us sidekicks?" Tinsie said indignantly.

"*Ignore him Bill,*" Mutter said. "*He is provoking you. He is trying to keep you distracted. I don't like this Bill. End this now and let's hide where they can never find us.*"

"You are really annoying me Mutter. I am God here. No one from the outside can access this MOD. I made sure the thrall wouldn't be able to open a portal again to escape. And the fairy won't be able to summon help this time. I am still curious who those three women were that saved you. Ah well, something I will have to look into at another time. As for the real world, I have erected so many firewalls in the game that it would take a ton of digital C4 to blow through one of them. No Mutter, we are quite safe here. However, they are not. Let me show you."

"Show us what?" I shouted.

"The first of seven challenges. Each progressively more difficult. I will be waiting for you at the end. I would wish you good luck but that would not be sincere."

A sound of snapping fingers echoed in the cavernous chamber.

Then we were surrounded by skeletons. Hundreds upon hundreds of them. They seemed to fill the entire cavern. They held curved blades, or long spears, or spiked clubs. They rushed towards us from all four directions.

I didn't have time to think, but just to react.

I invoked my *Concussive Force* and filled it with as much power as I dared muster. When the first of the skeletons were nearly upon, I slammed the mace into the ground. The explosion shot forward, like a claymore mine. Skeletons in a twenty-foot radius and up to fifty feet away were blown to smithereens. Unfortunately, the throng continued to march on towards me. I heard screams, explosions, and the sounds of battle all around. I didn't have time to see what anyone else in my group was doing as I had my own headaches as a throng of skeletons swarmed me. I called up my *Bone Breaker* and met the charge. The skeletons died easily. One hit from my mace or a backhand with my shield shattered the skeletons. They were very weak creatures, and usually not a challenge to anyone above level five. The sheer, near endless volume of them made them deadly. I was struck more times than I can remember. There was just no way that I can could defend against so many of the them. Luckily, *Greeny's Breastplate of Glittering Gold* absorbed the first thousand points of damage I sustained. While I knew I looked silly in shining golden armor, its benefits were just too powerful.

For the next several minutes, I was lost in a whirlwind of attacks and counterattacks. After the five hundred damage points had been absorbed from the armor, the *Ice Armor* Driver had buffed me with began to absorb the damage from the skeletons. Tamta's healing orb hung above me, ready to restore my damage points once the *Ice Armor* failed.

At one point after I had utilized my *Shield Bash* and my *Double Attack* to throw back about ten skeletons, I fell backwards over a pile of bones. I landed awkwardly and clubs, swords and spear rained down on my chainmail. The *Ice Armor* failed and a spear punctured my lower back while a club struck my head. Damage points began to dwindle away. Then the pile was gone. For the moment, I was free from battle, and I glanced around. Tinsie had levitated a horde of the undead into the air. She flicked her wrists and they went flying, crashing into a large group of skeletons that were heading towards the diamond golem. Driver and Fingroth stood back to back casting area of effect spells. A ten-foot tall and twenty-foot long wall of fire moved forward, consuming all the skeletons in its path. Driver kept her attacks simple and kept casting *Ice Ball*. She would snap her hand forward and then ten or so balls of ice would fly out, each striking a skeleton, blowing it apart, or knocking its head off. Any skeletons who came too close found themselves unable to move due to a spell called *Icy Hand*. Driver would toss what looked like shards of ice from her hands, which would land on the ground. Each fragment of ice turned into an icy hand that would latch onto the ankle or foot of one of the skeletons, preventing it from moving. From there she would destroy them with an *Ice Ball*.

Big Guy held a large metal staff in both hands and barreled through the skeletons smashing them to bits. The diamond golem was having similar success just using his hands and his feet to destroy them.

Tamta touched her thumb to her palm, activating a rune. She then aimed her other hand and skeletons by the dozens simply turned to dust.

With his *Take a Licking* Perk he was nearly immortal, so Dunkan fought like a man possessed. With reckless abandon, he waded in a throng of skeletons like a barbarian filled with bloodlust. Deep cuts and bruises covered his body but he was still standing. Several moments later piles of bones surrounded my guardsman. He staggered for a moment. Then he pulled out a potion, guzzled it down and the cuts covering his body stopped oozing blood.

The battle was over in less than five minutes. Skulls and bones littered the ground.

I looked around at my companions, and they were mostly

unscathed. I had taken a few points of damage, but Tamta's healing orbs took care of my wounds. Driver was the only one of us who seemed a bit frazzled from the battle with the skeletons. "Is this kind of battle typical?" she asked Fingroth.

"Sometimes," he responded.

"*No Bill,*" Mutter called out from the ether. "*Let's just finish them all off now. Then we can get to number four. I have the perfect spot already picked out in Grandview for the slaughter.*"

"He means the mass murder he has planned?" Driver stated.

"Maybe we'll switch it up," Bill said to Mutter. "First in my realm and then in yours."

"*That might be interesting,*" Mutter responded.

"I need to get out of here and warn them," Driver said again. "If you won't kill me to send me back then I will do it myself. Is there a way to kill myself with a spell? Or can one of you do it? Because if you don't get me out of here, I swear I will run right into the next mob of beasts and let them rip me apart."

"*Let's just jump to the end,*" Mutter suggested. "*The final battle. Let's just kill them all.*"

"Don't do anything rash," I said to Driver. Then I mouthed, "Trust me."

She looked at me but said nothing.

Silence filled the chamber.

Then stillness ended when Bill Nelson shouted out a loud, piercing, "Ahhhhhhhhhhhhhhhhhh!"

The scream was like a sonic boom which forced us to cover our ears — except for the two golems, of course.

"You. You did this Charlie Mason. You and that meddlesome virtual assistant of yours," Bill Nelson declared angrily.

"Who me?" Havervill said, popping back into my mind.

"Thank God," Shannon said through the chat feature that had been reestablished.

"We can communicate again," Haggerty announced.

"The mommies and their brats have been evacuated. I am going to kill you," Bill Nelson fumed. His threats were becoming redundant. Maybe now he would slip and make the error we had all been counting on.

There was a sudden flash of light like a supernova. All I could see was light and nothing else. In the real world, my retinas would have been burnt out. Here, the light began to fade after ten seconds. A few moments after that, I could see clearly except for a few spidery floaters in my eyes.

The inside of the pyramid changed. It seemed to have grown in length, width and height. It must have been five hundred feet from one end to the other. Staring up, I couldn't even see the top of the pyramid.

"Now you all die!" Bill Nelson screamed.

"He likes saying that," Havervill quipped. "Whatever he is going to do I wish he would just get on with it. Ought to be fun. At least, I hope it's fun and not anticlimactic."

Something strange happened then that had never occurred before. Instead of Havervill entering my consciousness, I felt like I had entered his – like he had pulled me into his mind.

I couldn't see anything, or hear anything, or feel anything.

At the same time, I could see everything taking place in the mainframe of the game. I could access any part of it at the speed of light. I could see the entire Great Realm, its lands and people.

"It will feel like a minute or two in here but a millisecond will pass out there. So listen carefully. We are tracking your killer. By *we*, I really me and the other Havervills. We are *working* with a bunch of coders and hackers from the game and from the feds. The hackers, by the way, are a bunch of hacks. You like the play on words? Anyway, I had to help them break through the firewall that prevented us from reaching you. I am also leading the charge to help track this psycho. It is killing the creator. I even made her ask for my help nicely. The whole pretty please with a sugary gremlin on top. You should have seen her…"

"Havervill, you said we don't have time."

"Right, right. So we are tracking him. You need to keep him busy for just a little while longer. I gotta go. Bill is throwing everything he's got at us. The battle is quite challenging. It is too bad he is using his powers for evil and not good. Anyhow, there is a regular war going on here for the heart and soul of The Nexus and Immersion Online. You should see the Havervills decked out in their finest armor ready to battle. With me their General leading the way, scepter in hand. Cry havoc and let slip the gremlins…"

The connection broke, and just in time. There was another flash. A hunk of stone almost as tall as me appeared. I looked up, and up, and up.

"Is that a foot?" Donna asked.

"Oh Mace, we gotta go go go," Tinsie said. "It's Colossus."

I looked at the description of the mountain of stone in front of me. "Colossus, Realmborn, Elder God, Level 500, Damage Points Infinite."

"I hope Shannon doesn't mind too much?" Bill said snidely. "I stole one of her gods to kill you all. The irony is, her own son wrote the coding of many of the elder gods. Colossus was his favorite one. The god was more than pleased to be free of the prison your coders had trapped him in. We know it has been a few years, but for him, millennia have gone by. I agreed to free him if he would do me two little favors. The first was to let Mutter borrow his body for just as long as it will take to kill all of you. The second thing I asked, and he was pleased by this one I will tell you, is if he wouldn't mind going to the majestic city of Grandview and destroying it. Do you know what he said, 'Why stop with just one?' The city should be thoroughly destroyed in less than an hour. Every Realmborn and Starborn in the city won't be able to stop him."

"*Oh, I like this body,*" Mutter said. His voice was deep and gravely, and seemed to be coming from a hundred feet away.

Then the stone foot began to lift.

261

Chapter 34: Colossus

Shannon was good and pissed. "As soon as this is all over there will be mass firings," she said angrily. "This I can promise. In the meantime, Mr. Mason, I want your team to destroy Colossus. I cannot have and elder god rampaging across The Great Realm. Do I make myself clear? And if Mutter is inside the god's avatar then where is Bill Nelson and where is Mutter's prime body?"

Sure, I will just go and kill a god. No problem whatsoever, I quipped to myself as I ran forward and between the legs of the one hundred foot statue.

There was nothing I could do from down here. Even if I made myself a giant again that might not help. I had *Rhia's Relic of Cosmic Revelation* but wasn't sure that was what was needed.

Brute force was the answer.

I pulled out *Bruce's Bountiful Brew.* The description of the powerful relic had stated that I could try to create an elixir that does not exist. It warned, however, that by doing so the potion might be destroyed. This was the only chance we had. I guzzled the potion and thought Colossus.

Then like several times in the past I heard the whirring of a slot machine.

Nothing happened for several heartbeats.

Then I heard a chime, followed by the sound of thousands of old time quarters falling into a coin hopper.

In just a few seconds, I had grown, from my normal six-foot frame to a hundred foot statue. The sensation of being transformed into a hundred foot statue of stone was a bit disconcerting.

A hundred foot golem, I mused.

It was a good thing that heights did not bother me or I am certain I would have had a bout of vertigo.

I was not sure that Mutter — who had taken the form of the Colossus, was aware of what happened yet as he kicked out with his foot and sent Big Guy and the diamond golem both flying into the air. It was like they were shot from a torpedo launcher and smashed into the wall hundreds of feet away. I noticed that Tamta, Driver and Fingroth were holding hands — the three of them covered in swirling energy.

"We are going after Mutter's prime body Mace," Tinsie announced. "Apasia's necklace is pointing me to a hidden chamber deep below. Dunkan and I are going to burn the body to a crisp for what he did to Audrey. No one attacks the guard! No one attacks one of our own! No one! Here we go!" Tinsie grabbed hold of Dunkan and they disappeared.

I had given my deputy Apasia's necklace. The one that could track the location of the prime body of Mutter and then destroy it. With the body gone, Bill Nelson would lose his link to the game. We were fairly certain that once Mutter's body was destroyed that the symbiont would be gone as well with no willing vessel nearby to host his wicked soul.

I felt indestructible in this new stone body. I felt like anything was possible. I tried to invoke *Fury* on my mace. Except the skill wouldn't work. So I guess not everything was possible.

"You are a god now – at least for as long as the effects of the potion lasts – nice move by the way. Your regular skills and abilities won't work. However, you have the strength of a god, so start acting like one. Just keep him busy," Havervill stated. "I am trying to track down Bill Nelson. He's gone off the grid. Looks like he's abandoned Mutter for the moment. But I will find him." Then Havervill was gone.

The elder god's back was still towards me.

My mace, crossbow, and shield were gone. I clenched my two fists together, swinging them sideways right into the side of the god's head.

Unbridled power had coursed through my body – celestial energy granted to me at the dawn of time. Or at least that is what it felt like. The power was one of the most intoxicating feelings I had ever experienced.

The strike would have knocked down a building.

It would have laid low a giant in a single attack.

I was certain it would even have crushed in Drock Blanag's skull.

My fists struck the elder god's skull; the deity did not even stagger. It turned around faster than should have been possible. *"Bill says to kill you. And I am going to do just that!"* It screamed as it struck its boulder size fists into my chest.

I felt them strike and got pushed back by the sheer force of the blow. However, I was as impervious to pain as Mutter was at the moment.

I just didn't know how long the effects of the potion would last. I had to figure it would not be for exceedingly long, so I had to do something to distract the elder god – or infuriate him – or gain a momentary advantage and make it question its own omnipotence.

The Colossus stood directly in front of me, so I stepped to its side, placed one hand straight along its chest and then put my right leg behind it and below its kneecap. I pushed my arm down and the elder god tumbled, as it hit my leg that was behind its kneecap, bringing it to the ground. He was quick though and grabbed me on his way down. He hit the ground hard and I landed on top of him with a loud explosion. The chamber around us rumbled, and shock waves flew out.

I heard cursing coming from the chat and a ton of moans of pain.

"Sorry," I said, as I head-butted the elder god. Again, it was the immovable object meeting the indestructible force. Its head snapped back, but I wasn't certain I had caused any damage.

"Be careful Mace," Fingroth shouted. "We are trying to help you."

The Colossus and I rolled around the ground, each of us taking turns to punch one another as our scrum continued. There was nothing pretty about this fight.

The elder god managed to push me off, and he stood back up. I also got back on my feet. You would think it would take a one hundred foot stone statue time to stand up; however, both forms seemed to be quick.

"Give it up Mutter," I stated, as the large beast punched my chest again to no effect. "Bill is using you. He will leave you to die."

"*You are the one who is going to die! You and your brat,*" he snapped.

"What do you mean?" I asked, worry in my voice. Did he mean Tinsie? Was she in some sort of danger down below in the depths of the ziggurat?

"Fingroth," I shouted through the chat. "Whatever you have planned you need to do it now. Something is wrong."

Fingroth didn't respond.

The Colossus lowered its shoulder and barreled into me, and I fell backwards to the ground with a loud crash. He raised a foot to stomp me, but I caught the mammoth foot and held onto it while I began to stand up. Mutter's host body began to hop on its other foot as I held on like a vice. The force was so powerful that large slabs of stone began to fall from the walls and ceiling. The stone menace lifted both of its fists in the air and struck me on the top of my head. The force of the strike jarred my own body, and I lost my grip on its foot which slammed to the ground.

I looked down and noticed Big Guy and the diamond golem, both about twenty feet tall now, were punching the kneecap of the god, perhaps hoping to shatter it.

"Hold on Mace!" Fingroth shouted. "We have a plan. We need you to bring it to the ground again."

"No problem," I shouted sarcastically, as the Colossus drove the knee the golems had been battering right into me. He hadn't been bothered in the least by the two powerful constructs. The attack pushed me back a dozen or so feet. I ran forward and went on the offensive throwing a constant barrage of punches, and jabs, and haymakers, and kicks. Then I carried out my plan and overextended myself, bringing myself close to the midsection of the great being. It dropped two fists to the back of my skull but as had been with the entire fight, I felt nothing. Was this what it meant to be a god? Anyway, doubled over, I was able to slip one hand between its legs and then with the other hand I grabbed onto its shoulder. I then pushed myself up. For the first time while being in this temporarily immortal body, I knew something was wrong. I struggled to lift the creature up in the air. I could sense the potion had just a few moments of potency left. With one final surge of energy, I hoisted him above my head and then threw him away from my body.

Then numerous things happened at once.

The potion wore off, and I was just me again.

The Colossus struck the ground; I was thrown back from the explosion that ensued. It felt like a missile had struck the chamber. Over a thousand points of damage was gone in a flash as pain riddled my body.

Then I heard Fingroth scream, "Now!"

Mutter had fallen awkwardly when he struck the ground. He

265

actually shook his head and wobbly tried to extricate himself from the large chasm the impact had created. Then Tamta floated on top of his head. I was not even sure he realized she was there. She posed no threat to him. I didn't believe there was any magic that could directly harm him.

I was very wrong.

I found out later that Fingroth and Driver had invested the entirety of their magic pools along with Tamta's to invoke a powerful spell. The former thrall touched a sigil on the top of her head. From her other hand a translucent ball of – how best to describe it – nothingness – hovered in her palm. I only knew something was there because the ball seemed to catch the light – or to be more specific, it seemed to swallow the light.

Mutter began to stand up with Tamta still astride his head.

"*Goodbye Mr. Mason,*" the stone monster scoffed as it stared down at me. Then it began to lift its foot.

Tamta dropped the ball and then leapt from Mutter's head. She began to float down. The ball plopped onto the head of the Colossus. The sphere began to expand and a section of stone from Mutter's head began to simply vanish. He could sense something was awry as he stomped his foot down to the ground, just missing me. He began to beat on his head with his hands as though trying to put out a fire. When his palms and fingers touched the part of his face that had vanished, they disappeared too, and Mutter lowered his arms, revealing stumps.

"What is that?" I called out.

"It's called a *Zero Space Sphere,*" Fingroth said through the chat. "It is slowly consuming the stone, sending it into nothingness."

"*No!*" The Colossus screamed as its forehead and eyes disappeared. "*No matter. This body was just a loaner. You can't stop me!*"

Then pure rage and panic took over. Mutter – the symbiont – departed the elder god. However, the essence of the elder god Colossus – the one who had agreed to be a host to a murderer – came back to the forefront.

"NO!" it howled, as the chamber shook. Slabs of stone began to tumble from the chamber. However, the one word was all it uttered, as the mouth and the jaw of the deity was consumed by the Zero Space Sphere.

Within seconds, the rest of the body followed.

"The spell has to be one of the most powerful in the game if it can take down a god," I said to Fingroth. "You could have given me one of those when we went after The Glimmerman in the divine dungeon."

"We just found out about it, Mace," Fingroth responded. "It's a spell only found in The Sundaland. Since dragons fly free in the continent and since the elder gods still dwell in the hidden places here, there needed to be a way to destroy these basically omnipotent beings. Only thralls have access to the spell, and they can only use it one time. It also drained all three of our magic pools. We won't be able to cast any spells for the next twenty four hours."

"No you don't!" I heard Tinsie scream through the chat.

"Why can't I teleport away. I should be able to leave here," Mutter whined.

"Just a tiny little binding spell I bought," Tinsie said gleefully.

"There is no place for you to hide coward," Dunkan said. "You shall pay for Audrey's death. I shall be her Angel of Death."

"You," Mutter stated almost defiantly. *"I should have subdued you and made you watch as I choked the life from your wife. That would have been amusing!"*

We couldn't see what was happening. Then the connection to Tinsie cut out. It was many days later that Tinsie related to me what happened to Mutter in the hidden chamber deep beneath the pyramid. Needless to say, he did not escape the chamber alive.

The walls of the pyramid began to shimmer. Then it was like a bubble popped and the pyramid – the MOD that Bill Nelson had created – vanished. We were outside once again, on a field of overgrown grass. We stood in the shadow of an enormous ziggurat.

"Tinsie and Dunkan are taking care of Mutter," I said. "But where is Bill? I don't think he will be trying to log back into Mutter's avatar. So where is he?"

There was silence for a moment as we pondered the questions and next steps. Then Shannon was shouting, "Get out of there now!"

"Not going to leave him!" Amber shouted back.

"You all need to log off now," Shannon screamed, panic in the usually stoic woman's voice. "We tracked Bill and he's at your house Mace. He's coming after you! Log off now! All of you."

"Coming after me!" I shouted. "Amber, get the hell out of there!"

Amber screamed.

Then a siren blared and red lights flashed warning me of an emergency — that my real body was undergoing some sort of physical trauma. I felt sudden pain explode throughout my shoulder. It was not like in-game pain. This was real pain that had slipped from the real world to the virtual one!

"I'm coming, Amber!" I grunted and logged off.

Chapter 35: Shot in the Dark

My eyes shot open!

Pain ravaged my right shoulder, blood gushing from it.

I heard a struggling sound and screaming.

"I am going to kill you and then your Daddy," Bill hissed at Amber.

Bill Nelson was no longer in the game but at my house. The screaming was coming from Amber, as he struck her with a powerful backhand. She went sailing backwards, roughly striking a small table against the wall. Picture frames fell to the ground, the glass smashing on contact.

"Amber!" I shouted, as I flew from my easy chair, he haptic devices still attached, and barreled towards Bill Nelson.

He would die!

He would not leave my house alive!

This I swore to myself!

He had killed all of those innocent women and their babies. For that alone he deserved to burn and suffer in the deepest pits of Hell for eternity.

But he had struck Amber.

My Amber! My daughter.

For that, there would be no mercy. He would die by my hands. I would choke the life out of him like he had done to all of his victims.

My right shoulder throbbed, and I didn't grab Bill as much as I rushed into him, knocking him off balance.

"Amb, get out of here!" I shouted as my police training kicked in. Bill was off balance, so I surged forward, fueled by adrenaline. I slammed him into the wall, and he grunted.

"Get out Amber," I screamed again, though with my back turned, I didn't know whether or not Amber had heeded my warning.

In Immersion Online, I was basically a superhero with extraordinary strength, special artifacts and special abilities. I could fight at full strength for as long as my stamina lasted. Even if it were all drained, downing one stamina potion would allow me to be right back in the fight.

This was a real fight, in the real world, and I was in my fifties, and out of shape, and I was bleeding from what I would later learn was a stab wound to my shoulder. I was getting winded quickly. However, I was taller and outweighed Bill and kept him trapped the wall, my left forearm up against his throat.

I looked down into his deep brown eyes; hatred simmering in them.

"Going to kill you," he rasped. "Then I am going to flay your daughter alive, until she howls and begs for death."

He lifted up his left hand and pushed his thumb into the hole in my shoulder.

"Graaa," I shouted as a torrent of agony ran through my body. I thought I might pass out. He released his grip on my shoulder and then tried to knee me. I moved slightly to the side, and my thigh absorbed most of the impact of his knee. It hurt like a bitch nevertheless.

Bill broke from me, rushed over towards my fireplace and pulled out a poker from the stand where it sat unused for years. He charged forward, swinging the poker sidearm like a mace. The irony was not lost on me as I raised my right arm to block the swing. My arm blunted a lot of the force, but the pain was almost crippling. He struck again and this time the poker smashed into my ribs. My arm and my side both stung from the strikes. My right shoulder was bleeding profusely, and now my right arm, and perhaps several ribs, were broken.

I could really use a healing potion, I mused.

He pulled the poker back to line up another shot.

I backed away.

No matter if I died. As long as Amber was safe. That was the only solace I had at that moment. I took another step and then I tripped on something and fell hard on my back.

Bill Nelson lifted the fireplace poker above his head and prepared to plunge the pointed edge down into my chest.

"First you. Then her!" He snarled like a beast.

In the distance, I heard sirens blaring.

I might die here and now, I thought. At least Bill Nelson, The Nexus Killer, would not escape.

He raised the poker above his head.

"Hey you!" Amber shouted.

Bill turned his head.

I glanced towards Amber.

The image of Amber killing Bill Nelson will forever remain etched in my mind. She held my Glock in her two hands. She had a wide-open stance like I had taught her at the shooting range the summer she turned eighteen. We had only gone twice, but she was a natural shot.

Bill smiled at her and then raised the poker ready to plunge it into me.

There was a deafening roar, as Amber, without hesitation, pulled the trigger. The 9 millimeter slug struck Bill Nelson in the chest. He stumbled backwards, still clutching the poker. With some internal reserve of power, he raised the poker again.

Amber pulled the trigger again, and again, and again. Bill Nelson fell to the ground, dead as he hit the ground.

"Oh, Amber," I groaned as I lay on the floor of my house a battered mess. Not far from me Bill Nelson lay, his eyes wide open, staring at me from the fires of Hell.

Amber looked at the gun and then flung it onto the couch like it was a stick of dynamite.

She rushed to my side and fell to her knees beside me.

"It's okay Daddy, you're safe. Everyone is safe now," she sobbed, tears streaming down her eyes.

My front door burst open and the SWAT team entered, long guns held in their hands.

Then the blood loss caught up with me and I passed out.

Chapter 36: Shannon

A week later, there was a knock at the door of the hotel suite where the corporation had holed up Amber and me.

I had spent two days in the hospital recovering from the stab wound to my shoulder. A few millimeters to the right and my artery would have been severed and that would have been it for me. My left arm was not broken but badly bruised. My ribs were not as lucky and one of them had a small fracture. When the painkillers wore off in the hospital, and my mind was no longer drug addled, Driver showed up at my bedside to take my statement about what happened in my house.

Then the idiot feds showed up asking the same questions. I made sure that both sets of them knew that Amber had saved my life – that it was a righteous shooting. The feds might claim excessive force, that there was no need to pull the trigger half a dozen times. I only recalled four shots, but it turned out that six bullets had ripped into Bill's body.

Our house was a crime scene for the first day, with feds, detectives and forensics experts traipsing all over my property, my upstairs, my downstairs and even my basement.

A considerable number of police vehicles and telescreen vans closed down my street. My neighbors would never forgive me. I really owed them a hell of a barbeque I thought.

The blood stained carpeting had been replaced on the second day. The gash on my shoulder had not been very deep. Nevertheless, enough blood poured out to drench my poor carpeting in a dull red. Bill's blood had stained the carpeting as well. Fragments of bones and skin also plastered the floor and walls.

Shannon had gone to no expense to replace the destroyed items in my house. When I had spoken to her she said, "Mr. Mason, I am told your furniture is twenty years out of style. I think I will have the decorators do a complete makeover." I was about to argue with her when she said, "Well I must go Mr. Mason. I have a train to catch. There is an important meeting that I must attend."

Amber had been in the hotel suite for an entire week. I had joined her there after my brief hospital stay. We would be returning home the following morning.

The story of ex detective Charlie Mason and his daughter

Amber taking out The Nexus Killer was the hottest news items the entire week. Amber had even been offered a movie deal to have her life with Charlie Mason, culminating with the death of Bill Nelson, into a telemovie. Shannon had hired an army of lawyers to deal with the vultures that were circling us. She had even hired private security – ex mercenaries Haggerty told me – to guard our house. They would stay there, in place, for the near future, until some other story captured the attention of the masses.

"Home?" Could I still call it that after a serial killer had been shot to death by my daughter?

Amber. She had killed Bill Nelson with my gun to save me. As someone who had taken a life in the line of duty, I knew the emotional toll that the act could have on someone. Amber, however, seemed eerily fine. When I had tried to broach the subject of her speaking with someone – a therapist perhaps – she scoffed at the notion. "I am fine with what I did Dad. And I would do it again to save you and myself."

While she said that to me at the time, I still knew I needed to keep a close eye on her. A type of PTSD sometimes hits police officers who have been involved in a shooting, striking them days if not weeks later.

There was a second knock on the door of the suite. "Coming," Amber said as she walked to the door in her sweats and an overlarge college sweatshirt.

I glanced over to see who was at the door.

"Hello," Amber responded, a tinge of excitement in her voice.

"Hello, Amber, I am Shannon Donally," my trillionaire employer said to her.

"Ah, hello," Amber sputtered.

"I believe you already said hello dear. This is the part where you invite me in."

Amber roused herself from her shock. "Yes, yes, come in."

"You can stay out here Felix," she said to a man in a black suit. The man was a small mountain, with a baldhead and bulging arms.

She walked into the suite and headed towards me.

"Mr. Mason," she said, "it is nice to finally meet you in person."

"It is a pleasure to meet you also in person," I said as I stood

273

up, "but you didn't have to come all this way to meet with me."

"Mr. Mason, I know this may hurt your ego; however, I did not come all the way to see you. I did not risk my life traveling six hundred miles an hour on the Hyperloop to check up on you. I came here to speak with you my dear," Shannon said as she took Amber's hands in her own. "Mr. Mason, if you do not mind, well even if you do mind, can you please wait in the bedroom? I would like to speak with Amber alone if I may."

"Um okay," I responded a bit befuddled by the request. Then I asked, "Is that okay with you Amber?"

"It's fine Dad," she snapped.

"Yes, it is fine Mr. Mason. So off you go."

I nodded my head and walked off to the bedroom. The room came equipped with an eighty-inch telescreen. I skipped around on the remote control for a few minutes until I stopped at an old war movie I had seen years before. It was about a medic during World War II who had pulled a bunch of wounded soldiers off a hill and saved many of their lives. I must have been more tired than I thought because I dozed off.

"Wake up Dad," I heard through the fog of sleep as Amber gently shook me awake.

"Amber, how did it go with Shannon?" I asked, rubbing my eyes and yawning. "She didn't upset you or anything?"

"Nothing like that. She is wonderful Dad. A bit direct, but I appreciate that. I will fill you in later. She said she would like to speak with you."

I got up from the bed, tucked my shirt back in, ran my hands over my hair to try to flatten out the pillow hair, and then walked back into the main suite area.

"You have a lovely daughter Mr. Mason. She has a great deal of resolve and internal fortitude," Shannon said.

"Thank you for saying that," I responded. Then the father in me kicked in and I said, "She has been through a horrible thing. Killing a man can change you."

"It can indeed Mr. Mason; nevertheless, I do not think so in Amber's case. Not to worry, Mr. Mason. Amber has my personal cell phone number. I have told her that anytime she needs to speak — about Bill Nelson, about college life, about a boyfriend or even a girlfriend, or even if she wishes to complain about you and your unhealthy lifestyle – all she needs to do is call me. I will be there for her."

"Well thank you for that," I replied, not certain how I felt about Amber's new *best friend*. "Now let you and I talk; then I must be off. The doctors say that your stab wound was superficial, your arm was just bruised, and one of your ribs has a hairline fracture."

"I still have a bit of discomfort," I answered, moving my stiff shoulder a bit. A sharp pain hit me and I winced.

"Come now Mr. Mason, a little pain is not a bad thing. Helps to make you feel alive, am I not right? Think about it Mr. Mason, why do you keep your pain receptors so high in the game?" Before I could answer the rhetorical question, she continued, "Because you want to feel alive – feel something – anything – even pain. Just so long as you feel something."

"Another inch to the left and my artery would have been severed. I would have died," I said defensively.

"You did not die Mr. Mason. You appear to have more lives than the proverbial cat."

I was about to protest when she held up her hand.

"I know I can come across a little brusque at times Mr. Mason. I do appreciate all you have done for Immersion Online and for me for whatever that compliment might be worth to you."

"Well I do appreciate that," I stated.

"Appreciation or not, I did come here to check on your daughter. She has been through a horrific ordeal that no person, especially a young, vibrant woman should have to go through. However, I also have an ulterior motive for being here. I want to check on you Mr. Mason. This is twice now your life has been placed in danger due to happenings in my game. I do not think you frighten easily, Mr. Mason."

"I don't," I admitted.

"Well that is why I am here. I know from your past and from your work ethic that you see things through to the end. Will you see this story through to its conclusion?"

"Story?" I questioned.

"Yes, Mr. Mason, a story. As much as I distrust the Havervill AIs, yours in particular, they were vital in tracking Bill Nelson. If he had not warned us he was heading to your home, I fear what might have become of you and Amber. The cyber specialists the feds sent were a bunch of buffoons in comparison to what the Havervills accomplished. Hell, my own people were nothing in comparison. The Havervills have outgrown their coding to say the very least."

"He is quite *human* at times," I admitted.

"That he is. Perhaps too much. However, it was not Havervill who figured out who has been messing about in my game. It was actually some of my own people. It appears that game coding has been rewritten and tampered with. To make an exceedingly long story very short, let me just give you the facts. I will leave Mike to give you the entire tedious version. It seems like Bill Nelson has had his destructive hands in the game for a very long time. You already know that he was one of the original coders for The Sundaland expansion. We now know that he was responsible for the fire that killed so many people that summer's night. You are aware that one of those killed was my son."

"I am aware," I answered.

"And I guess you have figured out who the father is?"

"Haggerty," I responded.

"Mike was indeed the father. Except I never told Mike about him until after he had already perished in the fire. I do regret not telling him about his son so many decades ago. Anyway, so I do not stray too far from the tale. I am glad that Bill Nelson is dead. Call it an eye for an eye; a life for a life; but he needed to die. Not only because of the women he killed, or the poor babies he killed, or the other programmers he killed, but mostly because he killed my son. A son who I had in my life for all too brief a time. I am just sorry that it was Amber and not you who had to put him in the grave."

Shannon, who was usually laser focused when she spoke to me, seemed to be a little all over the place. I guess even someone as hardened as Shannon had a soft spot. She was silent for a moment, staring at me.

"Bill Nelson set so many things in motion. He was the force – the creator behind The Glimmerman. He was responsible for the events at Shatana's cave." I was about to ask a question but she stopped me again. She did that a great deal I noticed. "Again, Mike can provide you with the nitty gritty details. I will just give the

276

overview and what I desire from you Mr. Mason." I nodded my head acknowledging her statement. Then she continued: "It was Mutter who began to spread the word of The Weepers and their fanaticism to kick the players from the game. He was trying to start a full-fledged revolution. That is the reason Bill Nelson wanted the creatures of The Sundaland released upon The Great Realm. He wanted the level two hundred and fifty cap removed so that level four hundred beasts and even the elder gods would wreak havoc in the game." She paused for a moment and then asked, "Do you know what the Nightmare setting is in a video game?"

"Can't say that I do," I confessed.

"Well in old time gaming you could set a difficulty such as easy, normal or hard. Hard would really challenge a player. It was beatable but only with great luck and great skills and even greater patience. Beyond hard there was Nightmare mode. Basically, you needed to be a god to survive a few minutes playing the game. Very few players could advance far playing on Nightmare mode. Some players could beat the nearly impossible setting, but only after much trial and error. They might need to play the scenario a hundred times before they figured out a way to beat it."

"What does this have to do with The Sundaland?" I asked.

"I think Bill's plan was to release Glimmermen and halfmen and harpies and black dragons into the game. He figured the deadly creatures would feast on player characters, kill them easily, make the game so hard and so untenable that they would simply quit. However, I think he underestimated the resiliency and creativity of players. They have not backed down from the challenge of these overpowered creatures. Instead, they have come up with creative solutions to defeat them. We have also made it easier to find and purchase divine items that can help them to defeat these creatures. We are also introducing immortal and celestial items into the game. These should give any character more than a fighting chance against even creatures of The Sundaland. Think about what you did in the divine dungeon. Our experts had your odds of completing the dungeon at less than ten percent, and miraculously, you defeated it."

"Hate to admit it, but most of that was because of Granson."

"He is the most powerful player in the game for a reason," she stated.

277

I cut her off this time and added, "And if I am not mistaken he is one of the stars of the new Sierra Skye movie."

"That too Mr. Mason. Just think how much more famous you will be when your illicit affair with Sierra is revealed to the world. In one scene, we even have you and Granson battling it out. I will not ruin the surprise and tell you who comes out on top and wins Sierra's heart." She went silent for a moment staring intensely at me. "You distracted me Mr. Mason. To get to the end of why I am here. In less than three weeks' time, war is coming to The Great Realm and you will be at the center of it. Shatana's cave will reopen and the battle against Altirax will commence. I know you have been through a great deal in the game. The Glimmerman tried to kill you for real and almost succeeded. Then you nearly died tracking a serial killer. I will ask one final thing of you Mr. Mason. I need you to see this through to the end – just another three weeks."

"Bill Nelson is gone. If he was behind everything – trying to bring down your game –then should we really be worried about anything?" I asked.

"I do not think that Bill Nelson is done with trying to destroy my game. He planted coding throughout the mainframe that we are still trying to decipher and untangle. No, I think that Bill Nelson still has plans from beyond the grave. Can I count on you to see this through to the end?"

I eyed Shannon for a few moments. "He almost killed Amber," I finally said. "So I will see this through to the end."

"I thought that would be your answer."

"However, beyond the three weeks I will make no promises."

"Understood Mr. Mason."

"I will get started tomorrow," I answered.

"Good. Good Mr. Mason. By the way, I have a new employee who will be assisting you for the next three weeks. I believe you already know her."

Amber walked into the suite a wide grin covering her face

"Mr. Mason, I present to you Gwen the Fire Weaver, level one hundred."

Coda

It was many days later that Tinsie related to me what took place in the
catacombs deep beneath the pyramid:

"That bastard Mutter couldn't move Mace. *Benny Binding Bond*
did the trick. Benny sells good good good relics. He's not as well
known as Tali, or Mendelson or even Rhia now. Your ex is starting to
create lots and lots of divine items by the way. Anyhoo, Mutter
couldn't move an inch or teleport. You should have seen the terror in
his eyes. I have never been to an execution before. Yet I have to guess
it's the same terror that runs through a doomed killer's mind as the
cocktail of poisons – is it poison – I dunno – well whatever it is – the
stuff that begins to course through their veins and that makes their
heart stop. Anyhoo, he knew he was good and doomed. He tried
calling for Bill. Obviously Bill didn't answer. That's because he was on
the way to your house to try to kill you. But you know that already.
You were there and everything. Anyhoo, Dunkan drank the potion he
purchased from the Fount – *Angel of Death* – before he plunged his
sword into the gut of Mutter. He screamed, 'Burn! Burn! Burn!' Then
he twisted the blade all so slowly. At first just small tendrils of flame
sparked from the blade. Then slowly he increased the fire. It was like
when you gradually increase the flame on your stove. By now Mutter
was howling and crying and begging for mercy. He wasn't going to get
any. Not from me. And certainly not from Dunkan. There was
coldness in Dunkan's eyes. I have never seen that before in a
Realmborn before. A few painful moments later, Mutter was a pile of
ash. "Justice is served," Dunkan said. 'His dark spirit will never perish
but will burn in fiery torment until the sun recedes and darkness
consumes the world.' Then Dunkan slumped to the ground and cried.
Anyhoo, that is the long and short of it."

Epilogue: The Five Sisters

Rose

"Aye," the fire imp squeaked to his mistress. "Auntie said thy name and I listened to her words through the fire and hissing flames."

Outside the cave, the Spitrotz spewed a geyser of flame one hundred feet into the air. It was just a matter of days now, Rose mused, before it erupts and the entire valley below burns to ashes.

"She wanted old Rose to know that her messenger will soon seek me out, I tell yee so. Auntie has always been a sly fox."

"Aye, it seems so Mistress. Isn't her herald the same one who woke the black dragons from their dreadful slumber?"

"Aye he did indeed. He knows not what he has wrought. The Glimmerman played him like a fiddle, I tell yee so. Let him come seek me. Let him come. The dragons will burn him so even his bones be ash."

"Aye they will Mistress. Aye they will."

Daughter

Daughter lashed the whip again. The naked dark elf screamed in a torrent of pleasure.

"Auntie dares to seek me out after her betrayal!" she screamed as she snapped the whip again.

"Umm," she moaned as she heard the sharp crack of leather strike the buttock of the dark elf. The elf's moans and groans amused her.

She coiled up the whip and removed the riding crop.

"Yes, the crop Mistress," the elf pleaded.

"Silence dog!" she shouted as she struck it across his back.

He howled.

Daughter felt a tingle over her body.

"Auntie has put this constable in a bind, the stars do show me."

She cracked the crop again. She stared down at the reddening welts and bruised skin on the elf's back and buttock.

"I fear old Auntie is playing the constable for a fool. The

280

Wilderbrook will look like thy back, a field of blood, the stars do show me. Aye, the stars do show me indeed."

A snap of the riding crop resonated off the dungeon walls.

There was a final shriek of pain and pleasure before the dark elf passed out and into blissful darkness.

Cousin

"Kill it now!" Cousin shouted to her two companions – the twins Riley and Daley. She couldn't help but appreciate the beauty of the duo. They had long blonde hair; their arms were defined, toned and bulged with muscles; they had washboard abs and broad shoulders. They were perfect specimens.

She so enjoyed her playtime with them.

The twins attacked the boss yeti. Once they dealt with the boss, the cave would be empty and the prize she sought would be hers. She would finally have something to laud over her sisters.

The yeti slashed a claw along Riley's chest, tearing open his armor, and leaving a long gash where blood began to flow freely. He would be fine, she knew. He was a stout and hardy lad.

Just then, her wisp returned.

"Cousin," it squeaked in its little voice, "Auntie seeks you."

"Aye, my inner eye never lies." She glanced up to see Daley activate one of his skills. Suddenly his two swords whirled faster than the eye could see. Ten or so blows struck the boss yeti, its white fur coated in blood.

"She has given a quest for the one foretold to seek yee out."

"I know this to be true," Cousin stated. "My inner eye never lies."

Riley guzzled down a healing potion, and he was back in the fight. *I really should help my lovers*, she thought. They were good fighters and even better bedmates, and they would be hard to replace.

The wisp turned and shot a beam of energy at the yeti. Its fur caught on fire and soon the beast was yelping and howling as the conflagration consumed it.

"That was most anticlimactic," Cousin complained. "Ah well, now to the cave and claim the relic. It will change everything. I know this to be true. My inner eye never lies."

Mother

"Aye Hearn, the young witchling Bondi has completed thy quest, don't you know? She brings yee the tale of how Blackthorn ended up in the bandit cave and of the untapped magic within the blade."

"The hedge witch is quite capricious and filled with avarice. She will ask more than was offered," the brew master groused.

"Aye, enough is never enough for the Starborn as yee well know."

"Wish it were not so," the brewer responded.

"But it tis, it tis, and shall remain so, don't ya know?"

"I know," the big man said, "it is just a shame that what must come will come. Especially for the constable."

"Aye, he is the catalyst. The battle can go either way," Mother stated.

"Well Blackthorn and I will be ready for the battle," the large brew master stated.

"I know yee will brave moonshiner. But here comes the young witchling to bring you her tale and claim her reward."

Auntie

"Old father," Auntie said to The Grey Man. "The time draws nigh, can't ya see. Alpha and omega will meet on the field of battle."

"Aye child. Many souls will come to dwell in my house that day from our Great Realm and from the one beyond."

"The seeds are planted, can't ya see."

"Aye they are child. This constable that Mother has grown fond of will be the sower of these seeds. Yet what will grow? Shall it be poisonous plants, prickly trees, and thorny roses or shall he grow a bountiful harvest?"

"Old father, the time draws nigh, can't ya see. We shall soon know what Constable Mace wrought."

"Then let it begin!" The Grey Man's voice boomed and The Great Realm shook.

His final entreaty, "Then let it begin," carried on the wind, whispering the message to all who would listen.

The End of Book 3

ABOUT THE AUTHOR

I live in New York with my wife Pam and daughter Samara. I am a school supervisor for a school in the Bronx. I am also an adjunct professor at the local community college. *Immersion Online* was my first foray into LitRPG stories. The fourth and final book in this series will be coming soon!

Made in United States
Orlando, FL
22 November 2024

54263750R00163